12th Man for Death

12th MAN FOR DEATH

Gregory C. Randall

Amazon Print Version

Printed in the United States of America

Windsor Hill Publishing, Inc.
Walnut Creek, California 94596

ISBN: 978-0-9656510-5-9

*This book is dedicated to the other
and most special redhead
in my life,
Bonnie*

ACKNOWLEDGEMENTS

The America's Cup race is real and has been contested on the high seas since 1851. In the Twenty-first century it has morphed in international event with preliminary races called the World Series using 45 foot long catamarans that are fast and temperamental, in 2013 they will change to 72 foot giants that can rip the heart of the ocean. It is these races that form the backdrop to this story of invention, creativity, and international intrigue. I wish to acknowledge Anthony Sandberg with OCSC Sailing for his comments and insight into sailboat racing. The concept of a high-tech catamaran is mine but the reality may not be too far into the future.

The Internet is now ubiquitous. Through Wikipedia, the free encyclopedia, I was able to quickly research the America's Cup, participants, and locations for this novel. In fact, using Google Earth I was able to locate scenes in Venice and Paris. All the major characters in this book are fictitious except for the high-tech genius Larry Ellison who is one of the most exciting and creative people in America's Cup history, he is also the dynamic head of the Oracle Corporation.

And lastly, a thank you and a big kiss for my publisher and companion of the last fifty years, Bonnie Randall, for her insightful questions and ideas for the story, the book is better for it. She is the other redhead in my life.

Walnut Creek, California

Fall, 2012

Chapter 1

"She's flying," Catherine Voss screamed into her headset. "Twenty-five, thirty, thirty-five knots, Mike, thirty-eight incredible and wonderful knots. She's flying!"

"I see you, incredible," Mike Stroud yelled back into his microphone as he stood on the bridge of the chase boat, binoculars up and alert. "Watch the wind shift off the beach, watch it."

"I'm watching, the hard wing looks good, real good, but she's a beast in this wind."

The thirty-six foot trimaran rode high on its thin hydrofoils mounted under each of the outboard hulls; these blades angled in like knives as they cut the heart from the waves. With each burst of wind, the boat's speed increased; she rose higher and higher on the blades until she seemed to skate on nothing but the thin runners constructed of hard carbon fibers. Catherine, snug in the boat's cockpit, flicked the control stick. Every servomotor on the sailboat responded. Lines came in taut in milliseconds, tightening the sail's grasp of the wind. Other lines eased out. Every second, a hundred adjustments were made to the sails, the rudder and the angle of the hydroplane's runners. She toggled the stick to the left, the boat corrected for the offshore wind's kick, she eased it right, it corrected again. The *Cheetah* responded like the wild cat the trimaran was named for.

"The program is just right, *magnifique*, superb. God damn it, Mike, I'm flying. You *can* sail this boat single-handed."

The hydrofoil raced across the San Francisco waterfront, tourists on the piers pointed at the strange craft, hundreds took snapshots. The setting was perfect with Alcatraz floating in the background. Catherine shaped her course into a large arc that would bring her near the Golden Gate Bridge. Even from two miles away, Catherine could see the fog boiling over the deck of the bridge. She increased her speed.

"Forty-one knots, Mike. Forty-one," Catherine said calmly as she stroked the glass smooth hull of her pet. "She's wonderful, Mike. Wonderful."

"Watch the fog, it's starting to lower!" Mike answered.

"I'm watching, damn," Voss said as she carved a broad arcing U-turn across the length of the Golden Gate Bridge, "It's dropping fast."

Catherine Voss had practiced well that late afternoon. Running a thirty-six foot trimaran is not easy on the best of days, they usually had a crew of at least five, but single-handed sailing tested her on everything she had learned during her fifteen years on the water. The boat performed well; she had designed it. She knew it would. Her prototype, unique and innovative, cost two hundred thousand euros, but it was hers and she knew it would make millions when produced in quantity. She designed it to be sailed by one person, one very insane pilot with an unquenchable passion for speed. The boat might perform better with three people as backup and to help balance the weight. But today she drove the *Cheetah* alone, it was her baby.

She knew the growing mania for the next America's Cup, taking place on these same San Francisco Bay waters, would create hundreds, if not thousands, of buyers. The new boats designs for the upcoming America's Cup were different; they were catamarans with two gigantic hulls built for speed and agility. They could also explode into the most spectacular slow motion disasters imaginable, one pontoon would slowly rise out of the ocean, tip over on itself like it was flipped by Poseidon himself, throwing crew and rigging into the sea like a dog shakes fleas. Catherine's boat was half the length of the contending AC-72s, yet still held thirty-six feet of sinewy muscle, speed, technology, servomotors, and cold wave slicing terror.

The radical finish on its carbon fiber hull sloughed off the cold San Francisco Bay water better than the warmer water of the

Mediterranean. She was amazed by what a few degrees colder made to the trimaran's ability to pull speed from its hulls. The bay's 56-degree water was perfect for her pet.

For three hard hours she had practiced, ignoring the warnings from her support crew about the fog. Cell phones, telemetry, phone, GPS and a dozen other dials and lights told her and her crew everything they needed to know. Mike said there was more data flying back and forth than the first moon landing. The new lithium batteries still held reserve power. Catherine wanted to test everything without the incessant blinking of lights and metrics; she let him know it. Mike said, "No! Not on your life."

She wanted to feel the boat through her ass and her hands. Now her ass was sore and her callused hands, raw. The exhilaration was indescribable. But the fog was winning; the soup became incredibly thick; she suddenly lost sight of the trimaran's bow not thirty feet away. It appeared and then disappeared. The last time she had looked north, Angel Island stretched across the deck of the Bay, its flanks hidden in the fog. Now she saw nothing.

"I'm about a quarter mile west of Alcatraz," she said to Stroud, her crew chief and lead tech, the cell signal was surprisingly strong.

"Roger that, we lost you about twenty minutes ago. Jesus, when that stuff drops, everything is gone. You okay?" he asked.

"I'm good Mike, she performs great. I shut her down to wait for you. And that finish does make her faster, not sure why yet but this cold water makes a difference."

"Thought it would," Mike answered. "You stay put and the tow boat will find you."

"Where the hell do you think I'm going?"

"Just sit tight, eat something. We'll be right there."

She aimlessly drifted. The hard sail, with its fixed radical wing shaped design, dumped the light breeze that carried the fog. There was no need to make it harder for her boys to find her and no reason to crash into the rocks of Alcatraz Island. The boat had so little steel in its construction that its radar return was minimal, lost in the clutter of the bounce from the islands and the mainland. The deep gut-turning foghorn on the south tower of the Golden Gate Bridge gave her intermittent comfort and helped her find her bearing. Drifting on the incoming tide, between the blasts from the Gate, she listened for the soft scratching sound of waves on the rocks of Alcatraz.

Catherine Voss chewed on an energy bar. She had been becalmed before. The first time, in a dense fog like this, she was twelve. Alone, off the huge jetty of her home in Marseille, she had cried from fear, the fear of never seeing her family again, especially her twin brother. But an old man and his fishing boat found her and towed her in; her brother was the first to grab her and hold onto her tight. They both cried. Catherine still went sailing the next morning. She loved the sea as much as her twin, Jean-François. The foghorn snapped her out her thoughts; she heard an engine.

"Finally," she said out loud to the sound of the approaching launch. She ran down the evening's schedule: a brief interview with that reporter from LA, dinner at Boulevards with the crew, then a long and luscious evening with Bobo. The black launch eased itself up to the port hull, scraping the gunnel of the sailboat.

"Hey, what the hell are you doing?" she yelled as two lines were silently thrown from the launch. Their loops expertly snagged cleats and secured the hydrofoil to the side of the launch.

Stunned, Voss just watched, not believing what was happening. Without warning, two men, dressed in black wetsuits, expertly pitched themselves over the launch's railing and landed on the port pontoon of the *Cheetah*. Each carried a machine pistol and both were pointed at her head.

1b

The next morning the fog still hung low over the Bay, so low that the waves tickled the fog's belly. The upper structures of the old federal island prison, Alcatraz, now a tourist trap, were visible and floated like an ethereal, yet surreal, castle atop the thick grey goop pushed through the Golden Gate. Fog is a death shroud that, for ten thousand years, has given sailors the willies. Was that surf they heard, or the waves on rocks, or the wave carving bow of a container ship? In thick fog, everyone believes in God.

The thirty-six-foot trimaran no longer drifted in the soup; its rigging clanged schizophrenically against the carbon fiber mast, beating out a weird rhythm. Its main red hull and one pontoon were caught on the coarse chunk of reef that extended westward from Alcatraz. It was called Little Alcatraz; but to every San Francisco Bay sailor it was a chunk of rock that would gut your hull as soon as show its face at low tide. The trimaran was now a prisoner of the 'Rock'. The receding tide left it anchored among the sharp barnacle-covered boulders that were gnawing through the brilliant red finish of its starboard hull. A night's work of chewing had left a gaping hole and now water sloshed in its forward compartment, the port pontoon had settled into the cold water of the Bay about three feet, wedging itself and the boat tighter in the reef's grip.

A tourist from Detroit, on a two-week RV trip, had just arrived on the first Alcatraz tour boat with his wife; he was the first to see the boat on the rocks. He waved at the park ranger, signaling her to look where he pointed.

"It was there, officer, there, thought I saw something."

"What, sir?"

"A boat or something; it's stuck on the rocks."

"Fog's too thick, you sure?"

"Pretty sure, it was there," he said again, pointing.

"Harold, please leave the officer alone, she has other things to do," Mrs. Harold RV said.

The fog opened and even Mrs. RV could see the trimaran hung on the rocks.

"My lord, it is a boat," Mrs. RV said.

The park ranger was already talking into her microphone when the hole in the fog closed.

The Coast Guard cutter rounded the island in less than twenty minutes; they had been out most of the night in the thick fog looking for Catherine Voss. The cutter launched a Zodiac; the two Coast Guardsmen slowly approached the catamaran.

"Nothing sir, we see no one on board."

"Anyone on the rocks, Ensign?"

"No sir, nothing there either."

"Let me try to get a line on her before she's busted up worse than she already is; that's a good looking boat. Strange hull configuration, never seen anything like it, looks more like a plane than a boat."

"Hold a moment sir, I see something," Ensign Grant said.

Grant grabbed a line secured to the hull that disappeared into the Bay water and slowly drew the hawser to him. On the third pull it stuck, he gave a hard jerk and Catherine Voss exploded from the cold waters of the Bay. Ensign Grant and Seaman Hines screamed like little girls. Catherine Voss missed the press interview, never had dinner with her crew, didn't do the nasty with Bobo and now she had foiled the San Francisco Bay crabs of their dinner.

1c

"I hate sailboats," Sharon O'Mara said, looking out to San Francisco Bay and the Bay Bridge from the deck of the La Mar restaurant on the Embarcadero in San Francisco. She turned to her friend, Claudette Leclair, "Out there it's cold, wet and my hair is a mess for a week, then there's the added bonus of all that salt and sun."

"But sailboats are so romantic," Claudette answered.

"Romantic? If your idea of romantic means hanging over the side with wave after wave of cold water slamming into your face, soaking you to the bone and getting seasick, go for it. My idea of romantic is sitting in a deck chair in the stern of a motor launch, a scotch in one hand, a guy in the other and the sun setting over the marina. Now *that's* romantic."

"Well, I suggest you keep your thoughts to yourself. JF makes his livelihood from sailboats. He's had his hands full since the death of his sister. She was the face of their business and, for him, the creative brain as well. Now, he's trying to make sense out of all the chaos; that's why I want you to meet him. He needs your help."

"What kind of help?"

"He didn't say, just that there's trouble and he needs answers. He asked me if I knew someone who could make inquiries and dig deeper than the Coast Guard or the police. He's sure that his sister's death wasn't an accident."

"That's not what the papers said."

"I know, but he's certain there's more to it. That's why I suggested you to him."

"Me? What do I know about sailboats, especially catamarans?"

"Hear him out, please. And it's a hydrofoil trimaran, very high tech, not a catamaran."

"For me, lunching here is special, I'll listen all afternoon. But I promise nothing. Damn sailboats, I don't care whether they have one, two, or three hulls," Sharon said as they headed to their table.

They ordered a crisp chardonnay from Chile and watched the Marin ferry *M/V Mendocino* pull out of the terminal. She revved up her waterjet engines, threw a foamy broth from the stern of her twin hulls and jumped toward Marin County.

"Goddamn catamarans," Sharon mumbled.

"What?"

"That ferry is a twin-hulled catamaran and it's about the only one I would board. It has a bar."

"Be patient, JF sounded depressed," Claudette said as the server poured the wine.

"Who wouldn't be? I understand that Catherine was the driving force behind their company; it must be worth millions. Without her it's worth a lot less."

"I can tell you it's not money that's the problem; they have a lot of it, old family money. The twins inherited it all when their parents were killed. They made a lot more since then. But she drove the company as fast as she drove her boats and crew. I watched her race out of Marseille; she was good; she was very good. But she burned money faster than JF could make it. They used my software to run their company's business; I customized it for them. And this new boat runs with a lot of software, stuff way beyond me; I gave them contacts. They have been my friends for a long time. That's why I'm here, to attend Catherine's memorial service and see Alain; he's not doing well," Claudette said, changing the subject in mid-sentence.

"He's tough. I saw him last week; I think he's just about finished reorganizing his companies and putting things right with his life. Since the return of the paintings, he seems more relaxed and settled."

"*Oui*, I think he sees the end. He told me he's ready but doesn't want to rush anything."

"Who does when it comes to dying?" Sharon raised her glass to Claudette.

Claudette raised hers and nodded.

Alain Dumont was Claudette's grandfather. A billionaire high-tech investor, Alain needed Sharon's services to return four valuable Impressionist paintings confiscated by the Nazis. Alain had stolen them at the end of the war. Sixty-five years later he found their rightful owners and gave them back. Sharon only had to deal with Twenty-first century Nazis' to make sure they were returned safely.

Sharon watched a Navy guided missile cruiser, on a one week visit, slowly head toward the Golden Gate, the brilliant noon sun flashed off its rigging as it crossed the churned wake of the ferry.

"Now that's a ship," Sharon said as the *USS Cape St. George* slowly turned toward the Golden Gate, the number 71 painted boldly on its bow. "That cruiser has enough fire power to waste a small country. She's beautiful."

"And expensive," Claudette said.

"That's a small price to pay for freedom on the seas."

The death of Catherine Voss occupied one week of newspaper columns, then faded at the same time as her memorial service ended. The most common question was: How could an experienced sailor such as Voss drown in the rigging of her own boat? There were no satisfactory answers forthcoming. The Coast Guard and the police chalked it up as an unfortunate accident. Maybe the boat pitched in the fog from a ship's wake, maybe she fell, there was a bruise on her forehead and one on her shoulder, maybe she grabbed the line and then passed out. There was water in her lungs; the autopsy said she drowned. *Maybe* she did.

After the Coast Guard retrieved her body, they helped the crew of her towboat pull the sailboat off the rocks and tow it to the America's Cup pier at San Francisco's waterfront near Pier 80, the temporary headquarters for the upcoming America's Cup races. A cursory check of the trimaran found nothing looked suspicious. It was finalized as a profound sad accident that claimed the life of one of the world's premier catamaran skippers. Her team members from the small, yet convenient, yacht club in Bora Bora were stunned by the loss. The mining billionaire and the Bora Bora yacht club commodore, Ellis Turner, led the eulogy at the small chapel in the Presidio. Turner's racing team was hoping to challenge for the America's Cup, assuming they could win in the smaller AC45s that were competing in the America's Cup World Series. It was there, among the dozen or so international contenders, that the final challenger to the Americans would be selected. Ellis Turner's reputation as a tough negotiator and her take-no-prisoners attitude within the coal and iron ore industry preceded her; even the international commodities huge all-consuming maw that was China paid attention to her. Her boats raced hard within the tight and narrow harbors in which they competed.

Claudette's call surprised Sharon. She'd had many conversations with Claudette in San Francisco and Paris. Since the shooting at Alain Dumont's Broadway mansion that ended the possibility of a return of the "New Reich," their conversations had been brief, mostly about Claudette's grandfather and the disposition of the gold treasure key stashed in Claudette's Paris safety deposit box. The key now sat in the luxurious panic room of Alain Dumont's mansion. Dumont gave Sharon a smaller replica, also in solid gold, as a memento. It sat in her own safety deposit box, a photo of the original sat on the mantle of the fireplace in her cottage, next to the photos of the Toulouse-Lautrec painting and other Impressionist's art she had saved; the art had once, for a brief early morning, graced her small parlor; both the cottage and the safety deposit box were in Walnut Creek, just twenty-six miles east of San Francisco.

Sharon and Kevin Bryan, her closest male friend, confidant, 'last second' rescuer and dog sitter detective, who worked with the Lafayette, California police department, spent a week in Paris, recovering. During that week, they retrieved the gold plate with its secret numbers locating the largest gold hoard of the Nazi SS, a treasure that was never officially found. That week in Paris was everything they could ask for: food, wine, galleries, and the City of Light. Even a curmudgeon like Bryan agreed that the vacation was worth the effort. Claudette entertained them with two dinners in her apartment overlooking the Pont Neuf Bridge. Its narrow terrace, with its western view of the Eiffel Tower, wrapped the upper floors of the apartment building. They returned, rested, on Alain Dumont's private jet, a Gulfstream G-4.

Now Alain Dumont was dying and Claudette's friend, Catherine Voss, had drowned. She was stressed; Sharon could see that; she knew she would try to help her as much as she could.

But Claudette Leclair neglected to say how extremely good-looking the French industrialist, raconteur, and sailor, Jean-François Voss, was.

Sharon turned to Claudette, "Is *that* him?"

"*Oui, c'est Jean-François Voss, votre nouveau client. Magnifique, n'est pas?*"

"If you just said: 'That's my new client and he's magnificent,' all I can say is thank you very much," Sharon said, as she stood to greet her new client.

"To his friend's, he's JF; his name gets a bit garbled by you Americans."

"My guess, it's his looks that do the garbling," Sharon said, staring.

The six-foot-four Frenchman walked toward Claudette's table, his black hair ended in a wave that dropped over his right eyebrow, a Roman nose centered his deep tanned face and his ice-blue eyes glistened. His smile (ignited when he saw Claudette) knocked three girls off their stools at the bar. One would need medical attention.

The diminutive Claudette disappeared in his arms when he hugged her. As he bent down to kiss both her cheeks, another girl at the bar fainted. Sharon could feel her own tongue begin to tie in a knot with envy.

"Jean-François, this is Sharon O'Mara, a close friend, the woman I told you about," Claudette said, never taking her eyes off the man.

"*Enchanté*, you are even prettier than Claudette said you were." JF took Sharon's trembling hands and kissed her on both cheeks as well. Sharon's cheeks colored almost as red as her hair.

"Sit, please sit, I need a drink," JF said, turning to look for their server, who, after seeing JF, collapsed and was now being helped by one of the male servers, he was handing her a damp towel to cool her cheek; even he was stunned by the man. The young girl recovered and hurried to the table.

"A double Macallan 12 on the rocks, *s'il vous plaît*, I'm parched, young lady, parched."

The server, stunned by the order, nodded and retreated to the bar, passing the three girls frantically waving their menus across their collective faces.

Sharon smiled at the man, pointing her finger at JF, "Damn, I knew I would like you."

1d

Jean-François, dressed in elegant grey gabardine slacks and a soft coral shirt, open at the neck, sat down with his back to the Bay.

"Sit here, the view is better," Claudette said as she moved her napkin.

"The view is better from here," JF said. "And the sunlight highlights your two faces; besides, I see too much of the sea."

Sharon caught herself staring and quickly looked past the Frenchman toward a lone seagull standing on the rail being teased by a young boy. The scene made her smile.

"You have a beautiful smile, Sharon. May I call you Sharon? Ms. O'Mara is far too formal."

His English was accented with an educated French lilt. *"God damn he's charming,"* she thought.

"Yes, Sharon is fine, and thank you for asking," she answered.

Claudette had never seen Sharon in such a state. She tapped the top of Sharon's hand. It snapped her back from her reverie and some very embarrassing thoughts that were bouncing around in her head. She looked at Claudette.

"A beautiful day, isn't it?" Sharon said.

Claudette looked a Sharon, then JF. "Stop it you two, it's indecent."

JF laughed. "Thank you for coming to lunch. Since Catherine's death, it has been crazy, I'm beside myself. I'm still jet-lagged; with the memorial service and everything else I find myself very tired. The two of you have energized me."

The server brought the scotch and with a shaking hand, she set the tumbler on the table.

"Thank you, another one please," he said and took a long sip from the glass. It was half-full when he set it back down on the table. The server quickly left, she had lingered for two seconds more than normal.

"Much better, now." He raised the glass and saluted the girls. They raised their wine glasses to him and smiled again.

Sharon, almost giddy, could feel the muscles in her cheeks; it had been a long time since she had felt this way.

"Okay, down to work," Claudette said. "This is a business meeting, not a blind date."

"*Absolument*, yes, a meeting," JF said. "Now, Claudette says you may be able to help, can you?"

Sharon took another sip of her chardonnay and looked into JF's blue eyes, "You think there is something more to your sister's death. Why?"

"My sister was an excellent sailor and she could swim for miles. She also has a habit, I mean, Jesus I still can't believe she's gone, had a bad habit of pissing people off. But I never thought that someone would kill her. I am certain that she was murdered. I know it deep in my soul. I need to find out who did this and why. And when I find them, I intend to kill them."

"I'll consider that last remark the emotional outburst of a brother who has tragically just lost his twin sister," Sharon said.

"As you wish, but I meant it."

"I'm sure you did, but I'm not in the business of arranging revenge killings. Do we understand each other?"

JF smiled and raised his glass to her, "*Je comprends.*"

"Excellent. Claudette gave me copies of the police reports," Sharon said continuing. She saw seriousness, deadly seriousness in his face. "She said that you gave them to her. The authorities don't give these up easily, how did you get them?"

"Simple, actually, I met with a delightful Coast Guard lieutenant, quite pretty in fact, after a brief conversation she gave me a copy. I usually, just like my sister, get what I want."

"Why am I not surprised?" Sharon said. "But from now on, stop it. Simply put, they said she hit her head and fell into the Bay, possibly caught a line as she fell, tried to wrap the line around herself and then may have passed out, then drowned. Fairly believable."

"Anything is believable if composed properly. As I see it, her death was too simple, too convenient. That's why you're here, to make it inconvenient. Something happened out there," JF pointed over his shoulder toward Alcatraz. "I need you to find out what that was."

"May I see her boat? Maybe I will spot something that the Coast Guard missed," Sharon said.

"It's on a trailer at the pier we're using as a temporary base. The final America's Cup competitors' docks aren't ready, won't be for a few months. We can go there after lunch."

The server returned with the second drink, she took away the first glass.

"Mike Stroud," JF continued, "is Catherine's team manager. He has secured the boat from prying eyes and cameras. I told him we would be over to take a look."

"You knew I would take the job?"

"Claudette said you were good, that's all I needed to know. But let's make it official: Will you continue the investigation?"

JF's blue eyes caught Sharon's green eyes. She felt as if a spell were being cast upon her, she blinked.

"Yes, I'll take the job. I get five hundred dollars a day plus expenses, not negotiable. I will need full cooperation from her crew and you." She waited for a negative reaction, seeing none, she added, "If there is criminal activity and the perps are arrested, I get a $5,000 success bonus. If prosecuted and convicted, I get another $5,000."

JF looked at Claudette across the table, "She talks like an attorney, only cheaper. But," JF turned and looked at Sharon, "a lot prettier - done."

"I hate attorneys," Sharon added.

"And so do I," JF said, adding his comment about the second oldest profession.

"She also hates sailboats," Claudette said.

"So do I, now," Jean-François answered. "Now, let's eat, I haven't had a bite since last night. *Je suis affamé.*"

Lunch, composed of various small plates of Peruvian specialties, filled the spaces of their conversation. A second bottle of Chilean wine appeared. JF explained the structure of their company, a simple partnership that developed exciting new designs in the thirty-six foot class of racing catamarans and now this trimaran. That was what she was testing; a boat that could be sailed single-handed or with a small crew. It was a new, technologically brilliant, design for a market that they knew would explode as the new boats raced in the America's Cup. Their goal was to develop a trimaran that an experienced sailor could pilot and still afford. What they were also exploring was a new finish that shed water better than the usual paint. With the new design and its high tech finish, their boats would dominate for at least a season or two; the others would catch up eventually.

"It's like anything high tech," JF added. "You may take the lead for a while but then the competition will build a better design. We know we will have to keep improving or die. I didn't realize how personal our competitors would make it."

"Claudette also told me your sister was the skipper of Ellis Turner's America's Cup challenger," Sharon said.

"She is, damn, I mean, she was. She could out-sail almost everyone, even the Americans. Turner hired her a year ago; she had been racing Turner's 45 in Europe and New Zealand. Catherine was here trying to do both, the testing for her own boat and training Turner's crew. I never knew her to be happier. But Turner is a ball-buster; she never accepts second place. Turner often told the story of Queen Victoria when she asked, a hundred years ago when the English lost yet another race, 'Who was second?' 'There is no second,' was the response. That's how Turner and Catherine race. There is no second."

Chapter 2

JF, Claudette and Sharon walked up the Embarcadero toward the touristy area in San Francisco known as Fisherman's Wharf; a sad misnomer. There were fewer and fewer fishermen making a living off these docks and piers. Now these docks trolled for tourists.

Near Pier 23, an old, but treasured, bar and restaurant, they stopped.

"The new facilities for the America's Cup will be built right here," JF said pointing to the long wharf that jutted into the Bay. "This pier will be rebuilt to hold new shops and venues for the visitors. Some of the race crew operations will be here as well; they want visitors to see everything that's going on. Or at least those things we want them to see." JF turned to the girls; his smile implied more than just happiness.

"Ah yes, secrets upon secrets," Sharon said. "I remember that this silliness has had spies and intrigue in its past."

"Absolutely, I remember one team, a few races back, even hired divers to secretly check the hulls of the competitors trying to find out everything they could," JF said. "Since its start in 1851, it has been very rich men building very expensive toys to compete against other equally rich men. Sadly, during the last few years, I believe they have spent more on lawyers then they have building the boats. But this wasn't the first time there was litigation, it's happened often."

"Rich men, expensive toys and lawyers, sounds like an unholy triangle to me. My guess is that the attorneys are the only ones to win or at least make a profit."

"I think you're right but it's not going to change anything.

They do what they will do." JF pointed at the piers that curved north and then toward the touristy end of the Embarcadero. "Until the final docks are rebuilt along here for the competition, Larry Ellison and the Golden Gate Yacht Club, the current holders of the Cup, are using Pier 80 as the temporary location for the American's boats. All the others have found space where they could. The Bora Bora Yacht club found a small vacant warehouse halfway between the Bay Bridge and Pier 80 and that's where Catherine's *Cheetah* is trailered. It's lost among the numerous vacant piers and wharves that line the San Francisco waterfront south of the bridge."

At one time, up until the end of World War II, San Francisco's waterfront was the busiest on the West Coast. But San Francisco's politics and egos let it all go to hell. Now, Long Beach is busier, especially with the invention of the shipping container industry; even Oakland, across the Bay, has surpassed San Francisco. The historic wharves are now repair yards and small marinas stuck in between the huge, empty buildings that extend out into the Bay. Where other West Coast cities revel in their waterfronts, cities like Vancouver and San Diego, San Francisco's waterfront is hidden behind these ghostly structures that continually remind the City, like a nagging grandmother, of its past glory. Ellison wanted to change all that and while the politicians gave lip service to his dream, they didn't make it easier.

As usual, committees were formed, pronouncements made, demands listed, lines were drawn in the sand, or as in this case, lines were drawn along the waterfront. The America's Cup committee still didn't understand that there were a lot of people that didn't want these rich people mucking about on *their* waterfront. Tourists were one thing; they could be fleeced and they even enjoyed it. These guys were different; they sent out vibes that they were the fleecers, not the fleecies. The residents on hills above the waterfront, with its signature Coit Tower, were some of the most critical of change.

"The Cup is the oldest championship in sports," JF said. "It's this big silver trophy shaped like a silver pitcher, the damn thing can't even hold water. The bottom has been added to hold the names of the winners. But it's not the Cup they want; teams fight over the bragging rights. Sure there's nationalism but not much, these guys are in it for themselves. Now there're some women competing, tough women and Ellis Turner is one of toughest."

"How did Catherine get hooked up with Turner?" Sharon asked.

"She was racing with a crew in Auckland," Claudette said. "She stood out, being the only woman; her looks didn't hurt either. With her athletic body, quick mind and sharp tongue, she and Turner quickly connected."

"Yes, she had a sharp tongue, she didn't suffer fools," JF added.

"Turner asked her to join her catamaran racing crew; Turner knew this would be the boat design choice for the next Cup. It was a good guess. The giant trimarans that Ellison raced in the last series morphed into smaller catamarans. The idea emerged to have a series of races, a World Series competition of forty-five foot catamarans, all identical, all racing each other in various ports around the world."

"Expensive, very expensive," Sharon added. "Boys and now girls, with their toys."

"You are always the cynic," Claudette said.

"Who, me?"

"They have raced off the coast of England, San Diego, Naples and even Venice. The winds were different in every port," JF continued. "That's part of the reason for the catamarans, watching normal sail boats race in the Mediterranean, with its light winds, is like watching seaweed grow. Most fans watch the start, go to lunch, take a nap, then show up for the finish. Cats are faster and more exciting. We Europeans love speed and style, no one would show up for a race between Toyota Priuses, throw in some Porches and Ferraris, millions line the race tracks."

"And what is your angle?" Sharon asked.

"Our angle?"

"Why were you and your sister building these boats, they

aren't competitors."

"Simple, money and style. Both of us love speed and this boat of hers is a marvel, wait until you see it. Her variation of the trimaran set the speed record for a sailboat. A larger version has exceeded fifty knots, all pushed by the wind. They are more like airplanes than boats."

"Fifty knots, now that's speed! Even power boats have trouble going that fast with all the hull resistance," Sharon added.

"We can be lighter and faster; our goal was to make the boat handle with a very small crew or even just one pilot. All the lines and the rudder are controlled with servomotors, sensors and technology, fly-by-wire, like the new jet planes. Everything is anticipated and controlled through a single joy stick."

"Like the one used to play video games?"

"Yes, if you like. The software and hardware make the adjustments, small and large, all based on various sensors. The large single sail makes it easier; not having to run sails up and down reduces crew demands, just a jib and gennaker. Using a trimaran design allows for a more balanced stable boat, the pontoons provide the balance but in reality they are there to hold the hydrofoils."

"Hydrofoils?"

"Yes, Sharon, our boat doesn't really sail through the water, she flies over it."

2b

Sharon drove her Jaguar. Claudette sadly begged off, she was going to see Alain Dumont at four then board an overnight flight back to Paris.

"Claudette says that somewhere around here you got into a gun fight with some Chinese gangs," Jean-François said as they passed 24th Street.

"Claudette loves to tell stories. Yes, it was just over there, brings back memories I would like to forget."

"I'm even more impressed, turn here."

The broken asphalt and old railroad tracks led toward another empty waterfront building, it angled diagonally out over the Bay waters. Three SUVs, all shiny and dark blue, were parked in an area enclosed by an eight-foot chain link fence topped with coils of razor wire.

"Damn secure," Sharon said.

"It came this way with the month to month lease, even the port knows we'll be moving," JF said. "Imposing and scary, don't you think?"

"It's more than that; it says something's here. I wonder what? It might encourage trespassers."

"*Oui*, there's that too."

She parked next to the last SUV.

They walked toward the large door cut into the shore-side wall of the building, a bull of a man stood at the entry wearing a dark blue windbreaker, a bold logo stitched on its left side.

"Mike, I want you to meet Sharon O'Mara," JF said as they approached the man.

He extended a huge weathered hand. "Good to meet you, Ms. O'Mara, name's Mike Stroud. JF said that you were coming."

"A pleasure Mike, Sharon's just fine," she answered as she looked at JF.

"JF told me you might need to see the boat; it's inside," Mike said leading them into the building. "Follow me and be careful, this wreck of a building has holes everywhere, the rot's extreme. We can't wait to find a better home." Sharon noticed his obvious Scottish brogue.

"Quite an international crew, JF. Mike, I assume some of the crew are from Bora Bora," she said with a knowing grin.

"On the contrary, not one of them. We have men and women, all tough as leather," Stroud offered. "And surprisingly most of them are from Australia, as am I. I jumped ship when I was on an old tramp steamer in Perth years ago, was tired of the cold northern oceans. She's been my base for the last twenty years; the warm waters of the Indian Ocean suit me just fine."

They carefully walked the length of the five hundred foot

pier; Sharon saw the Bay sloshing around through some of the largest holes in the deck. A construction trailer stood to one side; new plywood decking had been laid over the old timbers providing the only safe route to the boat's location. Dark tarps had been spread over the trimaran's hulls, hiding the main hull and the outriggers.

"Can we pull these off?" Sharon asked.

Stroud looked at JF, the Frenchman nodded.

Five minutes later, the crisp red lines of the trimaran sparkled in the shafts of light streaming through the high broken windows.

"We dropped the single main wing, she's over against the wall," Stroud said pointing to the tall mast and its hard triangular sail, its top cut off at a hard angle. "She's made of carbon fiber, Kevlar, and some other stuff. I'm a sailor, not a scientist."

Sharon looked closely at the sail; it was a far cry from the nylon sails she was vaguely familiar with. "This isn't your old fashion sail is it?" she asked.

"Hardly, this is a rigged sail or wing; if additional sail is needed we let out a jib or gennaker, a bit more traditional."

After a cursory inspection, she turned to the trimaran. "Simply beautiful, hard to believe that this can do what you say it can, amazing," she said looking at JF. "It's like a marriage between a catamaran and a small jet plane. All the hard angles and those two blades connected to the cross bars, striking. I assume those are hydraulics for the hydrofoils?"

"Yes, they adjust the angle and depth of the hydrofoils. The damn thing can almost fly under the right hands," Mike said. "She can do forty knots with the right wind but she will bite you in ass if you're not careful. I don't know how many times I've almost flipped her. She demands respect, if you don't, as I said, she'll make you pay."

"How many times have you had her out?"

"Twelve times here in San Fran, the winds, currents and tides are tricky. We are trying to get the feel of how she performs in all kinds of conditions and weather."

"You check her out after every sail?"

"Like a baby's bottom. Since Catherine's death, she's been on this trailer. Coast Guard hasn't officially released her to sail again; they will give the okay in a few days. She needs to be packaged up and sent back to Marseille, they tell me they are moving this model into production." Stroud looked at Jean-François, the Frenchman nodded.

"So soon?"

"It was Catherine's last order as we were lowering it into the Bay, 'Time to get this back to France, I want ten out by the end of the year; we have orders for eight,'" Stroud said.

She walked slowly around the trimaran, looking at every edge and fitting. "The hole in the starboard hull, it's not been repaired?"

"They will do it in France; the carbon fibers are tough to repair. It will be easier at the factory. We also made some modifications that they can duplicate on the new boats. It's not the first time, she took a knock in Marseille but it was only about 100 centimeters, this one is much worse."

Sharon ran her hand along the starboard pontoon, then along the port side. She stopped and walked back to the starboard side, then back to the port. She looked closely at the sharp edge of the port side pontoon again.

"What color is the tow launch?"

"Blue, why?"

"Did the tow launch strike this pontoon when she was towed in?"

"Don't think so and the outboard hulls are called amas."

"Amas, got it. There's a crease of paint here," she pointed at the edge. "Looks black, you sure something didn't just touch her in the tow?"

"Positive, it would be like hitting my own child, I'm sure." Stroud looked at the mark. "Damn, missed that. Damn sure it wasn't there when she went out, does look black. Damn."

"My guess is that something came alongside and just nicked her, left the paint."

Sharon turned to JF. "Something or someone hit this boat; it wasn't from the rocks or the launch. The Coast Guard's boats are usually white, not black, and the Zodiacs wouldn't leave a mark. Whoever hit her may have been the last person to see Catherine alive."

2c

The paint posed more questions than answers. The obvious question was: How did it get there? The second, where did it come from? Sharon mulled these and other disturbing issues over in her head as she drove back across the Bay Bridge to Walnut Creek. She had dropped JF off earlier at the Taj Compton Place Hotel; he asked her if she would like a cocktail; every fiber in her body screamed yes, her head said no.

"Later then," he said as he leaned across the stick shift and kissed her on the cheek. "I had a great time, for a first date. Dinner, tomorrow night? My treat."

Sharon smiled and tried to mumble a no, it came out as, "Yes."

"Are you sure, you seemed to hesitate."

"Very sure, just trying to get my head around all of this and you're too damned distracting. Yes, dinner tomorrow, where?"

"Here, I'll call you." Jean-François Voss exited and passed in front of her car. He waved as he stepped up on the curb. Two women, shopping bags hooked in their hands, stood blocking the door of the hotel; they stepped aside and let him enter in front of them. One checked him out from behind; the other turned to look at Sharon. One look was all that Sharon needed to boost her ego, the woman's face said it all, *you lucky gal!*

Basil damn near jumped in her lap when she sat down in her small living room. Basil sniffed at her slacks and harrumphed; he knew she had been with another male.

"Yes boy, mama's been out." She scratched behind his ears; he grudgingly began to forgive her. "What the hell am I going to do? Haven't felt this way in years, too many years."

She poured two fingers of Lagavulin, neat, into a crystal

tumbler; its peaty aroma filled her nose as she lit a cigarette. "Basil, today's a day to celebrate, mama's had a chance to strut and I like it. There's something about that man that's comforting, too comforting, he's a goddamn Adonis, even if he's French."

She sipped the 16-year-old scotch, inhaled its muskiness, in her mood it was an aphrodisiac. Every nerve tingled; she stood and looked at herself in the hall mirror. She couldn't see what was happening inside, but she felt it. Her body hummed and vibrated. It would be a long night.

She woke early, feeling better than she thought she would. Her tossing and turning made her think of the onslaught of a rough morning. But after a light breakfast of yogurt and coffee, she went to the shooting range and scored well. Then she went to the gym for a hard workout, her phone rang while she was doing push-ups.

"You aren't doing anything special are you?" Jean-François said.

"Sweating, trying to get you out of my system, almost made it too."

"If you're going to sweat, at least don't do it alone."

"I'm not, there's at least fifty others here sweating with me," she said looking around the gym.

There was a pause on JF's end. "Got it. Called to confirm dinner here at the Compton at seven. I will meet you in the bar. I have reserved my table."

"My table? Who has their own table at a restaurant?"

JF paused for a second. "Is that a rhetorical question?"

"I guess it was, sorry. Just in a bit of a mood. Yesterday was interesting."

"Personally, I thought it was fun and even stimulating. Thanks, after the last week I needed that."

"So did I, it was a pleasant surprise. Tonight at seven."

"Seven it is."

Chapter 3

3a

Sharon slowed to a stop by the valet stand in front of the Taj Compton Place. The boy, in a crisp white shirt, smiled and welcomed her after a casual, yet thorough, scan. She could tell he approved, the short black leather jacket over a very dark green dress put her in a stylish mood. *"It's fun to get dolled up,"* she thought. She entered and took the few steps up into the restaurant. The small, yet *tres chic*, Compton Place restaurant was to the right; the bar was to the left. She turned left. It had been four years since she had been to this restaurant, consistently on most five-star lists. Then it was only for a drink, a goddamn, salute-to-herself, life-saving drink. She had promised herself that the first scotch she would have when she got back to the States was going to be in this bar. She had promised it while she leaned against a mud wall in a brown dirty drift of a village north of Kufah. A village with a name she didn't want to remember and couldn't forget.

* * * *

Near Al-Kufah, Iraq, Summer 2005

Sharon was there with her squad to pick up three Iraqi locals. The local chieftain swore they were al-Qaeda. He said they were causing difficulties in the village and like the good loyal supporter of the Americans that he was; he pointed them out to an American patrol. They passed on the word.

She arrived with her men, met with the village leaders and immediately knew something else was up. They acted nervous, scared shitless nervous.

"Sergeant Sanchez, I want everyone on their toes. I don't

know what we are getting into here but be careful, real fucking careful. Watch the roofs and windows. I want no one dead today."

The two Humvees idled in the courtyard; their 50 caliber machine guns swiveled across the face of the buildings. She could see the tops of palm trees over the unfinished roofs of the houses. The village was snuggly nestled within the expanse of irrigated fields south of the Euphrates River. Her men secured the courtyard corners; she went inside with her interpreter, a twenty-four year old corporal from Kuwait by way of Atlantic City, New Jersey.

"Where are they?" she demanded.

The corporal asked the three men fidgeting with their beads, their long white beards softened their hard eyes and leathery faces. Words were exchanged between them and the corporal.

"Lieutenant, they say the three escaped last night. Someone helped them, they don't know who."

"Bullshit," Sharon said. "Tell them they forfeit the reward, no bad guys, no money."

One of the elders said in reasonably good English, "We were promised."

"Sir, you were promised a reward if you produced al-Qaeda. No fucking bad guys, no fucking money," she answered. "Habib, make sure they all understand."

"Yes sir," Corporal Habib answered.

The elder of the group stared directly at O'Mara. No woman ever talked to him in that manner, it was as if he had been bitch-slapped - infidels. He started to take a step toward her. She smiled and put her hand on her holster, he paused, looked at the corporal who shook his head. The elder backed away. She noticed a ragged touch of scarring on the right cheek above the elder's beard.

"Bring me al-Qaeda and you will get your reward, simple. Got it?"

The elder turned to the others and said something; Sharon caught the words infidel and something about her parentage.

The men laughed, the corporal started to chuckle.

"Don't you dare, corporal. I heard what they said."

The corporal stiffened, "Yes, sir."

The village elder looked hard at Sharon over his sharp hawksbill nose. She knew he understood what she said and he knew she spoke Arabic. He raised his hand and motioned to her to step toward him. She lifted the flap on her sidearm, but didn't remove the pistol. She came within inches of the man. He began to speak to her softly, in English.

"Please leave now, this is a trap. Please leave, may Allah have mercy on me."

Sharon stepped back; no one else heard what the man had said. If any of the other Iraqis heard or even understood, they didn't react to the man's whispered words.

"We're out of here, this is a fool's errand," Sharon said to the men standing behind her. "I'm not sure they even had someone locked up. They seem too nervous for my taste. Corporal, out." She turned to the three men and looked at the man who spoke English. "No money and I will not be back. Peace be with you." The last she said in perfect Arabic.

He mumbled, *"Wa alaikum assalaam."*

She bowed to the men and turned into the bright sunlight.

"Saddle up, Sanchez," she yelled as she left the building. The squad slowly worked its way across the courtyard and back to the two trucks. The 50 caliber machine guns continued to cover the buildings.

"I don't like this one fucking bit," she yelled into her head-set. "Not one fucking bit."

The two Humvees kicked up a cloud of dust and headed toward the opening wedged between the two-story mud build-ings. The first bullets dinged off the hard edges of the Humvees as the buildings closed in around them.

"Faster, God damn it; make this fucking thing fly," she screamed. The eight-cylinder AM General engine roared like the devil himself had squeezed its balls. More slugs hit the trucks; some left rays of sunlight through the dark cab. They made a

hard turn to the right, the buildings were now one-story der-
elicts, low walls connected them, good cover for IED's and an
ambush.

"You know your way out, private?"

"Yes sir got it all in my head. Not going out the way we came
in. Those assholes will be waiting for us, I just know it. Three
more fucking blocks and we're free of this shithole."

O'Mara's headphone buzzed, "We are on your tail. There
were at least four on the rooftops as we saddled up. They hit the
deck when Hernandez sprayed the roof, saw one almost explode
when he got hit by the 50 cal. Good call, Lieutenant, getting us
out when we did; it was a fucking trap all the way."

"No shit, Sanchez, no shit. Your boys ok?"

"We're fine as long we get out of this fucking dump."

Sharon looked out the window, field after field of irrigated
desert extended out from the edge of the village just one block
away. Palm trees lined the road like columns with green feath-
er dusters stuck to their tops, suddenly great puffs of dust and
debris exploded from their trunks. The gut turning bawling of
the vehicle covered the sound of the explosions that sheared off
three palm trees a hundred feet ahead of them. They fell across
the dirt road.

"Hard left, hard left," she yelled. The private was already
ahead of her; he knew what to expect. This wasn't the first time
they had been ambushed. They cut left then right, paralleling
the row of palm trees. For good measure, the 50 calibers ripped
a hundred rounds through the thick underbrush that paralleled
the road near the explosions. Two men tried to cross the road;
they fell under the fusillade.

"Too fucking close, too damn fucking close, those sons-of-
bitches. God damn them," Sharon said to no one.

"Everyone ok?" she asked calmly into her headset.

"Not a scratch, damn lucky, I guess."

"Roger that."

The ride back to the base seemed surreal; the two Humvees
were caught up in the day-to-day traffic on the Iraqi highways

not unlike a typical American suburb, except for all the weapons. Roadblocks clogged the intersections. The Iraqi army tried to maintain some sort of order but the truly dedicated soldiers, those that can make a difference, weren't used for traffic control. The government couldn't afford to lose their best soldiers to suicide bombers at traffic stops. Iraqis watched as the Humvees paralleled the mixed bumper-to-bumper queue of cars and trucks, kids waved, one pretended to be pointing a rifle at them. The women, many fully covered in black chadors, walked along the rough sidewalks. Sharon smiled when she saw a flash of blue jeans and Nikes under one obviously younger woman's hem. *Style will win out.*

They were back at the base in forty minutes. The bundle of American dollars sat jammed between the front seats on the floor next to her. She knew the money was more than a year of her pay; hell, it was more than a year's collective pay for every man in the truck. The bundle was to be traded for the al-Qaeda prisoners, the same prisoners, she was sure, had probably bought or intimidated their way out. Telling an American infidel to fuck off was a lot easier than having your head sawed off with an eight-inch knife. Seeing what she had seen during the past year, the old men had a right to be scared.

* * * *

Taj Compton Place, San Francisco, California
"Black Label, rocks," Sharon said to the bartender.

Like the valet, the bartender noticed everything and liked what he saw. She smiled and spun the ice around in the glass with the tip of her finger, her version of stirred, not shaken. She saw him reflected in the mirror behind the bar. She turned around on the stool and watched Jean-François Voss talking with the maître d, his cool elegance obvious. He was dressed in a dinner jacket. The staff said hello as they passed. JF shook at least three hands in the restaurant. One very good-looking blond stood and kissed him on the cheek. For some reason, Sharon felt jealous. *What the hell was that? I don't even know the man.*

"Are you waiting for someone?" the bartender asked as if insuring the caliber of the clientele at the bar.

Knowing his intent, she smiled at the bartender, "Be careful, young man, in a few minutes Mr. Voss will be joining me and we don't want to make a scene, do we?"

Properly chastened, the man began to pour a Macallan scotch into a crystal tumbler holding one large ice cube. Sharon couldn't see scotch's age, his hand obscured the label.

"This is for Mr. Voss," the bartender said as he sat the glass next to Sharon's Black Label.

"Thank you and I apologize."

"And I do too. Mr. Voss is well known here and he treats this hotel well."

JF walked through the intimate lounge to the wooden bar, smiled and kissed Sharon on both cheeks. Her light makeup hid her blush.

"Henry, please meet Sharon O'Mara, she's a good friend."

"Good evening, Mr. Voss, and good evening, Ms. O'Mara."

"Henry," Sharon said raising her glass to the man behind the bar. He tipped his head. Sharon was now a sanctioned member of the bartender's club.

"I take it that you stay here often?" Sharon asked turning back to JF.

"Every time I'm in the City. Which, during the past few years, seems to be every other month. It's a wonderful hotel. Claudette's collection of software designed for the boat needs operating hardware and some of the best and strangest hardware guys are located in Silicon Valley. They put together the computers and the servomotors. My meetings are about marriages between the software and hardware." JF's eyes never left Sharon's, even as he gently touched the back of her hand.

She lingered in his look for a moment and quickly decided to change the subject, "Did Mike find out anything else after we left?"

JF's knowing smile returned her look. "No, you were right about the paint; it doesn't match anything in the yard nor is it from any boat that came close as they towed her in. He thinks it either happened during the launch, there were a few boats tied up along the pier, or, as you suspect, somewhere out near Alcatraz before the Coast Guard found her. He says he'll keep looking."

"Good man," Sharon said.

"One of the best, we've known Mike for almost ten years. These guys are like, what's the word for hired soldiers?"

"Mercenaries?"

"Yes, mercenaries. They're all very competent and skilled; they offer their services for the best price they can get. Strange to see boats from Korea and The Emirates with New Zealand and Australian crews but that's the way it is. These races wouldn't exist if it weren't for them."

"Why New Zealand and Australia, water is everywhere," Sharon said, signaling to Henry, she pointed at both glasses.

"The sailing is tougher there, bigger winds and seas. They're better trained and experienced. The Mediterranean doesn't have the water and wind mix to make great sailors. They are good, very good, but the real hard asses come from Down Under." Jean-François sipped his refreshed scotch.

"Mike hired the rest of the team?"

"It's more like recommended; his working for us on the hydrofoil is a separate agreement. Ellis Turner handles all the final crew decisions for the America's Cup. She hired him, added whomever else she wanted, looked at his recommendations, and set the crew. Catherine also suggested a few people, for both onshore and the boat. Takes a big crew to pull this off, a crew who expects to be paid promptly and well. This is not a game for millionaires, only billionaires can fund an attack on the Cup holder these days, people like Larry Ellison, mining conglomerates, Emirates Airlines, or with a collective host of other sponsors. It's really silly if you ask me but it's also a hell of a lot of fun; boys and their toys!"

"And big girls," Sharon added.

"And girls. Damn I miss her. Catherine and I were so close;

she was twenty minutes older and wouldn't let me forget it. She was a force of nature. I followed her, cleaning up the messes she made but they were glorious messes. She thought up more brilliant ideas in an hour than some people think up in a lifetime. I took on the job of sorting out the best and trying to make something of them. The hydrofoil is the best she has ever come up with; I will make it happen." JF paused a second, looked into Sharon's green eyes, and sighed.

"I know how you feel, there are people in my life I miss, some I never knew but I still miss them," Sharon said, not knowing why.

"Enough of this maudlin conversation, dinner? *J'ai faim, je suis très faim.*"

"*Moi aussi,*" Sharon answered.

"You speak French?"

"*Un pue*, just enough to understand."

JF took Sharon by the arm and led her into the elegant dining room, a room critically judged as more European than American. Softly lit walls, with small delicate paintings hung high wrapped the room. Banquettes flanked the left wall as they entered; a glass sculpture of white and red flowers floated high in the center of the room. The place settings were perfect.

"That sculpture is by Nicholas Weinstein, a local California sculptor whose works in glass are just astounding; Catherine had a whole bouquet of his flowers."

The maître d' showed them to a table in the back, it was set for two.

"Can't fit in those booths, not enough leg room, besides the view of the room is better from here," JF said, looking at both the sculpture and Sharon.

"I agree," Sharon answered.

They ordered and a bottle of French white burgundy appeared. Their conversation was light and extemporaneous. Interests and hobbies, nothing was said about their business arrangements and Catherine Voss but she was definitely sitting in the empty chair at the table.

As they sipped coffee and debated dessert, a commotion intruded through the arched entry into the dining room, the patrons all turned. A woman, dressed in a black knit dress with a short jacket that sparkled with sequins, commanded the door. Another woman, powerfully built and tense like a jaguar, stood immediately behind her. She was dressed in black also but she wore slacks and a long sleeved jacket, the collar of the white starched shirt stood high over the jacket's lapels. Two nondescript men stood behind them.

"Sharon, that is Ellis Turner," Jean-François said.

"Which one?"

"The woman in the dress with the 'I'm-the-head-bitch-around-here' look," JF said with a grin.

Ellis Turner surveyed the room like a lioness surveys a herd of wildebeests. Where are the weakest, lame or infirmed? Her eyes darted from table to table. Everyone in the room, with only a few exceptions, knew the act and returned to their dinner; this was a dining room full of predators; most knew they could take her. The rest went meekly back to their soup.

3b

"Jean-François!" Turner loudly announced to the room, heading directly toward Sharon and JF.

JF stood and waited for Turner to reach their table, after the obligatory double cheek kiss, JF said, "Ellis, meet Sharon O'Mara, she is a friend I've known a long time. Sharon, this is Ellis Turner."

Sharon smiled at his slight exaggeration, "Pleased to meet you Ms. Turner."

"Call me Ellis, my dear. Please. And JF, how have you kept this Sheila hidden from me all this time, are you being naughty?"

"Sharon and I have had some business dealings in the past and after Catherine's death she is assisting with some family issues," JF said, adding more to the cover story. "And how are you Eva?"

The woman gave JF a bitter death-stare, unlike any that Sharon had ever seen.

"I am well, why do you care?"

JF let the question slide, "Sharon, this is Eva Karg, Ellis's assistant. I'm not sure about all of her other duties, but wherever you find Ellis, you will find Eva close behind."

Sharon caught the motion of an arm to her right; the two men that had accompanied the women sat at their table, one beckoned to Ellis with an exasperated wave.

"Shortly, Bobo, shortly. How long are you in town? I would have thought you'd be returning to France after the service."

"In a few days, I have to get the prototype into its container and clear up a few things here, then yes, it's back to Marseille," JF said.

"I understand the boat is spectacular. I believe that it could be the next big thing in sailing," Turner said.

"Maybe, we accumulated a lot of data from Catherine's last sail. I have to look over that before I make any other decisions."

Again Bobo waved, Sharon could see impatience building in Eva and her body language screamed that she wanted to be well away from JF.

"I am ready to fund the project, just let me know when. It will be Catherine's legacy. Ms. O'Mara, a pleasure and I hope to see you again," Turner said as she left the table and walked across the room to theirs. Eva followed.

"So that's the world famous Ellis Turner," Sharon said to JF.

"Yes, she reminds me of the white shark her home country is famous for and Eva is like a remora, always hanging on, close by, feeding on scraps."

"You two seem to have a history."

"Yes, it was fun for a few weeks, then she returned to Ellis. Eva is, putting it nicely, Ellis's lover."

"You're kidding, right?"

"No, it's well known in business circles and Ellis would squash and ruin anyone who tried to use the knowledge to better their position in a deal. Eva, on the other hand, is dangerous as well as confused. Not a good combination."

"Dangerous?"

"Yes, Eva Karg is very dangerous. It's rumored she was a special operations officer with the South African security forces."

"She was a 'Recces'?"

"A what?"

"A Recces, South African Special Forces Brigade. That's the name they call themselves, like our rangers in the army. Carry out the heavy lifting for the government of South Africa. Last I heard, the whole military structure was a disaster waiting to happen, corrupt and all. I thought that they didn't allow women. I need to do a little checking; what do you think?"

"Thought she might pique your interest; they make such a cute couple, don't they?"

"Yes, like you said, a shark and a remora. I didn't know you were going back to France."

"Have to, business, I have to start working on the production schedule for the hydrofoil, that's the least I can do for Catherine."

"Is Turner funding the development?"

"No. I have other investors, French investors, I hope, but possibly Russian as well. I would never enter into a partnership with Turner. Her general history is like the camel and the tent; soon she owns the tent and you're left out in the desert. No, she'll never get a piece of the *Cheetah*, I'd sooner shut it down then let her even have a taste," JF said as he caught Turner's attention, lifting his glass of wine toward her. She returned the toast with a quizzical look.

After a calvados in a brandy snifter, Jean-François and Sharon said their goodbyes to Turner and Karg and took a brief turn around Union Square. The fog had started to obscure the upper floors of the St. Francis Hotel; it swirled and eddied in the shadows of the buildings.

"Would you care to come up for a drink? I have an excellent

bottle of Dom on ice."

"Would like nothing better, but I have a rule and you are certainly its toughest test. No affairs with clients," Sharon answered.

"I see, and that rule has never been broken?"

"Never."

"And how old is that rule?"

"Thirty seconds, it's one of my oldest."

"I see, and are you making up any other rules?"

"As I go along! JF, there would be nothing more exciting then spending the evening with you; you have been a delight. But I also need to keep some perspective if we are going to sort this out." She ran her fingertip along his cheek.

"Is there someone else?"

"Actually, there is but he has four legs and a tail, and I promised him I would never let a man to come between us."

"Promises are made to be broken." JF nuzzled Sharon's ear. "I think he might understand."

"I doubt it; we go back a few years. He does get jealous and he will kill to protect me."

"And so would I." He caressed her throat, she shivered. "See, there is electricity here."

"Yes, and with that said, I need to go." Sharon quickly kissed Jean-François hard on the lips, and held his face in her hands; she finished with a soft kiss to his cheek, sighed, turned and walked sharply away. Her heels clicked on the sidewalk as she quickly walked to her car sitting by the valet stand at the entry to Compton Place.

JF watched her walk away; it was his turn to feel a jolt of electricity.

3c

A black BMW 650i pulled away from the valet stand as Sharon approached. The streetlights reflected off its wet German finish. The windows were too dark for her to see who was inside; it quickly turned onto Stockton Street from the alley and disappeared. Her Jaguar sat parallel to the curb near the valet stand; she thanked the young man for retrieving it.

"Mr. Voss took care of it ma'am, no worries."

"That was a sexy car that just pulled out of here," Sharon said.

"She was Ms. Turner's friend, said she was in a hurry," the valet said, a look of disappointment on his face.

"Stiffed you, did she?"

"Not going to say, ma'am. Not my place."

"A man's got to make a living no matter what he does; a service should be paid for."

"I get my hourly, it's not so bad."

"Hourly's never good. You going to school?" Sharon asked as she slid into the leather seat.

"Yes, ma'am, studying hotel management at SF State. One day I want to work inside."

"You will with that attitude, keep it up." She slipped him a twenty-dollar tip; he beamed and checked her over once again.

"Thank you," he said.

"Young man, be careful, you never know who you're dealing with," she said with a laugh. She felt good, real good; the best she had felt about herself for a long time. For once, a man liked her, tickled her senses, made her feel like a woman. It had been a long time. Jeans and sweatshirts were comfortable but an honest to God dress that shook a man's soul was something else. The months in the gym after the Nazis helped. But it was more of an attitude adjustment, the sense of accomplishment that she enjoyed; beating down evil and raising the good. But the need to be wanted, to be held and kissed, and maybe, maybe being loved, that was different, very different. And she liked it.

She shook herself and smiled a self-satisfied grin in the rear view mirror as she settled into her Jaguar. She had an affinity for the brand since her days in that Rockies high school, the strange school where her foster parents sent her when she was fifteen, a school where no one had a past and most kids, she learned, were grateful to even be alive. Colorado was hard on young girls. The father of a young man she had a crush on drove a Jaguar, years later she still wasn't sure if she'd had the crush on the kid or the car. All she knew was that the car stuck but she couldn't remember the boy's name.

She clicked on the Pandora app, selected Pat Matheny and pulled out onto Stockton Street. Matheny's tight steel string guitar filled the leathered cabin with notes that only a master could pull from six strings. She tapped her finger on the steering wheel, crossed Market Street and headed toward the Bay Bridge. *"The world is a delightful place,"* she thought.

In twenty-five minutes, she would be home. She hated the Bay Bridge as any Bay Area resident did. It was as unpredictable as California rains. Tonight it was clear, the traffic was light and even the slight buzz she felt left her awake and alert.

The seven mile-long bridge dumps East Bay travelers into the west side of Oakland, but it's an Oakland seen from thirty feet above the streets, below lay a gridded mess of politics and gangs. The nightly news, repeated on the early morning television news, scares the hell out of the commuters as they head to their safe villages beyond the tunnels drilled through the hills to eastern Contra Costa County. The suburbanite sighs of safety can almost be heard above the highway din as the freeway opens up into the wealthy village of Orinda. Here, on a steep winding downgrade, Sharon noticed the headlights from the car stuck hard on her tail. Its high beams were on and close, too close for comfort and at eighty miles an hour, too damn close. They felt like search lights probing for weak spots, trying to find an opening.

She pulled to the far right lane and slowed, the headlights followed her. She slid left, the lights followed.

"What the hell!" she muttered. "Some damn fool kid playing games, I'm too damn tired for this crap." She slowed, so did the headlights. She blew by the Orinda exit and headed up the grade toward Lafayette. She accelerated, the Jaguar XJR leaped at the chance to show its power, ninety jumped to one hundred, the headlights held tight to her tail.

"God damn it, this is too much. Shit." She yelled *"phone"*, the screen on the dashboard lit up. "Kevin Bryan," she yelled. In two seconds, the ringtones of detective Kevin Bryan's phone filled the interior. Three rings were answered with, "Why the hell are you calling me at this time of night?" was all Kevin Bryan offered.

"Kev, I am just passing through Orinda, I have a crazy ass driver on my tail, I'm doing one hundred and five miles an hour; they're doing 106. In about three miles, I will be crashing through your jurisdiction and I don't think I'm traveling at a safe speed."

"No kidding, I'll let dispatch know. You okay?" Bryan said as he punched in the number into his desk phone. "You seem to have a way of collecting traffic violations. Maybe it's someone you pissed off; probably cut them off in the tunnel."

"Yeah, right, I don't think so and you'll pay for that. Damn."

"What happened?"

"I swear the son-of-a-bitch just nicked my fender, just a nudge but I felt it. I'm off at the next exit; this is bullshit. One mile."

"Be careful." The adrenalin was pumping through Kevin Bryan just as fast as it was through Sharon. "Where are they now?"

"They have moved to my left rear fender, we're still doing 100. They're close, too damn close."

"Are they behind you?"

"No, half a lane over, left."

"Slam on those fucking English brakes, hard. Hold tight, hit the pedal, let them pass you."

"Now why the hell didn't I think of that?"

"Takes a man to make these decisions."

"Fuck you, Kevin Bryan."

She took a deep breath and held the steering wheel tight. One second she's looking out the front window, the centerlines were lit like a runway; a split-second later she's looking out her windshield at the side of a black car, 'BMW' flashed in her head, before the spinning Jaguar pointed her back the way she had come, then a series of impossible 360's spun her off the freeway onto the road's shoulder. The dust from the dry gravel engulfed the Jaguar; she pumped the brakes, turned the wheel toward the opposite direction, the car slid to a stop. She saw the red taillights of the BMW disappear into the dark night.

"What the hell was that? You okay?" Kevin screamed.

"That's was a crash, Kev, but any crash you can walk away from is a good one, right?" Sharon answered, just a little shaken.

"Crash, what the hell do you mean, crash?"

"I think I was hit in the left rear quarter panel by the son-of-a-bitch, tried to make me lose control. Was ready, didn't flip but spun off the freeway. I'm okay."

Dispatch hadn't wasted time, flashing blue and white lights filled her rear windshield. Sharon took a couple of deep breaths and swallowed a handful of Altoids just to be safe, the last thing she needed was a breath test. She secured the Beretta, from her handbag, putting it under the seat in its discrete hidden case, pulled a flashlight from the glove box and slid out of the car. Ahead, a caring citizen had pulled over after seeing the Jaguar spin. A dapper man in a dark suite was walking toward her car, a police cruiser pulled up immediately behind her. She waved the flashlight over the rear corner of the Jaguar.

"Damn," was all she said after seeing the eight-inch dent on the rear quarter panel. "God damn it."

A flashlight waved about from the direction of the police car.

"You okay, ma'am?" a deep voice said over the intermittent roar and swish of passing cars.

"I'm fine. Look what the son-of-a-bitch did to my car," was all Sharon could lamely offer.

"Hit and run?"

"You think?"

"Ma'am, be civil," the cop said as he passed the flashlight over

Sharon's face. "Great, just what I need. Is that you O'Mara?"

She washed her flashlight over the cop's face, "Santinni, great. Of all the cops in Lafayette, I get Tony Santinni, now I won't have any secrets," Sharon said.

"Oh won't Bryan be thrilled, can't wait to tell him."

"Tell him what," a voice said from inside the Jaguar. "Tell me what?"

"O'Mara, don't tell me Bryan's inside?"

"Only his big mouth, the rest of him is somewhere else."

"I heard that."

The citizen stood to one side, not sure what was happening.

"Why are you standing there? Were you the guy who hit her?" Santinni asked as he flared his flashlight over the man.

"I was following her car as it came through the tunnel." He pointed at the Jaguar. "Just as we cleared the tunnel, a BMW roared by me and pulled up tight behind her, jamming itself between us. Then they took off like it a scene from a movie, you know, like that film *Fast and Furious*, they both just bolted. I hit my breaks and slowed. Sure wasn't my business, I didn't want any part of whatever was going on, then I saw the headlights start spinning and the cloud of dust. So I pulled over. You okay, Ma'am?"

"Why is everyone calling me ma'am, I'm not that fucking old."

"Calm down, O'Mara," Santinni and Bryan said at the same time.

"Did you recognize the car or catch a plate number?" Santinni asked the citizen.

"The plates weren't California, sure of it," the man said. "But the car was a BMW, a real new BMW 650i, black convertible, black windows, a very nice car. I can't believe they would knock you off the road using that car."

"Me neither," Sharon said as she looked up Highway 24, east toward Walnut Creek. "Me neither. Just look at my car, Reggie is going to be pissed."

"Reggie, is he your boyfriend?" Santinni asked with a leer.

"No and it's none of your damn business, Santinni," she answered.

"Santinni, it's her mechanic, her God damn English mechanic," Bryan said from inside the car.

"No shit, you have your own English mechanic?"

The concerned citizen looked at the two people standing in the glare of the headlights, threw up his hands and said, "You're all fucking crazy!"

"Probably," Sharon said, looking straight at Santinni. "Yes, I have my own English mechanic, don't you?

Chapter 4

Still pissed, Sharon rolled into the center of Lafayette, parked and walked the three blocks to Geno's. She needed all three blocks to kill a cigarette. She breathed in heavily and blew the last blue smoke into the night air outside the best bar in the county. The electric whine of a BART train, its tracks high above the village, cut through the damp late summer air; she didn't know which way it was going, she also didn't care. She pushed open the door as two politicians spilled out. They were well known, but more for the other spousal company they kept. Sharon watched them hugging and squeezing as they walked down the street; all she could do was shake her head.

"O'Mara, I see you, get your butt in here," a voice called from deep inside the bar. "And my God, don't you look good. I knew there was a woman under that stuff you usually wear."

The ten or so patrons, evenly split between male and female, looked toward Sharon. The women watched in mild unease, the men in awe. One woman smacked her husband across the back of his head.

"Hi Gina, thanks. Been quite a night. The usual, please," Sharon said.

"Already pouring, babe, the ice is in the glass."

Gina Cavelli owned Geno's, or at least held it in trust for her family and their reputation. Gina, known for her wild black hair, which was beginning to look like a salt and pepper fight, had inherited the bar from her father after he passed on to one of the better barstools in heaven where great bartenders are served forever. She still carried herself like the love child of Sophia Loren but with the humor of Gina Lollobrigida. She joked about their common names and the fellows admired the physical similarities. But the locals knew that she could recite Giant's baseball stats all night and they also knew the old Louisville Slugger under the bar hit a pop fly more than once on someone's head who thought the bar was a bank.

"What's your trouble girl, you look bothered, out of sorts," Gina said.

"I just had a wonderful date, and …"

"You had a date, with whom? I knew you would breakdown and join some dating service, I just knew it. Which one, Date Watchers Anonymous?"

Sharon looked at Gina as she sipped her Johnny Walker. "You don't think I can get a date on my own?"

"For you, taking Basil for a walk and getting ice cream is a date. You never date. You never go out. You spend too many lonely nights here. I was almost sure that someday you would look like my spinster great-aunt: old, bitter, wearing nothing but black, smoking cheap cigarettes, gun in your lap, drinking red wine wrapped in a basket."

"Screw you, Gina Cavelli. Yes it was a date with a hunk of a Frenchman, he's single and he's rich. We had a wonderful dinner at Compton Place, took a romantic walk about town, and, to my own shock, I turned down his request for a nightcap in his room. For my penance I got run off Highway 24, the Jag had its butt kicked in, and Mr. Kevin Bryan was on my car phone the whole damn time."

"During your date, too?"

"Funny but no, not during the date. He called Santinni and it was Tony who caught up with me when I was forced off the road."

"Anthony Carmine Santinni, this only gets better. And then what my dear?" Gina said, hardly controlling herself.

"I came here to be abused and underappreciated." Sharon said.

"*Au contraire*, you are always appreciated here even if there is some abuse, but you do give what you get," Gina said as she moved down the bar, pulling two beers from the ice. "Hold your horses, Duane, I'm coming."

Sharon took another sip and watched the tumbler shake as she held it. She sat the glass next to the two other rings she had left on the mahogany surface. *Shit, that asshole could have killed me.* The car spinning flashed in her mind like a strobe light. Red taillights flashed to headlights, then back to red. Her mind suddenly grabbed an image; it hung there like a black and white photo. *BMW 650i, it was a 650, no mistaking that side silhouette, nothing else like it. Two in one night, now that's just a little too coincidental and I don't believe in coincidences.*

"Did you say something?" a deep male voice said from somewhere over her head.

She looked in the bar mirror and smiled. The head floated above her red hair, his black hair tousled and twisted like he had just gotten out of bed. He towered over almost everyone in the bar.

"Hi Kev, knew you would show up," she said.

"Don't I always," Kevin Bryan said.

"Yes you do, you always do."

"The usual, Kevin?" Gina asked as she headed toward the pair.

"No, not tonight, working. Wanted to see how Sharon was doing, looks okay. You okay?"

"I'm fine, just pissed. I always get pissed when my car gets dented."

"As often as your cars have been busted up, shot and blown up, now I know why you're in this perpetual dark mood."

"What is it tonight? Pick on Sharon O'Mara night! Anymore of this and I'll go home to my dog. He, unlike all of you, understands me. I will be consoled there," Sharon said twirling the ice in the almost empty glass.

"It's only because he knows that you feed him, other than that, and he's told me, he'd rather have male company."

"It's just that when you take care of him," Sharon answered, "he gets the chance to roll around in the exotic smells of your little bachelor cottage. He's told me the aromas are just divine, unlike anything he could ever find at my house. Something about old socks and underwear, but please, I don't want to go there."

"Stop it you two, you're driving the customers out, even I'm disgusted, old socks, please Sharon," Gina said standing across the bar from the two Bickersons. "You two better keep it down, there's some here who might think you're married."

Kevin leaned over and kissed Sharon on the cheek; she squeezed his hand. Their relationship was extremely complicated. In a way, they loved each other like a sister and brother, yet were often thrown into the roles of comrades in arms, more often through her own complicated devices and adventures. More than once, Bryan had shown up in the nick of time. She also helped him with some police matters especially when dealing with kids. Kids were the main reason why Kevin Bryan left the Oakland police force, escaped through the tunnel and landed in Lafayette. He had been first on the scene for too many injured and or shot children in Oakland; it was killing his soul. Now, at least, on this richer side of the hills, most of his murders were committed for jealousy and money. He hadn't been to a good revenge killing in years.

4b

Sharon parked the Jaguar on the short driveway that paralleled her stucco cottage in Walnut Creek. The one car garage's single door slowly climbed into the old rafters, the grinding of the garage door motor could wake the dead. At this moment she didn't care. She leaned against the car, Basil stood silently in the window facing the driveway, he was patient; his mistress was home. She smiled at the Rottweiler-Shepherd mix and waved, the dog smiled back. She lit another Marlboro and blew smoke into the black sky; the stars fought for attention, each one screamed, "Look at me, at me! Make a stupid wish!"

The moon was in its crescent phase, one large star hung just out of its reach, to the right. She hated that crescent shape. All the other phases of the moon played their part in her life. Full, half, waxing or waning, even the dark of the moon, held secrets, desert secrets. But it was this crescent, this Islamic moon, that she hated. It was, to her, the death moon.

* * * *

Green Zone, Baghdad, Iraq, 2005

"Lieutenant, there's an old man here to see you, says he met you three days ago. He's agitated and upset. I think it took everything for him to come here," the corporal added. "Scared shitless, I think."

"Where is he?" O'Mara asked.

"We have him in the trailer; he said he couldn't go in the main building. But the trailer was okay."

"Know what he wants?"

"No, said he would only talk to the Lieutenant woman and he meant you."

"Did you frisk him?"

"He's clean, stinks a bit, but they all do here."

"Corporal, some days you're no joy to be around either." She stood, strapped on her service pistol, adjusted her uniform and strolled out into the yard. The trailer stood off to one side just inside the gate. Every Iraqi ass squeezed tighter when they walked up to this gate, scared to go in and even more scared to be seen going in.

The corporal opened the door of the trailer, the old man stood in the center of the room. Sergeant Sanchez stood beside the door, armed. She could see the old man was agitated, the aroma of a Turkish cigarette hung in the room. Sharon looked at Sanchez.

"Said he could smoke sir, seemed to need it."

"That's okay, did he say anything else?"

"No sir. He kept repeating that he wanted to see the Army woman, the one who came to see him."

Sharon turned to the man, *"Asalaamu alaikum."* She tilted her head at the man.

"Wa alaikum assalaam," Lieutenant," the man said.

"Your name?"

"Hakim al-Jamil."

"Mr. Jamil, please sit. Corporal, coffee please," Sharon said.

"Yes sir, will you be alright?" the corporal asked.

Sharon looked at the man with a withering glance. *Never reduce my stature in such a meeting*, it said.

"Yes, sir."

After the corporal left, Sanchez adjusted his position in the room, she turned to Jamil. "What may I help you with, Hakim al-Jamil? After the other day, I would have thought I would never see you again since we walked into that ambush you helped to create." She offered al-Jamil another cigarette, he took the Marlboro; as he held the butt in his shaking hand, she lit it. She lit one for herself. He took a drag, it seemed to calm him.

"Lieutenant, they made us do it. Three al-Qaeda forced us into setting the trap. After they told us what to do, five or six more showed up. We have seen too much death in the last twenty years, we did what they wanted."

"How old are you?"

"Lieutenant, I am seventy-eight years old. I lost one son in Saddam's war against Iran; I lost another in the war with Kuwait, a suicide bomb in the village market killed my eldest daughter's son three years ago. My heart has been torn apart so much that it was all I could do not to give in to these scum. But I had no choice."

The door opened and the corporal sat two cups of coffee on the table, the Starbucks green logo was obvious.

"You always have a choice."

"Yes, to live or die, those are my choices. I can make that choice but my family can't. I must protect what I have left."

Sharon paused for a moment and sipped the coffee, "You speak English very well."

"Thank you, before Saddam, I was an engineer with an American oil company. I was trained in Houston and Saudi Arabia. But my home and family called me back just after Saddam took power. I now raise beans and chickpeas."

"A farmer, nothing better."

"Yes, if you love poverty, farming is great."

"Why are you here and what can I do for you? I would think those men would have left by now. They knew we would be back for them, and soon."

"Yes, they did leave, but they took something more precious than my life. They said that they would remain hostages for the time being, in case we collaborated further with the Americans."

"They, who?" Sharon said.

"Those foreign scum took my twin granddaughters; they are only seven years old. My daughter is inconsolable, she cries all day. You must help me. They are all my family has left."

"Took a lot for you to come here."

Sharon looked at the man, he desperately fingered his beads, he took furtive drags on his cigarette, quick, nervous drags; he could barely stay seated in the metal chair.

"Hakim al-Jamil, what would you have us do?"

"Find my granddaughters and bring them back to their mother. They are all she has now; she is the youngest of my daughters. Her husband is in the army and is stuck in a base on the Jordanian border. He knows they have been taken but cannot leave his post."

"I understand, if he were allowed to leave, thousands would leave for home as well," Sharon said. She turned to the sergeant. "Get Major Simpson's aide on the horn; tell him I want to talk with the Major. Tell him it's an opportunity."

"Yes, sir."

"Mr. al-Jamil, I will be talking with my superiors, alerting them of the situation. We'll see what we can do. Do you have pictures of the girls?"

Hakim al-Jamil reached into his rough and torn black sport coat and slowly drew out two photographs, one was of a family gathering, the other a close-up of two incredibly beautiful young girls, their straight black hair glistened in the sun; their soft faces carried smiles that only seven-year olds could wear in this forsaken country. Their eyes were as blue as the desert sky. The child on the right held up a drawing of the crescent moon and star.

* * * *

Sharon closed the garage door and walked through the kitchen, Basil nudged her butt as if he knew something was wrong. She found a bone in the bone jar; Basil took it and curled up on his bed in the corner of the kitchen, watching his mistress. She poured a cold glass of water from the refrigerator and took two Oreo cookies from the stash she had hidden from herself in the cupboard. She sat, took a deep breath and bit into the chocolate brown cookie, the filling squeezed out of the layers. She licked at the white frosting and sighed.

"What the hell am I doing? One minute I'm happy, the next I'm getting run off the road. Again I'm caught up with a band of crazies. This time, rich crazies, rich bitchy crazies, shit. Hell, there has to be something better in this life than helping a bunch of excessively rich over-achievers figure out a way to one-up another. Who the hell cares anyway?"

Basil put his huge head in Sharon's lap, his eyebrows flicked from left to right, left to right. It was his turn to sigh.

"I know, I know, we got to make a living. You need a roof over your head. I think I have this facilitating bit down but, good Lord, why can't they at least be simple reasonable people with simple problems. High tech sailboats, billionaires, Frenchmen, world travelers and now someone who wants to play brinksmanship with automobiles. Basil, old boy, one bad spin and you would be at Kevin's about now. And I wouldn't want that for anyone. Outside one more time and then to bed, I'm exhausted. Life in the fast lane will kill me yet."

4c

The next morning Sharon took BART into San Francisco. An hour earlier she'd met with Reginald, her Jaguar mechanic; it went well. At least he didn't cry like the last time she'd brought in her car. He was hardened when he took her calls; he was prepared when she drove into his shop now.

"Well, the damage isn't too bad, dearie. You have done much worse, much worse," his Cockney accent hung in the oil fumes of the garage like the odor of fish-and-chips. "Will take a couple of days, but I can make it look as good as new, the paint's in good shape and it will be easy to match. May even have some left from last time."

"I know you'll be kind to me and I can deal without it for a couple of days. I can work around it."

"Good, you can take my Vauxhall if you like."

"No, once was enough. I'll manage; can it be ready by Friday?" she said hopefully, not in a demanding tone.

"No problem, Friday at noon. See you then."

She walked the three blocks to the Walnut Creek BART station and took a cab from the San Francisco City Center station to Alain Dumont's mansion on upper Broadway. Peter Brass, his assistant and personal medic, opened the door. After a brief kiss on the cheek, Brass took Sharon into the study. Alain Dumont, now ninety plus, sat in his wheelchair, smiling. He put his hand up to stop them both, pointed to the huge black man and pointed at the door. Brass smiled and left the room. He pointed at Sharon and twirled his finger. Sharon did a slow pirouette; Dumont put his hand over his heart.

"You're still a letch, you old fraud. Is that all I mean to you; cheap thrills so you won't have to change the batteries in your pace-maker?"

"Sharon, my dear, you have no idea how you manage to keep me alive," Alain Dumont said. "Your visits just keep me going, what more can I say."

"You can give me a kiss and tell me what you know," she answered.

"Claudette tells me that you are working with JF Voss, he's one of the good guys. I've known his family a long time."

"You've known everyone a long time," she quipped.

"So true, outlived a bunch to boot as well. Catherine was

a rarity, smart, good-looking, an adventuress, well-educated - such a loss."

"Yes, would have liked to have met her, now I'm trying to find out why she died and or who may have killed her, all over a boat and a race. It's such a tragedy."

"Drink?"

"It's eleven in the morning, Alain."

"It's eight in the evening in Paris and the weather is delightful there, I miss it. The offer still stands."

"Pass for now. Do you know anything about the America's Cup?"

"Sharon, my dear, the America's Cup is one of the silliest international races conceived by man, actually by rich men, very rich men with huge egos. I can have Peter make you a cocktail."

"No," she said, emphatically.

"I seldom take no for an answer, so I'll ask again in a few minutes. Anyway, since its inception in 1851, when the schooner America won a hundred British pounds in a race around the Isle of Wright, beating a fleet of British vessels, it's been a race of challengers and losers and for 132 years no one bested an American boat. These men have spied, stolen and even, now this is a rumor my dear, killed to take the Cup and to keep it."

Dumont took a deep breath, the oxygen nose prongs fed him an enriched oxygen mixture; he took another measured breath and visibly relaxed.

"I put a couple of million into the damn race maybe thirty years ago, a silent partner then. I was talked into it by some friends from the San Francisco yachting crowd, had to keep up with the Jones, as they say. . . was fun, some great parties and even prettier women. There is a reason they are all females."

"The boats?"

"Yes dear, the boats. They all have great lines with great full sails and they cost a lot of money. Yes, woman and boats have a lot in common."

"Incorrigible," Sharon said.

"Ain't it the truth?" Alain said. "Anyway, for years the race was held off the East Coast, mostly focused on Newport, Rhode Island. Then the Aussies won the damn thing and off it went, Down Under. You would have thought that they had stolen the Holy Grail or something. Well, young Dennis Conner won it back and moved it to San Diego for a couple of races, then New Zealand took it and held it twice down there about ten years ago. Then, of all things, a Swiss group out of Lake Geneva won it and took it to the Mediterranean, it was right about then that the traditional mono-hulls were unceremoniously dropped and faster catamarans and trimarans came to the starting line."

"Two hulls are always better than one," Sharon said with a smirk.

"Don't interrupt!" Alain said. "These weren't your fun little Hobie Cats, these were honest to God monsters that grew into multi-hulled giants when Larry Ellison caught the bug, big ninety-foot boats that could tear the heart out of the ocean. He blew away the Swiss. Now it's moved to the big time with international preliminary bouts and billions being sent all over the world. Ain't it fun watching the rich at play?"

"You old cynic!"

"Don't I have a right? Don't all my years allow me a little room to laugh at all this? But I'll tell you the technology in these boats makes my heart jump with joy, all the sensors and information gathered, just amazing. My first sail, back in the thirties, was in a twenty-foot wood-hulled dream, I busted her up on the rocks, got lost in the fog somewhere off Maine. She was my first and last sailboat, only dabbled with them from then on."

"Millions spent in the America's Cup isn't dabbling," Sharon admonished.

"Tisk, tisk, Sharon, boys and their toys. Hand me that glass, please."

Peter walked into the room, "Mr. Dumont, pill time."

"I'm ahead of you, already got it," Sharon handed him the glass; he swallowed a blue pill.

"Was that what I thought it was?"

The old man smiled, "And what do you think it was, my

dear?"

"That looked like a Viagra!" Sharon said.

"Oh that, yes it was, I knew you were coming so there you are."

"Oh please, you are an irredeemable letch, what more can I say?"

"The pill has other uses besides the advertised one; the docs say it's good for my heart. But it does surprise me sometimes and I get real light-headed."

"I wouldn't be surprised, all that loss of blood to the brain."

"Ain't it the truth, ain't it the truth."

Peter served an early lunch. Sharon watched Dumont slowly eat a plate of the most disgusting ground-up food she'd ever seen.

"The old stomach has troubles dear; you eat for both of us. Peter certainly does."

Lunch was crab salad sandwiches; Peter joined the two in the sunroom that overlooked the Bay. One of Dumont's own Sancerre's was served. The discussion was light; it revolved around seaside villages they had been to and which one was their favorite. After an hour, the host won out with Positano - it was the food, always the food.

As Sharon left, she asked Peter how Alain was really doing.

"He's waiting to die, actually he's quite happy about it, not that he wants to rush it, he just wants to move on. He feels trapped and handcuffed. Once in a while one of his tech friends stops by to say hello, most have moved on or died. He barely understands this new world and all that's going on and he knows it and bitches about it."

"You're good for him, thank you."

"It's you girls visiting that really brightens him up, he was beside himself when Claudette stayed here. She is more than the love of his life; right now she is his life. And by the way, he likes you too."

Chapter 5

5a

Sharon navigated around the numerous holes that pierced the old wooden deck of the pier. The bay water sloshed under the rotten flooring and slapped up against the black, tar-covered piers. The last thing she wanted to do was go through this rotten deck. If no one saw her fall through, she was sure she would never be found. The noise and echo of banging and slamming metal on metal filled the end of the warehouse.

"Is that you, O'Mara?" a deep voice boomed near the source of the noise, the unmistakable Scottish brogue left no doubt who it was.

"Hi Mike, wanted to talk with you, you available?" Sharon said as the big shape of Mike Stroud appeared in the glare of the open warehouse doors, looking out at San Francisco Bay.

"Give me a minute, we're loading a lot of the gear from the trimaran into a container, needs to be at the port tomorrow to catch a ride to France. Anything I can help you with?"

"Maybe, I wanted to take another look at the boat, see if anything else was missed by the police. That okay?"

"Absolutely, but you only have about an hour, then we load her," Mike said. "She's been broken down into three primary pieces; the container was designed to allow her to be easily slipped into the box. At least the hulls can stay in one piece. When we move those AC-45s, we have to literally break-up the hulls and pontoons, the containers are too small so we have to make them fit."

"A lot of work."

"A lot of headaches. Lord knows that when the big girls are built, all seventy-two feet of 'em, they will have to be assembled on site. Ms. Turner is expecting, beyond a doubt, that her boat will be challenging Ellison."

"She's that confident?"

"She doesn't expect anything less. The death of Catherine has thrown her into an ocean of hard choices. She needs to find a skipper in the next few weeks to remain competitive. They have to train together as well. And most of the good guys are already pulling checks from one of the other boats."

"Anybody being considered?"

"Down to two, another Frenchman and a hotshot from Auckland. Both are good, in fact both are very good. Jimmy Doolan, the kid from Auckland, was working with the Chilean group but they pulled out so he needs a gig. The Frenchman is from Nice, worked on the big boats all around the world and knows the Mediterranean where the racing will be later this summer."

"What's his name?"

"Guillaume Boutin, but almost everyone calls him Bobo. He's been hanging around the races off-and-on for the last six months trying to find a boat. Lot of experience but he's mercurial, blows up at a the slightest thing, tough for a captain; no one gets more from their crews except that by the end of the race they want to kill him."

"Hard to be a leader if the team wants you dead," Sharon said.

"I was exaggerating a bit but just a bit. He cuts hard and deep during a race, both on and off the boat. You can't sail with him if you have a thin skin," Mike offered.

"Is Bobo dark, thick-browed, rough black hair, pony-tail, about six-one, big shoulders?"

"Yes, that's him, looks like that actor in the movie *Black Swan*, Cassel, I think?"

"Yes, Vincent Cassel, he does look a lot like him but harder with a deeper edge," Sharon added.

"That's what being on the high seas will do to you, why do you ask?"

"I saw him with Ellis Turner the other night; they were having dinner."

"Doubt it was a date, Turner was probably interviewing him. Karg there?"

"Eva Karg? Yes, that was a dinner I wouldn't have wanted to be a part of, too hormonal and too much bitchiness for my taste. May I look over the boat?"

"Absolutely, I've got a few things to do in the office trailer; if you need anything just holler. Say goodbye before you leave, okay."

"Yes, sir," she said as she headed toward the pile of carbon fiber and fiberglass.

The boat was disassembled into two small hulls and one larger hull. Thanks to Wikipedia, she found out that the terms for the boat's parts are Malayan. The central hull, the vaka, was big enough to stand alone; it's just that this boat's shape was very different from the usual mono-hulled sailboat. It was narrow and shallow with what appeared to be shoulders across its midsection. This was where the connections, or akas, were secured to hold the smaller hulls, or amas. These outriggers were where the conventional stopped. Secured within these narrow hulls were the hydrofoil blades that would be lowered and raised hydraulically to hike the whole boat, except for a long rudder, into the air. At this point, the boat became more like a plane than a Polynesian canoe.

Running her hand along the edge of the smaller hull, probably the port hull, she noticed the line of black paint again and a slight ding at its starting point.

"Here's where the initial tap occurred," she said out loud to no one. "Then the boat slid a few feet, leaving the paint behind. My guess is they fended it off, minimizing the impact, with a gaff or a pole or maybe someone simply leaned over and pushed it away."

She got down low, looking closely at to glasslike finish of the ama; looking at the end of the paint transfer, she noticed a smudge.

"Thought so," she said.

She reached into her handbag and drew out a small plastic zippered bag containing a fingerprint kit. After opening it, she dusted the spot on the hull lightly with a salt-shaker. It left the hull sprinkled with a fine black powder. Then she extracted a small, yet very soft brush and gently dusted away the loose powder. She blew away the last bits. Looking closely, she noticed the rewarding shape of a palm print and three fingertips set against the dark red hull.

"Gotcha, you little bastards," she exclaimed softly.

She drew out three small sheets of paper, each with a plastic face. Pealing one back, she gently placed the sticky side down on the black swirling patterns, pressed gently, and slowly pealed the plastic away from the hull. Folding it back on the paper, she smiled at the perfect transfer of the three fingertips. She repeated the process on the palm using a slightly bigger paper. In three minutes she was done.

When the boat was in the water and all the hulls were connected, a net-like structure was stretched between the main hull and the two outriggers; this made it easier to move from one side of the trimaran to the other. She wished the boat were still assembled; there might have been something left in the netting, something, anything. But now it was too late.

Sharon looked at the port ama again, now with a noticeable black smudge in its mid-section area. A metal cleat was secured to the hull; two pulleys were attached to the long cleat. She looked closely at the gearing and noticed something missed by the Coast Guard. A long buff-colored hair had wrapped itself around the shaft of the gear.

"And what do we have here?" she said, as she extracted a pair of tweezers from her case. Working slowly, she extracted the hair; it was buff with a slight change in color toward its tip, easily seven inches long and, wonder of wonders, it held a dark almost invisible bulb at one end.

"I love it when DNA comes together," she said with a smirk. She dropped it into a plastic zippered bag that she had also taken from her magic kit bag.

"Find anything more?" Mike asked as he walked back to the hulls.

"Maybe, won't know for a week or so, but maybe something."

"Good, ever since you pointed out that black smudge, I'm certain that someone did hit the boat and then someone killed Catherine. If I find out who the son-of-a-bitch is, I'll personally cut his throat and not think twice about it. It's not worth killing over, none of this shit is worth it but I swear I'll gut him."

Sharon was sure he would and would never get caught; he just had that air about him.

"I know how to do it; no one will ever find out."

"Don't spread that around, Mike, the police take threats seriously."

"Yeah, like the investigation they did. See you found something," Mike said looking at the black smudge.

"Maybe a print, I'll find out." She said nothing about the long hair. Mike's was hard black and grey, cut close, yet curly, a far cry from the straight blondish seven-inch hair she found twisted in the pulley. But she also knew there couldn't have been three reasons why that hair was there, only one. She knew it could only have been left by whoever pulled the rope through the pulley, just before they put it around Catherine Voss's neck and threw her into the cold salty water of San Francisco Bay.

5b

Over a sandwich, that included corn beef and bribery in one of Lafayette's better noontime bistros, Sharon slid the large white envelope across the Formica top toward Kevin Bryan.

"This had better be the one million dollars you owe me, O'Mara, I've waited long enough," Kevin said as he ran his fingertips over the paper surface.

"You still have to wait; I told you I'm short this week. Yah just gotta give me a week, just one more week. I just knows my pony's gonna come in, just one week, Mr. Bryan. Then it's gravy time."

Kevin scrunched his eyebrows at the obscenely bad film noir antics of his best friend.

"I've already given you more time than I would any two-bit flunky, no way, pay up. If not, it's the river, just like Bugsy. I know you're the one who did it. I got it on you, so pay up."

"The river? Please, that one was used last time – not the river."

"Okay, okay." Kevin paused. "If not, it's the quarry, you did it before - I can make you do it again."

"Never, I won't, I just can't. You can't make me!"

Kevin stared at the redhead sitting across the table. "I have ways."

"You've tried them all and you know nothing works except, of course, Italian food and red wine."

"I told you not to go there; I've told you a thousand times. The greatest gift that God gave to man was making Christopher Columbus accidentally run into America and discovering the tomato. A billion Italian mommas have thanked him since 1492."

Sharon shook her head. "He did not run into America, it was some godforsaken island in the Caribbean and he did not discover the tomato. The Mayans had been making pizza for over a thousand years when he landed but he might have been the first to sell it by the slice."

"And I suppose red wine wasn't discovered by Italians?"

"No, I only think they perfected it. Then they sold the patents to the French who, to this day, believe they invented red wine. Me, I have it on good authority that it was Socrates, a Greek, who, after drinking a really bad batch of the stuff, said something prophetic, became famous, then died. And besides, the Irish owe their collective success as a nation of gastrophobes to Columbus as well, he also discovered the potato."

"Gastrophobes?" Kevin asked, not wishing for the answer.

"Yes Kevin, the fear of good food."

"You win, I can never beat you. You're just too damn smart. And after you have bribed me with corned beef, Ireland's national meat, what can I do for you and what is in the envelope?"

"Hopefully, some answers, though I think maybe more questions," she said running her finger across the envelope. "I'm working with the Voss family, investigating Catherine's death, they think there's more and after that bit of foul play on Highway 24, I'm beginning to think so too."

"They connected?"

"Maybe and if not, it's a big coincidence. I saw two BMW 650s that night and both were black, with dark glass, convertibles, so maybe I'm paranoid or the same person tried to knock me off the road. Maybe, I just don't know."

"The envelope?"

"Some things I pulled from Catherine's trimaran, a palm print and fingerprints and a long hair, blond with maybe a touch of DNA. So could you slip it in the next bag to the county and see if anything pops up?"

"Maybe I can tie it to your accident, perhaps. But you, more than anyone, know that the captain wants you and me to be at least a million miles away from each other. He says you're no good, could catch my death if I hang around you."

"Little ol' me? Why sir, I'm hurt."

"Well, let's just keep this on the q.t. I'll check them out and let you know. May take a week or more, okay?"

"Will have to be, could be nothing or maybe it will pry the door open a bit; let's take peek inside. Won't know till we know."

"Profound."

Sharon walked around the boot of her Jaguar trying to find the eight-inch dent. She ran her hand over the green rump of her car, and caressed the rear quarter panel.

"Good lord, Reggie, it's gone, like it never existed."

"With my skills, it never did. I wished it away and it vanished. My skills are legendary. Here's my bill."

"Don't care, thank you. It's wonderful."

"I also serviced it, saved you a trip later, dearie. Will be good for another five thousand miles or until you damage my car again."

"Your car?"

"Sharon, when you are in my hands, every car is mine. I only let you drive them so be careful. By the way, did you know there was a small caliber bullet hole in the rear door panel?"

"What?"

"Small caliber, maybe a twenty-two caliber," Reginald said. "One very neat hole, rear door mid-panel, I filled it. But I did take some pictures. I also found the slug imbedded in the inside panel. Whoever fired it left me no doubt that they wanted to do more than just dent your fender."

Sharon took the slug from Reggie's hand and rolled it around in her fingers; the steel of the door had mangled it beyond recognition. Only the hole in the door gave it size and substance.

"Didn't go through?"

"No, was caught inside the far rear door panel. I guess it was a lucky shot."

"For who? Me or them?"

"You, dearie, you."

Sharon talked to Kevin and brought him up to speed on the bullet in the door and the repair.

"Drop the slug off and I'll have my gal check it out. Maybe she can get a make on the ammo."

"That's possible, no rifling left or at least no grooves. Later."

"Be careful Sharon, looks like it was more than bad driving. Someone wants more out of you than a dinged fender."

"Thanks for the heads-up."

"Anytime."

Now it was personal, she hated it when it got personal. She knew she could lose perspective. She could develop a serious complex if someone was after her. She'd been there before and didn't like it. Now it wasn't just an accident with someone leaving the scene; seems the son-of-a-bitch wanted to involve her in a drive-by shooting.

She slid into the leather driver seat of the Jaguar and headed back to her cottage. She needed to think this out a bit more, get her head wrapped around the accident, Ms. Karg and her BMW, the damaged trimaran hull, JF Voss and the fellow, Bobo. Her unique Irish heritage was picking up vibes but trying to get them to sing the same song was a different matter.

Ellis Ann Turner was born in 1955 to a young husband and wife in the outback of Australia. The young man, Jack Turner, was a metallurgist with an uncanny ability to find iron ore in the hard lands of Western Australia. He found iron ore at Kooly-anobbing. For thirty years he worked for the company that spotted him his first stake; he paid it back within five years and eventually took over the small iron mining company. When Ellis was thirty, her father had expanded into coal and gold. In 1998, while flying through a dust storm, his plane crashed. It happened while they were going to their daughter's forty-third birthday. Both of her parents were killed and the next day she owned the largest mining company in Australia. Twelve years later, she owned the second largest mining company in the world. Forbes set her personal wealth at $22 billion dollars, US dollars, not Australian.

Sharon shut the computer off, closed it and sat back in her desk chair, "Not bad ol' boy, not bad," she said to Basil. "Have to admire her, she inherited the pile but has spent the last fifteen years making it bigger and bigger in the big boy's world of iron and coal. Hard enough anytime, but today it's a bitch. Walk?"

Basil jumped to his feet and spun around like a dervish, he never needed to be asked twice, too many new smells in the neighborhood, too many bushes to stick his nose in and too many new places to pee.

Cinched up with his new leash and collar, Basil and Sharon quick marched around the neighborhood. Her loose sweatshirt, emblazoned with the SF Giants logo, contrasted with her tight black gym shorts. He had to contend with short and fleeting sniffs of the shrubbery. Only once, where the delicious aroma of a dead something in a bush caught his attention, was he able to pull Sharon up short.

"Now what?" she said watching Basil. "No way, get your face out of there. I'll not have you stinking up the house."

She gave him a quick pull; he turned and looked at her as if to say, *"This is my time, not yours. You get to have all the fun and that dead possum smells divine."*

"Now, out of there," was all he got for his efforts. He har-rumphed and led the charge down the sidewalk again, Sharon briskly in tow. *He'd show her.*

Two blocks later, she jogged in place waiting for the light to change; Basil sat as he was told, waiting as well. As the light changed, he bolted into the intersection, whip-sawing Sharon around, only the leather strap wrapped tightly around her wrist prevented her from flying through the intersection. The screech of tires caught them both up short. Sharon quickly turned and looked into the panicked face of a twenty-something girl, cell phone clenched to her face. Relieved that the brakes on her Prius worked well, preventing her from running into the woman and her dog, she held onto the steering wheel for dear life, her heart thudding loudly in her chest. Sharon, feeling as though she just lost about ten years of her life, looked at the girl, took a deep breath and offered a weak smile. Basil couldn't figure out what the holdup was.

They walked the remaining three blocks home. Basil was nothing but a gentleman. As she keyed the lock, her eye caught a flash off the glass panel high on the door and only then did she notice the van at the curb across the street. The van hadn't been there when they went for their jog. A red and black magnetized sign was stuck to the door panel. She read 'ARNIE'S PLUMB-ING', in large letters, no address or phone number.

"Obviously Arnie doesn't want to expand his business" she said to Basil. The rear windows look painted over from the in-side. A small hole in the painted window's finish looked black and then flashed with a bright light, then back to black again.

"Basil, ever seen a surveillance truck, especially a very bad one? Well there's one for you to pee on. Shall we go take a look?

Give me a second."

Sharon opened the door and Basil followed her into the living room. She slid the Beretta out of her handbag and slid it snug into the back of her shorts. The sweatshirt covered the pistol. Then she gripped the leash tightly and went back out the front door. She waved at the truck and immediately started to walk directly toward the van. Whoever was inside jumped into the front seat, gunned the idling engine and bolted down the quiet suburban street.

"Well I wonder who that was and why he didn't wait to say hi?" She noticed a smoldering cigarette butt on the curbside where the van had sat. She gently snubbed the butt out and collected three others, all with black filters and paper. The labels were a brand she hadn't seen since Iraq, Indonesian Djarum; there was also the heavy aroma of cloves.

"Shit, if you're going to smoke, smoke real goddamn cigarettes, not some fru-fru shit brand. Amateurs, damn amateurs."

5c

Green Zone, Baghdad, Iraq, 2005

The smell of cloves and tobacco drifted in the thick air of the trailer; even the air conditioner on the roof couldn't break the fog. The heat hung low with the added haze from O'Mara's and al-Jamil's co-mingled cigarettes, in layers to the ceiling. In another hour, the room would be too hot to sit in, in two hours, too hot to even think in. The corporal handed her the phone.

"It's Major Simpson's aide."

"Ginny, O'Mara here, can I talk with the Major? . . . Yes, I'll hold . . . tell him I may have an opening in the al-Kufah region," Sharon said, waiting.

Five minutes later, she heard Major Jebadiah Simpson on the other end. "O'Mara, what do you have?"

"A chance, sir. Seems the al-Qaeda have kidnapped a local chieftain's twin daughters. Finding and returning them could help us a lot in the area. It's been hard to get those people in the swamps to listen, most want us to leave and then maybe the al-Qaeda would also go, or so they think. This guy knows it's wishful thinking. He's been educated in the US but he keeps a low profile. We help him, maybe he can help us."

"It's a possibility. I'll pass the word to question any detainees that we pick up in the area about the kids. I missed it, boys or girls?"

"Twin blue-eyed girls and they're as cute as all get out. I'm sending a picture to Ginny; she'll get the prints to whoever needs them."

"Good, sure as hell would be nice to have a few of those families down there working with us. What village?"

"Near the shrine at al-Kufah."

"Shia?"

"Yes. No love lost between the al-Qaeda and the Shia. Shit, the Sunni and Shia go back over a thousand years, killings been almost non-stop."

"They using the kids as leverage perhaps?" the Major asked.

"Seems likely, we help them then maybe they can help us. That work for you, Major?" Sharon said, already knowing the answer.

"Works just fine. We'll spread the news to the southern bases. Anything else?'

"I want to be there when they're found. I owe it to the man; he saved our hides last week."

"I heard. Was it his village?"

"Yes sir."

"If I can, I'll call you. Sometimes these things happen faster than we want."

"Don't I know it, Major. Don't I know it."

* * * *

Walnut Creek, California

Sharon placed the clove cigarettes in a plastic zip-lock bag; she knew that these had to come from outside the US. In the infinite and all-knowing wisdom of Washington, they had been outlawed in the US by the FDA, one of their many Olympian efforts at reducing the number of kids who smoked. US companies didn't fight the effort too strenuously, not many of them made the flavored cigarettes. Their source was mostly foreign, especially from Indonesia. O'Mara knew that if nanny Washington went after menthol cigarettes; there would be hell to pay.

"Kev, seems they want to look into my windows now," Sharon said after Bryan returned her call. "Amateurs, real amateurs. Reminds me of one of your stakeouts, the ones where fast food wrappers are left lying about with empty coffee cups on the curb."

"I would never do that, never, you know that. What makes you think it was a stakeout?"

"They bolted when I started to walk up to their van, a cheap sign on the door, poor disposal habits when it comes to smoking; everything said 'amateurs were here'."

"More than one?"

"Couldn't tell; only saw one man in the front seat. Had a camera or something taking pics through a small hole in the rear panel. Maybe two men; can't be sure."

Kevin wasn't too concerned about Sharon's safety. He knew she was better prepared than most of the men and woman in the Lafayette police department. When he brought up the thought of her joining with one of the local police departments, she'd told him more than once, "If I wanted a boss again, I'd go work for the government. I like being my own girl, independent. And besides, I'm tired of uniforms."

"What do you need?"

"One more DNA test; seems they left a few cigarette butts lying about. Just a little more information might help. That okay?"

"Sharon, if the captain finds out, I could be working with you permanently."

"Not a chance, no employees needed or wanted. The insurance would be too high, couldn't afford it. You'd have to be an independent consultant, that way if you're shot up or worse, I wouldn't be liable."

"Pleasant thought. Yes, you're right, never could work for a woman anyway."

"I'll hold onto that thought, might come in handy later. Can I drop this off?"

"Better than that, I'll stop by, will you be home around 6:00?"

"See you then and yes, I'll cook. You bring the wine. I'll surprise you."

"I just love your surprises," Kevin said as Sharon hung up.

She found a pound of ground sirloin in the refrigerator, along with enough greens to make two salads, two day-old ciabatta buns and some sharp cheddar from Sonoma. She left out enough meat from the two patties to cook up a small piece for Basil. He sat and watched her every move.

She chopped a red onion into fine pieces and worked them into the meat. Then she split each burger into two pieces, inserted a slice of Brie between the pieces and knitted them back together into a patty. When she went outside to let Basil do his business, she lit the mesquite charcoal in the grill. *When you need it done right, best to do it right, no gas tonight,* as the briquettes started to heat up and grey over.

Basil quickly turned at the first sound and lumbered to the front, he knew that knock intimately.

"Sharon," Kevin said, as Basil, who nuzzled his hand, escorted him down the hallway.

"Kitchen, just in time," she said as she sprinkled balsamic wine vinegar and olive oil over the greens. "You know where the cork screw is; I hope you brought a wine that needs a cork screw."

"Very funny," he said as he started to remove the cork, he was ten seconds ahead of her. "Anything more about the stakeout?"

"They've not been back. I went through the video from the front door camera. Not much more to say, but it does look like two men, dark complexioned driver, nothing on the other but a shape, maybe a man or a woman. The envelope on the front desk has the cigarette butts in it. Maybe they'll turn out to be nothing. But thanks."

"Burgers," Kevin said as he spied the patties on the counter.

"Brilliant detective, just brilliant. You can put them on after you pour me a glass."

Kevin poured the cabernet into the two glasses Sharon had left out on the table. He sniffed and tasted the wine, "Excellent," then headed out the door with the meat, Basil in close pursuit.

* * * *

Green Zone, Baghdad, Iraq, 2005

The aroma of barbequed meat rose into the dusty grey-blue sky over their small spit of heaven within the almost four square-mile American Green Zone. Sharon stood at the top of the low earth dike that enclosed the compound she and her men used as their billet. The dike separated them from the Tigris River. She watched an Iraqi patrol boat speed up the greenish brown river; the rooster tail spray exploding from the stern of the small craft obscured the man standing behind the 50 caliber machine gun mounted mid-hull. The noise from its motor masked the urban sounds that normally echoed across the ancient river into the Zone. She scraped her foot across the new asphalt poured recently at the base of the dike and left a track in the dust deposited by the sandstorm the day before. The smell of beef, American beef, hung in the still air. She closed her eyes and for a moment tried earnestly to believe she was back in California.

It was Friday. The voices coming from the speakers hung on the sides of the hundreds of minarets piercing the skyline began their calls to prayer as the patrol boat disappeared. The *muazzins* call to prayer rolled around the canyons of the city until they mixed with the urban sounds, resulting in a muffled cacophony. Nothing was distinct, just like with the sandstorm, everything blended together into a dusty reddish yellow haze of gritty Arabic confusion of sound and city.

"Your burger, lieutenant," Sergeant Sanchez said holding out a plate.

"Thanks Sanchez, beer?"

Sanchez reached behind him and pulled a long neck Budweiser from the small of his back where he had stuffed it. "Burger okay?"

"Can't get much fucking better than this, Sanchez."

"Yeah, this is heaven, lieutenant, fucking heaven." He clinked his beer against hers.

"Heaven, Sanchez, heaven."

The two soldiers stood shoulder to shoulder, Sharon's red hair was pulled up under her field cap and dark wrap-around sunglasses covered her eyes. She held an American hamburger in one hand and America's beer in the other; the miasma that was Baghdad lay out before them.

"What would you be doing right now Sanchez if you were home?" O'Mara asked.

"The same thing I did every Friday night, pick my daughter up from school, then pick my wife up from her job, then pick up a huge pizza, a six pack of beer and a bottle of coke. We would sit in the back yard and tell stories," Sanchez said between bites and sips.

"Nice, what does your wife do?"

"She's an assistant for an attorney, always was smarter than me, I do what I can. But the army will be my life, I think, but two tours in this shithole are more than I can or want to put up with."

"Good job, always marry someone smarter than you. Yes, two tours are more than I bargained for as well." They tapped bottles again.

As one, they scanned across the river, east toward the Sahid Mosque and Firdos Square marked by the towers of two hotels; the haze obscured the lower portion of the mosque's dome and the upper portion sparkled in the late sun. They blinked twice as a huge fireball climbed up into the grey sky, four seconds later the explosion reached them like distant thunder. It rolled across the river in echoing waves.

"Fuck," O'Mara said as the smoke billowed and roiled high over Baghdad. "The sons-a-bitches are killing themselves again, if it's not al-Qaeda, it's the Sunnis and then it's the Shiites. Sanchez, sometimes I think we're policemen involved in an East L.A. gang war, you never know what will come next."

"Seems to me that L.A. is safer, Lieutenant. None of my homies could get RPGs and explosives like they have here."

"Thank God for small favors," Sharon said as she took another swig from her beer.

A private walked over to the two soldiers.

"Shit, killing each other again," he said, watching the smoke drift over the brown city. "Major on the horn, Lieutenant." He handed Sharon the phone.

"O'Mara ... Yes, Sir ... Firdos ... Yes, I know, just saw it, ... Roger, thank you, Major, we'll check it out. The locals are sweeping through now; I can hear the sirens from here ... Yes, Sir, ... Roger, I'll let you know. Out."

"Party's over, Sanchez, mount up. We're going to take a look at that shit," Sharon said as she turned her back on the river and pointed over her shoulder at the remains of the explosion, its cloud slowly drifted over the river. As if the sirens were a cue, a second explosion ripped through the air in almost the same location as the first, this one larger and louder.

"Fuck, now they want to kill the rescuers," O'Mara said. "This is one fucked up country."

It took thirty minutes for her patrol to reach the small market area near Firdos Square. The smell of the explosions lingered in the still air. They passed a smoldering, burned out emergency vehicle; it had been blown into another truck. Iraqis sat dazed and bleeding against the walls and along the sidewalks. People moved among the living and dead, trying to help as best as they could.

"Main blast occurred around the corner, Lieutenant, came in over the radio from the locals."

"Thanks, private. Sanchez, bring your people to the left and flank us. We'll take a look-see at what's left. Remember that this may be nothing more than bait to lure us out here. Be fucking careful."

"Roger, Lieutenant," both vehicles answered.

The three Humvees split and navigated between the tipped cars and building debris thrown into the street, most of the bodies had been removed already. When Sharon's Humvee turned the corner, they almost ran into the crater the first bomb had created.

"Car bomb, can't tell whether it was parked or there was a suicide driver. If it was a suicide, hope the fucker can put himself back together for those virgins he was promised," Sharon said into her radio.

"Virgins are so overrated, Lieutenant," Sanchez said.

"You still a virgin, Sanchez?" another voiced quipped over the radio.

"Keep your minds on the job and you, Nolan, shut up and watch the roofs," O'Mara said as they pulled to a stop and dismounted from the Humvee.

It was eerily quiet, no traffic noise, but people were rummaging about amongst the debris. A woman's wailing cut through the dust still drifting along the edges of the arcade. A neon sign flickered, its Arabic letters busted and disfigured. The Sheraton and Palestine Hotels stood high over the one and two story buildings; the stalls within the market below them were blown away.

For the next two hours, they walked the streets and alleys around the square that was made famous when Saddam Hussein's statue was pulled down. O'Mara arrived in Baghdad less than a year later. The traffic circled the square as if nothing had happened; a fatalistic attitude develops among people in a war zone. They still have to move on as best as they can with their lives. She knew the American presence pissed a lot of people off but those same people were glad they were there; if not, the millennium-old war between the sects would break out again.

"Sanchez, get your people out of here, we're done. The beer

should still be cold. Nolan load'em up," Sharon said into her microphone.

"Don't have to be told twice, Lieutenant. I feel like a target in a shooting gallery out here," Private Nolan said.

They wound their way through the maze of streets to the relative safety of the boulevard that paralleled the Tigris River embankment; the 14th of July Bridge crossed the Tigris ahead of them. In ten minutes, they were across the bridge and back in heaven again.

Chapter 6

6a

Eva Karg paced back and forth across the marble lobby of the hotel; her man was late and he was never late. Her phone buzzed in the pocket of her short black riding jacket.

"Where the hell are you?" she asked, after checking the screen. "Well okay, told you to be careful … Did she see you? … Good, anything else … No? Email me the pictures. I will be back later this afternoon … None of your business, but if you care, I'm riding." She hung up.

If there was one thing that Eva Karg could pull off without much difficulty, it was the head bitch effect. She stood on the hotel's hard stone floor dressed in a full-cut white blouse with open bodice, a large collar and tight cuffs. Her tight, ass-enhancing riding britches disappeared into her polished black riding boots. A small cap tried to contain the mass of blond hair she was known for; an honest-to-God riding crop finished the look. She tapped the crop against her boot, making a hollow tapping sound, expressing her impatience.

She didn't have to wait long. The elevator opened and a dark complexioned male with a three-day beard walked into the lobby, his riding outfit was similar, but masculine. He didn't wear a cap, his black ponytail made enough of a statement.

"You're late," Karg said.

"We're going riding, not catching a plane. The car's out front, you'll be on your horse in an hour. Patience."

"Patience my ass, Bobo. And he's a better ride, too," Karg said as she turned toward the doors, her black BMW waited in the courtyard.

"Bitch," Bobo said under his breath, as he followed her

through the double doors.

The riding stables were located in a valley snuggled between one of the low foothills at the base of Mt. Diablo. Riding trails extend up to its summit as well as encircling the whole mountain. Some claim that from its peak you can see more of America than anywhere else in the United States. Eva Karg could not have cared less.

Her ride was a palomino mare; Bobo's was a chestnut mare. This was her third ride on this horse; she liked its seat and was thinking of making an offer to buy her.

"Why the hell do you want to own a horse, Eva. They're just a double pain in the ass, money-wise as well as ass-wise," Bobo said as they started up the trail.

"Very funny," Karg answered. "Always wanted a horse since I was a kid in South Africa. But we never settled down long enough. We moved from one mining town to another. I learned to ride but never stayed in one place very long."

"I rode all over the hills behind Aix," Bobo said. "I grew up in the country but we were just a few kilometers from the sea. During the summer, we would sail in the morning and ride in the afternoon."

"You were rich. We had almost nothing."

"Sure we had money but we were hardly rich."

"Yes, all the rich people I've known have said the same thing."

"I'll bet Ellis doesn't say that."

"She doesn't have to, I know her roots."

"She's made a point of letting everyone know her roots, her biography leaves little out of the picture. Must have pissed you off when she outed you."

"Couldn't have cared less, was out long before that, and you don't seem to mind how I go. Boys or girls what's the difference?"

"I don't care who you screw but just don't wrap me up in one of your little sick games," Bobo said.

"Games, I don't play games," she answered. "Games are for

children. Mine are for real; there are real winners and real losers. And I would suggest that you stay out of my way. Besides, you didn't mind being selected as Ellis's new driver. I would say that when the opportunity presented itself, you were there to grab the line and hang on tight."

"Yes, I was. And it's a damn shame about Catherine Voss. I liked her."

"Yes, just like I like this horse," Karg said as she tapped the flank of the palomino with her crop and set off on a trot, Bobo followed. He knew then that he wanted Eva Karg riding in front of him, not only was it easier to watch her ass but it was also easier to cover his own.

They rode for another hour before turning back to the stable. They crossed the old span of the Bay Bridge in the dark; the new bridge span that flanked the old one was scheduled to open about the same time that the America's Cup races began. This old eastern structure would be demolished and shipped off somewhere, probably to China, where it would be melted, rolled, punched and eventually come back on a container ship under this same span's ghost, as a million washing machines.

6b

"Next week, Sharon, I can't get any of the results until next week. The lab's already backed up and even though this is important, there are other cases that have top priority - political priority," Kevin said.

"I understand, let me know as soon as you can," Sharon answered. She was disappointed but the state lab was good, pushing it might cost her and Kevin their only leads. If his captain found out, he'd pitch all the samples and then they would have nothing.

Her phone rang again, a few brief bars of *La Marseillaise* were heard, she smiled.

"Good morning Jean-François, how are you?" she asked.

"It's afternoon here," JF said. "And I don't have good news."

"What happened?"

"It's missing."

"What's missing?"

"Catherine's boat, the hydrofoil. The container never made it to the railhead."

"Railhead, I'm confused. I thought that Mike was going to send it by boat."

"Yes, it was going by boat. But first, it was going by rail to Newark, New Jersey then by boat to Marseille. I just got off the phone with Mike; it never got to the railroad. After it left the dock, it disappeared. That was yesterday. Mike didn't learn about it until this morning. He never got confirmation from Union Pacific. They said it never arrived. This is not good."

"No, it isn't, I'll call Mike right now and find out all I can. I will get back to you."

"Call me no matter what time it is."

She sat the phone down on her desk and thought out the logistics of the problem, she had a lot of experience with the Port of Oakland and its attendant rail facilities. There were millions of boxes coming and going at the port, it would be easy enough to lose one or two. But she was fairly certain that JF's box never even made the port. It could be in a million places; the box would just disappear in the visual clutter of the many highways and warehouses.

"Mike," she said after Stroud answered. "Just got off the phone with JF, what else do you know?"

"Not much, the driver has also disappeared, a Latino fellow, Julio Flores, according to his boss. Never late, has driven for him for five years, Lived near Stockton, no union card. The company says he was one their best drivers, never lost anything and never had an accident. Now this happens and he's gone."

"What time did the box leave?"

"Yesterday at two; slated to be transferred in Oakland to get on a railcar to leave this morning at 5:00 AM. I got the call at 11:00 last night. Said they were holding a spot, couldn't wait for the box. Shit, I should have followed the damn thing, but Turner showed up all pissed about something and I couldn't get away. And you know she's not too thrilled about my association with the Voss's anyway."

"So it was either high-jacked or this fellow, Flores, is a part of the deal. I'm leaning toward the container being high-jacked. Whoever wants the boat has the means to get what they want."

"It's just a goddamn boat, O'Mara, who the hell would want to go through all that trouble for a boat?"

"Mike, look around you, how can you say that with a straight face? Hell, the millions, maybe billions being spent just to ride around in the cold ocean - racing each other. No Mike, there's a lot more to this than just a boat, there's something else going on. I'll call you later."

Basil snuggled his wet muzzle in her lap, she scratched the hollow behind his ears.

"An enigma inside a mystery, inside a shipping container, déjà vu all over again, right old boy? But mama's got to get to the gym and then to the range. Then we'll see what we can find out."

She found out on the ten o'clock morning news while watching the screen positioned over the elliptical trainer.

"The driver, Julio Flores, was found dead in the cab of his truck," the blond anchorwoman said. "The truck was found parked along a side street in the warehouse area of West Oakland. The Oakland police believe that he may have been a victim of a high-jacking. He was reported missing by his company early this morning; Flores had worked for the company for many years. The investigation continues. Now, the weather with Carmelita."

6c

Green Zone, Baghdad, Iraq, 2005

"Lieutenant, we may have something about those girls," Sanchez said as he hung up the phone. "Seems that an Iraqi patrol found a house near Karbala that may have contained the girls. They found some of our posters in the house along with a teenage kid. The boy says he was given the poster by some American soldiers. The men in the house wanted it so he gave it to them."

"Smart kid," Sharon said. "But how does he know they had the girls there?"

"Said he saw them and watched them leave in an old Mercedes," Sanchez said. "The two girls were wearing black clothes, like chadors, so he's not positive; but they were smaller than him and he saw tennis shoes under the clothing. Four other men with guns had circled the girls. They left in a hurry."

"What else did the Iraqis find?"

"They had been there a while, left a lot crap and food lying around. No weapons. But there was a torn road map of the al-Kufah neighborhood where we were ambushed. Can you believe it was a fucking Google Earth aerial photo, maybe shot from before the war, but an aerial none-the-less? Whose side are those high tech assholes on? The Iraqis dropped it off with the kid; one of the soldiers said he had the balls to ask for a reward."

"Nothing changes here, that's for damn sure, we use them too," Sharon said.

"Yeah, I know Lieutenant, but shit, they're supposed to be on our side."

"Is the kid here?"

"Yes sir, they transferred him to us when I suggested it was in our best interest to have him, not theirs."

"Good. Not sure what the locals would do to him? I don't trust them any more than a Wall Street banker."

"Yes sir. You want to talk to him?"

"Did the fucking sun come up this morning, Sanchez?"

As she waited for Sanchez and the kid, she wondered about why al-Qaeda might want the girls. The obvious reason was to control the village and al-Jamil, but there had been a lot of ransom kidnappings recently; they needed money and this was one way to get it. It didn't matter how poor the village was, families would find a way to get the money together. She knew of two instances where families became kidnappers themselves just to get the money. *What a lovely country.*

Sharon could see that the kid was about thirteen and he needed a bath. He stood proud and defiant in front of her and Sanchez. The interpreter stood off to one side; he said something to boy. For a moment Sharon could see a slight change, even with all the bravado, this was one very frightened young man.

"Ask him about his family," she said to the Corporal Habib.

The man asked him a string of questions in Arabic.

"Lieutenant, he says that he doesn't have any, lives on the street. Says he's a tough guy. Nobody messes with him."

"Tough guy? Ask him if he wants some ice cream."

The kid's grin said it all and also that he understood some English.

"Sanchez," Sharon said.

"Already on my way, you want one too?"

"You come back with only enough for the kid, you better not come back at all and I'm sure Corporal Habib would like one also."

Habib's grin confirmed Sharon's assumption.

"Now, tough guy, what made you think the girls were the ones we are looking for?"

"How much is it worth to you?" the kid said in a mauled form of Arab accented English.

"You speak English?"

"No, American, learned it from some people at the school. I want to go to America - that's my price. I'll tell you what I know, then you give me a plane ticket."

"Well, tough guy, that won't be that easy. We are mighty particular about who we let into our country."

"Not that particular, my uncle lives there and he's an asshole."

"No fucking swearing," Habib said.

Sharon looked at the man and cocked her head.

"What sir? What?"

Sanchez came through carrying ice cream bars.

"What's your name?" O'Mara asked.

"Abdul," the boy said as he watched Sanchez cross the room.

"Well Abdul, tell me everything you know about the house," Sharon said as she handed Abdul a chocolate-covered ice cream bar.

"They took over the house about two weeks ago, it was empty." The ice cream, in the heat of the trailer, had begun to run down Abdul's arm; he licked the bar and his arm as fast as he could. "They kept to themselves but everyone knew they were bad guys."

"No one said anything?" Sharon said.

"Why? If anyone said anything they would be dead or worse. So everyone ignored them. I made a few dollars from them, getting them some food and rice; I only take American dollars. They seemed okay, not old, but nervous."

"Why were they nervous?"

"Not sure, but everyone in the neighborhood is nervous, so I'm not surprised. Then they disappeared for two days, that was the end of last week then they slipped back into the house. That's when I saw the girls the first time."

"Why didn't you say something then?"

"Didn't want my throat cut and it was before the pictures were handed out. After that I started wondering. Maybe it's the girls they're looking for, maybe Abdul can make a dollar or two and maybe I can get to America."

"Then what?"

"Stood on a stack of boxes outside one of the windows and looked in."

"That was a very bold move," Sanchez said.

"I needed the money. Anyway, I saw them sitting on the floor, very pretty for girls. One man sat on a chair with a rifle. They didn't see me. They left a few hours later in the Mercedes. Didn't think much more of it until the American soldiers came through; I told them what I saw. And, Allah be Praised, here I am, going to America."

"Not so fast, Abdul, a lot more has to happen and your chance of getting to America is smaller than a grain of sand."

"The soldiers promised."

"Iraqi or American?"

"Iraqi," Abdul said, then raised his eyes the ceiling. "The bastards, they would tell me anything, wouldn't they?"

"Seems so, but here you are and now we have a little more information than we did before," Sharon said. "What color was the Mercedes?"

"Silver, dirty with bullet holes on the driver's side. The windows were all dark."

"Did you see a license plate?"

"Yes, but I don't remember anything about it. But one of the lights in the back was gone."

"Do you mean it was burnt out?"

"No, I mean gone. Looked like it had been ripped off or something, you could see into the trunk. One of the men threw a long box in the trunk after they put the girls in the backseat. Then they left."

"You getting that, Sanchez?"

"Yes sir, I'll let our road blocks know about the Mercedes, maybe something will turn up."

"Well, Abdul, you've been a big help. You want some dinner?"

Sharon could see that the tough guy was very hungry, the ice cream lasted one minute, at best.

"Got burgers and fries?" Abdul asked.

"Absolutely, then tomorrow you can take us back to the house so I can look around. Maybe they left something that was overlooked."

"Maybe yes and maybe no. Everything is maybe, maybe I get a reward, maybe I go to America and maybe I get my throat cut. Maybe, maybe, maybe," the Iraqi teenager said.

Chapter 7

"I have the results from the lab. Lunch, you buy." Kevin Bryan said over the phone. "The usual place in Lafayette, I need to be back at the city hall by three."

"Anything interesting?" she asked.

"We'll talk then; the captain's been walking the halls and beating the bushes. Something's really got him, just hope it doesn't include me."

"See you at 1:30," she said and hung up. "*Just what he needs, more shit from his captain,*" she thought as she dialed the restaurant Postino's number.

The Captain had issues with Sharon and Kevin. Separately, he didn't have any problems; it was only when they were together that the trouble started. Usually either one of them got shot, was shot at or had to shoot back and he blamed Sharon for all of it. She protested but she knew Kevin would do anything for her and her for him. More than once, he had showed up in the proverbial nick of time and saved her ass. It was this fact that annoyed the captain more than anything else.

Bryan was habitually late, lifesaving not-withstanding. She knew he would be delayed; she hoped he wouldn't be but he always was. Fifteen-minutes late, Kevin walked into the restaurant, chatted up the girl at the front desk and then headed directly to Sharon. As he sat down, he handed her a manila envelope.

"The captain needed to talk, he was concerned," Kevin said.

"About us again, the samples? Sharon asked.

"No, for once it wasn't us. It was about budgets and politics. He's been ordered to reduce costs by thirty percent."

"That's cutting it close to the bone."

"Too close, this time it may be clean to the bone. The council won't cut their pet programs and besides, they often ask, why do we need such a large force patrolling these quiet suburbs? All I know is that a lot of the men and women are tired of looking over their shoulders. They may get their wish, fewer cops; I think some are ready to move on."

"They're good people. They need to take care of themselves," Sharon said.

"Yes, but most of them like it here and don't want to start over. So, there you have it."

The waitress interrupted and they ordered. Sharon tapped on the envelope impatiently. When the server left, she bent the tabs back and slid out a thin stack of papers.

Two minutes later, she looked at Kevin incredulously, "No way!"

"Way! I had them check it twice."

"I was sure we would get something from the hair, I just knew it. But I sure as hell didn't expect this."

"I wouldn't think so. It's not every day that you find a hair like that out in the middle of San Francisco Bay."

"A horsehair? Light blond color, says the animal might be a palomino; its DNA isn't in any database they have. They have a DNA database for horses?"

"Guess so, you never know when you want to ID a horse, hard to take their fingerprints."

"Nothing on the fingerprints either?"

"Sorry, no match to anything available but the cigarettes came up with a positive, they got a match," Bryan added.

"It obviously isn't from a horse," Sharon said looking at the report. "The DNA matches a piece of murder evidence from about a year ago?"

"Yes, San Francisco PD has been looking for this guy since they found a man beaten to death on one of the piers. There were bits of skin found in the dead man's teeth and that skin DNA and your cigarettes' DNA match. So the interest of the SFPD is also piqued, they had to be told," Kevin added.

"Understood and who says piqued now days?"

"It's a legitimate word."

"Please. Anyway, why the hell was this guy watching my house and why was there a single horsehair stuck in a pulley on a boat stuck on the rocks at Alcatraz?"

"I have no idea but you always attract the nicest and most interesting people. At least we know that these guys are real and not phantoms. Too many coincidences," Kevin said.

The server brought their sandwiches.

"My client had his boat stolen a few days ago," Sharon said.

She caught Kevin in mid-bite on his grilled chicken. "What?"

"They had loaded it into a large shipping container to go back to France; somewhere between the San Francisco docks and the Oakland rail yards someone high-jacked it. The driver was killed; they found him in his truck."

"That man in Oakland was the driver? Another senseless killing."

"It was Voss's only working prototype. It's a radical design and it's the same boat that Catherine Voss was sailing when she died. I found signs that it might have been something more than accidental, these reports begin to help prove it was more than just an accident."

"She was murdered?"

"Possibly, but the boat's gone. Her twin, Jean-François Voss, is coming back from France to help with the search. He added that to my *'To Do'* list. Now, not only do I need to find her murderer but also the boat she was killed on."

"Because of the dead driver, a BOLO was issued, that might help."

"Hope so, maybe some fool will get caught moving the container, could get a lucky break. I'm thinking that the boat was stolen for other reasons, not just the technology."

"Ransom?"

"One possibility, the other is, and I'm going out on a limb here, insurance. And I'm assuming that it was insured for quite a large sum."

"Worth more lost than found?"

"Maybe."

"Not nice to think that about a paying client."

"I know but this whole thing is hinky and now, with a killer parked in front of my house smoking Indonesian cigarettes, it's even stranger."

"If it was ransom they'd contact Voss, right?"

"Probably," Sharon answered.

"Then I'd wait and see what happens, no rush. I'm more concerned about your stalker and his game. You watch yourself. Whatever these guys want, they aren't shy about using force to get it."

"I can handle it," Sharon said as her phone buzzed in her back pocket. The screen said *Stroud*. She looked at Kevin and put a finger up, pausing.

"O'Mara … Mike, you okay? … Yes, I know, I know … Yes, I can be there … You're kidding! … Really, I'm flattered, I think. … Tomorrow morning at nine, see you then." She clicked off her phone.

"For some unexplainable reason, I'm going sailing tomorrow. Ms. Turner has invited me as a guest on her racing boat. Not sure why, but I never want to miss a chance to rub up against billionaires."

"But you hate sailing," Kevin said with a chortle.

"I know, I know, but sometimes you have to swim with the sharks."

7b

All Sharon could see when she walked into the poor excuse for Bora Bora Yacht Club's international headquarters was Mike Stroud's ass sticking straight up out of a huge steel utility box. Piles of ropes and cables were strewn about the floor; Ms. Ellis Turner stood over Mike yelling at him.

"I know the Goddamn thing is in there, I saw it fall."

A garbled reply came from deep inside the box and then Mike slowly stood as his great frame went vertical. He opened his hand in front of Turner like a child whose mother demanded to know what was inside it. The contents sparkled in the morning sun.

"Your earring, Ellis," he said.

"Thanks Mike, had that a long time, don't know how the bloody thing fell off. It was a prezzy from an old mate, years ago. Would hate to lose it."

They both noticed Sharon.

"Well dearie, glad to see you could make it," Turner said, checking Sharon out. "Thought you might like to see what all the yabber's about. I have an empty seat today and I want to be on the tender. This will be Bobo's second run with the boat and I thought, 'Let's give JF's Sheila a chance to see what it's all about. You game?"

Mike was looking over Turner's shoulder, directly at Sharon, a big smile hanging between his ears.

"Always, I just love to sail,' Sharon answered, feeling quite uncomfortable. Even Turner could see through her lie as she smiled at O'Mara

"Well dearie, don't worry, you don't have to do any work, in fact you'll have the best seat in the house," Turner said as they headed toward the huge triangular panel of sail that extended high above the pier. "You'll get the sixth seat, right there amidships between the two hulls. Takes five to crew her. You, as they say, are sitting in the catbird seat, nothing to do but watch and enjoy."

"And get wet and seriously screwed up if she flips," Mike Stroud injected.

"Oh Mike, that's not going to happen, she looks athletic and nimble, she'll have a fair go at it."

"A Buckley's chance, I say," Mike said not letting up.

"Mike, I've offered. It's up to the Sheila to say yes or no," Turner said looking at Sharon with an "I dare you to back out now" grin.

"Oh, I'm going Ms. Turner, I would never pass up a chance like this."

"Ripper. Told 'ya, Mike, she'd do it. Since I saw her that night at Compton's I knew she was a gamer, she's no wowser."

"You ready?"

"Not sure now, Mike. What's this sixth man business?"

"For many years, I think since the San Diego races, the America's Cup rules have permitted one person to sit in the stern of the boat and go along for the ride," Mike said. "Probably started with an owner or someone who backed the boat but couldn't participate or even help. They were there for the ride and the thrill. Ellis usually takes the seat but with Bobo as the new skipper, she wants to watch from the tender."

"That gives me a lot of confidence," Sharon said.

"No worries, dearie, just want to see what Frenchy can do," Turner said. "Got a lot of money riding on this race and I want to make sure he's the right man for the job. And we're leaving for Italy in three weeks for the Naples and Venice races, so there's a lot to do and learn before we go. You just sit back and enjoy the ride, dearie." With that, Turner did an about-face and walked down the pier toward the five people in bright yellow jump suits that had just exited the building.

"The tall one is Bobo," Mike said. "The other four are from Australia and New Zealand, the one on the right is Barbara Brown; we call her Babs. She may be the best sailor of the lot, including Bobo. She and Catherine were mates, real tight, they worked their way up through the ranks on boats all over the world. They're all good but I'll reserve judgment on Bobo; he's always struck me as a loose cannon. Too much yelling and screaming for my taste but he's been seeing Eva Karg so I'm sure the road was paved with gold bricks for the bastard."

"Not a fan of either Bobo or Karg, I take it?" Sharon asked.

"No, and I'll leave it at that. Still like my paycheck and this gig. In three weeks, we'll be practicing in Naples, then Venice. Not bad on someone else's ticket."

"Do I need some gear?"

"Follow me, I have a suit that'll fit you and keep you afloat if you fall off. I suggest you don't. Ellis may leave you there until after the race is done."

"Pleasant thought," Sharon said. "It will take more than five people to sail those big seventy-two footers, won't it?"

"They will carry a crew of eleven and the seat stuck high in the middle between the hulls will carry the twelfth man. Kind of like a jury, twelve men and all. Who knows what verdict they'll come up with?"

"That's one hell of a boat, seventy-two feet of raw power and speed."

"Sure as hell is and they have yet to build one," Mike said. "The Golden Gate Yacht Club and Ellison are supposedly building theirs in some secret location but everyone knows it's at Pier 80. Ellis Turner says that hers is also under construction, but that's not part of my job description. Where she's building it, even I don't know; there are some rumors about Oakland or somewhere in the East Bay but I honestly don't know."

"She's confident enough to be spending the money, got to be millions. If they don't win the AC45 World Series and the competition, it could be all for nothing," Sharon said.

"She can afford it. My guess is she'll sell it to the Cup competitor, whoever that'll be, but it will take at least six months to build so the sooner they get started, the better. Go get into your gear; she's scheduled to be towed out at 10:30."

Sharon, all dressed in foul weather gear, could hardly see the two hulls for all the advertising plastered all over the graphite composites. By her count, she saw three high tech firm ads, one Swiss watchmaker, two heavy industries and maybe a partridge in a pear tree. Her perch between the hulls wasn't a chair, or for that matter, anything like it. Spread between the hulls, hanging on a black pipe that connected the two hulls, was a netlike contraption. This would be the home for her butt for the next few hours. Sharon stood looking at the net, then the bay, then the net, *"What the hell am I doing?"* kept bouncing around in her head. She'd ducked rocket propelled grenades, dodged AK-47 rounds and even survived a rollover thanks to a roadside bomb but staring at the catamaran, she actually started to hyperventilate, *"What the hell am I doing here?"*

"You okay, Sharon?" Mike said from just behind her. "You look a little peaked."

"Yeah, just fine, just don't like to get wet."

"The suit looks good on you, can't say that anyone else has ever looked as good in it as you do."

"Thanks for that," Sharon said.

"One more thing," Mike said as he brought forward a black round shape from behind his back. "Your helmet, absolutely required; no helmet, no ride."

She thought about it for a long five seconds and then took the helmet reluctantly, stuffed her red hair under it and pulled the strap tight.

"Blimey, don't you look great. Like a pro," Stroud said.

"Just shut up before I change my mind."

"My, my, don't you look all sexy in that thing, O'Mara," Ellis Turner said. "The girls will be envious, and the boys, well, let's just leave them out of it."

All that Sharon got out of Ellis's remark was another very uncomfortable feeling.

Ten minutes later, she sat well secured on the netting, the crew had begun preparations and the tender began to slowly tow them out into the bay. A light but steady breeze blew across the Mission Bay neighborhood, west toward Oakland. The sky was a California blue, sharp, crystal clear, not a cloud in sight. She took a deep breath and said out loud to no one, "Let the games begin."

As if on cue, the two hulls exploded through the water like the catamaran had been kicked in the ass. She was used to sails banging and fluttering about, rigging rattling, but now there was almost no sound. The single seventy-foot tall hard triangular sail-wing caught the wind and pushed the two hulls forward. To Sharon it was eerie but a little exhilarating as well. The cold salt water of the Bay ripped along not more than five feet below her. Then the space became six feet, then seven, then eight, and then held. She hadn't noticed but now she and the boat were canted over at least twenty degrees, she could almost feel herself flying. The five crew members had all aligned themselves along the port hull, which was now more than ten feet out of the water, Babs was closest. She nimbly slid over to Sharon.

"First time?" she asked.

"Like a virgin," was all that Sharon could think of.

"For now, slide up the netting toward the hull that's rising, I'll signal with my hand when you're up far enough. When the Skipper yells that we're coming about, be prepared to slide or crawl the other way. All of us will be jumping across the trampoline to the other hull. Gotta go."

Sharon watched as the nimble and, from the obvious size of her thighs, strong Babs Brown, along with another crewman, let out the first sail she had seen, a jib. Again the boat lifted and increased speed. She looked behind them and saw the tender quickly receding. Only a high-speed drug runner could keep up with this boat and, remarkably, she was still dry.

The Bay Bridge flew by overhead; they had transferred to the starboard hull. The open bay, ruffled by white caps, lay ahead. The calm of the west side of the Bay below the Bay Bridge gave way to the stiff and incessant winds blowing straight through the Golden Gate. Sharon was actually enjoying the ride, Babs signaled her and she slid down across the netting to starboard. Bobo was screaming at the crew and now Sharon was getting drenched. Water streamed off the blunt nose of each hull and it was thrown at her at almost thirty miles an hour, it stung her cheeks. The boat came about again.

"Get your ass to port, O'Mara," Bobo screamed. "I need your fat ass over there."

Sharon looked at the man who was screaming at her; she heard every other word. But she climbed across the netting toward Babs.

"Pay attention, girl. Bobo wants your head, it seems," Brown said with a huge smile.

"How fast?" was all Sharon could say before a slug of salt water slammed into her mouth. She coughed hard and through the salt water dripping down her face, saw Alcatraz quickly gaining on the port side. She had to admit to herself that this was fun.

"Thirty-two knots,' Babs yelled.

"Just past Alcatraz we'll turn back toward the city, everyone, be fucking ready," Bobo screamed again, not because he liked to yell, which Sharon was sure he did, but because the wind had picked up even more and the boat was almost flying, Sharon was only ten feet away and couldn't hear him. She watched both hulls lift out of the Bay until they were completely out of the water, bouncing from wave to wave; only the long white knife-thin rudders touched the surface of the water. Bobo ordered the larger gennaker sail out. She didn't think this boat could go faster; it was now going faster, insanely faster.

The starboard hull cut through the swells pushed through the Golden Gate; Sharon caught a quick glimpse of the international orange twin towers of the iconic bridge and then lost them in the spray. The wind continued to rip across the bay slamming into the semi-transparent hard wing, lifting the boat even further.

"Cut the jib, cut the jib," was all she heard from Bobo over the roaring of the wind.

"Can't, the block's jammed," someone screamed.

"I said cut the jib, God damn it."

The hulls continued to drive through the cold water; the waves now washed and submerged the forward part of the starboard hull. Sharon crouched now, holding tight to the black spreader, she watched in abject fascination as the right hull continued to drive deeper and deeper under the waves, until, for a moment, it was totally submerged. The drag of the submerging hull fought the lifting of the wind, the port hull rose higher and higher. The five crewmen were holding on for dear life, knowing nothing could stop the inevitable.

"Oh shit," was all Sharon could say as the two hulls slowly

came perpendicular to the cold bay water; the boat's wing sail hovered, not vertically as it was designed to do, but horizontally, like a large hand passing over the waves. Her world was literally turning upside down.

"We're going, going, she's going over," someone yelled from a less than secured spot on the capsizing catamaran.

"Fuck," was the last thing Babs Brown heard from Sharon as Sharon fell past her, hit the bay and disappeared.

7c

There was no explosion or crashing sounds like a highway collision makes, almost nothing to hear except for the screaming and cursing from the crew, some dangling from their security cables like Christmas ornaments on a bizarre tree.

"What the blooming hell happened, Bobo?" Turner bellowed as she and the tender came along side. "You know better than that. Is the wing okay?"

"Where the hell's O'Mara," Mike yelled from the stern of the launch.

"She fell in about there," Babs Brown screamed back at Stroud. She pointed toward the bay.

As if she had been summoned from Neptune's lair, Sharon exploded out of the sea, coughing and flailing her arms.

The first thing Stroud heard was Sharon yelling at him, "I'm going to get you, you Scottish bastard. Sometime, when you don't expect it, I'll get even."

All Stroud could do when he heard Sharon's curse was laugh. His laugh was contagious, everyone, including Ellis Turner, started to laugh.

"Let's get the damn thing upright," Bobo said. "Everyone on the starboard side, you too, O'Mara, we need the ballast."

Sharon had been called a lot of things in her life: bitch, bastard, son-of-a-bitch and something in Arabic she still didn't understand, this was the first time she had been called ballast.

"Bobo, you're an asshole!" she yelled as she started to climb up the webbing of her catbird seat.

Bobo looked hard at Sharon, said something under his breath and pointed, "I need you up there. The free ride is over."

As Sharon climbed, she saw a line thrown from the tender and tied off on the upright hull of the catamaran. The powerboat slowly turned into the wind and pulled the twin bows toward the Golden Gate, lessening the drag on the sail; in seconds the sail was vertical and the boat horizontal.

For the next hour, they ran a figure eight course out to the Golden Gate Bridge and back, all along the Marina Green and past the Golden Gate Yacht Club, which Babs pointed out, "Should really piss off the old farts holding their lunchtime drinks at the bar."

Even Sharon had to admit that it was fun, a blast to ride this thing. The final leg home was quiet and uneventful even though the boat was hiked up at almost a thirty-degree angle for most of the ride.

Other than general sailing directions and orders, Bobo said nothing to the crew during their return to the pier. Sharon could see that he was fuming. After they tied up, Bobo climbed up to the pier and waited for one the crewmembers to join him.

"This won't be pretty," Babs said to Sharon.

She couldn't hear what was being said, except the opening remark, "You God damn asshole," Bobo screamed at the man; his French accent mangled the phrasing. Then Bobo pushed himself into the man after hearing his response, in a split second Bobo found himself decked. After slugging Bobo, the man turned and left the pier.

"That's been coming to him for a week, ever since Bobo got the job," Babs said to Sharon. "They haven't liked each other since the Falmouth races, bad blood, real bad. How about a beer? There's a great little bar not too far from here."

"Mission Rock Cafe?"

"You know it?"

"For years and years, long before this area started to get all toney and highbrow. Great breakfast and lunches as well," Sharon said. "Give me ten to get out of this gear and try to do something with this mess of hair. I'll meet you out front, I'm famished."

An hour later, after crab cakes, salad, and two Anchor Steam beers, Sharon began to feel better. She had been able to wipe some of the dried salt water from her face but it would take an hour under the shower to really clean her hair.

"How do you put up with all this testosterone," Sharon asked Babs.

"Not easy, hard to get a crew to work together, so many have histories together in this business, comes out like it did today."

"What happened to the man?"

"Ellis had a talk with him, they came to an agreement," Babs said. "He'll be there tomorrow. He knows it's his fault that the winch jammed. Wasn't paying attention and the line slipped. Was his job as grinder to make sure it didn't happen, it hung up and we flipped. No biggee, done it lots of times. In a race though, no recovery, and that's what Turner wants to make sure doesn't happen, stupid mistakes like that."

"I understand that, but why are you here? Probably a lot of other opportunities?"

"Some, but Ellis and I go way back. I grew up in Sydney, sailed like some girls chased boys. Couldn't get enough of it. Saw an advert for a crewman on her yacht, really a luxury sailboat, 120 feet long and I spent two years there. Sailed it from Australia to Nice. That's where I met Catherine Voss; we raced against each other a lot there. And as they say, the rest is history. Ellis wanted to race in the America's Cup and I offered to help, she said yes and here I am. I also did some work with Catherine. Still pisses me off about her dying, so strange."

"What do you mean?"

"Well, she and Ellis got along fine, Catherine knew so much about sailing that Ellis turned over most of the responsibilities for the upcoming Cup races to her. She set the crews, the schedules, made sure the boat was being built to specs in New Zealand, everything. Then when Catherine started to work on her own project, her hydrofoil, things started to go wonky. After a lot of tension and arguments, Ellis wanted to stop all the "non-sense," as she called it. Wanted her to focus on Turner's boat, she even offered her a ton of money to stop manufacturing the thing. Catherine told me it was a lot of money, but JF, that's her twin brother, said let's think about it. Catherine said no and two weeks later she drowned. Sharon, that girl couldn't drown in a hurricane."

"You think it was something other than a accident?"

"Absolutely, I think somebody killed her, wanted her out of the way. Don't know why, but that's what I think."

"Do you know Eva Karg?"

"Good God yes, now's there's a piece of work. Not sure what she does. Shows up here and there, sometimes with Bobo, then Ellis. Heard a lot of strange things about her, sexual things, but I stay way away when she's around. "Bitch in heat" is what comes to mind first."

Sharon smiled, "You think she may have had something to do with Catherine's death?"

"Never thought about that," Babs said taking another sip from the bottle of beer. "Maybe? She certainly has the skills from what I understand. South Africa and all."

"She's from South Africa?" Sharon asked, trying to draw more from Brown.

"Yes, and we Aussies know a real accent when we hear one; she's from Cape Town or certainly nearby. Couple of the fellows told me she was with their special forces or something similar. Not surprised. She walks with a swagger that says a lot. And she's been dating Bobo. I think that's what really pisses me off about the whole thing. Catherine was seeing Bobo, not sure why other than he's a fellow Frenchman and as soon as she was dead Bobo shows up with Karg."

"I thought that he was seeing or was at least with Turner," Sharon offered.

"No, not hardly. Turner probably accepts it, but I just don't know. He's definitely with Karg and she's not particular when it comes to partners; in fact, my guess is she'd find a way to screw a horse if she could."

"Now there's an image I don't want in my head."

"Well she rides a lot and I understand she goes to a stable somewhere out that way," Babs pointed across the Bay toward Oakland, Mt. Diablo loomed over everything. "Near Mt. Diablo, whatever or wherever that is."

"It's that mountain over there," Sharon said pointing. "Lots of stables and ranches around it. Good country for horseback riding."

"That's all I know but she's tough and strong and doesn't play well with others. Like I said, when she's around, I try hard to be somewhere else."

"Got it."

Chapter 8

Green Zone, Baghdad, Iraq, 2005

O'Mara crushed the cigarette out with her boot and watched the rest of her squad gear-up. Abdul leaned against the wall of the trailer, he was smoking as well.

One hour earlier, Sergeant Sanchez had handed O'Mara a message from Major Simpson to give him a call at ten that morning.

"A Mercedes that matches your description was spotted by a local policeman north of Karbala, parked near a small cluster of houses," the Major said. "There were rumors from the locals that there was an al-Qaeda safe house located at the edge of the cluster, not too safe if everyone knew about. They said that five or six men come and go, another Mercedes was also seen."

"The girls?" Sharon asked.

"No sign, but the car is a ringer for the kid's description. You still believe him?"

"Yes and no, he has a big agenda for someone his age. Want's to trade his info for a green card. Told him we'll see, seems satisfied for now."

"No promises, Lieutenant, you know that. Hell, if we hung that carrot out everyone would turn in their grandmother for a pass."

"Understood. Let's play this out," Sharon said.

"Quick trip in and out, command says a front's coming," the Major warned. "I'll bring in two Hueys as backup; you take your men and coordinate from the ground. Sixteen-hundred hours this afternoon, does that work?"

"Works. We'll need three hours to get there, only about seventy miles but I want time to prepare. I'll call for the copters when we're one hour out and then we'll coordinate."

"Good, keep this low profile if you can," Simpson had said. "No need to blow up the whole damn village."

"Wasn't intending to, but the element of surprise would be nice."

"Later, mind the front."

"Roger, out."

Every operation needed meticulous planning from ammunition to water; it's not a good idea to run out of either in the Iraqi desert. Her three Humvees were double-checked and loaded. Operations gave her coordinates as well as aerial pictures. The house sat on the northern edge of a cluster of other houses; all were constructed of the typical mud walls found among the houses in the agricultural areas fed by the elaborate irrigation system dug over five thousand years ago.

The land, mostly irrigated fields, was open to the south and west; groves of the ubiquitous date palm wrapped the north side of the compound. Irrigation canals sliced back and forth across the flat plain of fields providing the only life-giving substance that this forsaken country had. One of Saddam's gridded master planned residential neighborhoods sat a quarter mile to the south, entirely out of context with the historic informal ways of living in this country.

"You can't go, Abdul," Sharon said to the boy.

He took another drag on his cigarette; the smell of cloves filled the air. "Sure I can, seen lots, maybe I can help."

"Not a chance, you stay here. We'll be back before nightfall, I hope, with the girls."

"Then on to America!"

"As I said, we'll see. No promises," Sharon said.

"Promises, promises, you American's always promise."

"That's another issue to debate! When I make a promise, I keep it. You remember that."

"Sure, sure. Big promises, small kid, no fucking chance."

"You know what I said about swearing."

"Yeah, no fucking swearing, I hear that from all you guys, but then all I hear is fucking swearing. I'm a big guy, I can handle it."

"Yeah, tough guy."

"Yeah, that's right, tough guy."

The three-hour trip only took an hour and a half; the Iraqi commuter traffic was light that afternoon. The three Humvees pulled up about a mile east of the compound, turned onto a side road that paralleled a large canal and slid to a stop. Dust engulfed the vehicles.

"Always amazed how sometimes this country feels like the land south of Fresno, Lieutenant," Private Nolan said. "All these canals and irrigation ditches everywhere, seems the same as back home, except that the locals in California don't try to shoot you."

"You ever stumble onto a meth lab in California?" a voice over the radio said. "If you had, you would never have said that."

"Sure, Sergeant, but then again, you're a cop and have seen that shit. Me, I'm just a farm boy trying to make a living."

"Quiet, you two," Sharon said. She dismounted, stood outside the Humvee and sighted her binoculars on the compound. Open fields sloped down from the canal to the tangle of palm trees and grey brown buildings; the fields were crisscrossed with shallow irrigation ditches. One larger canal cut diagonally across their target, a straight shot from where they were standing. She scanned the top of the low earth dike along the canal's banks, she saw nothing. No lookouts. They had already mapped the attack. One group would parallel the large canal and then come in from the north. The second team would come up a dirt road from the south. O'Mara would take her team further west and sweep up the road from the southwest. She wanted the helicopters to sweep in from the west and set down in an open area among the date palms; this would push the insurgents toward either the south or east. *Traps are so easy to diagram and set-up, so easy, so fucking dangerous. All you need are willing rats.* She knew these people would not be willing.

She made the call to the Huey base at the Baghdad Airport, they were standing by. They confirmed, Sharon knew, with their normal cruising speed of 120 miles per hour, they would be there in less than thirty minutes. She would get another call from them when they were four miles out.

"Lieutenant, we got weather issues. A front is busting in from the south, will hit soon, my people say it's picking up speed. I need my people back here and on the ground in two hours," ground control said.

"Roger that. I want this over in one hour. Send them," O'Mara said. She knew the front he was talking about wasn't rain; maybe a dry front, like a dust storm.

She killed two more cigarettes. At the thirty-minute mark, she heard from the Hueys.

"Ten minutes out, O'Mara," a voice said, almost drowned by the roar of his engines.

"Roger. Sanchez, let's do this. First one to get the girls gets a case of beer," O'Mara said.

A minute later, they were busting down the hard road directly south of the compound, which poked its ugly roofline over a field of short gray green grass. Sanchez split off on the first dirt road and headed north. Sharon's Humvee slowed at the next road and began to turn north. Her radio blared in her ear.

"O'Mara, we got a problem. That front's not two hours out, it's fucking here." The static-filled reply grated on Sharon's ears.

"Say again."

"The front is about twenty miles south and bust ... Can't land ... wall of sand a mile ... sorry, going home, good luck ..." Static, generated by the sandstorm, erased any further chance of communication.

"Shit. Sanchez, we lost the copters. The front's busting in and it's a Goddamn sandstorm as well."

"Shit."

"Let's rethink this. Hold your position."

"Roger."

For two long minutes, O'Mara considered their situation. The sky to the south continued to darken and an eerie yellow haze began to envelope the colorless landscape. Shadows disappeared and the world flattened.

"They won't expect any kind of attack in this shit," Sharon said into her headset. "Same game plan, but this time we'll wait for the first winds, then hit them. Sanchez, you come in as planned. Rodriguez, you swing over and come in from the north side, I'll come in from the west. At the perimeter, dismount and push forward. Encircle and envelop, got it?"

"Roger that," came two replies simultaneously as static built in their helmet speakers.

Sharon tapped Nolan on the shoulder, "On my command."

The rest of her team sat behind her, three soldiers, one from Salt Lake City, one from Phoenix, and one from some place she'd never heard of in some forgotten part of northern Nevada; she lit another cigarette. Salt Lake tapped his boot nervously on the Humvee's deck. She watched the tops of the palms, they went from dead still, to waving, to leaning over in less than thirty seconds. The first burst of dust blew in waves across the fields.

"Now, go, go, go," she yelled, pitching away her cigarette.

Private Nolan pushed the accelerator to the floor and the thousand pounds of human military muscle and three tons of Indiana steel roared down the dirt road, racing the sandstorm toward the al-Qaeda compound. The wind masked the sound of its motor; they could barely hear themselves think inside its dark interior.

Nolan drove fast down the street that split the central core of the first cluster of buildings. He watched as mothers, dressed in black chadors, grabbed children and pulled them inside doorways. He could feel eyes watching their every move.

"Positions?" O'Mara yelled into the headset.

"Ready," Rodriguez said as the static began to interrupt his radio.

"Ready," Sanchez echoed.

As if Sanchez's affirmative response was a signal, an RPG appeared over the top of the mud wall of their target and then tore through a wave of yellow dust and exploded against the wall behind his Humvee.

"Lieutenant, I think surprise is no longer an option," Sanchez said.

"You think! Find cover and dismount, hit these bastards."

Nolan spun the Humvee into a narrow alley between two buildings a hundred feet from the target. Everyone dismounted and took covering positions forward and rear. Sharon could hear small arms fire over the increasing wail of the storm.

"Everyone okay?" All she got back was static. "Shit, this storm is screwing everything up."

With that invective still blowing in the wind, O'Mara watched their empty Humvee explode and fly ten feet straight up into the air before landing on its demolished undercarriage. Everyone on her team was flat on the ground, she felt the hard mud wall behind her; she couldn't hear anything. Dust and dirt filled her eyes and throat as the Humvee started to burn. Two men began to crawl toward the walls of the buildings; she could see Nevada's leg ripped open. Nolan didn't move, he was down and ten feet from the mud wall. Through the sand, O'Mara watched a man walk casually around the corner of the far end of the alley; he was partially obscured by the heavy smoke from the Humvee and the sandstorm. He held an AK-47; his head was wrapped in a red and white keffiyeh, his face was covered except for a dark opening for his eyes. He raised the weapon and aimed at the motionless Nolan.

Before O'Mara could bring her weapon up, Nolan quickly rolled on his side, scanned the alley and knocked the man down with three short bursts. The man's keffiyeh was the only thing preventing his head from exploding like a melon as the 5.56mm slugs slammed into it. Both Nolan and the dead man were immediately lost in the blowing dust, then, as quick as the dust filled the air of the alley, it left and they reappeared. Nolan signaled O'Mara, thumbs up, as he pointed to the wall, she covered him as he found safety next to one of his team.

For the next ten minutes, O'Mara heard sporadic gunfire but no heavy weapons or explosions. The storm's intensity increased until they were forced to crawl from safe points along the walls to other safe points, hopefully out of the storm's path. Nolan dragged Nevada to a safe location and triaged the man's leg, a piece of shrapnel had opened a six-inch gash on the man's thigh; it wasn't deep, he'd survive. She was also well aware that, under these conditions, one of her team members could be mistaken for the enemy by the other team; accidents might happen. The storm's static electricity completely shut down any radio communications; visual signals were all but impossible. She signaled to her team.

"We'll settle in against the lee side of that wall. Nolan and Hernandez take the ends," Sharon said. "We'll watch the center. As the storm subsides, we'll move to the right, toward the building. All we can hope is that Sanchez has his team holed up as well."

"Lieutenant, I'm catching something on my headset," Nolan said. "Wait a second."

O'Mara wiped the dust off her goggles and watched as Nolan listened, the man looked like a ghost, dust and sand covered most of his body. The other team members looked the same way; one had cleaned his goggles and it produced the strangest look imaginable, as if a stone sculpture had goggly eyes that moved.

"Got you Sanchez," Nolan said directly into O'Mara's ear. "Yes, Sarg," Nolan continued, "we got one injured, one enemy down, IED killed the Humvee ... yes ... yes, Sergeant. Got it." Nolan went back to O'Mara's ear, "Lieutenant, he says to move to the building, they have the far side secured ... two enemy down ... maybe three left, they may come our way."

O'Mara signaled to the team and they slid along the wall, she could see the top of the buildings again. As quickly as the storm hit, it was leaving as dust twisted in small tornados in the courtyard.

Her experienced eyes scanned the building; she looked at

each window and potential hiding place. Clear. She signaled to the men behind her, they moved in a cover formation, leap-frogging the courtyard to the building facade. Nothing showed. If the girls were inside, she couldn't rake the building with cover fire or toss grenades inside it. She would have to settle for a room-to-room search.

"Lieutenant, Sanchez is at the back. The third team is providing cover for him. It's quiet back there."

"On three, bust the door - get the count to Sanchez."

"Roger," Nolan answered and spoke into this headset.

O'Mara scanned the courtyard past the walls to the roofs of the hardscrabble village that stood beyond the dust-covered palm trees and dead trees. Nothing moved except some fronds tossed by the dying breeze. Nothing moved as O'Mara looked across the courtyard again, nothing at all.

"Nolan, I want you to cover us and watch those walls; this stinks and I don't want to find out they've moved behind us. Tell Sanchez. No one goes in yet. After the Humvee, this building may be nothing more than a bomb waiting for us. Tell him."

"Roger," Nolan answered.

Thirty seconds later, Nolan responded, "He felt it too, he is holding."

"Watch for an end around to push us into the building, tell him," O'Mara said to Nolan.

"He's pulling back."

At Nolan's comment, gunfire erupted from the far side of the building.

"Shit," O'Mara said. "Everybody, hit the deck."

At "deck," bullets exploded into the mud walls over their heads, new dust churned by the impact started to fill the air. The team opened up and returned fire. Insurgent rifle barrels popped up and disappeared over the walls of the courtyard, not concentrated fire, just erratic and unfocused. The enemy was trying to force them to find cover inside the buildings.

"I want four grenades over that wall; Nolan, get them ready."

One team member continued to fire at the pop-up AK-47s, the insurgents kept below the wall.

"Any time, Nolan, anytime. One of those sons-of-bitches may get lucky," O'Mara yelled.

"Now, frag out," was all she heard as four M67 grenades flew high and over the wall. Four concussions, no AK-47s popped-up.

"Check it out," O'Mara said.

Nolan zigzagged across the courtyard and gingerly looked around the end of the wall. He held up two fingers and then pointed to the ground with his thumb. "Clear," he yelled as he ran back to the wall and his team.

"I want eyes in this building, can you get a man through that window," O'Mara said, pointing to an open window ten feet above them.

"No problemo, Lieutenant," Nolan answered.

She watched as two team members hoisted Nolan up to the window's ledge. He grabbed the ledge and pulled himself in. All was quiet for twenty seconds and then one shot echoed through the downstairs windows.

"Nolan?"

Private Nolan stuck his head out the upper window. "One man left, badly injured now. He was going to set off an explosion. Looks like an explosive charge in the center of the downstairs' room. He won't now, Lieutenant. And no girls here."

"Shit. Be careful, there may be redundant trip wires," O'Mara said.

"Roger that," was Nolan's response. He disappeared into the building.

"Lieutenant," Sanchez said into her working headset. "Move or hold?"

"Let's get inside and stop being moving targets."

O'Mara reached the closed front door and checked the jam for any visible wires. Nothing was obvious. "Nolan, we're coming in."

"Hold a minute, Lieutenant, think I've found something,"

Nolan said from inside.

"Be fucking careful," she answered.

Three heartbeats later, the interior of the lower level of the house exploded outward through the windows and doors. O'Mara, standing directly behind the heavy wooden door, was thrown thirty feet into the courtyard. The door lay across her legs, she didn't move. Other team members were luckier, they were between the blown out windows, only their ears rang. Sanchez came around the corner of the building and ran to O'Mara.

"Get the medic over here," Sanchez yelled.

The medic was with the third team and it took a precious minute for him to reach the courtyard. Sanchez had already removed the door and was beginning to check O'Mara out for injuries. He didn't see any blood but there could be internal injuries. He looked at her dirty face, she blinked.

"Sargent, if you touch me like that one more time I'll have to marry you and your wife wouldn't like that at all." She coughed. "My ears are ringing like a fucking super loud alarm clock is going off. Everyone okay? Nolan?"

"Not sure, the men are inside trying to find out," Sanchez answered.

O'Mara slowly sat up and waited for some form of reality to return. She felt like she had been beaten with a baseball bat, everything tingled and vibrated. Pain was worse across her breasts and shoulders where the impact of the exploding door hit her first. She looked back toward the house; one of Sanchez's team walked out the door and signaled the Sargent.

"Help me up, Sarg," O'Mara said.

"You just sit there," he answered.

"Not a chance, give me a hand."

Sharon reached up and grabbed Sargent Sanchez's forearm and, with locked hands, she rose shakily. The world spun around her, she felt Sanchez's strong hands steady her; the world came slowly back into focus.

"You sure, Lieutenant?"

"Damn sure," she said as the two slowly went to the house.

The soldier stood just outside the destroyed doorway. He was grey orange from the storm's dust, his face said everything.

"Nolan?" O'Mara said when they reached the man.

"Dead Sir, the explosion caught him coming down the stairs, probably missed a trip wire or something. He's pretty busted up, was dead instantly, for whatever that's worth."

"God damn it, son-of-a-bitch," she said. "The twins, he said he didn't see the twins."

"Nothing Sir, but they may have been here. The upstairs room has some bedding and blankets thrown around; there were some personal things that girls their age would wear, along with some papers with drawings on them."

He handed Sharon a piece of paper. The drawing was of a rough house with doors and windows high over the house; in yellow crayon, there was a crescent moon and stars.

8b

Basil laid his head on the edge of the bed and looked into the closed eyes of his mistress. On his third warm breath, as he breathed into her face, Sharon opened her eyes and stared into furry jowls and dark eyes, a spot of drool hung on a corner of his mottled lip.

"I know, I know," Sharon said as she slowly swung her legs out toward the floor. Everything was stiff, "This is what I get for living a life of such dissipation, Basil. I wake up stiff and sore with only a furry roommate to have breakfast with."

Basil nudged her naked hip and took a step back, then nudged her again.

"I know, I know," she said as she pulled an Army tee shirt over her full figure; they headed down the hallway to the kitchen. Basil headed out the door and into the back yard. Sharon made a cup of instant coffee and sat at the kitchen table.

"Just one, just one," was all she could think of.

Habits are hard to break, that's why there're called habits and some are worse than others. There's the usual drinking and drugs, your choice. And then there are the compulsive sexual things and the need to collect and store everything you touch. There are many that are just socially undesirable, such as nose-picking, thumb-sucking and hair fondling. Then there's OCD, bulimia, and Internet porn that can be just plain annoying not to mention dangerous. And then there's smoking, the most politically evil bad habit of all.

Sharon ran her fingers over the red and white box sitting in the middle of the kitchen table. All the tools were there: her Giants zippo lighter, an ash tray from a small hotel in Paris where she and Kevin had stayed, an open box with eight cigarettes left and her cup of instant Starbucks coffee, Columbian.

Her habits sat at the three other chairs around the table and encouraged her. *"What the hell's the difference,"* the one on the right said. *"With the way you live, someone will shoot you someday and look what pleasures you gave up."*

"Not that I'm bragging," the habit directly across from her said. *"But we have cut back on the drinking. That's a good thing. So why not?"*

The last habit, TO SMOKE IS TO LIVE written on his tee shirt, just sat there and joined Sharon in staring at the box; finally it looked at Sharon, smiled and said, *"Yes, what the hell."* With that she lit up, took a deep breath and relaxed. They all agreed it had been a good discussion.

After a light breakfast, she searched the Internet for stable locations around Mt. Diablo, surprisingly, there were more than she thought, but they were all fairly close together.

"Good morning," she said to the first stable operator on the list. "I'm hoping to find out some information about your stables. We are moving to the area from Colorado and have two horses. A friend of ours, Eva Karg, suggested a stable in your area, but for the life of me I can't remember which one. So I'm a bit embarrassed to be asking."

On the third call, she snagged a potential winner. "Oh yes, Ms. Karg rides here, tell her thank you for the reference. I don't know her that well, in fact she was here just the other day. She has been riding with us for almost six months. You said you had horses?"

"Yes ma'am, two, a mare and pony my daughter rides. We have been relocated to the Bay Area and Ms. Karg mentioned your place and now I do remember the name. I apologize."

"Oh dear, with everything on your mind and the move, we can help," the woman said. "I have an excellent shipper who can handle your horses and move them safely here and we have room. And the hills and trails around here are excellent for riding."

"Excellent, may I come out and visit? I'm in town for just a few days before heading back, this afternoon?"

"That would be fine, I'm here all day. I live in the ranch house. Just ring the bell, plenty of parking out front."

The ride through Walnut Creek's suburban neighborhoods quickly changed into rolling hills and small open valleys, Mount Diablo, a double peaked chunk of rock 3,864 feet high, looms over its five surrounding counties. Its flanks folded and spread outward from the base of the cone shaped upthrust of rock. Not an extinct volcano, as some think, it's more of a leftover from the turbulent and shaky history of the California coastline that includes two massive plates of the earth's crust grinding and pushing against each other. With the way the two plates grind against each other and the northward thrust of the western Pacific plate, someday Los Angeles will replace San Francisco as Mount Diablo's urban area of choice.

The stable sat in a pleasant valley between two of the ridgelines that extended out from Mount Diablo like broad roots from an oak.

A stout yet strong looking woman met Sharon at the door to the simple ranch house, its covered porch extended across and then around the one story building. Two rocking chairs separated by a low table sat on the deck.

"Good morning, can I help you?" the woman said as she dried her hands in a towel.

"I called about boarding my two horses; I'm moving from

Colorado," Sharon said.

"Oh yes, yes, yes. Just a sec, let me put this dishtowel down. Be right back. Coffee or anything, just made some?" The woman's voice died as she headed back into the house.

"No, thank you, I'm fine," Sharon answered and looked around the ranch's compound. Corrals and low buildings filled the area and a large fenced pasture extended out toward the mountain. She counted at least ten horses in the corrals; she guessed others were still in their paddocks.

The hard tap of boots on wood preceded the woman as she rounded the end of the house. Cowboy boots, jeans, belt with silver buckle, and a checked shirt supported a pleasant face and tangled head of blond hair. She stuck her hand out as she approached Sharon.

"Emily Chase, ma'am. Glad you could make it, came from around back."

"Sharon Moss," O'Mara replied. "Thanks for meeting with me on such short notice."

"Oh don't worry about that, I'm here all day long and people come and go as they please," Chase said. "Two people are out riding right now and the boys are always moving the horses in and out."

"Quite a place you have. Didn't realize there were so many stables up here," Sharon said.

"We are the leftovers, last edge of old California. We keep all the suburbanites from building right up the slopes of that old mountain. So you said you had a couple of horses?"

"Yes, a mare and a pony. My daughter just loves to ride and I've had the mare a long time. Would hate to leave her. She might even like the weather here, kind of like retirement for her," Sharon said with a laugh as they began to walk between the fences of the first corral.

"I understand, that fellow there is almost fifteen; he came from Wyoming when his owner moved here. Added a couple of years to his life, to the man and the horse."

They walked into the first stable; a long double row of paddock doors lined the brick paved hallway. Another open double door cast light from the opposite end. The smells were unique. The full aroma of urine and manure instinctively conjured something primal in Sharon, as though she had been here before. Men and horses have been working and living together for over ten thousand years, they are both genetically linked. Both depended on each other.

Halfway down the hall, the full head of a Palomino stuck itself out over the stall's gate to see what was happening. Her nose flared and she shook her mane. Sharon remembered the strand of hair from the hydrofoil.

"That's a handsome horse, Ms. Chase. In fact gorgeous," Sharon said as she walked over to the mare.

"Careful, she's full of spirit and herself. Her name's Madigan, she occasionally gets in these moods, when she was a colt, one of the boys yelled that she was mad again, it stuck. We're not real creative when it comes to naming horses."

"I think it's great," Sharon answered as she raised her hand toward the horse, it jerked away and spun back into the stall.

"A little shy, but more often testy," Case said. "Horses are like humans, same nervous issues and traits. I never get tired trying to figure 'em out. And I'm sure they are trying to outsmart us. By the way, that's the horse that your friend rides."

"Ms. Karg? Oh yes, I can see she would fit her. Did they ride recently? I only just got back in town."

"Maybe a couple of days ago, as always she was all business, had a friend with her this time. Good-looking fellow, had a dark outdoors tan, not that fake paint-on stuff I see, black hair, pony tail, which suited him and a French accent. Actually pretty good-looking if you ask this old farm girl, kind of took your breath away. Out for a couple of hours, Madigan came in well lathered so my guess is they went at a good pace. Madigan loved it, I could tell. Ms. Karg hinted that she might be interested in buying the horse. I'll wait and see."

Sharon watched the horse swing its full flanks in a half circle and then come back to the gate; it looked directly at Sharon. She put her hand up and the horse didn't shy this time. She placed her palm against the jaw line, slowly rubbed her and felt the strength of the mare. Though her touch was light, she could feel the horse's power and energy. She ran her hand through the mare's mane, and dug her nails into the hair. The horse nudged her.

"Amazing, she won't let some people near her. You're a natural, can see you've been around horses. Well, back to business, let me show you some open stalls," Emily Chase said as she headed toward the far open door.

"Right behind you," Sharon said as she patted the horse with her left hand and gave a short jerk to the mane she had gripped with her right. A small handful of maybe twenty hairs came away. Madigan didn't even flinch. She carefully twisted the hairs into a tight coil and slipped them into a small zip-lock bag she had retrieved from her back pocket. She gave the horse another pat and followed Chase out the rear door of the paddock.

After another fifteen minutes of walking the stable grounds, Sharon was satisfied that Chase didn't suspect anything more than a prospective client. She left her cell number but no address. Twenty minutes later she rolled up the driveway to her bungalow.

"Kevin, I have one more sample to test," Sharon said over her cell in her most businesslike voice.

"You are going to get me fired, O'Mara. All the favors I do for you and all I get is another request for another favor," Kevin said.

"Poor boy," she answered. "This one is critical. I think I found the horse that matches the hydrofoil horsehair."

"No kidding, how'd you do that?"

"Intense detective work," Sharon said.

"And luck."

"Yeah that too; anyway, can I drop them off? I think there are enough bulbs on the hairs to get DNA; if they match I'm a couple of steps closer."

"I'm in all morning, paperwork. The Captain is out for the next two days at a conference in Sacramento, it's safe."

"Like he scares me," Sharon chortled.

"It's not you I'm worried about," Kevin said. "I just don't need the friction."

An hour later Kevin took the hairs, still in their bag, placed them in another, more official, evidence bag and posted a number on its label. Sharon's little car accident had an evidence trail that was now longer than some strong-arm robberies.

"Thanks," Sharon said as she kissed him on the cheek.

"Don't do that," Kevin said. "Not here!"

"Kevin, everyone in this room," she scanned the area designated for detectives, all three desks in one corner of a large open floor, currently empty, "knows me. They can keep a secret. Later, I have a meeting in Oakland." And she walked out, leaving Kevin holding the bag.

8c

As she passed through Orinda, heading toward Oakland, Sharon's phone rang. It didn't really ring; it played a few bars of the *La Marseillaise*, then repeated itself. Warmth grew in her breast; she answered.

"Good morning Jean-François, *comment allez-vous*?"

"*Je suis tres bien* and your accent needs work."

"Don't I know that, are you back?"

"Yes, you are my first call; I'm in a limo heading to the Compton, then meetings all afternoon in San Jose. The tech people want to show me some new gear and pulleys, all remotely controlled. Are you free for dinner?"

"Let me catch a breath," she paused for a moment and turned down the radio. "Dinner would be delightful. Where?"

"A special place on Folsom between 7th and 8th, Italian."

"Rocco's? Just love it."

"You know all the good places," JF said.

"I know more about the cafes and pizza joints than high-end restaurants; that's why I have you around," Sharon answered.

"7:30, see you there," JF said.

"7:30 it is."

She hung up just as she exploded out of the far right westbound bore of the Caldecott tunnel that connected the near suburbs of Contra Costa County and the urbanistas of Oakland and Berkeley. The view, as she weaved her way down Highway 24 into Oakland, was, as always, spectacular. The city of San Francisco, with it hills and skyline, spread out across the left side of the panorama. The Bay Bridge and the Golden Gate Bridge looked almost connected and Alcatraz floated, like a ship, on San Francisco Bay. No fog obscured the picture framed by the windshield of her Jaguar. After a brief stop at a Starbucks, she pulled into a visitor's stall at the Oakland police department and headed to Major Crimes, Section 1, Homicides. An hour earlier she had called and made an appointment to see Sergeant Danny Chang.

"Sergeant Chang, please, Sharon O'Mara, I'm expected," she said to the officer at the desk as she sat two grande coffees on the desk.

The officer, a young woman, smiled at Sharon and punched a few numbers into the ancient phone on her desk. She said something into the phone and then said to Sharon, "Please take a seat, Sergeant Chang will be right with you."

Sergeant Danny Chang had worked with Sharon on an earlier case involving the Chinese sex slave trade that resulted in the collapse of an Oakland Tong as well as putting a serious hurt on one of the local Mexican drug cartels. She learned more, as a result, about the shipping container business than she ever wanted to know. Now she needed Chang's help again; he had been reassigned to homicide.

Sharon watched Danny Chang push open the door from the back offices into the lobby. As experienced cops go, this man hadn't acquired the usual bad habits of a thick physique and a fluorescent light inspired pasty face. He was tall and trim; walked with an athletic grace and she had never seen him without at least a trace of an ironic smile. Irony spread from ear to ear this mid-morning.

"Damn Sharon, it was good to hear from you, but then again, every time I see you something happens. Should I call backup?" Danny asked, as he hugged her quite unprofessionally.

"No, I think we're safe here, but I need a little information and a little help. Do you have a minute or two?"

"Absolutely, the left interview room," Chang said and then turned to the desk officer, "I'll be in Two, ring me if you need me."

The officer nodded and then looked at the coffee cups, then at Sharon.

"Refreshments, Sergeant," she said as she picked up the coffees and handed one to Chang. The desk officer looked seriously disappointed.

They settled into the hard well-worn, battle weary wooden chairs.

"How's your mother?" Sharon started.

"She's well, the tea room keeps her occupied and Mei and Jiao are in school now. It was a close one for those girls; if it weren't for you, I don't know where they would be. You need to see them again."

Mei and Jiao were two girls kidnapped in China and smuggled into Oakland in shipping containers. Sharon, Kevin and Chang had rescued the girls before they became two more drug-addicted prostitutes in Oakland's darker alleys.

"I know, it's been too long, I promise," she said.

"You said help," Chang said.

"What can you tell me about the dead trucker found last week near the port?"

"You know I can't discuss ongoing cases," Chang answered.

"I know, but I'm looking into a possible connection between the man's death and a missing boat. We might be able to unofficially trade information."

"Missing boat?"

"Yes, my client is developing a new style of sailboat," Sharon said. "It was placed in a shipping container to be taken back to France where it's being manufactured. The driver, Julio Flores, was to take the container from a pier in San Francisco to the Port of Oakland. There it was to be loaded on a train and sent to the East Coast and then transported by boat to France. But, before Flores could get to the port, he was murdered and the container was stolen."

"We know that, give me a couple of minutes," Chang said as he left. Two minutes later he returned with a binder and a laptop. He laid both on the grey Formica; he opened the binder, when he lifted the lid of the laptop the screen lit-up. Sharon could see the edges of crime photos and section tabs in the binder; she could not see the screen.

"Can you help me?" she asked.

"Not sure, but maybe you can help me?"

Sharon squinted at Chang, "Me?"

"We know that Flores was killed somewhere else, put back into his truck and left where we found it. It wasn't until we got the APB on the missing truck that we found it; a patrol car spotted it late on the same day the APB was issued. Nobody paid attention to the truck or the driver all day; he looked like he was sleeping. We get a lot of truckers doing that near the port between loads. Our men banged on the door and found him dead. Coroner says he'd been dead maybe fifteen hours, shot once in the heart. Damn shame, left a family."

"Always a shame when the innocent get caught up in evil," Sharon answered.

"We haven't found the primary crime scene, not sure we ever will, could be anywhere. The keys were left in the cab, no fingerprints, none, even from Flores, wiped clean, handles, steering, everything. The odometer tells us nothing. His company logged in the miles before his shift and it fits his trip into San Francisco, then back to Oakland, seems there might be a two or three mile anomaly. But shit, he could have gotten lost or had to take a piss or something. A couple of miles are almost nothing."

"Almost?"

"Yeah, almost. As I said, the primary crime scene is somewhere along the route between the piers and where Flores was found. Not a lot of leeway, considering the mileage. We caught a break; his truck had a transponder that let the Port know about his comings and goings. We found out that he never entered the port so that area was eliminated.

"How come you couldn't find him through the transponder in his truck?"

Chang looked through the photos and slid one across the table to Sharon, she saw a small grey box, its case cracked open with wires sticking out at all angles.

"They busted it up," she said.

"Yes, it was found on the street near the truck. All the information we have is from the company's computer files, timed about fifteen hours before Flores was found. Works with time of death. I have three men working on this. The men at the port are worried and the union isn't helping since the guy was non-union. Me, I think this is specific to the theft, not a general threat to the drivers. But the unions are using it for leverage and their own purposes, way out of bounds crap if you ask me."

"No kidding," Sharon said.

"We have also spliced together a short video from cameras in and around the port," Chang said and turned the laptop so that both he and Sharon could see the screen. "Thanks to Homeland Security, we have worked with the port to install about twenty cameras at the entry area of the port's gates and along major routes in and out. The short shots take us from the end of the Bay Bridge to within a few blocks of the port."

"That all makes me feel so warm and cozy, Sergeant," Sharon said.

"I know, I know. Not my call. The Feds are all concerned about terrorists and the port. They wave money and technology at us, we bite. Anyway it does help with the crime in the area, car thefts, break-ins, general vandalism is down almost 20 percent. Funny how different you act when mom's looking over your shoulder."

"Yeah, real funny," Sharon said.

"Anyway, let me run this and you will see what we have, the number 053 is painted on the cab's roof, makes it easier to follow. Ready?"

"Go for it," Sharon said. "Does it have a lead-in that says Big Brother Productions?"

"Jesus, Sharon, I only work here, please," Chang answered just a bit too defensively.

She looked at the laptop and pointed, "Action, Sergeant, action."

Chang pushed the enter button, the screen came alive.

A high overhead view popped up on the screen, cars raced from the bottom of the screen toward the top, the off ramp from the Bay Bridge softly curved to the right, trucks, cars, vans, and motorcycles did a deadly dance amongst each other as they headed toward the road's split, north to Berkeley and south to Oakland. A digital display clocked seconds in the corner of the image.

"At the twenty-one second mark, 053 passes by the camera," Chang said as he counted up, "nineteen, twenty, twenty-one. There."

The cab, with 053 painted on the roof, drove into view. Its forty-six foot, dark blue container was secured on a trailer. Two more tractor-trailer rigs followed 053. They watched as it kept to the far right lane and eased from their view. This off ramp headed toward Oakland and the port. Cars and mini-vans surrounded the trucks, the dance continued.

"The clock jumps here to the time stamp of the next camera," Chang said.

The next image showed the rig slowly going down Maritime Street, the primary access to the port. The next camera picked it up near the rail terminal.

"It should have turned here, but it didn't. It continued on into the Acorn area of Oakland and then past these cameras near the Nimitz underpass. This is where we lost it. Flores was found on a side street in the Produce District. We found one quick shot of his cab, without the trailer, passing by the Amtrak station on 1st Street; it was heading south toward the Produce area. No visual on the driver, you can see it on the screen as it passes the station."

The red bobtailed truck cab, 'Port Shippers' on its door, passed by the camera's view, then disappeared.

"The time stamp says it's almost two hours later than the Nimitz shot; that correct?" Sharon said.

"Yes, I confirmed it, all the cameras' digital clocks are checked often, actually they are all monitored through a security center; all images are sent directly to the hard drives; this new equipment is just amazing."

"Yeah, amazing," Sharon answered. "I just hope that some-day scratching your ass or picking your nose in public doesn't become a criminal office, hell, they might go back years to con-vict you."

Sergeant Chang tilted his head and opened his palms up-ward, "Please, Sharon, it's just a video, my head hurts from all the crap I get from Homeland. To them, this is all a game. So please ..."

"I'm sorry, Danny, anyway, looks like we have two hours missing, not too much additional mileage and, wait a second," Sharon said pointing at the laptop. "Back the video up."

Chang stopped the video; making a series of clicks he played the video back to the start where the cab passed the train sta-tion.

"There," Sharon said. "Freeze it."

The image came to an abrupt stop.

"Gotcha," she said. "Danny, what's that following the cab?

Chang studied the screen, "Black BMW, maybe a 650 from the looks."

"Go back to the beginning please," she said.

The tractor and trailer slid into view, followed first by a grey and then a white car, then a black vehicle appeared, a black BMW ragtop. It followed the trailer with its dark blue container as it turned south to Oakland. During the next three camera shots, the BMW showed up in all of them, following the container with the hydrofoil tightly packed inside.

"Coincidence?" Sharon asked.

"I don't believe in them," Chang said. "Let's go through it one more time, maybe I can grab a plate number."

In two of the five camera shots, they could see a license number on the BMW, not Californian. They both agreed it was the same BMW.

"Right there, does that front right corner look damaged?" Sharon asked.

Chang studied the image; they ran it back and forth a couple of times, "Yes, a slight indentation, but the headlight's still good. Give me a second." The sergeant left the room and Sharon watched the video one more time.

"The license plate was reported stolen a month ago, also from another BMW 650 visiting from Nevada," Chang said when he returned. "These guys are good and meticulous. What's with the damage on the car?"

"This may have been the same BMW that tried to knock me off the road a few weeks ago, too many coincidences."

"I would have guessed they'd have repaired the ding by now. If it's connected to the murder, we may be looking at the car that picked up whoever was driving the truck. They needed some way to leave after dumping the truck and leaving the driver. We identified Flores from his driver's license but the press got his name from someone, we're not sure from whom. It was leaked before there was a confirmation; his wife found out from the news. Everyone's upset about how it went down."

"It was done to mess up the police and the storyline, now you have to spend more time defending the story than finding the killers," Sharon said.

"Could be, but you've given us a clue and a possible murder suspect, thanks."

"No worries, now I just need to find a goddamn sailboat in a box."

Chapter 9

9a

Outside Karbala, Iraq, 2005

"We know the girls were here, Major" O'Mara said into the radio. "Everything points to it, but they sure as hell were waiting for us."

"No shit. Damage?" Major Simpson asked.

"One KIA, Private Nolan, killed when the building exploded. Another with a leg wound," Sharon answered.

"Enemy?"

"We count seven dead, but in the aftermath of the storm some may have slipped away. Photos and prints are on their way back to you and Intel. Maybe we can find out who these guys are. A lot more sophisticated than your usual al-Qaeda thugs. They knew we were coming."

"Get your ass back here. Let's figure this thing out," Simpson said.

"I want a Bronze Star for Nolan, Major; he saved our asses out here twice and his family should know it."

"We'll talk about it when you get back. Out."

"Out."

It was a classic screw-up of the worst kind. Bravado mixed with overconfidence, seasoned with the sandstorm, led to a cluster-fuck that left Private Timothy O. Nolan dead. They stripped everything of value from the wasted Humvee; another crew would try to retrieve the remains sometime later. The ride back to the Green Zone was hot and crowded; Nolan was in a bag on the floor between the men, O'Mara sat next to him.

"Maybe it was the loss of the helicopters," she thought. *"Maybe they would have seen something from the air. Maybe they shouldn't have gone down that alley, maybe, maybe. Maybe the whole thing was*

fucked from the start. And where the hell are those girls?"

The debriefing took the rest of the day and went on into the evening, Sanchez talked about what happened from the east side and O'Mara from the west, they left nothing out. The operation, other than being screwed-up, went as planned.

"We didn't find the Mercedes," Sanchez said during the interview. "Maybe that was something important we should have seen. But hell, they could have hid it or something. We know that as soon as the shooting started we were close to something, we crashed in. These guys were experienced with tactical. Wanted us in the house, tried to push us in, but they failed. If it weren't for that wire on the stairs, Nolan would be waiting out in the hall with the rest of the squad. It was a fuck-up, but not sure if anyone's to blame; after all, anything can happen in this shit hole of a country."

O'Mara and her men were held close to the base for the next few days. The usual hurry up and wait; they cleaned their gear and tried to get their collective heads around what had happened. They went to the airstrip with Private Nolan for his trip home; there were three other caskets on the tarmac below the ramp leading to the C-17. Maybe fifty soldiers were standing in tight formation honoring the men who had died for their country.

Abdul was waiting for them when they returned to their billet.

"I'm sorry about the soldier, Lieutenant," Abdul said. "He was very kind to me; we talked a lot about my home and your country. He was very nice."

"Yes, too damn nice to die here," O'Mara said as she studied the boy, he was calm and engaging, no evasion, full of sincerity. "Have you thought of anything else that might help us since we came back? Anything about the car, the men or the girls?"

She watched the boy as he thought through what he had seen, "No, I told you everything I remembered, the car, the girls in the room, the men standing about talking to the old man, everything."

"What old man, you never said anything about an old

man?"

"An old man came to visit; I stood on the crates and looked through the window. The girls ran up and hugged him," Abdul said. "One showed him pictures and the other just danced around. After all Lieutenant; they're just kids and they act like kids, just girls."

"Was he tall or short?"

"Maybe like the sergeant," Abdul said pointing toward Sanchez as he walked over toward them.

"What did you see before the man went inside?" Sanchez asked.

"Let me think, he arrived in a car, a Toyota, white. Nice car, someday when I'm in America I will own that car, no damage, it was very nice."

"Back to the man, Abdul," Sharon said.

"Yes, yes. When he drove up, the soldiers standing out front came to attention and then a man came out of the building and greeted him, kissed him on both cheeks, like he was somebody important. He was the big deal, is that the right words?"

"Close enough, then what?" Sanchez asked.

"He lit a cigarette, the wind blew the smoke to me, smelled like my brand," Abdul said. "You got a cigarette, sergeant?"

"Don't smoke kid."

"They smelled like your cigarettes?" O'Mara asked. "The ones with the clove taste?"

"Yes, they taste much better than the plain kind, except for your Marlboros, those are real good. Lieutenant?"

"No way." O'Mara looked at Sanchez. "You thinking what I'm thinking Sarg? Get that stack of photos."

Sergeant Sanchez returned to the Lieutenant and the boy, laid the pictures on the table, said nothing and stood off to one side.

"Abdul, I want you to look at these photos, if you see anyone you know, just point to the photo."

"Yeah, sure. No problem." Abdul walked to the edge of the table and began to scan the photos starting at the top row, then the next and so on until he stopped at the last row. He pointed at the third photo in from the left.

"That's the old man," he said with his finger on the photo.

"You sure?" Sanchez asked.

"How do you say, damn sure?" Abdul said.

"That'll work; do you know who he is?"

"No, but I expect that he is the big man, their leader."

"You have got to be kidding, I can't believe it," Sanchez said. "The man would use his own granddaughters as bait to lure us out."

"After what I've seen, I can believe anything in this country," O'Mara said. "I suggest we pay Mister al-Jamil a visit."

9b

Rocco's is one of those San Francisco restaurants; every city has at least a dozen, hidden, yet in plain sight. Narrow, like a shotgun shack, seats fifty customers if lucky, tall full front glass windows on the street and at night, reminds you of the restaurant in the movie *The Godfather* where Al Pacino finds the pistol behind the toilet and shoots the mobster and his enabling police captain. And, to no one's surprise, they all seem to be Italian.

O'Mara arrived early and parked on the street. While the neighborhood, to the casual suburbanite, seemed a bit on the seedy side, it was full of homes, apartments, and high tech start-ups. When the high tech industry started, over fifty years ago, they pushed out their first computer bytes in now famous backyard garages. Today, they start in lofts and warehouses on the south side of San Francisco, where good food and pizza can be found on the first floors of the same buildings that hold nascent Facebooks.

Jean-François Voss sat in the window seat fully engaged with the restaurant owner in an animated conversation as Sharon passed the window; she waved. The usual crowd filled the doorway as she pushed herself through the mix to JF's table.

"You're early," Sharon said, a touch of surprise in her voice.

"You are right on time," JF answered. "I've known the owner a few years; I come for lunch once in a while. Good spot to meet some of the young tech guys, a couple of the guys have shops not more than a block from here."

"One of my favorites," Sharon said, and as if to prove the point, a glass of red wine arrived. "You are beginning to annoy me, JF, you and your assumptions."

"And don't you look good; it's refreshing to see a woman dress up even if for a casual place like this. To you," he said as he raised his glass and smiled. Two girls at a nearby booth giggled; their boyfriends were not amused by the attention they paid to JF.

"You do cause a stir wherever you go," Sharon said, as one of the boyfriends pointed his finger at his date, she answered with a less than amused look.

"What do you expect one to do?" JF said.

"Now that's a line of bullshit if I've ever heard one," Sharon answered. She sensed that he was worried about something. "What's the problem?"

"The missing hydrofoil is setting us back at least six months; there was some data left on the hard drive in the boat that could not be sent on ahead. Mike hadn't the time to retrieve it after the Coast Guard released the boat. We were going to download it when the boat arrived in France; that data is critical."

"I may have a lead on the boat," Sharon said. "We've traced it to an area near the Port of Oakland. There is a two hour window that we are trying to open but we are closer now."

Jean-François paused a few seconds, "Near the port, near the area where it was to be unloaded onto the train?"

"Looks like it, we have video of it coming into the area and then we lost it. Then a few hours later the cab turns up without the trailer." His reaction caught her attention, something buzzed in the back of her brain.

"Did they see anything else suspicious?"

The buzz became louder; it was her turn to pause, she held back, "No, just the truck and then the cab, nothing else. Whoever took the trailer with the container doesn't show up on the video. One minute the cab and trailer are there and then two hours later, no trailer, no container, just the cab and the dead driver."

An antipasto plate arrived and they nibbled on the olives and salami. But Sharon was sure something had changed, there was some type of shift in JF's mood and attitude. She couldn't place it. Then he changed the conversation to France and Provence. They shared a Caesar salad and a plate of linguine and clams; they both sopped up the juice with the French bread. For a few minutes, she forgot about his pause and reflection, but only for a few minutes.

The owner stopped by twice and brought them an aperitif the second time around, a glass of anise rich liquor, Pernod.

"I have a friend that enjoys this very much," Sharon said, thinking of Evelyn Luca, the high-end handbag designer.

"It is an acquired taste but it's a European drink and quite an industry. Did you know that it was the invention of the man who made absinthe, "the green fairy," of Parisian fame, Monsieur Henri Pernod?"

"Yes, as a matter of fact I did but I'm a scotch drinker, the anise flavor just doesn't appeal to me."

"That is a shame but for now, *bonne chance*." JF tilted the glass toward Sharon and then sipped the green liquor.

"Tell me more about the videos, they showed the truck and the trailer?" JF asked, returning to the subject they had dropped.

"Yes, we followed it from the Bay Bridge to the port, then we lost it," Sharon said repeating herself. "It pops-up later near the Oakland Amtrak station. It was found about ten blocks away by the police with the dead driver still in the cab."

"Shocking, but at the same time surreal. Like one of your reality TV shows."

"Yeah, but more deadly. And I'm sure that Mr. Flores would rather be on *Dancing with the Stars* than on one of those cop shows."

"I'm sure you're right," JF said with a touch of distraction in his voice as he glanced at his watch. "I sadly have to call it a night; I have to be in Sunnyvale at 9:00 AM tomorrow, some new software to look at. Do you need a lift?"

"No, I'm fine. Parked just around the corner," she added.

The owner walked over as they stood and shook JF's hand, he also smiled at Sharon. "I've seen you here before," he said.

"I've been here often but tend to stay to myself, still the best Italian in the City," Sharon offered.

"Thanks for the compliment, we try."

The two exited into the fresh evening air, a cool breeze washed down Folsom Street from up in the hills west of downtown. The traffic on the street was remarkably quiet as they walked arm and arm to Sharon's car.

"Why did you become distant in the restaurant when I brought up the videos?" Sharon asked. "You hired me to find out what happened to your sister, this is all part of it, like it or not."

JF again paused before he answered; Sharon lit a cigarette.

"Those will kill you, you know."

"You're the second person to say that to me today," she answered, remembering her earlier four-way conversation with herself.

"You should pay attention to us."

"Yeah, there are a lot of things I should pay attention to; I'll just add it to the list."

"What's the matter with you?"

"You're evading my questions and from your body language you know more about this than you are telling me."

She waited for an answer, when none came, she pointed a finger at JF's chest. "Damn it, JF, if you're involved in this, I'll walk away right now, I will not be lied to. To hell with your boat and the whole race, good night!" She opened the door to her sedan, pitched the cigarette to the ground and slid into the seat. JF reached in and tried to grab her arm.

"Don't try that unless you want to eat left-handed," she said, loud enough that JF quickly yanked his hand back.

"I don't get it, what's the matter?"

"We'll talk later, I'm done for tonight. Thanks for dinner, I'll call you later," Sharon said as she started the Jaguar, in two minutes she was on the east bound on-ramp of the Bay Bridge and heading for home.

9c

"Men are bastards," Sharon said as she nursed a real drink at Geno's. "Just when you get stars in your eyes, they kick sand in your face, they're all bastards."

Gina just stood in front of her friend and allowed her to vent. This was one of her forms of therapy, listening. Usually the problem resolved itself with only a little coaching and a little more scotch.

"Yes, I agree that he's a *stronzo*, but then again all good-looking, very rich men are *stronzos*," Gina said. "I know the type and the attitude; they are all worthless pieces of ..."

"You talking to me?" a male voice asked from near the door.

"I rest my case," Sharon said as she patted the stool next to her. Kevin Bryan sat and smiled at the girls. "Therapy session?"

"Fuck you, Bryan, I came in here to drown my broken heart and you have to walk in. I honestly believe that God wants me punished, I don't know why yet but I'll find out."

Kevin kissed her cheek.

"That's not going to help. All you men are bastards, plain and simple. You say one thing and then you just go about your merry way doing what you want, regardless of who you hurt."

Kevin looked at Gina for an answer. She shrugged and shook her head.

"All right, I won't defend myself or the male of the species. God knows, from what I've seen, that's a lost argument anyway but something else set you off. You want to tell me?"

Sharon drained the tumbler and pointed at Gina.

"Sorry girl, you're cut off for the night. Don't like where this is going. Talk to Kevin, I'll be back." She headed to the far end of the bar.

Sharon put her fists on each side of her face and stared into the mirror behind the bar, "Kevin what have I gotten myself into? I had dinner with Voss tonight and at one point, while I described watching videos of the truck hauling his boat, he acted like he already knew what went down. Not in so many words but I can read people and from that moment on, the whole conversation went another way. He wanted to know what else we saw, not the truck; he didn't care about the truck or the driver, he wanted something else. And I know what it was."

"What?"

"A black BMW."

"Why?" Kevin asked.

"The BMW kept appearing in almost every shot, it followed the tractor trailer rig from the bridge to where it was found. The plates are stolen and there is only one person that I know of, amongst this collection of stellar human beings, who owns one, Eva Karg."

"Did you clue him in?"

"No, he can stew about it. He can wonder about what we know."

"I've got the DNA results in my car, be right back," he said and left. A minute later Kevin laid an envelope on the table; it was similar to the envelope from the last response by the state C.I.U. lab.

"You were right about your hunch," Kevin said. "The DNA from the sample you gave me the other day and the one from the boat match, the same horse provided both samples."

"So now I have a black BMW, a match to a Palomino horse and a Frenchman who went from client to suspect over a plate of linguine. Kevin, this whole thing is screwy. As I said before, what have I gotten into?"

"It's no different than any other complicated case; you collect the evidence and then see where it leads you."

Gina sat a glass of water and two aspirin on the bar.

"Take these, drink that and then go home, get a good night's sleep. Everything will be clearer in the morning, right Kev?"

"Seems to work for me, sometimes," he answered.

Sharon gathered up her coat and handbag and slid off the stool. With her back to the bar, she waved her hand in the air as she walked out the door.

****

Green Zone, Baghdad, Iraq, 2005

"Major, the kid identified the tribal elder as the leader of this group; this whole operation was a setup from the start. They got us to their village and then, because of the Mercedes, we were led into trap," Sharon said.

"You think the kid is involved?" Major Simpson asked.

"Not sure, everything is on the table in this country, wouldn't surprise me but it would disappoint me."

"You like him?"

"Yeah, he's smart and intuitive. Learned English from the street and speaks it well. Always on his toes but he's still a thirteen-year-old when it comes to some things, like his fancy for ice cream."

"I'm not thirteen and I fancy ice cream, Lieutenant," the Major said with a laugh.

"You know what I mean, he's seen a lot, been through a lot and it's hardened him. He's defensive and expects a prize when he gives the right answer; maybe they offered him something more."

"Not seventy virgins, I hope."

"No, I think he's actually too smart for that. Not been through the religious schools, it's almost too late to get him indoctrinated. Right now he just wants to go to America."

"Keep him going with that goal," the Major said.

"What? Hanging that out there may only make matters worse, when he finds out that he's being lead about, he'll shut down and we won't get anything."

"Who said I wasn't working on the request for him to go to America, O'Mara?"

O'Mara looked at her Major, "If you weren't my commander, I'd give you a kiss, then again, screw it." She gave him a peck on his cheek.

"I'm not making any promises; this will be kicked upstairs before it happens. Keep an eye on him and keep him out of trouble. Now get out, I've got work to do."

Sharon O'Mara climbed the bank of the levee that paralleled the Tigris River and looked over the skyline of Baghdad. The morning heat had started to build after the long night; it was like the heat in Phoenix, except that here, along the grey river, the humidity rose with the heat, the moisture was sucked from the river and it lounged along its flanks like hot steam over a pot. She saluted a young private on guard duty and walked along the wide road that capped the levee.

This was her second tour and she knew it would be her last. She had three months to do before going home, wherever the hell that was. She knew why she liked Abdul, even though she couldn't tell anyone, especially the Major. They had similar backgrounds. Until she was eighteen, she bounced from one foster home to another; always stubborn and independent, most of the homes tired of her and her inflexible nature very quickly. They wanted to help her, to change her and mold her into the perfect young lady. One even had her go to ballet classes. Her own view of life formed during long hikes and horse rides in the foothills behind Colorado Springs. She had an almost intuitive view of everything she saw; she could look into the heart of something and see all its possibilities. She was smart and studied hard. In high school, she learned math and calculus quickly and picked-up the rudiments of French and Spanish. One of her friends was Mexican and she coached her until her Spanish wasn't too bad for a "Gringo."

She learned to hunt and fish from books and videos. At seventeen, she lost her virginity to someone named Bob or Rob; she couldn't or didn't want to remember his name. When she turned eighteen, she bought her first hunting rifle; at nineteen she took her first and last deer. There was no satisfaction in the kill; in fact, she was profoundly saddened. She dressed out the animal and lived on venison for a year. She honored the animal before every meal. Never spiritual or religious, she read everything from science fiction to Sartre. When she turned twenty, she loaded up her small pickup, moved to California, found a small house on the east side of Sacramento, took a job as a waitress and went back to college, a small JC near her home. She majored in criminal law and history and audited classes in art and literature; she also joined the school's Army ROTC program. They would help her pay for college and she was able to spend time at the pistol range. For the first time in her life, she knew she had a purpose, to learn to be a leader of men.

"Excuse me Lieutenant, I have a message for you," a private said, handing O'Mara a folded piece of paper.

"From who?" O'Mara asked.

"A boy left it at the gate; it had your name in Arabic on the front. They removed the letter from the envelope to clear it."

She unfolded the paper and looked at the signature at the bottom, Hakim al-Jamil. The note was in English.

My dearest Lieutenant,

Thank you for your efforts and those of your soldiers to try and find my granddaughters. I am very saddened to hear that one of your men died while trying to help. I am sure he is with his God; please pass on my condolences to his family.

I have received a ransom note from the kidnappers; they want 10,000 US dollars for the return of my grandchildren. We are a poor village, we have nothing and we cannot pay this. They will kill them, I am sure. This war has taken everything we once had and turned it to dust. They gave us one week to find the money, once again I ask for your help.

Hakim al-Jamil

O'Mara looked across the river toward the numerous minarets that punctuated the reddish grey skyline of one of the oldest cities in the world, a city where nothing is or was as it seemed, an open hand could not be trusted, a kiss on the cheek may be a lie and a grandfather's love was most probably a tool for treachery.

She climbed back down the levee and headed toward her quarters, her pistol needed cleaning.

Chapter 10

10a

"Sharon, please meet me at Alain's this afternoon," Evelyn Luca said. "The doctor's tell me that he is dying."

"They've been saying that for years," Sharon answered.

"He is bleeding inside; there is nothing that can be done. I will be there at 2:00."

Sharon sat the phone back on the table and looked out her office window into the backyard. Her whole life it seemed that death was always just around the corner. Her parents died when she was just a child, a neighbor just about her age died when she was ten, Iraq and countless lives wasted and now again in this freakish profession she had chosen. It's a door that beckons everyone and a door we must all go through. She felt Basil nuzzle her hip.

"That's a good boy," she said. "Walk?"

Basil reacted like she had said "unlimited bones for life." He took off down the hallway, pulled his leash off the countertop and trotted back to Sharon.

"Now where's my shoes?" she said to him. He cocked his head and looked at her, then scanned the room. "Shoes?"

Basil, leash still in his mouth, turned and walked into the hallway; Sharon followed, sliding her phone into her back pocket. In her bedroom, he stopped by the bed, sat, looked at her sneakers, then at her. She was sure that, if her boy could talk, he would have said, *"There they are, same place you left them, now put whatever they are on your feet and let's get going, I'm already late for a bush."*

Five minutes later he had marked, for maybe the thousandth

time, every bush and shrub on their circuit and a few garbage cans with rollers set in twos and threes along the street, it was trash day.

Since the surveillance truck incident a few weeks earlier, she never went anywhere without her Beretta, now couched in its holster snug in her back. A white shirt, long tails out, covered the weapon. Black jeans and sneakers finished the look. But Basil was more than enough protection if any close quarters work had to be done.

On the second tour of the block, she noticed something new, a van parked at the curb in front of her cottage. Department of Sanitary Services, with its elaborate Contra Costa County seal, was painted on its side. No one was in the front seat or anywhere around the vehicle.

Perhaps she was more sensitive and aware of things in the neighborhood since the clove guy, this was probably nothing, but she couldn't just leave it alone.

"A little peek, don't you think, old boy?" she said as they stepped off the curb and headed to the van. At fifty feet away, she saw two boys on bikes heading toward her in the middle of the street, they couldn't have been twelve. She couldn't understand their banter but it was loud and full of classic early-testosterone bravado, as well as a few, "we're so fucking cool," curse words. She smiled.

She looked back at the van, then the boys. "Shit," was the first thing Basil heard, then "Run." But she wasn't running away from the truck, she was running toward it. She dropped Basil's leash and waved frantically at the boys who had pulled up short, three cars were parked on the opposite side of the street from the van; *maybe* was her best hope.

"I need you to get out of here fellows, now!" the tone in her voice said it all, besides, she looked pretty crazy to the two bikers and the dog would have put fear in the eyes of the devil himself.

But these were tough suburban twelve year olds; no one was going to push them around.

"We don't have to do what you say, you're not my mom," the taller one said while straddling his bike. The other, not to be left out, said in full voice, "Yeah."

Since her first fears had not immediately materialized, Sharon approached the boys with a more measured tone, "Men, I'm an ex-Army officer and I live right there in that house," she said pointing. "I need you two to leave the area. It's very dangerous at the moment and …"

"What's so dangerous?" the shorter of the two said, interrupting. "Don't see nothing."

Stubborn was not what she needed right now. "See that van over there," again she pointed. "There's a chance that it's not what it's supposed to be and I really don't know, but it may be very dangerous."

"Like spies and stuff, maybe it's an IED, what do'ya think Pat?" the taller one said.

"What do you know about IEDs," Sharon asked, her impatience rising.

"I watch TV, I know all about 'em but they're not around here. No terrorists around here but Dad says to be careful around town, lots of foreign people," the smaller of the two added.

Paranoia everywhere and with too much casual knowledge. "I want you boys to leave here now, I'm calling the police. I want them to find out why that truck's there and until I know what's going on, you two must get out of the area," she paused and looked the boys, Abdul flashed in her memory. "And I mean it, right now."

Startled by her sudden, very loud order, they started to saddle-up, the taller spun his bike around. As the shorter boy began to spin his bike, all three saw the man appear, striding down the narrow walk between Sharon's cottage and the one next to it; he was carrying a metal toolbox. The boys looked back at the crazy woman but all they saw was the automatic pistol in her hand and the dog ready to lunge. They looked back at the man as they heard the sound of the crashing of metal on concrete; he had dropped the toolbox and also held a pistol. It was aimed at

Sharon.

"Boys, run behind those cars, now. And stay down. Basil, hold."

No bravado this time. They dropped their bikes and ran behind the cars as instructed.

Sharon hit 911 without taking her eyes from the man. She slowly raised the automatic and aimed it.

"Your emergency?" a voice said over the phone.

"Shots fired," she said, anticipating the future; she then gave her street address. "Two people on the street, one woman and one man. The woman is plain clothes." She knew she'd get in trouble but if it went down as she hoped it wouldn't, better to be safe than sorry. Nothing brings police faster than, "Shots fired and officer on scene."

The man held his ground but she could see him inching his way down the walk toward the van. He was strongly built with narrow hips and wide shoulders. His complexion was dark, black hair, a two-day-old beard and black eyes. He looked at the cars where the boys were hiding.

"Don't even think about it," Sharon yelled, Basil stood very still, his eyes never left the man; he waited for the order. "Just throw the weapon on the grass, drop to your knees and interlock your fingers on the top of your head." She knew that was not going to happen. She continued to watch the man. Out of the corner of her eye, she caught movement and then the sound of a diesel truck, took a quick peek, a garbage truck. "Shit."

The truck picked up speed and headed toward her. She hoped the driver would see her standing in the road with a pistol in her hand but then again that's not exactly what you are looking for on a quiet tree-lined suburban street; the truck kept coming. Her target was ten feet from the van, "I said stay where you are," she yelled.

The truck had enough room to pass between her and the van; the first sirens could be heard over the increasing rumble of the garbage truck's engine. The boy's bikes, still lying in the street, would force it to move to the right, *then what?*

She heard the engine roar suddenly. *He's seen my gun; he's trying to get the hell through this area as fast as possible, good.* She looked back at the man; he was almost at the van and cover. She could tell he heard the sirens, fight or flee was all over his face. She stood fully exposed in the middle of the street. The truck roared by directly in front of her, hiding the van for maybe two seconds. As it passed by, the van roared to life, its rear wheels spinning on the asphalt, tire smoke filled the wheel wells. The van lunged forward and took off after the garbage truck. At the corner, the garbage truck paused, its brake lights flared and then it went left; the van, on almost two wheels, went right, no brakes. Five seconds later, a patrol car sped around the same corner, lights flashing, siren screaming. O'Mara turned and watched two more prowlers approaching from the other end of the street. She slowly lowered her pistol to the asphalt.

"Boys, you can come out now," Sharon yelled. From behind the cars, the two boys stood and slowly walked to their bikes as the patrol cars slid to a stop; the trio was now flanked by black and whites. The sirens suddenly faded, not a sound filled the street. The door to the first arriving prowler opened, a large man stood, adjusted his gear and looked at Sharon.

"Goddamn it, O'Mara, I just knew it had to be you when I got the call and heard the address," he said as he walked toward the group. "What the hell's going on here?"

"Good morning, Sergeant," Sharon said. "May I?" she asked, pointing to the ground and her Beretta.

"Yeah, go ahead, any shots fired really?"

"No, Glenn, but I thought there would be," she answered as the two of them were surrounded by three more cops. Two others, one was a woman, were talking to the boys.

They moved the bikes from the street to the small patch of lawn that extended to the sidewalk in front of Sharon's cottage. She noticed a couple of people standing in front of their houses, looking at her and the police. *Not going to help my already poor standing in the neighborhood,* she thought as she explained everything that had happened over the last five minutes. Sergeant

Glenn Stack was not amused by her telling dispatch that there were "shots fired and officer on scene;" he was not amused at all. The man's toolbox sat where it was dropped on the sidewalk.

"Don't ever do that again, O'Mara. Jesus H. Christ, my people might have reacted differently, who knows what would have happened." He also knew that it worked and the boys were lucky to be involved in nothing more than a good story to tell at school. It could have been worse.

"I saw the ass-end of that van when I turned onto the street," he continued. "We might be able to grab a shot of its license from the dash camera. What did he look like?"

"Dark, swarthy complexion, might be Greek or Middle Eastern, maybe six one, grey uniform, something that a county inspector might wear, nothing suspicious," Sharon said. "I was cautious until he pulled his gun, that's when I told the kids to get behind the cars."

"Why so cautious? Why is your radar heightened over a sanitary van parked at your curb?" Sergeant Stack asked.

Sharon told Stack about the earlier surveillance van, the clove man and the DNA hit and the SFPD's interest. Even she had to admit it was all a jumble with a couple of big pieces sticking out; large pointy pieces that explained nothing.

"Should I get the bomb people out here to look at the toolbox?" a patrolman asked Stack. They all looked at the blue metal box lying on its side on the sidewalk.

"Don't think it's going to explode," Sharon said. "He dropped it down hard on the concrete just before he pulled his Glock. It sounded like a toolbox. May I?"

"Be my guest, it's on your property and I still don't know if there's been a crime committed other than a false police call," Stack said.

Sharon walked over to the box and nudged it with the toe of her sneaker, the patrolman blanched a bit. She smiled at him, bent down, grabbed the handle and uprighted the box. A single chrome plated clasp connected the lid and the case; she flipped the hasp and slowly opened the lid. Inside were electrician's tools, wire cutters, screwdrivers, black electrical tape, coils of wire, two small empty boxes and two crumpled wax paper wrappers with no labels. Basil stuck his nose into the open box and harrumphed.

"Interesting, follow me, Sergeant," Sharon said as she headed to the backyard. She scanned every inch of the cottage's walls, even the fencing between the houses. Basil led the way; he stopped near the Jaguar, his nose high in the air.

"Nice car," the patrolman offered seeing the Jaguar parked in the driveway.

"Thanks," she said turning to the car. She looked at Basil. "What do you smell, boy? Where?" She got on her knees and felt along the car's undercarriage. "If he left anything here, I should be able to feel for it, he was bigger than I am and there's no way he could get under this car." She continued to feel about, getting more and more pissed as her two hundred dollar shirt collected dirt on its sleeves. Basil nudged his way toward the area where she had her hand under the car. "You smell it too, don't you, now get back."

"One of my men has an inspection mirror, do you need that?"

"Maybe ... wait, got something," Sharon said, after a few seconds she withdrew her hand. "Now, Sergeant, you can call the bomb squad, I suggest we clear the area."

Two hours later, the tech from the bomb squad held up a small rat-sized device by its tail, another small pencil-shaped piece of metal in the other. "My guess is about six ounces of C-4, blasting cap, cell phone activated, taped near the gas line. Saw something similar in Afghanistan, simple and very effective, six ounces or six pounds, doesn't matter. Ma'am, that would have blown the car up and probably killed you."

"Thanks, Jimmy," Stack said to the officer. "Well, Sharon O'Mara, I now have a crime scene and you are it."

"Well, lucky me."

10b

After the morning's events, the last thing Sharon wanted to do was visit Alain Dumont. And it was the only thing she *needed* to do. Alain had become almost like a grandfather to her; he was, like her, an orphan. He was a true self-made man, even with the kick-start of forty ingots of found gold at the end of World War Two. At ninety-four, the billionaire had been involved in almost every high tech venture since the invention of the transistor. He lived in a fine mansion on upper Broadway in San Francisco and had lived well, sired a beautiful, but damaged, daughter who OD'd on drugs but left him a granddaughter, Claudette Leclair. Claudette met Sharon as she climbed the steps to Dumont's front door, they kissed and then hugged.

"He's resting peacefully," Claudette said. "Evelyn's with him."

They walked the length of the hallway, past the parlor, to the library. There, amongst one of the greatest private collections of art, first editions and small Impressionist statues, lay Alain Dumont on a hospital bed. A large black man stood directly behind the head board and smiled at the women as they entered. Evelyn Luca sat on a low velvet footstool near the bed. She held the right hand of her godfather. The bed had been adjusted allowing Dumont to sit more upright.

Sharon kissed Peter Brass, Dumont's nurse and bodyguard, on the cheek. "How's he doing?"

"As well as can be expected, the medication has softened the edge but he's still with us." Peter said.

"Damn straight I am," a hoarse voice mumbled from directly below the two. "As long as I'm breathing, I'll be a pain in the ass. How are you, my dear?" Alain Dumont said as he slowly raised his free hand toward Sharon.

She took his hand, kissed his sallow cheek and saw that he was even thinner than the last time she visited; he was almost translucent.

"I missed you Alain; are you comfortable?" Sharon asked.

"As best as I can be, not much else I can do."

"You rest," Evelyn said.

Dumont took in a large breath, his eyes brightened. He turned his head to take in the three women in the room; calmness seemed to soften the hard edge to his cheeks.

"A man could ask for nothing more than to have you three with me, you are like my Valkyries leading me to Valhalla," he chortled then coughed, not a deep cough but a laughing cough. "

"Quiet now," Claudette said.

"Granddaughter, soon I'll be quiet forever. It is my hope that my love will meet me at the gates, I have missed her for more years than I can remember." He took in another breath.

After Alain Dumont fled the army at the end of World War Two, by faking his death and changing his name from Robert Alan Dupont, he moved to Paris and became a very successful, if not creative, importer of goods for desperate Europeans. He also found and married the love of his life, Dominique, Claudette's grandmother. The gold that he and two fellow soldiers stole or, as the case was, liberated, gave him an excellent grubstake. One of his fellow thieves died in the war and the other was reunited with Alain almost sixty years later when Sharon helped Alain find the family that originally owned a Toulouse-Lautrec painting that was confiscated from them by the Nazis; it too had also found with the gold. Now he was dying.

"I'm sure Dominique has missed you as well," Evelyn said squeezing Alain's hand.

Alain sighed heavily, "I know that my daughter will be waiting as well, all our lives leave small tragedies for others to deal with and I hope I have left few behind. Sharon," he looked at O'Mara, "I want you to watch over these two and keep them out of trouble," he squeezed her hand and Evelyn's. Sharon was amazed at his strength. "Claudette, let these girls help you and you help them - I know of no better three women than you. Take care of each other." He inhaled raggedly.

"Rest, we will be right here," Claudette said wiping a tear

away.

Sharon's involvement with death, violent death, hadn't hardened her as Alain lay dying. Her heart ached. She was sad because she had only known the man for a short time and she would have loved to have been near him, like Claudette and Evelyn were, for her entire life. There were few people in her life that she loved; Alain Dumont was one of those few.

For the next few hours, they sat and talked, Peter made coffee and even found some small sandwiches, they nibbled but the tray stayed full. Sharon told Claudette about the events with Jean-François and the missing trimaran. She didn't say anything about the suspicions that were gnawing away in her gut about JF's possible involvement with his own missing sailboat. Her gut had been wrong before but then it was in Iraq and she might have had food poisoning.

* * * *

Green Zone, Baghdad, Iraq, 2005

"I can't get my head around al-Jamil and his granddaughters," O'Mara said to Sanchez as they sat in the afternoon shade near their billet. "Why would the son-of-a-bitch put them in jeopardy just to get to us? Shit, we're sitting ducks most of the time, IED Central, wait long enough and we'll pass every potential bomb planted in this wreck of a country. Why all this intrigue? I just don't get it; there has to be something else he's after."

"Can't say I don't disagree, seen a lot of strange shit here, two plus two don't always add up to four with these people," Sergeant Sanchez said. "If he's out there moving the al-Qaeda around, assuming they're al-Qaeda, then why would they deal with him? He's Shia and they're Sunni, true believers, like oil and water. Historically, they have hated each other since the seventh century and that's a lot of hate and vengeance."

"What you said about assuming they are al-Qaeda makes me think, suppose they aren't; maybe we're dealing with something else. Maybe we want to believe they are al-Qaeda, perhaps he's using that to make us his tool." She lit a cigarette and stared at the flame of her lighter for a moment. "Sergeant, I hate being a tool."

"I don't like being a tool either, Lieutenant. My mom didn't raise me to be the tool of some fucking asshole in some God forsaken part of the world. No sir, I'm not a tool."

"Shall we go and pay Mr. Hakim al-Jamil a call and this time it won't be social."

"Yes Lieutenant, I'll get the plans together."

O'Mara took a long pull on her cigarette and wondered what tomorrow would be like.

* * * *

San Francisco, Today

"I'm going have a smoke," Sharon said to the group as she walked toward the library balcony.

"I'll join you," Evelyn said. She always smoked when she was stressed and now was one of those times.

The view across the Bay from Alain's balcony was breathtaking. This particular afternoon was clear and sharp; Alcatraz sat like a coarse cruise ship heading toward the Golden Gate as ferries scurried about minding their own business. Their business and their passengers' business didn't include dying or even thinking about dying today. For Sharon, that's all she was thinking about.

"Something's eating you. I can tell," Evelyn said bumming a cigarette.

Sharon paused as she slowly let out a mouthful of smoke. "I've seen so much death that sometimes I think I'm past caring, past even thinking about it. Friends and enemies are all the same dead, they don't care anymore but we care, those that mourn for them. I think that's the reason for all the pomp and the lengthy ceremony, not for the dead, but for us, the living."

"Guess that's the way it's always been, we never know what they know."

"I will miss Alain a lot, he is very dear to me and I only wish I could have known him longer. You two are the lucky ones."

"Can't disagree, he has been everything to me and Claudette, a friend, a father, a mentor and a shoulder to cry on, I'll miss him forever."

"What a beautiful day, everything considered," Claudette said, opening the door to the balcony. *"That's what Grand-père would have wanted, sun and blue skies."*

Sharon and Evelyn smiled at Claudette's comment. Yes, sun and blue skies, especially blue skies.

Peter Brass tapped on the window and motioned to the girls, they followed him to Alain Dumont's side. His breathing was very shallow; Claudette took his hand and noticed how warm it was and how strong it was. Alain opened his eyes and looked at his granddaughter.

"Dominique? Dominique?" Then his hand softened and the only strength left was hers.

10c

For the next week, all was organized chaos and confusion. The outpouring of sympathies, obituaries and phone calls astounded Sharon. She was most amazed by the half-page obit in the Wall Street Journal that put the visionary financier and venture capitalist in the same league as Hewlett, Packard, and Jobs. *"While Alain Dumont never invented anything and there is not one patent under his name, he provided the capital and the means to make most of todays technological marvels happen. There is no one else like him in our time nor will there be for a very long time."*

Sharon could only shake her head. She, along with only three or four others, knew that Alain Dumont was a fraud, that his real name was Robert Alan Dupont. She found that thinking of Alain Dumont as Robert Dupont's pen name made it all seem better. He was to be buried in his native country, France, with great pomp and circumstance; she had to smile since she knew he came from Pennsylvania. And, according to his wish, he would be buried not too far from Jim Morrison's grave in the Père Lachaise Cemetery. Dumont had always been a rebel and a pirate; this, above all, was why she'd loved him so.

"Hello, O'Mara here," she said holding her cell phone in her sweaty hand; it said 'number blocked' on the screen.

"Good morning, Sharon," Jean-François said, breaking her exercise routine on the elliptical machine. "Are you okay, you are breathing most peculiarly?"

"I'm at the gym, JF, give me a second." She climbed down from the machine. "Now what can I do for you?"

"Awfully brusque these days, we haven't talked in weeks it seems."

"Been very busy," she said.

"Yes, I'm sorry to hear about Monsieur Dumont; I met him a few times and admired the man for many years. He will be missed."

"Yes, he will; thank you for that. Now, what do want? I've heard nothing more about the sailboat and nothing about the investigation from the Oakland PD," as if she would tell him anything, at least for now.

"I'm sorry to hear about that but I know you'll find out what happened," JF said. "We are proceeding with the development of the trimaran using a second prototype being built from the earlier molds; I have a new investor from Russia who is very interested in the boat and its technologies. His offer has been very generous and I need to stay here in Europe until it's finalized."

"So it may be a while until I see you again," she said, hoping that was the case, more out of trying to avoid him rather than making a definitive decision to resign from the case.

"I miss you too, so here's my offer. Next week, the America's Cup World Series is in Venice, I will be there staying at a friend's villa; it's on the Grand Canal. There are two first-class Air France tickets waiting for you at the Compton Hotel. I would like you to join me for the races, we can discuss business and then you can tell me if Fidor Balanca, the Russian investor, is okay. And we can also have a wonderful time, it will be fun."

"Venice? *Two* tickets?" she was more than shocked, catching her breath she asked, "Who do you think I would bring, even if I could go? I've got too much to do around here, other cases."

"No you don't! I'm your priority. It's important that you come and see me, I miss you and besides, it's Venice, *mon cheri*. Great wine and food, elegant people, Venice! What better way to spend a week? I thought you could bring that tall Irish fellow, Kevin O'Bannon. He's fun and it would be my entire treat."

"His name's Kevin Bryan, JF. And he's a cop and I don't think he can take the time off."

"Well, ask him, if not him, you pick a girl friend or someone else, it will be fun."

"You said that twice," she said.

"Well it will be fun, let me know."

"Wait a second; your number didn't pop up on my phone, why?"

"Lost the damn thing, fell off my boat a few days ago, this is one I picked up. Here's the new number." After she noted his new phone with its French identification code, she asked him one more time. "Why me?"

"I miss you, let me know soon, see you next week, fun's waiting." JF's line went dead.

Sharon stood in her Army gym sweats; looking at her phone, then noticed the stinky sweating bodies that surrounded her. Venice? It had been almost seven years since she had stayed in Venice, on an R&R trip to Italy. Then it was all new and strange, one day she was in the dust and crap of Baghdad and two days later she was sipping rich Italian espresso on the Grand Canal. Yes, the world was strange then and even stranger now.

"Kevin, got a minute?" Sharon said into her cell phone.

"Now what? What trouble did you get into?" Kevin asked.

"Why is it you always think I'm in trouble?"

"Every time you call me, it's to ask for something or it eventually gets me in trouble, so …"

"Kevin, I'm hurt," she feigned indignation.

"Stop it, what's up?"

"Can you take next week off?"

"Why?"

"Before I say what it's about, can you take next week off?"

she asked.

"Actually, and I'm sure you're going to ask me to do something exotic and potentially illegal, no."

"No, that's quick and awfully strong. Why not?"

"I have, starting Monday, two cases going to court; juries have been selected and I need to testify. You know the two, that felony hit-and-run with the drunken kid and the other about the kid whose parents are suing each other and the kid got in trouble, I have to help him - he needs everything he can get. So, no. What did I escape?"

"Venice."

"I can go to Southern California anytime, let's plan it later."

"Italy."

"Damn, just knew it wasn't SoCal. So why are you going to Venice," he paused; there was a sigh in his voice, "Italy?"

"Jean-François invited me and sent me two first-class tickets."

"First-Class! With leg room?"

"More than even you need. Yes, the venues for the next stage in the Cup races are taking place in Naples and Venice; he's there for some meetings, wants me to meet him. Paid vacation, haven't had one of those since we were chased on bikes through Paris."

"That was not a vacation. All I remember was having a sore ass for the next week."

"Don't remind me, so you're out, *quel domage*."

"Why would he want me there anyway; third-wheel and all?"

"He mentioned it in passing, not sure why. But I think I'll go, maybe tease more out of this confusion, I just need to find a partner."

"Stack, at Walnut Creek PD, tells me they have more info on the bomb, the wiring was common, in fact, it matches a spec and drawing on the Internet. The C-4 came from a Croatian manufacturer; batch is about two years old, the whole thing smells like Eastern Europeans. Still don't know why they think you're so dangerous."

"Me neither, just don't get it and if JF is involved, it makes it even more bizarre. So maybe a few days in Venice will help me figure it out."

"You be very careful, understand?"

"Don't worry, I will," she answered.

"That was a wonderful service for Alain, I'll miss him. He was quite a guy," Kevin said, thinking of the man that he and Bobby Gillis saved from being killed by a bunch of very real neo-Nazis.

"Thanks, there was never a dull moment around Alain, never. I'll call you later, good luck with the trials," she said as she hung up.

She thought of asking either Evelyn or Claudette but she knew they were too busy with their businesses and making the final arrangements for Alain in Paris. The French government had taken over much of the pomp anyway; he was an important Frenchman to them, even though his primary home had been San Francisco for the last forty years. There was even talk of a parade but Claudette would not allow it. If his real past ever surfaced, she wanted to make sure that few officials would be embarrassed. So, the simpler the better.

After a quick three-mile run and a shower, she dressed and headed to Lafayette for a burger at Geno's. Gina had been pressured by her customers to serve a better menu than salty chips and pretzels so she cleared an area in the back, added a small kitchen with a real chef, a few more tables out front and after six months of permits, started selling hamburgers, hotdogs and, on Fridays, fish and chips. To Sharon and Gina's surprise, it was a hit; her gross revenues jumped 32%. She also took on a manager; she was getting tired of spending every working hour in the bar.

"Hey girl," Gina said while throwing some ice in a glass. "How are you doing, been a rough week?" She sat the tumbler of scotch on the bar.

"Very rough, but this will help," Sharon said.

"You bet, did you get my flowers? I wasn't sure what to send to a billionaire's funeral."

"They were beautiful and Claudette says thank you, she was glad you attended the memorial. She wants all of us to get together when things are quieter."

"I'll be there, you know that," Gina said. "Haven't seen Kevin for a week or so, you talk to him?"

"Just an hour ago, he's busy with a couple of trials but I'm sure you'll be seeing him in the evenings; you know how they go."

"Don't I know it! They really grind on him." Gina saw an old-timer sit down at the bar's last stool and signal. "Be right with you, Jimmy. The usual?" He nodded. "Be right back," Gina said to Sharon as she headed to the far end of the bar, dragging the bar rag across the century-old bar her grandfather had salvaged after the San Francisco earthquake.

Sharon sipped on her scotch, as always it warmed her heart and quickly settled her head. She turned on her stool and looked out the window, Gina was highlighted by the late afternoon sun as it streamed through the glass. It suddenly hit her.

"Gina, get down here, I need to talk to you now, it's an emergency," Sharon called out.

Gina sat the large glass of cold milk in front of Jimmy and quickly headed back toward Sharon. Jimmy smiled. Even at his advanced age, he could admire Gina's Sophia Loren-like figure and the wild hair of Lafayette's leading libationist.

"Now what's got you all wound up?" Gina asked, standing arms on hips directly across the bar from Sharon. "You still have your drink so I know that's not it. So, what is it?"

"You speak Italian, don't you?"

"Yes, but they say I have a California accent, why?"

"How about one week from now you and I sit in Harry's Bar and have a drink?"

"I don't know Harry's Bar, is it new?"

"No. The same Harry's Bar that Hemingway frequented," she let it sink in. "That Harry's Bar."

"The only Harry's I know is … no way!"

"Absolutely, in Venice. I have two first-class tickets and I can bring anyone, and I am asking you."

Gina thought for few seconds, "Just can't, need to watch this place."

"No you don't, you have Bobby, that fancy manager you hired, to take care of things and that new chef, if that's what you call him, they can handle things for a week. I'll have Kevin stop by just to make sure they aren't stealing you blind or burning the place down."

"Bryan, a babysitter, that's rich. Why didn't you ask him, or did you? Ah, the trials, so I'm second fiddle?"

"No, you are the first girl I asked, it's different. It will be just the two of us and JF and a very rich Russian and all those billionaires and their toys."

"Jean-François? They're his tickets?"

"Yes, he's invited me and, through me, you."

"Wonderful, we go to Venice where you will spend all your time with a rich Frenchman and what do I get? Borsht. But it is Venice, magical Venice, *sarà fantastico!*"

Chapter 11

"Good morning Mike," Sharon said after punching in Mike Stroud's number. There was an odd delay.

"Sharon, what a surprise; actually, it's evening here," Stroud answered.

"Evening? Where the hell are you?"

"A warehouse in Naples. We're loading up Ellis' 45 and then hauling it across Italy to Venice," Stroud said. "Been racing here all week, the Venice prelims are next week, then the Venice stage of the races is the following week, busy as a hell. What can I do for you?"

"I thought you were still in Oakland. Venice?" she asked.

"Venice. Ellis is coming into town next week; she was only here in Naples for one day. Bobo's doing okay, in fact, he placed second in two of the races here, even the crew is beginning to like him, somewhat, any more news on the boat?"

"I've got nothing more on the trimaran. The police are still looking but there's a good chance I'll see you in Venice. JF's asked me to come over; I should be there next week. We can have a beer together."

"Rippa, looking forward to it. JF knows where we'll be, he can show you," Stroud said.

"I'll call when we get in," Sharon said.

"You bringing anyone?"

"A girl friend, she owns a bar."

"Single?"

"Yes."

"Then you must introduce me. A Sheila that owns a bar, the good Lord is looking down on me. Just a second," Stroud said with a lilt in his Scottish-Aussi accent. Sharon could hear commotion and yelling through the phone, "Something's come up and I've got to go. Next week, hooro!" Stroud hung up abruptly.

Sharon stared at her phone. *What the hell was all that about?* The voice in the background sounded like Bobo, a very upset Bobo. She'd never forget his voice after her tour on the bay on the 45, especially since he screamed at her about being ballast. She poured another cup of coffee, punched in Venice on Google Earth and scratched Basil's head.

"Sorry fella, mama's going away for a few days. Kevin will take good care of you. And you can wreck his place for a week," Basil had spent so much time at Bryan's house that he thought he actually owned it and there was that cute poodle that he got to sniff occasionally through the boards of the fence.

Her phone rang again, "This might be interesting," she said noting the number while she still scratched Basil's head. "O'Mara."

"Good morning, Sharon, Sergeant Chang, Oakland PD, I have some more news but I think you would rather see it than hear about it."

"Absolutely, Sergeant; where?" She jotted down the address, slipped into jeans, a crisp blue shirt and serviceable go-to-crime-scenes shoes. She kept the Beretta in her handbag, a big SKIA bag that Evelyn had given her after the take down of the Chinese Tongs; it was the same nasty nest of slavers she and Danny Chang had taken down.

The warehouse was a few blocks from Jack London Square in Oakland, the Acorn District, near the spot where they last saw the container still coupled with the cab. Three Oakland squad cars and a van with 'Oakland PD Crime Lab' painted on its panels were parked along the front of the metal building. Based on its design, Sharon guessed it to be from the 1950s. Sergeant Danny Chang was standing in front, talking with a technician in a white throwaway lab suit. They were both wearing blue booties.

She parked directly across the street. Times had been tough in this area and most of the buildings were empty, parking was easy. Just six blocks south, hundreds of new condominiums and lofts had been built for the ever-expanding techie horde that now commuted to San Francisco and Silicon Valley. They wanted the urban experience but not at San Francisco prices.

"Good morning, Sergeant," Sharon said as soon as Chang acknowledged her.

"Good morning, Ms. O'Mara," Chang said after dismissing the tech.

Sharon arched an eyebrow due to Chang's formality; she knew Chang had noticed.

"Sorry about that, Sharon. New rules and regs in the city, the administration has been all over us; the last six months have not been good to be a cop in Oakland. So everything is by the book now."

Sharon knew the reasons for the changes; thanks to all the protestors, the on-going gang violence and all the political chaos in city hall. "I understand. I'll bet that I'm not supposed to even be here."

"For the record, you are not, but I have fifteen minutes before I have to be back downtown. I'll show you what we've found, for what it's worth. We can talk later. If anyone asks, you are not here. That work for you?"

"It works," Sharon answered. She knew that Chang could get in trouble so the quicker they did this, the better.

"Based on the videos, we searched this area hard. We questioned people and even peeped into a few dirty windows, finally we caught a break when one of our local bottle collectors said that she had seen a big truck pull into this warehouse about the same time our videos were tracking it. So we did a little more digging and found that this was leased on a month-to-month. The owner, an older Chinese woman who my mother knows, said the woman who rented it wanted it for storage for only a short time; she paid cash. No questions. It took my mom to get that much from her."

"I expect your mother could make a stone talk," Sharon said.

"That's for sure. Let me show you what we got," Chang said as they went through the steel door that the tech had disappeared into. "Put these on first," he said holding up pair of blue paper socks.

Sharon scanned the dimly lit room; large dirty skylights cast a grey gloom across the dusty concrete floor. Two objects sat a bit off center in the middle of the room, a blue shipping container and a black 650 BMW. Her observation and investigator skills immediately kicked in. Tire tracks and footprints created a confused and messy mélange of disconnected trips in and out of the box and the car. Three white-suited techs were taking pictures and sampling everything near the boxes. She saw, based on the tire tracks, that another tractor and trailer had parked parallel to the one sitting in the room. The container was on the floor, its double doors were open. The BMW was to her right; the second trailer had parked on the left side. What was remarkable was the complete lack of paper, packing materials or debris of any kind surrounding the two objects. The only object that was foreign was one yellow plastic crime scene marker with the number one on it. It sat about fifty feet from the BMW.

"What's with the marker?" Sharon asked Chang as they walked toward the box.

"One single shell casing from a 9mm, we also found blood and signs of a body being dragged. I'm making an educated guess, that's where Mr. Flores was executed. Shit, he was the driver, that's all, at least that's what I'm hoping."

"This is very neat and clean, in fact, way too clean."

"So is the BMW, our techs found nothing anywhere. No prints, no receipts, not even a hair. Like the container, it looks like it was wiped down and even vacuumed."

"It took hours to move the boat and its gear; the other container had to be rigged to accept the cradles and carriers from this box to the new one. Sergeant, these bars and cleats welded to the interior were used to secure the lines and cables needed to hold the hulls and boxes in place. Mike Stroud, Voss's man, was the man who did the loading; he explained the procedure to me as they were breaking down the trimaran to load it. The other box had to be set up in a similar way, if not, it would have busted up in transit. I don't think they would go through all this trouble just to have their prize get trashed on its way to wherever it was going."

"I'll buy that, but they sure as hell were neat, too neat from my experience. Nobody takes the time to cleanup a crime scene like this," Chang said.

"And leave the only real incriminating evidence, the shell casing."

"That too," Chang added.

Sharon walked to the car and checked its four corners, the right front fender area was damaged, the metal work was pushed in, yet the headlight looked operational.

"This may have been the car that hit me a few weeks ago; it wanted to play tag as I drove through Lafayette, it won."

"I'll have the lab try to match paint residuals on the BMW," Chang offered.

"Probably not worth it, it's more important to tie this scene to Mr. Flores and his murder, my little accident is not worth the time and expense but as long as I know this was the car, I'm fine," Sharon said.

She walked the room circling the container and the car; she studied the footprints in the dust and the tracks in and out of the box. She saw at least three sets of footprints, some with distinctive tread patterns, like work boots. Another set, one that crisscrossed all the others, was smooth and smaller, a woman's print. She looked back at the box and then at the floor. Another set of narrower parallel tire tracks bothered her until the light went on. *Damn it.* She imagined them opening the container and quickly moving everything to the new box, it was the moving process that caught her eye.

"Sergeant, they needed a fork lift to get the box on and off the trailers, see there, where there's a ghost on the floor, where the tire tracks and the prints start and stop, that was where the second box was set down for loading. They took this one off the trailer it came in, sat it on the floor, then loaded the other container and then sat the loaded one on the trailer the first box came on. They put the second box down where that ghost is before they had even stolen this box, they were very sure of themselves."

"Absolutely makes sense," Chang said. "We'll check on every forklift that was rented during the last three weeks, but there are thousands of trailers at the port so finding the right one, based on tread patterns, will be almost impossible, I bet there are hundreds with the same tires."

"No doubt, easy to take a trailer in and out, no questions. Then they have at least three options. Drive the container to a new drop point for safekeeping, load it on a boat headed somewhere or load it on a railcar and ship it east. But then we have to know the trailer and its number to even get an idea of its destination."

Chang and Sharon walked back into the sunlight; it was a crisp, clear day along the Oakland estuary.

"I'll have my guys recheck the videos, we'll see if we can find a suspicious box moving near this area the days before and after this box went missing. Maybe we can spot one and get its number."

As if on cue, two tractor-trailer rigs rumbled through the intersection each carrying a container. Sharon scanned the street and counted three more boxes on trailers; ten seconds later, another rig crossed the intersection; this time it was going the opposite way.

"Won't be easy," Sharon offered.

"No shit," Chang answered, watching another box blow through the intersection. "No shit."

11b

Green Zone, Baghdad, Iraq, 2005

Five army green shipping containers were sitting side by side near O'Mara's billet; these were used to store weapons and other items. There was enough firepower in just one of these containers to outfit twenty men for a week's worth of fighting.

Each of the men in her squad had been rearmed; Sanchez had gone over the maps and set up a strategic, yet simple, extraction process; all they wanted was al-Jamil. After the fuck-up of the last mission, this one was meticulously thought through, every possibility was considered. But it all came down to plan, pounce and pull out.

O'Mara was certain that al-Jamil thought he had convinced the Americans that he was the victim. She was also certain they would never find the girls. It's hard to find something that's not lost. *Hell, he could move them back to his village and we would never know.*

Again the traffic heading to al-Kufah was miserable, they were continually delayed at roadblocks and document checkpoints.

"Lieutenant, I'm not sure any of this shit makes a difference," Sanchez said over his microphone. "Everyone knows they are there, they can easily go around them. Besides, papers are so easy to forge, even my mother could pass for an Iraqi."

"I'd like to see that," another voice came over the speaker.

"You stay out of this, private," Mike said.

"You are the one that brought your mother up," the voice answered.

"Both of you shut up," O'Mara said. "I want eyes everywhere, IEDs are showing up more and more, sometimes these fuckers don't give a shit who they kill, as long as we're in the mix."

For the next hour, they circled south and then north to the village. Her goal was simple and she hoped al-Jamil would bite. Her men would set up strategically outside the village; three Humvees would cover the village's flanks. She and Sanchez would drive back into the center of the compound, dismount and engage al-Jamil. She would use the ruse that they had the girls, say they would take him to them, check for his reaction, ask him to get into the Humvee and leave. Simple, that is if anything is simple in Iraq.

As the two Humvees pulled into the main courtyard of the village, thirty children surrounded the vehicles, as always, almost all were boys. The young girls stayed with their mothers within the buildings. The more devout the village was, the fewer

the number of woman who appeared in public; that's why Lieutenant Sharon O'Mara was a double threat to the order of things
in Iraq and most Moslem countries, she was an American soldier
with its might and an American woman with her freedom. The
Iraqi men feared her more for the latter than the former, cultural
change is harder than war.

Al-Jamil appeared outside the door to his home. Simply
dressed, the man wore a dusty dark sports coat over a simple
open dress shirt and pants; he held a loop of prayer beads in his
right hand.

O'Mara intentionally stayed within the Humvees' shelter;
only one man in each Humvee was exposed as he stood behind
the 50 cals and scanned the rooftops and windows. Nothing
moved; she wanted al-Jamil to stew, to begin to wonder, to sec-
ond-guess. She saw him finger his beads frantically, "That's it,
get real nervous," she said to Sanchez over the microphone.

"I think he's about to shit in his pants," Sanchez said.

She waited another minute, the outside temperature was at
least 102; inside the Humvee, it wasn't much better.

"Now," she said.

Instantly, they heard the explosions from the flash-bangs
and the reports of automatic fire, al-Jamil spun toward the sound
quickly; that was the key for her and her men to dismount and
take control of al-Jamil.

"You need to come with us," O'Mara said as she walked toward al-Jamil. "I don't know who they are but my guess is that
they are coming for you; you're safe with me. We have found
your granddaughters, they are unharmed."

Al-Jamil again turned to the continuing sounds outside the
walls of the village, then back to O'Mara.

"I don't believe you, you don't have them," al-Jamil answered, suddenly understanding what was going on.

"Have it your way," O'Mara said. "Arrest him."

Before he knew what had happened, al-Jamil was on his
knees with a Plasticuff securing his hands. A woman ran out
the door; she stopped short when she saw the weapons and was

even more distraught when she saw the Lieutenant. Women just don't deal with men the way O'Mara did.

Al-Jamil looked at the O'Mara, "Why, what have I done?" he pleaded.

The village suddenly went silent, O'Mara's distraction was over. A few men stood in the shade of the buildings; no one could be seen on the rooftops. O'Mara's people continued to scan the buildings.

"Killed one of my men, for one thing, used your grand-daughters as bait and generally just pissed me off," O'Mara said, leaning over the man. "You, old man, will spend the rest of your miserable life in a fucking prison somewhere in this fucking country. If I can prove that you are al-Qaeda, you will be going to Guantanamo. Personally, I don't care; you lied to me, I don't like that, time to pay the bill. Put him in the truck."

Two of her men grabbed the man under his armpits, lifted him like he was weightless and carried him to the rear cargo area of the truck, a black head-cover was slid over his grey head. The others in her team watched the windows and building edges. The woman began to wail.

"I know you understand me," O'Mara said to the woman, looking directly into her eyes. "When I find out what's going on, he may be back, then again, maybe not. It all depends on him. Understand?" She hooked her thumb over her shoulder, the woman looked at the Humvee where her man had just been secured and she nodded.

"Good. Sanchez, mount up, we're out of here." O'Mara rotated her hand in a counterclockwise motion, her team slowly moved back to the Humvees. The 50 cals still covered the roofs and windows. Their exit was a lot quieter than the first time they left this village.

Ninety minutes later, Hakim al-Jamil sat across the metal table from Sharon O'Mara in the same trailer where al-Jamil had come to ask for help. Items found on the man lay about the tabletop. The stunned look on his face told O'Mara a lot, then again this man had lied about his granddaughters so she was cautious.

"Well that was fun," she started out. The man's expression changed to confusion.

"For who?" al-Jamil answered.

"Oh, for me," she said. "I just love going out into this heat and arresting sons-a-bitches who lied to me, who use me to do their bidding."

"What do you mean?"

"No, no, Mr. al-Jamil, let's get this straight, I get to ask the questions, only me," O'Mara said sharply. "You just answer them." She stared at the old man.

He paused, thinking, and then looked at the tabletop, "Cigarette?"

She slid his pack across the hard surface; she followed up with a cheap plastic lighter. She flashed on the strange thought that even in the worst shit holes in the world, you could find Bic lighters and those strange white plastic lawn chairs. She shook her head to clear the thought from her mind.

Al-Jamil lit his cigarette and blew the smoke into the air-conditioned air. The scent of cloves filled the air.

"How can you live in this cold air? This mechanical air will make you sick. Didn't like it in Houston even with the humidity. You American's are soft."

"Probably, but we carry a big stick. Let me tell you what I know and then you can correct me. Then, depending on your answers, I will decide what I'm going to do with you." She continued to stare at the man.

"Am I supposed to agree?"

"What did I say? No questions. So let's begin," O'Mara said as she slid his beads, his masbahah, across the table; al-Jamil slowly wrapped his fingers around them, they were his security blanket.

"Where are your granddaughters?" she began.

"I don't know, you said you were going to help me find them."

"A few days ago, you were seen with them, they were safe

then and you had a small army surrounding them. Where are they now?"

Al-Jamil paused, a bead slipped through his fingers and it occurred to O'Mara that if he were as devout as al-Qaeda, he would not be using the beads; to be as devout as the Bin Laden, he'd be counting his fingers, not beads. She watched him begin to slide the beads through his fingers faster. She had found his tell.

"I asked you a question; I'll ask you again, where are your granddaughters?"

Another thirty seconds passed, then he looked at O'Mara, "They are safe and I am sorry that your man was killed."

"Better, where are they?"

"They are with my family in another part of al-Kufah. I wish to Allah that I had not brought you into this."

"Into what? Hakim al-Jamil, what are you into?"

He slid the beads through his fingers faster, and then stopped. "I am just a trader; my family has been supplying the needs and desires of people in our country for many, many years. With Saddam's people in power, we had to be more secretive."

"You are smugglers?"

"Such a harsh term, but yes, we are. My connections and financial assistance allowed my family to provide everything from televisions to cars. We brought in goods from Iran and Jordan; we have friends everywhere, even Saudi Arabia and Kuwait. As I said, we have been doing this for many years, even Saddam turned a blind eye; we provided them with things they could not get themselves." He took another drag on his cigarette; both of his hands were occupied.

"And why drag us into your little criminal world?"

"From my point of view, it isn't criminal, we provide what was hard to get or forbidden, such is trade. The tariffs we paid were the bribes to officials, tariff or bribe or tax, it's just the cost of doing business. It has been that way here for thousands of years, it will be that way for thousands more."

"Don't get all business school 101 on me, al-Jamil." O'Mara

lit a cigarette, "Why drag us into this?"

"There is a group, actually the past local Baath party leader and his family, that is muscling their way into my business, they have killed three of my cousins. Muscling, that is the right word?"

"It will do but why should I care? You and they mean nothing to me."

"They are also supplying the local al-Qaeda, this I know for a fact. He is selling them explosives and weapons that he hid when you invaded the area. He has warehouses full of weapons and explosives; some are underground, others are not, some are stored in old bunkers from Saddam's days. But he wants more and is forcing my suppliers to deal with him; he is using American dollars to trade, something I have trouble finding. I was trying to use you to eliminate him, the compound you attacked was one of his transfer locations and he has others. We are too weak to stop him."

"Great, you have the United States Army caught up in a gang war." O'Mara said.

"Aren't they all gang wars?"

"Don't get philosophical on me, Jamil. Now I'm stuck, I've told my Major that you can be an asset to us, someone who can lead us to al-Qaeda and bring a small bit of peace to this part of Iraq. Now you admit to me that you are nothing more than a thug."

"Lieutenant, I may be many things, but I am not a thug. We used some of the money to build a small clinic and send some children, including young girls, to schools. I don't have millions hidden away, we have almost nothing. The rest we use to just survive. You may think I'm a gangster but I am not, I'm just a merchant." Jamil said as he continued to finger his beads.

"What a screwed up country," O'Mara said.

"All countries are screwed up, Lieutenant, in one way or another. We've just had our sins exposed to the world, wars and invasions do that. But most of us just want to live, raise our families and die in peace. For thirty years, Saddam used us, his own people, as cannon fodder, we died by the millions. Fear was everywhere, even now we are not sure what you will leave us when you go and you will go just like every army since Gilgamesh. We have so little, yet every great power has walked our land looking for something, now it is America's turn. But you will leave and we will still be here."

"Hakim al-Jamil, my job is to find and kill enemies of America, not bring peace and harmony to the world; that's left to others, we break things, they fix them. Right now I want to find these al-Qaeda and if they are connected to your competition, they will go down as well. It's very simple but someone will pay for Private Nolan, I assure you, that you can be damned sure of."

11c

Somewhere over Northern Ireland, after three scotches, Sharon fell asleep. She dreamed of sand dunes as high as mountains and then these mountains turned to great rolling ocean troughs, her Humvee turned into a burning catamaran, she felt herself hanging from a rope secured to the boat, she tried to reach the end …

"Wake up, Sharon," a voice pushed through the fog. "You okay?"

Sharon turned her head toward Gina, shaking the images from her head. "Yeah, I'm fine. Just a stupid dream."

"I guessed that," Gina said. "That is, unless you were doing exercises with your eyes closed."

"Just a dream, I'm fine."

She motioned to the steward, *"Oui, Madame?"*

"Café, s'il vous plait. Gina?"

"Coffee would be great, black."

"Oui, merci," the steward turned toward the galley.

"Now why don't we stop in Paris for a few days? We are only a short ride into town, then later, onto Venice," Gina said.

"The races start in two days, Jean-François hoped we would be early so we can meet people and get rid of jet lag. Never bothers me, but you, I've heard stories."

"They are, for the most part, untrue," Gina said. "But there was that one time at that small hotel after that non-stop Frankfort to Florence trip and that young cab driver and then something about a sun burn."

"Oh just shut up, relive your adventures later; I'm sorry I mentioned it. We transfer at Paris, then straight into Venice. Should arrive mid-morning, JF says he will meet us at the airport."

"This is sounding better and better the closer we get."

Four hours later, they pulled up to the gate at Marco Polo Airport. Their four bags were waiting for them; Gina was shocked.

"This never happens when I travel but then again this is the first time I've flown first-class. I just have to find a rich boyfriend," Gina said, pulling and extending the handle.

"He's not my boyfriend, Gina."

"Could have fooled me," she said looking through the glass of the terminal, out toward the Adriatic Sea. Venice sat, like a mirage, on the horizon.

They followed the signs to the water taxi stand. Gina spotted two men near the boats.

"Is that Jean François?" she asked with a gasp.

Sharon smiled to herself; *he is a handsome son-of-a-bitch*. Forgotten longings nudged her; she took in a deep breath as she pushed through the doors.

The roar of water taxis filled the air and the fumes of jet fuels and diesel mixed with the heady perfume from the North Adriatic. A light breeze blended them into a Venetian haze. Jean François Voss stood at the edge of the quay. He wore an open rose-colored shirt, cuffs rolled, dark linen slacks, gold watch with leather band, and canvas boat shoes. Another man, obviously eastern European, stood next to him just as elegantly dressed and an inch shorter. He seemed to be a darker, though just as handsome, version of the Frenchman. Two men, each as big as a Russian dacha, stood behind them wearing sport coats. Sharon had no illusions about who these men were and what was under their coats.

"That must be Fidor Balanca," Sharon said to Gina. "Jesus, what a pair and we look like we just got off the boat."

"We did, my dear. Just wish I'd powdered my face, damn." She sat her bags on the concrete.

JF walked briskly to Sharon and kissed her on both cheeks, "Welcome to Venice, *mon cheri*, welcome."

At that, three girls, heading toward the water taxis as well, swooned. One sat down hard on her bag, staring at JF; another patted her face with a tissue, and the third took a picture. They had been on the same flight from Paris with Sharon and Gina.

"Here's hoping all the men we meet look like that man," the one with the camera said, nodding toward JF.

"I'm into tall, dark, and handsome," said the sitter, looking at Fidor.

"And who says clothes don't make the man," tissue girl said, wistfully trying to imagine the Frenchman naked.

"JF, this is Gina Cavelli, a very close friend of mine, you must treat her right." Sharon said.

"Always and especially for someone this stunning," JF said as he kissed both of her cheeks. "Gina, this is a friend and associate, Fidor Balanca. Sharon may have mentioned him to you?" he said looking at Sharon.

"As a matter of fact, no, she did not," Gina fibbed. "She did mention that a friend was staying with you but nothing more. Fidor," she said extending her hand.

The Russian's hand was huge; hers was lost within its firm grip. "I am enchanted and delighted to meet you," his accent was educated, not tough, not the stereotypical Russian mobster's patois.

"Maybe I'm wrong about this guy," Sharon thought. *"Maybe I'm wrong about both of them."*

"The boat is this way, it's about twenty minutes to the palazzo; you can rest there. We will have a reception and dinner this evening to start the festivities but nothing really starts until tomorrow afternoon."

The bodyguards collected the girl's bags and took them to an elegant mahogany motor launch trimmed in polished stainless steel idling at the dock. The boat's driver, dressed in a classic horizontal striped pullover, welcomed them aboard in Italian; when Gina responded in kind, he lit up like an Italian Christmas tree.

He helped Gina into the launch and they began a conversation that Sharon had a devil of a time trying to understand. All she could see was that Gina was in her element, men and conversation; the man's eyes never left the full-figured Californian. *Italian men, must they always live up to their stereotype?* was all Sharon could think of. Then again, he was cute with his deep tan and hair as wild and curly as Gina's and he was very handsome.

Thudding on the launch deck brought her back to reality, the bodyguards had, not too gently, set their bags in the boat. JF's hand was reaching for her as she stepped into the launch, Fidor followed. In thirty seconds, they were racing out of the narrow corridor of channel markers, toward the campanile high over the Piazza San Marco. The wind threw Sharon's red hair about as if she was waving an auburn flag. The smell of the sea and the touch of salt water on her lips tickled her senses. She felt Jean François's arm wrap around her waist, pulling her a bit closer. It had been a long time.

"Warm enough?" he asked in her ear softly.

"Just right," she answered, placing her hand on his.

The launch quickly approached Venice from the north side of the island and entered the city through a small marina. A small opening almost magically appeared through the wall of buildings.

"How you say, a short-cut," the driver said as he slowed the boat to a couple of knots, the gurgling noise of the engine filled the urban canyon of brick and stucco.

Gina stared up toward the roof tops, laundry hung on lines strung across the canal, pots of flowers hung from windows and an occasional break in the buildings opened to a small courtyard or walkway that led from the canal. People were everywhere.

They were standing on top of every small bridge as the launch slid under them, they were wandering about and pointing cameras at every window and brick of this floating village, even her Italian blood had not prepared her for the experience. When they eased their way along a narrow canal between the ancient buildings and then out into the Grand Canal, she burst into tears.

"What's the problem?" the driver asked, holding her hand, trying to comfort her.

"It's so wonderful, I've dreamed of this my whole life and now I'm here."

She turned to JF, reached up to his face, pulled it down to hers and kissed him, not on the cheek but full on the lips, "Thank you."

"You're welcome," he said with a soft warm smile, "but look," he said, pointing as they rounded the next curve in the canal. The Rialto Bridge appeared in all its Renaissance glory; seeing that, Gina began to blubber. She collapsed on the cushioned bench seat and, like a child arriving at Disneyland for the first time, stared in wonder at all that stretched across the Grand Canal in front of her.

After passing under the Rialto Bridge, they cruised the right side of the canal; hundreds of boats busied themselves leaving crisscrossing wakes. Gondolas were tied to the iconic poles along the stone wharves. Peek-a-boo plazas opened to the canal and disappeared. Most building façades were a mixture of stucco over brick with carved stone lintels and balcony railings. Even though most structures were three or four stories high, no two buildings looked the same. Time and tide, literally, had molded these buildings into what they were, frozen façades from a faded age.

The launch slowed and drew up alongside a wooden wharf that extended perpendicularly into the canal from a particularly ornate example of high Renaissance Venetian architecture. Its glorious façade had been meticulously cleaned and repaired, the stonework was exquisite.

"Sharon and Gina, this is my friend's palazzo," JF said as

the driver tied the boat to the dock. As if this was a signal, two young boys exited the house and walked down the dock to the boat. The bodyguards transferred the bags to the dock and the boys quickly took them inside.

"My friend is in Argentina; his family has a ranch there." At the word 'Argentina', Sharon shuddered; the word 'Nazi' popped into her head but she quickly recovered. "They have owned this palazzo for four hundred years, through occupations, Napoleon, floods and wars. They have spread their wealth across the globe and invested in cattle, coffee and tea. They are one of the largest distributors of packaged foods in Europe. They are looking to expand into South America and America. With my American connections, I'm trying to help."

Pushing through an elegant door, they entered the palazzo. The interior was as beautiful as the exterior, light poured in from three sides from high windows; an interior garden was visible through the leaded windows of the main parlor. The girls stood there in wonder.

"This is Max," JF said as they entered what Sharon estimated to be the center of the palazzo. "He is the major domo and he runs this house with great efficiency. If there is anything you need, just ask Max. The two boys, Aldo and Lucca, live here and are also at your service, when they are not in school. Max?"

Max was a medium-sized man about sixty, silver-haired, dark blue eyes, with an almost Nordic construction. He was dressed formally as if jerked from the nineteenth into the twenty-first century; his silk waistcoat was black with white stripes.

"Ladies, your rooms are on the second floor; they face the canal," Max said. To their shock his accent was Scottish. "The lads have taken your bags to your rooms. Joanne, the upstairs maid, will take excellent care of you but be careful, she is very strict about things and she is also my wife."

"I expect that you would like to refresh yourselves and maybe even take a nap," JF said. "We have a dinner to attend this evening, we will leave about 8:30 PM, the launch will take us. It is formal so if you don't have something to wear, Joanne will help you."

"Formal?" Sharon said to JF. "You didn't say anything about formal; we thought we were coming to sailboat races and to do a bit of investigating, not attend formal balls."

"Sharon, this is only a quiet dinner with about fifty people, most are involved with the race and they will be retiring early. As I said, Joanne will help. Fidor and I have work to do so we will be back at six to dress. He wants to look at the new boat. We have brought the backup here for investors to examine. We rushed its manufacture; we couldn't wait for the prototype to be found."

Sharon looked at the Russian; during the whole trip he hadn't said more than two or three words and these were directed to JF. If she weren't such a suspicious person, she'd think he was shady but then again there was something about him that she couldn't place, something maybe less than shady.

"Ladies, if you will excuse us." At that, JF and Fidor retraced their steps to the dock, their huge shadows followed. Sharon could see the driver still standing on the dock, he held a line to the boat. With practiced efficiency, they boarded, within ten seconds the boat backed away from the dock and headed into the Grand Canal.

"Well that was rude," Gina said with a touch of sarcasm. "We seemed to have been abandoned in Venice, damn, let's go and check out our jail cells. Max, I assume there're stairs somewhere?"

"If you will, please follow me, and, if I may, I noticed that you seemed surprised by the announcement of the dinner this evening. You are not the first, I can assure you, who arrive and are not prepared for Venice. My employer is well stocked with dresses and gowns, for all sizes. My wife will help you select a suitable dress." During the conversation, they had climbed an ornate wooden stair that could have been featured in a TV show called *Castles and Counts*. A diminutive woman stood at the top of the stairs, the two boys directly behind her.

"Max, I will take over from here," Joanne said with a brogue even thicker than her husband's, it also had an Italianate edge to it. "Good morning ladies, I am Joanne. I gather, from Mr. Voss's description, that you are Sharon," looking at the redhead, "and Gina."

The girls looked at each other, smiled and then nodded. "Excellent, Ms. Cavelli, your room is here." They followed her into the first room.

Gina inhaled and looked around her room; it was gaily decorated in reds, gold tones and yellows.

"Sharon, this is the fairy castle I have always dreamed of and, without a doubt, something I will remember forever."

"Ms. O'Mara, please," Joanne said as the three entered the next room. It was as richly decorated as the first, this time in blues and greens. "Wonderful," Sharon said as she walked to the window and looked out over the late morning scene: boats and gondolas scurried about in the canal. Two lovers hugged each other as the gondolier's voice carried up to the room.

"Absolutely wonderful," Sharon said, "but Joanne, we have a problem…"

"Evening wear, I fully understand. You unpack and I will be back in ten minutes. Would you care for coffee or espresso?"

Gina looked at Sharon, then Joanne, "Two double espressos please, that should wake us up a little."

"Certainly, you should find everything you need in the bathrooms. Now, if you will excuse me." Joanne disappeared.

"My God, Sharon," Gina said, a tingle in her voice. "I have heard about these places but here we are in Venice, on the Grand Canal. I can even see the Rialto Bridge from my room's windows, what have you gotten me into?"

"I haven't a clue," Sharon said as she put away her clothes, "I didn't bring anything and neither did you; I expected saltwater and sailboats, not dinners and balls."

She waited while Gina unpacked. Precisely at the ten minute mark, Joanne walked into the room carrying a tray; the aroma of rich Italian coffee preceded her. She sat the tray on a low table.

"Sugar or milk?" Joanne asked.

"Black, please," Sharon said.

"The same," Gina echoed.

Joanne handed the cups to the girls and then asked them both to stand and turn around; they did as they were told. "Excellent, if you will follow me, I think we can take care of a few things." With that said, she headed out the door and down the hall, the two girls walked quickly to keep up but they kept looking at each other, wondering. Joanne stopped in front of another door and, after opening it, waved the girls in. It was as if they had entered into one of the greatest walk-in closets in the world. Rows and rows of dresses and gowns wrapped the walls, shoes were on display just like at Bloomingdales and mirrors caught the girls' reflections as they walked about the room.

"Your sizes, Ms. Cavelli, are here," Joanne said walking along one row. "Ms. O'Mara, yours are here. Please take your time; I suggest that you pick something simple and comfortable for tonight. Though formal, Mr. Voss says that it will be more business oriented. The formal masked ball is tomorrow night and ..."

"Masked Ball?" Gina exclaimed.

"Yes, the ball at the Peggy Guggenheim Museum, very chic and very chichi. I suggest something colorful; the Venetians love their color but we can deal with all that tomorrow. And, in another room, I have some delightful jewelry you may borrow; some of it is quite old. After we find your selections for tonight, we will find some matching pieces for the ball. I'll be back in an hour. I suggest a light lunch, then some rest. Jet-lag, you know, will creep up on you."

The girls spent the next forty minutes trying on dresses and touching the gowns, some obviously expensive, many still with their tags still affixed, tags that said Milan and Paris.

"I'm in a dream," Gina said standing in front of a mirror, the dark red dress she was trying on fit her like an Italian glove, every inch of her body displayed wonderfully, her ample bosom breached the bodice, revealing just enough to be tempting.

"I have never seen you look so alluring, you wench," Sharon

exclaimed.

"You look irresistible too," Gina said, looking at the elegant black chiffon dress that enveloped Sharon. "Oh, if the boys back home could see us now."

"This is our secret," Sharon said admiring herself in the glass. "There are times when a girl needs to feel like a princess, this is one of those moments."

A soft nock on the door preceded Joanne, who walked into the room.

She looked at the girls, "No one has looked as good as you two, my word; you look scrumptious. Those are excellent choices for tonight; yes, they will do nicely. Now, please follow me."

The next room was more secure and, from the door's construction, Sharon noticed, almost impenetrable. Joanne removed some keys from her pocket and, after fiddling with the locks, opened the door. Large safes lined the walls; low velvet covered tables stood in the center. She fiddled with a combination lock and opened one of the safes. Boxes lined its multiple shelves, what was in them was a mystery. She looked at the girls and their dresses and then extracted two small wooden caskets. She set them on one of the tables and slowly opened each. The girls looked over her shoulder. Their eyes grew as large as the colored stones that sparkled under the lights. Both said at the same time, "Oh my!"

Joanne took one necklace and held it against Gina's olive skin, "That will do nicely with these earrings and this ring will work just fine. Let me clip them on, there's a mirror there."

Then she extracted another necklace and offered it to Sharon, "And this should finish your look, Ms. O'Mara." Sharon held the emeralds and diamonds up to her throat; she had to agree they did look exceptionally well against her Irish skin. "And I have always had a fondness for this emerald ring," Joanne said as she slipped in on Sharon's finger.

"I have crazy desire this sing *I Feel Pretty*," Gina said, looking again at herself.

"I've heard you sing, so just hold the thought," Sharon said.

"But you can hum."

"Spoilsport," Gina answered. "But that bauble certainly brings out your eyes. Don't we make a great pair?" Sharon joined Gina in the mirror and they both began to giggle.

"Ladies, those pieces must remain here until you're ready to leave; I will bring them to you after you are dressed. I have had some sandwiches placed in your rooms so I suggest a light lunch and then a nap."

Like giddy school girls, they removed the jewelry and walked back to their respective rooms, "I'm sorry about the jail cell crack, Sharon, if prison was like this, I'd rob a bank just to get stuck here."

"I understand, Gina, my head's just spinning." She turned to Gina and added, "What have we gotten ourselves into, this is all so surreal."

"Surreal is just the half of it, I wonder what the evening will be like?"

11d

Green Zone, Baghdad, Iraq, 2005

O'Mara stood in front of the small flyspecked mirror in her billet, her face covered in stripes of black and green war-paint. Her body armor and Kevlar helmet were secured; this would be a fight. She checked its internal microphone and speaker. Whether these people knew they were coming was beside the point. They had to shut them down and secure the two warehouses full of al-Jamil's weapons and ammunition. Their location was what the son-of-a-bitch traded for his freedom. If one of her men were killed, she would hunt Jamil down and personally shoot him dead. She wanted to hold him but the Major said to release him. She was still pissed about that.

In Iraq, the night belonged to the US Army; every fighting soldier knew how to use night goggles and scopes. Surprise was their ally; fear of sudden night attack was as much a weapon as the MP5 was at close quarters. After millions of years of evolution, humans have instinctively feared the night, there were things that could sneak up on you, kill you and eat you. Night-time was possibly the main reason for the existence of civilization, the need for safety. A qualified sniper with a night-scope was like the hand of God, a God that showed no mercy.

Hakim al-Jamil had caved in; it was as simple as that. Sharon believed he was a good leader of his family, devout and strict but he also knew when it was pointless to go on.

"Now why should I believe any of this crap, Mr. al-Jamil," Sharon asked him, tapping her lighter on the hard table. "You have lied to me before and now you expect me to believe that you have not one warehouse, but two warehouses full of weapons. Where did you find such a treasure?" Al-Jamil stared at the tapping lighter, it was almost hypnotic, "Mr. Jamil?"

Al-Jamil looked at Sharon; beads sliding through his fingers quickly, "What more do I have to lose? I am lost to my family; they will have nothing if I don't return. Everything will be taken. They are defenseless. The weapons mean nothing to me now. After Saddam's fall, there were rumors of these weapons. One of my nephews was in the army; he told me about them. When you Americans came, everyone who knew about them ran or died. They were to be, as you Americans say, my 401K."

"Nice," Sharon said. "How were you going to convert these to cash? Almost anyone who wanted them could just take them."

"Very few knew about them. But there were rumors. My competitor from Basra, a man who is very cruel and heartless, kidnapped my granddaughters to force me to tell him about the weapons."

"Someone saw you with your granddaughters, they said it did not look like a kidnapping to them," she said.

"They gave the girls back when I told them about the warehouse. Even though the bastard is a thief, he is, at least, honorable. My men took them to a safe place and I went to see them. They are like water in the desert to me. I can't let anything happen to them."

"Where are these warehouses?"

For the next hour, Hakim al-Jamil used maps and photos to explain everything about the warehouses and the surrounding buildings. Sanchez stood behind O'Mara and asked technical as well as tactical questions. The streets were wide in this area, little cover available; most of the buildings were one story and close to each other, some were very close set. The building's doors were ubiquitous steel roll-ups. They couldn't just blow the doors in; the whole building might explode. A stray round was like a match to fireworks, care was critical. No choppers allowed in either, too noisy; they would come in for mop-up. This was a mission of stealth, cunning, and surprise. No shock and awe here, shock and awe would get them all blown to kingdom come. This would not be simple. Simple didn't like the plan. Simple said, fuck you.

The warehouses were across the Euphrates River from al-Kufah, just off highway 70. Her three Humvees would sweep in and secure the perimeter. Then they would work their way to the buildings, removing opposition as required. The goal was simple, take the two buildings and secure the weapons. She also had another goal, to make sure not one of her men got killed. She did not like the idea of killing al-Jamil; she was beginning to like the old coot.

Nothing is easy in Iraq. Invading armies have thrown themselves against her walls for four thousand years. If the people didn't kill you, then the desert would finish the job. The Iraqi desert was like the Russian winter, patient and impenetrable. Even with Humvees and Bradley fighting vehicles, the desert proved to be the real master. The heat destroyed the rubber and the fittings, filters often clogged and sand worked its way into everything, grinding away, eating bearings and gears. And the men inside these machines felt like they were being slowly baked alive. Night fighting was better, cold was better than heat when carrying fifty pounds of ammunition and weapons. Yes, a cool night was preferred to the shithole of an afternoon battle in the desert. And it was better not to be seen than heard.

Major Simpson agreed to the strike; he hoped it would be

fast and furious. "Go in hard, secure the buildings and then wait. I'll have bomb disposal come in when you call, but it won't be till morning. Secure those buildings and wait for morning."

"Yes, sir," Lieutenant O'Mara answered. It would be a long night.

The two buildings were new, at least by Iraq standards. They were metal corrugated structures, slight pitch to the roof, also metal. This was a break by O'Mara's standards; there was no way for the enemy to take to high ground. One single building about 200 yards away was three stories, only a pile of mud and wood. She would put two of her people on the upper floor, a sniper and his spotter. They could cover three sides from that location.

The sniper nest would be the edge of the perimeter; her three teams would work their way to the objectives, with cover fire as needed from the sniper. Once the warehouses were secured, they would hold their positions; she was more than glad to allow the bomb guys the opportunity to open the doors. She did not want to find booby-trapped doors the easy way.

Every operation consisted of three stages, the op itself, the ride in and the ride out. Every part of an op was potentially deadly in Iraq; roadside bombs could kill on either side of the operation as the enemy waited in the middle. They seldom brought the fight to the Americans. Today the ride was gratefully uneventful, but every soldier sat wrapped in his heavy gear, jammed in next to his buddy as the aroma of testosterone, sweat and fear filled every vehicle. Sharon smoked half a pack of cigarettes trying to cover up the cloying smell of her men, the open window helped.

O'Mara didn't know about, or particularly care about, the GPS system used in Iraq, she'd heard that it was a modified form or some other derivative from the type she knew in America; all she knew was that it worked, most of the time.

"How far, private?" O'Mara asked.

"Two miles sir, then we slide off the road and work through a tangle of buildings."

"Give me a heads-up at one klick."

"Roger that sir."

The driver sat next to her, his night vision goggles protruded toward the windshield, looking like the private was being given some bizarre form of reverse eye exam. Hers were also secured, the road ahead appeared an iridescent green, not a light glowed on the horizon or in any window of any building they passed. Her Humvee was lead, the others following in her dust. She hoped that an IED that missed the lead truck wouldn't light them up. Each Humvee driver wore their goggles, but the dust made it difficult. And there was no way to keep the dust out of the Humvee anyway, a totally sealed truck was still misery. The talcum-like sand found its way into every orifice and fold in a man's skin. Sometimes they felt like they were pissing dust.

At one klick, O'Mara signaled Sanchez and the third Humvee, they slowed to a stop.

O'Mara dismounted and walked to Sanchez as the dust slowly settled; a corporal from the third Humvee joined them. All had their goggles on and from one hundred yards away; they were invisible in the night.

"The last thousand meters, Sarg. How are you and your boys feeling?" O'Mara asked.

"Ready, sir, fucking ready as always." Sergeant Sanchez said with a big smile.

"Corporal?"

"Five by five, sir."

"You know the operation. Sanchez, get your men to the building, then take your position. Let me know when you are locked in. On my signal, we move. Quiet, no shooting until you have to, take them down physically if you can; I don't want rounds flying unless we have to."

"Yes sir, we know," the corporal answered.

"I know, corporal, just saying," she said looking at the young kid from Blythe, California, who once said he thought that his hometown in the California desert was the asshole of the world, until he came to Iraq.

The last thousand yards would be traversed methodically slow, no dust. She wanted to make sure the trucks that followed her could see. One hundred yards from the three-story building, they halted. Silently, her squad took their positions; the sniper and his spotter moved to the tall building. The whole complex was a mixture of industrial and warehouse buildings. No residential units around; the three-story building was a water tower. It had been misidentified. No civilians nearby made it easier; at least that's what O'Mara hoped.

They waited for the snipers to get into position, O'Mara's headset buzzed.

"In position, lieutenant," a voice said. She looked at the tower and saw two prone figures glowing green on the building's highest deck, a large metal tank sat behind them.

"Roger that. Sanchez, move them out."

She watched her squad break into teams and disappear into the night. She took the seven men that rode in with her to the middle spearhead location, between the buildings.

"On my count," she whispered into her microphone. "One, two, three, now."

Adrenalin pumped through the three squads as they moved fast along walls, providing cover as they leap-frogged each other. The streets and alleys were empty, nothing moved, nothing popped into her viewfinder. Nothing, nada, zilch.

"Levi, what do you see?"

"Nothing, lieutenant," the spotter said from high over the complex. "It's like a ghost town."

"Sarg, the old man said that he traded this shit for his granddaughters, wouldn't you think that there would be guards or some kind of security."

"Yes sir, that's what I'd do," Sanchez answered, breathing heavily through her earpiece.

"Me too, this is hinky and it stinks. Levi?"

"Still nothing." There was a pause. "Hold a second, lieutenant, something coming from the right." Another pause, this one longer. "Two soldiers, armed, coming around the back of the building, one smoking. Shit, lieutenant, they're Iraqi regulars, not some warlord's gang, these guys are real army." Another pause. "I also hear an engine noise from behind you."

"I hear it, shit." O'Mara said while she thought. "Iron and hammer, Sanchez, and we're the shit between them, God damn that old man. I'll personally put a bullet in his Goddamn ear. Get your men back, now."

She could hear orders being called out in the blackness. "Rally at the trucks, Levi?"

"Two more men have joined the original two soldiers, four in total," Levi said. "May be more inside the warehouse. Lieutenant, I spot three pickup trucks about five-hundred yards out, they've slowed to a crawl; they seem to be waiting. They probably assumed we'd open up on the warehouse and then they'd sweep in from behind us. Like jackals waiting for the lions to do the killing; then they take what they came for, the weapons."

"Looks like it sir, really fucked us this time," Sanchez said. "I don't like to be fucked twice."

"Me neither. Levi, change in direction," she said to the spotter. "I want a countdown as they approach, soon they'll begin to wonder what's up. So let's see if we can draw them in. The Iraqi regulars won't budge, I'm sure of that. I want noise and weapons fire for ten seconds, then hold. We'll see if they take the bait. At one hundred yards, we'll open up."

Private Elias Levi had been a soldier for six years and this was his second tour. He spoke Hebrew and French. He was from one of the tonier neighborhoods of western Los Angeles and wanted to be a cop when he got out of the army, just like his father and grandfather. He had sixty-three days until stateside and he would fight and kill anything that tried to prevent him from getting home. He tapped the head of his sniper, a young man who had been with the squad for three months. He was a soft speaking twenty-year-old from somewhere east of San Diego. He had learned well the arcane craft of killing humans from a thousand yards or more. Levi had spotted six kills for the boy, if it bothered him, he never said.

"Levi?"

"One hundred and fifty yards, suggest we light 'em up. From their body language, they are beginning to get confused."

"On my mark… one, two, three, now!"

Six flash bangs exploded three seconds after she called for action. Automatic weapons opened up in the shallow canyons of the buildings. One man in a Humvee swept the air with his 50 cal., its unmistakable sound ripped through the night. After ten seconds of noise, dead silence followed.

"Levi?"

"Like moths to a flame, they are coming quickly, one hundred yards. I count twelve, maybe fifteen; there may be more coming from behind the other buildings. They don't know that we know."

"Take them. Again, on my mark… one, two, three, now."

The sniper rifle barked, "One down," Levi said. Again it spoke, and again, and again, the sniper minutely swiveled the M24, acquiring targets in his night scope. Each round found a kill. "We'll cover you from here, Lieutenant, they are all yours."

"What do you see at the warehouses?" she asked.

"They ran for cover as soon as the first flash bangs lit up the night. My guess is they're calling frantically for support, even though they don't have a clue about what's happening."

"Good, I just want one fight right now. Keep your baby blues open, Levi," O'Mara said, she heard the rifle fire again.

"Sanchez, move them out," she said.

"Roger that." The sound was muffled, more of a whisper, the sand in her helmet grated against her ear padding.

She signaled her team and they soundlessly headed toward the enemy, along the walls as each man covered the man ahead, the last soldier watched their rear.

The American forces had learned that the opposing forces in Iraq often employed a tactic that had been used for a thousand years, Banzai-type charges. They had been common in the early days of the Baath Party regulars and now al-Qaeda. They would rush in and fire AK-47s at anything and everything until they were blasted to heaven and their virgins. This was no different, each of O'Mara's teams carried an M240 Machine Gun, heavy but effective, mercilessly effective.

The attacking force fired three RPGs into the alleys; the first one was only fifty yards ahead of O'Mara. The man leaped out from behind the building, took a solid stance and fired the rocket grenade; it ripped through the air, not twenty feet away from where she stood. The man, more intent on watching what it would hit, just stood in the alley, the next second she saw half his face disappear, thanks to a round from the M240. The launcher fell on his chest as he collapsed. She heard sporadic rifle fire, the whoosh of RPGs echoing through the buildings and explosions.

"Sanchez, status," she barked.

"Four down, third team claims six, Levi's count is seven," Sanchez called it like he was reading a scorecard. "Who are these fools? This is like target practice. I don't like it, Lieutenant. Not one fucking bit."

"Me neither, something else is going on, these SOBs are just fodder. Why?"

The why was answered five seconds later when all hell broke out from behind them at the warehouses, rapid fire weapons, the sky exploded as phosphorous grenades burst.

"Whoever they are, they don't seem to give a damn about the munitions in those buildings," O'Mara said. "Levi?"

"They came out of the fields, beyond the highway, maybe thirty or forty, hard to tell," Levi said. "I spotted three leading with goggles, the rest stayed close to them. They were following a lead team that started the initial attack."

"Sanchez, status," she said still hearing rifle and automatic fire.

"What's left of them is pulling back, they started pulling back when the second attack started. Shit, what the hell's happening?"

"We were suckered into this fight as decoys, Sanchez, and now I'm pissed. Those guys want the munitions warehouses and the weapons. Right now they don't know where we are or what our status is so let's use that. Rally at the trucks."

"Roger that," Sanchez answered.

"Levi, you are my eyes and ears, talk to me," O'Mara said as she ran toward the Humvees.

"They've swept in and surrounded the buildings, I haven't a fucking clue why they don't care about us," Levi said. "Hold a sec, I see five soldiers in Iraqi uniforms being led from behind the building. They appear to be prisoners or something. They are standing in front of one man, older, bearded. I can't believe it; the SOB's smoking a cigarette. He's pointing at the men, waving his arms about and, holy shit, lieutenant," Levi exclaimed.

O'Mara heard the shots.

"He just shot all five as they stood, executed them. Goddamn son-of-a-bitch, who does he think he is?"

"A man who believes that God or money is on his side," O'Mara said as the others joined her at the Humvees.

"It's that fucker Jamil, isn't it?" Sanchez said to O'Mara.

"Looks like it, he used us to soften up the guards and then he swept in. When we didn't bite, he flanked us, pushed in and took it himself. He may think we're pinned down or even dead. Sarg, that asshole will not leave those warehouses alive. Here's what I want you to do."

For the next two minutes, she quickly outlined a strategy that would allow them to encircle the warehouse with just her meager platoon of twenty men and herself. Levi would still command the high ground; she put two men at the tower's base to protect them. That left her seventeen. She got on the radio to Major Simpson, "It's all fucked up, I need you here as fast as those blades can get you here... Roger... Roger... And for Christ's sake, don't shoot us."

She turned to Sanchez, "Ten maybe fifteen minutes, you swing around the buildings and come in from the north; corporal, you sweep in from the south; I'll drive to the middle. Again, on my mark, we hit them like *we're* the fucking hammer of God, not them. That man is really pissing me off, Sanchez." She looked at her sergeant. "Saddle up boys; sunup is in one hour, I want this over before they can see us."

Chapter 12

12a

Jean-François and Fidor, dressed in formal jackets, crisp white shirts and black bow ties, waited for the girls at the foot of the staircase. The ladies did not disappoint them; the huge smile on JF's face told Sharon everything she wanted to know. Yes, again the sounds of *I Feel Pretty* filled her head.

JF took Sharon's hand as she reached the bottom step. Fidor reached for Gina, "You are gorgeous," he said, "simply gorgeous."

"I am beginning to like this man," Gina said to Sharon. "If he keeps this up, I just don't know what I'm going to do next."

"I'm sure you'll think of something, you wicked little wench."

Gina leaned toward Sharon and whispered in her ear, "Maybe, but tonight I'm Cinder-fucking-ella. Just remember, you invited me and I'm going to have a good time."

"The launch is waiting," JF said. "The party is on the island of Murano at the home of one of the Italian backers. I have heard that it is spectacular. Many of the international crews will be there, along with some very important politicians and business people. Personally, I'm going for the wine."

"And the vodka," Fidor said.

"You can talk," Gina said with a surprised lilt to her voice, "and what do you do, Mr. Balanca? From the looks of your, I must say, well-dressed associates, it must be something very important or very illegal. Please tell me, I'm all ears." She clung hard to his arm as they headed out the door into the soft warmth of the evening.

Joanne stood at the door and handed each girl a silk wrap that matched their look. "You will need these for the boat; it does get chilly at night."

The launch retraced their route from the airport and then raced across the short channel that separated Murano from Venice. To their left, the church of San Michel in Isola stood proud over the cemetery that had entombed Venetian dead for two-hundred years. Sharon remembered that Igor Stravinsky was buried there along with the dueling literary intellects of the unrepented, national socialist Ezra Pound and his arch opposite, another poet, Joseph Brodsky. She thought about their ghosts walking among the tombstones, throwing epitaphs at each other.

The boat carved its way past the waterfront of the Venetian island famous for its glasswork and its quite phallic lighthouse. Five minutes later, they pulled up to the quay in front of a magnificent façade that faced the setting sun. The rich butter yellow of its walls glowed in the dying light. Boats and launches were tied to the dock. The Oracle catamaran, all forty-five feet of her with its hard wing sail, was tied next to a huge motor yacht.

"I see that Mr. Larry Ellison has arrived," JF said, as the driver tied their boat to the pier. "Ladies, please follow me." JF climbed onto the quay and assisted the girls as they climbed out. A small group was gathered near the huge double doors that faced the canal. To Sharon's surprise and shock, Eva Karg turned toward the four of them as they left the launch and immediately turned back to the group. A second later, a voice split the air.

"Well, I'll be damned," Guillaume Boutin said, pulling away from the cluster, walking toward Sharon. He held a glass of champagne in one hand and a large cigar in the other. Sharon noticed that most of the group was smoking; *Things aren't much different here than in California, everyone is outside.*

"Well, if it's not my special sixth man, Ms. Sharon O'Mara. You are the last person I would have thought I'd see here," he said as he blew a large bale of smoke in the air. "And who is this delightful woman?"

"Bobo, this is a close friend, Gina Cavelli. We were just visiting Venice and happened to run into Mr. Voss."

"How happy for you. Ms. Cavelli, I am Guillaume Boutin,

you can call me Bobo."

"A pleasure," she turned to introduce Fidor but he and JF were nowhere to be seen. Flustered, she turned to Sharon. "Yes, Bobo, quite a surprise running into a friend of Sharon's."

Bobo turned to Sharon, "I suspect you are Mr. Voss's guests so I won't detain you any longer. Anytime you want to take another ride, Ms. O'Mara, just let me know. I am sure I can find some space." With that, he turned back to the group. Sharon noticed that Karg had disappeared.

They headed into the palazzo and were immediately handed glasses of champagne as small plates of h'ordurves passed by, their light lunch was a thing of the past. They both nibbled their way through the crowd. The celebrities and money people were all gathered at the far end of the ballroom, through the glass wall at the room's end the lights of Venice shimmered across the smooth lagoon. A few fireworks exploded above the island; in Venice there is always a celebration of some kind happening.

Sharon and Gina, two women as stunning as any in the room, stayed to one side of the room and watched. Elegant servings of finger food on silvered trays moved through the crowd, the girls were ravenous.

"I cannot stand that man," Jean-François said, as he cautiously approached the girls. "I'm sorry if I abandoned you, so is Fidor wherever he is, but there was no way I could even talk to that man, bad blood, very bad."

"Why, other than his being obnoxious and utterly stupid, what's the real problem?" Sharon asked, looking at JF.

"Just before my sister died, she told me she had been seeing that ass. I was shocked but not surprised; for all the great things my sister was, she made terrible choices when it came to picking her men. Then I heard from sources amongst the crews that he was bragging a little too much about her and that he was going to 'dump her,' according to one of the fellows. And to think that fool is a Frenchman."

"Would have been a little helpful if you had told me that when we started," Sharon said. "I asked you to tell me everything."

"I'm sorry, but by then I didn't think it would matter. She was gone; I was trying to figure out how to save the company. Now I'm not sure what's going to happen."

Fidor magically appeared, followed by his team of well-dressed oxen. "Ms. Cavelli, would you care to dance?"

Gina looked at Sharon; all she got was a scoot-along look from her friend. She turned to Fidor with her great Italian smile; he took her by the arm and they glided onto the dance floor. The oxen grazed at a small table while their boss enjoyed Gina's dancing talents. The Russian was shocked when a tango started and she took control. Gina was not going to let this night pass alone, no matter what the hell happened. *"I'm on fucking vacation,"* she said to herself, hoping her choice of words *would* become a double entendre.

"JF," a woman's loud voice said, breaking the silence that had suddenly been constructed by JF and Sharon. "And Ms. O'Mara as well, it's so good to see you. My, my, JF, I saw you from way over there, talking to this bluey, never saw her face, but, if you pardon me, you are looking really fine. Then damn, you turned around and it's you."

"Yes, Ms. Turner, it's me," Sharon said, looking at the most outrageous dress she had ever seen on a woman; it was a huge harlequin patterned thing that draped along the rich marble floor, all angles and padding, topped with a hat that could have only been fabricated from the feathers of a hundred birds, some probably on the endangered species list. She stood in wonder at the sight.

"Like my dress, it's an original," Ellis Turner said as she turned so that JF could see the whole ensemble.

"Yes, Ellis, it is an original and only you could pull it off and you have done it well. Don't you agree, Sharon, isn't it just something?"

"Yes, Ms. Turner it is so very you," Sharon said, fighting the laugh monkey as it climbed up her throat. "Yes, it is something."

"Well, anyway," Turner continued. "I still want to be a part of your boat, Jean-François, I understand that luscious Russian has brought his checkbook but if he, like all those other obnoxious oligarchs, walks away, just give me a call. I will always have your back. I know you and your sister were battlers so if you need help, just give me a shout. Now I have to find a beer, this French piss is just too much for this Aussie."

And with that, she swirled about and headed across the room, "Larry, Larry, I need to talk to you. Don't you turn your back to me, you bludger, I need to talk with you."

"Well that was a cyclone," JF said; they watched Ellis Turner disappear into the crowd and saw Larry Ellison trying very hard to outrace the harlequin outfit as it chased him through the room.

Two hours later, after a delightful and thankfully filling dinner, Sharon's feet were killing her, borrowed shoes can do that, the looming threat of jet lag hung just outside her consciousness. She knew she would be worthless in about an hour. She tapped JF on the shoulder.

"JF, it has been a long day and I'm about to hit the wall and, even though Gina won't admit it, she's about ready as well. Do you mind if we take the launch back to the palazzo?"

JF smiled and caressed Sharon's cheek, "Absolutely, in fact you have done much better than I expected; Fidor and I will take a taxi back. Have the driver go home after he drops you off. Would breakfast at 9:00 tomorrow morning be acceptable?"

"Eight hours of sleep will be divine, yes 9:00 is perfect, now if I can just pry Gina away from that mad Russian," Sharon said, looking at the two still on the dance floor. She turned to JF, "You wanted to know my opinion of Balanca?"

"Yes."

"I think he's okay but most Russians I've met are multi-layered, complex souls; it must be the cold winters and vodka. But he seems sincere and there aren't many that can put up with that Italian as well as keep up with her. I'll know more later, for now that's my assessment."

JF looked at the Russian, "Thank you and I agree. It's hard to believe that that man writes poetry as well; seems that every Russian I've met writes poetry. I think you are right, it must be the winters and the vodka."

Gina adamantly declined. "I'm having a great time, maybe the best I've had in years," she said into Sharon's ear over the loud band that played electronic hip-hop music. "You go. I'll see you for breakfast." At that she swung back to Fidor, wiggled her fine Italian hips and immediately caught up to the music.

As Sharon left the palazzo, she wrapped the silk shawl over her shoulders and lit a cigarette. The pack of cigarettes, a small lighter, her iPhone, some Euros and her passport were all that fit into the Givenchy clutch. There was a time when this small piece of the fashion industry meant nothing to her but a green cloth bag with ten full clips of 9mm ammunition did. The driver of the launch spotted her.

"Miss, Miss, here, here," he said while he waved. "Are the others coming?"

"No, just me. I'm exhausted. Monsieur Voss will be leaving later so it's just you and me."

"*Eccellente,*" he said. "My name is Vitorio. I am at your service. No worries about payment or tip, Signore Voss has been most generous. So where do you want to go? Venice in the moonlight is *spettacolare!*"

"The palazzo will be enough for tonight, Vitorio, this girl is dead tired."

"Si, si, the palazzo." After helping her into the boat, he released the ropes and slowly worked the mahogany craft into the canal; other boats were coming and going from the quay; some came just to see the America's Cup boat and its towering sail. When they hit the lagoon, the cool breeze combed through Sharon's hair. She took a deep breath and sighed.

"You okay, Signorina?" Vitoria said over his shoulder.

"Just super, Vitorio, just super," she replied.

The city's numerous towers were silhouetted against the dark sky, lit up from hidden lights as more fireworks popped up high over the city to the south. *"It's all so magical and surreal,"* she thought. *"Why didn't I stay with that man? It's been so long. Why? What's gotten into this hard soul of mine?"* She tried to clear her head, but couldn't.

"I've changed my mind, Vitorio," she said. "Drop me at the Rialto Bridge, I'll walk from there."

Vitorio looked at Sharon, then at her shoes, "You sure?"

"Yes, I'll be fine, I'll carry them if I need to," she answered, seeing his concern.

"You're the boss but be careful; there're more than tourists walking about this late at night," Vitorio cautioned.

"I'm sure I'll be fine," she said as the launch turned into the Grand Canal; it looked like gondola central. Vitorio slowed the boat to an idling crawl and worked his way through the late night romancers. He pulled alongside a dock just out of view from the most iconic bridge in the world. Jumping out, he helped Sharon onto the stone plaza.

"Through there and to the left is the bridge; do you know how to get to the palazzo?"

"Yes, it shouldn't be a problem. I can walk along the canal for most of the way and then follow the alleys to the palazzo. Thank you, Vitorio, I'll see you tomorrow."

"Buonanotte, Signorina, more boats are coming, I've got to leave. You sure about this?" Vitorio asked with real concern in his voice.

"I will be fine, tomorrow."

"Si, domani, buonanotte." He released the line he had thrown around a cleat and drifted back into the Grand Canal as he watched Sharon disappear between the buildings. At the quay, his spot was immediately taken by another taxi. A big man, dressed in a dinner jacket, got out and followed Sharon toward the bridge.

Besides Plaza San Marco and its tower, the Ponte di Rialto is all that is Venice. Its architecture, scale and even the curve of its arch against the hard slope of its roof is pure Venetian. The rich glow from storefront windows warmed the pavers at the foot of the steps that led up and over the bridge. She climbed the stone steps to the top of the arch and looked over the canal full of boats and gondolas. The lights from a thousand windows reflected off the water as she heard a gondolier serenading his customers, magic. She lit a Marlboro, turned back to retrace her steps and was suddenly shocked by the graffiti sprayed on the roll-up doors of the shops. Even here, vandals had to announce their isolation from society by defacing an icon. *Hell, why not stick a mustache on the Mona Lisa.* She immediately began to feel better, her cynicism was returning.

The quay was full of late night revelers, some wore masks bought at tourist's shops, others snapped pictures soon to be sent by phone and Facebook to friends and families all around the world. "See mom, I really am in Venice, I'm here right now!" Yes, the other magic of technology.

The quay ended and turned back into the city, the walkway paralleled a narrow canal lined with small boats, many wrapped with the ubiquitous blue tarp. *God, couldn't they have picked a better color,* Sharon thought as she passed the boats. Every time she saw that particular color, flashes of Baghdad's Green Zone flashed by; it was used to cover damn near everything, including the dead.

Near an empty courtyard flanked by Venice's rarest treat, trees, she stopped. A sound, muffled and repetitive, echoed off the old stone and brick walls. It contrasted with the clicking of her three-inch heels. She stopped again, it stopped, she started and a second later, it started. She slid out of her black satin heels.

Now what the hell am I going to do with these? Joanna will kill me if I lose them. For now, she decided to carry them.

Walking more briskly in bare feet, she crossed through the courtyard; the sounds started again, this time louder and more hurried.

If I am being followed, he might think I'm getting too far ahead. She slid into a deep black doorway at the end of the courtyard and waited. The dark shape of a large man rounded the corner and stopped. He surveyed the courtyard then quickly covered its width to the far side. Just before he disappeared, he turned and took one more look; the light from a streetlamp caught him full on. Sharon silently gasped; the last time she had seen this man's face, he had just left a bomb under her car.

"You son-of-a-bitch," she whispered. "I'm getting tired of these games."

As he turned and went down the path, she left the alcove and quickly followed. She had questions and this man would provide the answers.

She never let the man out of her sight; she could tell he was sure of himself, his body language and his actions exuded confidence. He took on the role of a late night party animal, laughing with a few couples that he met. He even stopped and took some photos with his phone. She knew he was talking with someone the whole time, someone who was telling him what to do, a black earpiece flashed in his left ear for a second as he stood under a lamppost. Her years of night training had honed her instincts, she knew when to stop and blend in; she had no problem even in the tight black dress she was wearing. She was very glad she hadn't gone with a lighter color, under these lights, she would have just glowed.

She watched him cross a small bridge over a narrow canal and then head into a dark slit between two buildings.

What are you thinking? She crossed the bridge, the gap, not more than three paces wide, was black. A rectangle of dim light could be seen at its end, maybe two-hundred feet away, the man's shape silhouetted in the light. "Got you," she whispered, she immediately turned to the right after she crossed the bridge, went three paces, then flattened herself against the wall and waited. Five seconds later, her tactic was rewarded; the man burst out of the gap and was immediately stunned by an elbow thrown hard into his jaw, she lifted her knee into his groin and then, as he started to crumple, placed another elbow to the back of his neck, traumatizing the Vagus nerve, not hard enough to crush it but with enough force to temporarily paralyze him. He hit the stone paving with a groan and thud. Two seconds later, she had her silk wrap wound through his arms, immobilizing him.

"There, trussed up like the pig you are," she said as she relieved the man of his shoulder pistol, the back-up in his waistband, and, after feeling down the man's tree trunk legs, a throwaway revolver on his left ankle. She pitched that into the canal. The man slowly recovered his senses; the numbness in his legs wouldn't go away for at least thirty minutes. Like your leg falling asleep, bruised nerves take that long to recover.

She looked up and down the canal; it was still empty, then she rolled the man on his back. She put her foot on his throat. "Why?"

His black eyes just stared at her.

"Why are you trying to kill me?"

The eyes blinked but still nothing; a small trickle of blood appeared at the corner of his mouth, her elbow had done an excellent job.

The sounds of laughter and footfalls came from the gap in the buildings. Sharon could see that the man's brain was working, "Don't even think about it. I should shoot you like a rabid dog but, then again, that would be too easy."

The noise was getting louder, she had maybe five seconds. "So here's the deal, if you continue to follow me, at some point I will kill you, capice?"

His dark eyes only blinked, he twisted under her foot against his Adam's apple.

"Capice?" He blinked. "I'll take that as an affirmative."

In a split second, she grabbed the man's arm and yanked it up, forcing him to roll onto his face, then she yanked his other arm and continued to roll the man over, releasing the silk wrap, after one more roll, the last with his face up, she asked, "Can you swim?" She did not expect to receive an answer. Just as the two lovebirds popped out of the alley, the man fell six feet into the brackish water of the canal. The splash was loud. As Sharon disappeared down the dark alley, all she could hear was splashing and the couple's screams for help echoing off the old stonewalls.

12b

Sharon sat in the ornate iron chair, sniffing the strong Italian coffee in the early sunlight streaming through the glass of the small conservatory in the rear of the palazzo. The banging of pots and clinking of glasses hinted that somewhere in the quiet house breakfast was being prepared; a heavyset man with a large bristly black mustache looked around the corner of the doorway. *"Altro caffé?"* he asked.

"Yes, Signore Bonafonte, yes," she answered as she watched the cook disappear, Max had not risen yet. The garden was in full bloom and the open windows of the glass house let in a soft breeze from the canal just visible through a gap in the buildings. She had slept fitfully since she returned to the palazzo, the coffee helped a lot.

She had met Max at the door to the palazzo when she returned, told him she was dead tired, said nothing about the man who tailed her and went off to bed. She unwrapped the two pistols hidden in her shawl and hid them in her room. She slipped out of the luscious dress and took a shower. The water, sliding over her naked skin, made her think, in a most non-erotic way, of JF and his involvement, if any, in this mess. Her mind, still spinning and reeling from the adrenaline and the excitement, wouldn't shut down. As much as she didn't want it to, it threw thoughts, like a frenetic strobe light, against the walls of her skull: insurance, Catherine, a competitor, the dead Flores, software, the thug, America's Cup, Ellis Turner, the cold Bay water, technology; they all bounced and collided into each other. "It's a rich man's sport that accomplishes nothing in this world except to say my dick is bigger than yours, or in Turner's case, her mouth. Then again, in that rich Aussie's case, maybe they go together." After three fingers of scotch she fell into a dreamless sleep.

Now, as the palazzo began to awaken, the thoughts started to return, one after the other, each waiting their turn in a line that seemed to stretch and disappear into a black gap between buildings. She lit a Marlboro, *one problem at a time*; her phone sat next to the coffee cup.

"You are up awfully early," a soft voice said from the doorway.

Sharon looked up, studied her friend for a couple of seconds and smiled, "And you positively glow, you wench."

"When we got home, the light in your room was out so Fidor and I had a nightcap."

"May I ask where?"

"His room, it is very nice and quite comfortable."

"You're blushing," Sharon said.

"Am not, just the sun from the boat ride yesterday," Gina said as she crossed the room and sat in one of the wicker chairs. She tried not to look at her friend.

Max followed her into the room carrying a silvered tray with a coffee pot and cups. "I see that you are taken care of, Ms. O'Mara, sorry I couldn't attend you but this old body needs sleep occasionally. Ms. Cavelli, coffee?"

"Thank you, black."

Gina looked at Sharon, the blush leaving her light olive complexion, "What a wonderful evening and, in case I forget, thank you for inviting me. I feel like I'm at Disneyland, complete with my own Russian Prince Charming. It's all so fantastic and wacky. And everything they say about morose and moody Russians, forget it. He even recited some of his poems to me," Gina said as she sipped her coffee.

"When?"

"None of your damn business, no worries, he was the perfect gentleman in all the right ways."

"A lot more information than I need this early in the morning, save it for one those late nights at the bar; I could use it then."

"What's gotten into you? You're moodier than normal."

Sharon poured more coffee into her cup. Max had also left some tasty-looking pastries on the tray. She nipped off the end of a croissant and took a sip of coffee. Steam swirled above the rim of the cup in the heavy air from the canal.

"After I left you last night," she began, for the next fifteen minutes told Gina what happened the night before, as well as what had happened in Walnut Creek.

"Holy shit," Gina said. "Do you think he was going to kill you?"

"Don't know about last night, but obviously he wanted me dead in California. Bombs are a little more final than a warning beat down. There is something a hell of a lot bigger going on here than a sailboat race. JF seems nervous and those guards are watching more than some Russian oligarch."

"He is more than that, a lot more," Gina interrupted.

"You're biased for the moment, so I'll let your romantic defense slide."

"You are so kind but I agree. The two of them keep disappearing and then reappearing. There is uneasiness in the air, a sense of immediacy."

"Good word, something is happening and fast. But I'll be damned if I can figure it out. Then there's this," Sharon said, sliding her phone to Gina. It said she had two messages.

"Did you listen to them?"

"Yes, they came in last night sometime during the party. One's from Kevin, wondering if we're having a good time," she looked at Gina. "Don't worry; I'll keep your dirty little secret. The other is from Sergeant Chang with the Oakland PD, you remember him?"

"Yes, his mother and the girls from China, nice guy."

"The same, he's investigating JF's missing boat. Wants me to call him but he left a message that has me mystified."

"He says they think they have a line on the container that was used to switch the trimaran. It showed up on street cameras the day the dead driver was found and later at the gate to the port. From there, it was loaded on a boat headed for Japan."

"Can't you have them stop it?"

"It was weeks ago, the container could be anywhere and

Oakland doesn't have the resources to follow this up. Mr. Flores, the dead driver, seems to be one more casualty in this bizarre story. But why would someone take the trimaran to the east? Perhaps somebody in China or the Far East is trying to copy the design? Hell, it's just a boat. It's not a damn cell phone or another high tech device."

"But it's my sister's boat, Sharon," JF said as he walked into the conservatory. "It was her dream and I'm going to finish it. Good morning, both of you look wonderful."

"Don't you just love French men in Italy?" Gina said looking at Sharon.

"Yes and Americans too, they are so charming, especially when they bring friends," Fidor Balanca said as he and one of the bodyguards followed Jean-François into the room. The last guard stood at the doorway, a cup of coffee in his hand.

"Getting kind of tight in here, JF," Sharon said, grabbing her phone and coffee cup. "I'm going out on the dock."

She balanced the cup on the wood railing of the dock and lit another cigarette. The sun streamed down the Grand Canal, gondolas full of standing people ferried back and forth across the canal.

"You have to have good balance to commute around here," JF said as he followed Sharon out onto the dock.

"No kidding, one big wave and you work in wet clothes all day."

"Mettre la rate au court bouillon!" JF said, using the old French phrase.

Sharon turned to the man and looked up into his eyes, "You are very wrong; it is very important and I am pissed."

"Pourquoi?"

She told him about the walk home, the thug and the call from Chang. JF walked to the end of the quay and stared out into the roiled water as two water taxis passed each other directly in front of the dock. Two tourists sitting in the backseat of one water taxi waved, Sharon ignored them. She stood behind JF, "What the hell is happening, Jean-François? People have tried to kill me before and as you can see, they haven't succeeded yet, but then, just like now, I want to know why. JF, now's the time or I'm on the afternoon plane."

JF turned to Sharon, "May I have one of your American cigarettes, I quit years ago; Catherine made me, but I think it's time to start again."

Sharon flipped the box open, handed him one and clicked the lighter.

"The day after they found my sister's body, I received a call from someone I didn't know. They didn't offer condolences or even a hint of sympathy; they said they wanted the boat."

"The coast guard hadn't released it," Sharon said.

"That's what I told them so they paused for a few seconds and then demanded that, once released, I had twenty-four hours comply. They said they would call me later with more information. I was confused and that's when I called Claudette, who then called you. But I didn't tell you the whole story and I'm sorry about that."

"I almost walked away from all this crap twice but when that driver was killed for no apparent reason and somebody tried to kill me, twice, my interest has gone up, way the hell up. Now, tell me everything or sure as hell I'm gone."

JF paused and just looked at Sharon, "Someone wants the hydrofoil, the whole hydrofoil. When I tried to load the boat and get it back to France, someone knew about it and that's when it was hijacked and the driver killed. Two days later, I got another call; they were very upset. They wanted the whole boat; I told them that everything was in the container, everything. They said they wanted a chip or something from the computer; they said the software was missing. I said I didn't know what they were talking about. They said I had two days or they would kill you."

"Would have been nice if you told me," Sharon said sarcastically.

"I know, I know," JF said. "But I didn't have the software. I didn't even have a clue about it because Catherine handled all the details including, most importantly, the technology. The *Cheetah's* as much about tech as it is strength and speed. She wanted to manufacture a boat that you could sail around the Mediterranean at thirty-five knots for days at a time, alone. And I think she did it. I don't know why someone would want it; it's just a toy, a rich man's toy for nothing but pleasure."

"The Oakland police told me that the boat is now somewhere in Asia, maybe Japan or China. They lost it. Who else knows about the software?"

"That would be Mike Stroud; he was closer than anyone to Catherine. He helped build the boat and knows it inside and out, with Catherine he suggested ideas about its design and how the motors and wires worked. It's as much his boat as Catherine's. When it disappeared, he was really pissed, but his job with Turner had him packing up her AC-45 and getting it to Naples. Then, after Naples, he had to get the 45 here. He's still pissed."

"I didn't see him last night," Sharon said.

"Mike doesn't like parties; he prefers being alone rather than with all the 'richies,' as he calls us. I don't begrudge him, he's more right than wrong; in fact, he's seldom wrong, especially about people. Said you're *ridgy-didge*."

"I hope that's a good thing."

"You're an original and you're genuine, he seldom gives praise."

"Where's Mike's pier?"

"Near the cruise ship terminal, all the boats are set up there."

"JF, I'll find out what's going on, I promise you. And I thank you for this trip, I have some ideas about what's going on but there are still too many holes. You go about your business today. I'm going to go see Mike, then I'll see you at the ball tonight, if we don't go, Gina will never speak to me again. Then I think we'll head back to Paris, Alain Dumont's memorial service is the day after tomorrow and I want to be there. I don't know what Gina will do but, JF, if your Russian friend hurts her or even upsets her in any way, I'm holding you responsible. She's a big girl but she can be hurt. Do you understand?"

"Yes, *mon cheri*, I understand. And I will make sure that Mr. Balanca does as well and, if I may say, he was quite happy with last evening and his time with your friend. I would also say the same thing to you, do not let her upset my friend."

Sharon grinned, "Such matchmakers this island has never seen."

12c

Sharon returned to her room with a cup of coffee, the huge breakfast prepared by Signore Bonafonte would hold her until dinner. The table had been filled with eggs, fruit, thin slices of Parma ham, small wedges of a rich Italian cheese and more pastries. She tried to remember when she had a meal like that, one that she actually sat down and enjoyed, it had to be days and days ago, of that she was certain.

Joanne was standing in the room looking a bit miffed. She held Sharon's dress, from the night before, draped over one arm, the shoes in her other hand, the wrap was folded nicely over the dress. The two pistols Sharon liberated from the goon the night before sat on the bed.

"From the looks of things, you had a busy night, young lady," Joanne said with no recriminations.

"Too busy," Sharon answered.

"The dress survived the ordeal, as well as the shoes; I was pleasantly surprised to see that they weren't scuffed. What shocked me were the two automatics, my guests don't usually return from a dance with guns."

"I can explain," Sharon said as she proceeded to give the housekeeper the short version of the previous night's activities.

"Well done you," Joanne answered. "But aren't you are faced with a dilemma?"

"Additional clips and ammunition," Sharon said.

"Yes. Fifteen rounds may seem like a lot until they are not."

Surprised at Joanne's knowledge, she said, "You are a lot more than what you seem."

"Aren't we all, come with me and bring those," she said pointing to the bed.

She followed Joanne down the hallway to another door; this one was as secure as the jewelry room. When they entered, she was stunned, the center of the huge room was populated by a dozen armored warriors, their silver finishes sparkling in the sun that spilled through a high window, lances, swords and other Renaissance instruments of war were neatly displayed and mounted throughout. Hundreds of ornate flintlock pistols wallpapered one wall and glass cabinets lined the opposite wall, each filled with more modern versions of the tools of war craft.

"Let me see what I have," Joanne said, going to a cabinet and pulling out drawers. "Yes, this should do. My dear, hand me the Beretta."

Sharon did as she was told as she watched Joanne quickly breakdown the automatic, remove its clip, examine it, retrieve another from the drawer, insert it and then remove it.

"The fool you took this from left a round in the chamber, good way to injure or kill yourself. You didn't check?"

"Stupid of me, I know better."

"The other, please?"

Joanne went through the same operation with the Gloch. "Why two different weapon types, that's strange. I like to stick with one; it's easier to remember things. You said he had a throw-away?"

"Yes, a small snub-nosed revolver, black finish, Colt Cobra, effective for close work."

"Yes dear, this fellow was as over-armored as you could get and all for poor little you? I assume, from the way you handled them, you have some experience with these weapons."

Sharon gave her another brief synopsis of her past career and experience with the tools of war. Joanne was impressed.

"When we left Scotland Yard," Joanne began. "Don't look so bemused my dear, yes, the Yard. Max retired first and then I followed a year later. Bored, we needed something to do and the Scots and British have always gravitated toward Italy, so both of us, being well organized and worldly, applied to this palazzo's owner, through one of the Yard's agencies, one that helps place us old buggers. It has been wonderful, I highly recommend it to you for your later years but you are too young right now."

"You and Max are amazing," Sharon said.

"Don't be silly, everyone needs something to do. Now I suggest that you leave the Gloch with me; the small Beretta is perfect for you, here are two more clips, they are loaded, full jackets - not hollow." She opened another cabinet and extracted two holsters.

"Just the one for my thigh," Sharon said. "I'll carry it in my handbag during the day, shorts and a tight top can't hide a pistol that well. I can wear the pistol under my dress tonight."

"Agreed, just don't let your man get too frisky, finding a pistol under your dress might confuse him."

Sharon and Gina climbed into Vitorio's launch; JF had many things to do at the pallazo, they would have the day and the launch to themselves. JF already had visitors that morning; the hydrofoil was not his sole business, all were well dressed Italians and Eastern Europeans and Balanca sat in on all the meetings. Sharon was slowly warming to the man again.

"A tour of Venice needs more than one full day," Jean-François said to the girls.

"Don't I know it, but then again, a day or two in Paris isn't too bad either, besides, I'm here for the ride," Gina said looking at the Russian.

"You have the run of the city with Vitorio until 5:00; then you have to be here to change. The ball starts at 8:00 but I would like you to have something to eat first, then cocktails at 7:00. The Guggenheim is just around the bend in the canal, we leave at 8:15."

"I just love a man who gives orders," Gina said.

"You love all men, whether they give orders or not," Sharon said.

"Not true, not true," Gina protested.

"True, true, out wench, out," Sharon said. Then to her own surprise, she gave JF a kiss on the lips and followed Gina to the dock.

"That was nice," Gina said as they sat in the launch. "That man's getting to you again, isn't he?"

"Some, but I'm still not sure. Too many things are going on and I have no answers yet."

"*Donne, dove vuoi andare?*" Vitorio asked as he pushed the launch away from the dock.

"Piazza San Marco," Gina said. "Then a drink at Harry's Bar and from there let's go through the whole city; then a picnic lunch in the plaza of Santa Maria della Salute, that's something I have wanted to do my whole life."

"Si, si, wonderful, *spettacolare!*"

Sharon had to admit that visiting Venice with Gina was fun, more fun than she had had in a long time. Through Gina's eyes, it was a new experience, something that a dog-tired American MP on leave for two weeks hadn't enjoyed. She was continually amazed at what Gina knew about the city and its history, even though she had never been there.

"Some people pick a city and learn everything about it. Me, I picked Venice when I was a little girl; I could even draw a picture of it, my mom has it somewhere, she drags it out during family things."

Their lunch consisted of thin sandwiches and a bottle of crisp Soave.

"I have always wanted to sit here on these steps with this great cathedral behind me and watch the boats come and go as the bell tower over Piazza San Marco looks over everything," Gina said. "So much history has moved through this canal, so much. Now what do you want to do?"

Sharon took another sip of wine, Vitorio stood near the launch, it was tied to the stone quay along the canal. "Try and figure out who's in that boat that has been following us all morning."

"Where?"

"Don't look, they are tied up at the far left," Sharon said. "I said don't look," she added as Gina immediately turned to the left. "They've been tailing us all morning and they aren't trying to hide. They don't look like the thugs I've been dealing with; these guys are whiter and more American, at least based on their haircuts. The boat handler isn't even Italian and considering the unions here, that's almost impossible. Military is my guess. Give me a minute."

"You sure?" Gina asked as she watched Sharon walk across the plaza toward the modern cruiser, her handbag draped over her shoulder. When she was fifty feet from the boat, the man on the dock jerked the line free of the cleat and nimbly jumped into the boat. The man at the wheel quickly backed the boat into the Grand Canal, then stopped for one long minute, then slowly accelerated and headed out into the lagoon, past Piazza San Marco.

"That was very strange," Sharon said as she sat down next to Gina. "The driver was on a cell phone, looking at me the whole time, while he idled in the canal and then he left, very strange."

"Well, we can't solve it here and I asked you earlier, what do you want to do?

"Let's go look at boats."

"There's hundreds everywhere, just look around," Gina said as she sipped the wine.

"True, true, but these are special boats; you saw one at the party last night."

"The Cup boats?"

"Well, their smaller sisters. I need to say hello to someone and he's just behind that big cruise ship," she said, pointing over the rooflines of the buildings.

Vitorio slowly cruised past the far southern side of Venice, through the Tronchetto-Lido di Venezia; the girls stood in awe as the buildings passed in review.

"There must be one church for every ten people on this island," Gina said as another small church appeared between the stone and stucco buildings.

"You're the expert," Sharon said as they slid by the ferry terminal with its high-speed catamarans and large mono-hulled ferries lined up along the quay.

"That's the first car I've seen since we arrived. How the hell did that get there?" Gina said, pointing to the parking lot near the terminal.

"I thought you were the expert," Sharon said. "Vitorio?"

"They come across the same bridge as the trains, then along the harbor and then here. It's the only place to get to the ferries."

Ten minutes later, they tied up next to eight catamarans with their huge sail wings and colorful decals; most prominent were the two Italian boats, with *Luna Rossa* painted on their hulls, *Prada*, written in large letters, vertically covered the wing sail. Reporters, cameramen and tourists were lined along the dock talking and taking pictures.

"Vitorio, we'll be at the one with the orange sail, the one with the Polynesian symbol on the sail."

"So that's what that is," Vitorio said. "One of the other drivers said it was a hex sign, something evil. Me, I thought it was just a pretty design, shows you what I know. You go have a good time; I'll be here when you get back."

The girls headed to the orange wing sticking up seventy feet into the bright blue Adriatic sky, two men and one woman in shorts, were on board the cat, two were pulling lines as the other watched.

"That should do it," Mike Stroud said to the other two, "Wrap it up, you have to look pretty tonight, as hard as that is to believe." He spotted Sharon. "Well I'll be damned, what the hell are you doing here?" He jumped from the boat to the pier and gave Sharon a big hug.

"Just being tourists," she said. "This is Gina, a good friend. We're staying with Jean-François. How have you been?"

"Busier than a dingo in heat, pardon me, ma'am," Mike said looking at Gina.

"You've got to be kidding, Mike, she owns a bar," Sharon

said.

"Mother of God, she's the girl you were talking about? Then she's a saint," Mike said smiling at Gina. "We were just testing some lines and gear, they were sticking. You remember Babs?"

The young athletic woman stood off to one side, waiting for a chance to say hi.

"Gina, meet Barbara Brown. She's one of the crew and probably the best of the lot. And a hell of a lot prettier than the rest," Mike said.

"A pleasure," Gina said.

"Mine too, it's good to see you, Sharon," Barbara said. "Fall off any more boats lately?"

"No, but the day is young. How have you been?"

"Like Mike said, busy. Races start tomorrow; we've been practicing for the last two days. I'm beat but we're all required to be at the ball tonight so I'm going to take a short nap. Are you going?"

"Yes, guests of Mr. Voss. Then we have to go home tomorrow."

"Too bad, the races will be interesting; the wind here is dodgy and swirling, not like the steady winds we get in California, will be quite a test. Mike, I'll see you tonight," Babs said, "And don't give me that frown, Ellis said you had to be there all dressed up like a sunburnt monkey. Can't wait to see what you look like in a clean shirt. Sharon, Gina, later."

"She's a great kid," Mike said as they watched Babs disappear into the warehouse that paralleled the pier. "Everyone's on edge about the Cup races and whether they'll be successful or not, crowds watching the race are up in one place and down at another. The cities we race in are nervous about the money they're putting out; don't want to make a bad investment. Me, I keep putting the boats together, then taking them apart, boxing them up and then unboxing them. Spent a week in Naples and didn't even get a chance to eat pizza."

"The Oakland PD thinks they know what happened to the *Cheetah*," Sharon said.

"No shit! What?" Mike asked.

"The boat was transferred to another container and then shipped to the Far East where it got lost," Sharon said. "After it reached port, in either Japan or Korea, it disappeared."

"Chinese?"

"Anything's possible, perhaps trying to make copies, seems like a lot of effort for something with high cost and low profit."

"I agree, our costs were astronomical. Catherine never told me what she spent but carbon fiber composites and the gear were easily hundreds of thousands; hell, the Cup boats cost a million each and hers used the same hull technology. The AC-72s are going for above eight million and they're stripped to hull and sail, they have some electronics but not as complex as the *Cheetah's*."

"JF said that the boat was worthless without the software," Sharon said.

"Not so, but you would need a crew of at least five, like the AC-45s. She's as temperamental as they come and can develop an attitude. At fifty miles an hour, a crash can be as bad as one on a freeway. The software did two big things, it sails the boat through the hands of the driver and anticipates the future. The radar would read what's coming, like boats and terrain, scan with sonar for underwater problems and then compute alternatives while it responded to the driver. Catherine's goal was to have it sail itself, like powerboats do, but with wind power only and at high speeds. We were close, damn close."

"The people who took it said it was missing software."

"Damn straight it was; everything needed to run that boat was on a 64 GB flash drive. Plug it in and the boat comes alive all on its own. No drive, it's nothing but a very cool boat; plugged in, it's a breathing living animal."

"How many copies of the flash drive are there?"

"One."

"Where is it?"

Mike smiled and pointed to his chest, "Here."

"Where?"

Mike reached up and drew out a leather lanyard that disappeared under his tee shirt; at its end was a red stick of plastic. "Here," he said, holding the flash drive like it was a small trout in a hook. "Everything to run the *Cheetah* is on here. Catherine gave it to me the week before she died. She said it was the latest version; the original software is in four pieces, each in a separate location on a different computer. She was a genius but she was also quite paranoid about the technology. She combined the separate codes in a sequence that she developed and then copied it onto this thumb drive. I don't know where she did the combining and mixing."

"Four pieces?"

"Yes, she had four different software companies working on it; one was in France, the others in Silicon Valley. All I know is that every time she gave me an updated stick, the boat got faster and better, as I said, she was a genius. Right now, this little chunk of plastic is worth more than the boat." He slid is back under his shirt.

"No one company knew what the other companies were doing?"

"Most likely, she kept them apart, they did what she needed, nothing more. As I said, she was a genius."

"No copies?"

"No, no copies or at least none that I know of. Catherine told me to take care of it and I am."

"Was it on the *Cheetah* when Catherine died?" Sharon asked.

"No, I load it into the computer then pull the stick. When the computer is shut down, the software disappears; each time the boat is taken out, the stick needs to be reinserted. My guess is that Catherine shut the boat down while she waited for the launch. She knew I had the stick, so no worries."

Gina had been standing near the two, listening, "Incredible, Mike, don't you think you should make a copy, just in case?"

"Probably, but I don't know where to put the copy and I've been too busy. Here, around my neck, is the safest place; if I copy it, then it's somewhere I can't keep my eye on it, simple as that."

"Yes, you're probably right, but still…" Gina added.

"I know, I know. After these races are over, we pack up everything and go back to California. But without a boat to plug it into, it's worthless. So I wear it more as a memory to Catherine than a piece of high tech jewelry."

"To some people, it's not worthless, in fact, it's worth maybe billions to someone and sometimes things are worth far more than money."

12d

The girls behaved like sixteen-year-olds dressing for their first prom. Joanne functioned as drill sergeant, mother, hairdresser and high fashion runway manager. The three reentered Cinderella's dressing room. They ran their fingers across the fabrics; Joanne opened a bottle of Presecco and poured the Italian sparkling wine into thin flutes.

"Are any of the gowns from Chanel?" Gina asked.

"A few but none in your sizes. When I was quite young and just starting with the Yard, I met Coco Chanel in Paris at the Ritz, where she had lived for years. The meeting centered around a difficult interview about some connections she had with a questionable man in Parliament. She quite naturally told me, in the most polite terms, "To bugger off." Her French was almost exquisite, she was quite old and frail then, this was sometime in the mid-1960s. She was a delightful a piece of work, a fashion designer, a tastemaker, a Nazi spy, anyway, I digress."

"I'm in heaven," Gina purred.

"Please don't break into another chorus of *I Feel Pretty*," Sharon replied, standing back trying not to show any interest.

Gina answered with a mischievous smile. While still looking for something for herself, she kept an eye open for something for Sharon.

"This would be perfect. The color, the style, it's so you!" Gina said, pulling out a green gown.

"Very pretty but it's just not me," Sharon replied shaking her head.

"Oh, come on. Please, just humor me, try it on." Gina spun on her heels; the light fabric of the gown caught the air like a great emerald-colored sail as it fluttered by Sharon and Joanne. "Pleeease, as they say in the movies, step out of the very boring box you live in."

"I don't live in a boring box," Sharon answered, knowing that Gina was probably more right than wrong.

Gina tilted her head and paused, "Right! Just try it on."

Sharon took the dress and walked toward an elegant Japanese dressing screen set in the corner of the room, Geishas and great chrysanthemums adorned its fabric. From behind the screen, as she slid off the tight jeans she had been wearing, she watched Gina searching through the racks. Joanne occasionally pulled something out and held it against Gina. Sharon thought this all quite silly. She heard Gina humming.

"What's that you're humming?" Sharon asked as she slid around the corner of the screen, still adjusting the gown.

"My second favorite song, *I Enjoy Being a Girl*," Gina answered as she looked at Sharon. Stunned, she turned to Joanne and then back at her friend. "You make it incredibly difficult for your friends to look beautiful." She put her hands on her hips and tilted her head to the full-length mirror. "See what I mean!"

Sharon's breath caught, her breasts perked. She had never looked this way. She had dressed up and she had looked good, she had even teased men with her looks. But now, standing in front of the gilt-framed mirror, this was the first time she had ever felt deliciously and beautifully elegant. Her red hair draped softly across the thin gathered strap of gown that crossed over her right breast and disappeared over her right shoulder, her left shoulder was bare. The rich green emerald fabric was gathered and tied in a crossing wrap across her flat stomach, the fabric then hung in thin folds that fell to the floor; her toes just peaked from under the hem.

"I have just the shoes for you, my dear," Joanne said, joining Sharon at the mirror. "You are stunning. We'll pull your hair up, like so," Joanna pushed Sharon's hair up on her head. "I have some beautiful earrings that just sparkle."

Sharon had to admit that, with her hair up, the dress did show her shoulders better, she was still not sure about the earrings. But she did smile at herself in the mirror.

"Now you," Joanne said turning to Gina half buried among straps, gowns and gossamer. She watched as Gina tugged and pulled out a dress, its blue fabric a deep rich sapphire.

"This is it! Perfect!" Gina exclaimed and then discovered the dark blue lace of the sleeves. "Oh my, oh my, this is absolutely perfectly wonderful." She quickly disappeared behind the Japanese screen.

Joanne fussed with Sharon; she tugged and tucked the gown. Then, pulling some pins from her pocket, she began to temporarily set Sharon's hair. "Just hold still," she ordered as the redhead began to fidget. "I said hold still."

Gina slid in front of the mirror, bumping Sharon over with her hip.

"WOW!" was all that Sharon could say.

"Do you think so? It is very pretty, but is it me?" Gina asked.

"It, and you, look absolutely fabulous! Wear it, please," Sharon answered. "I think your Russian will be even more impressed, even more, I'm sure, than he already is. You'll knock his socks off." She looked at herself and Gina in the mirror, "Correction, WE will knock their socks off."

Later, after relaxing in decadent bubble baths, Joanne helped to coif and dress the girls. She watched over their make-up and then hung incredible jewels from their ears and wrists and fingers.

Sharon stood in front of the tall mirror again; long diamond and emerald earrings almost touched her shoulders. "This really isn't me, Gina," she said as she admired the wide diamond bracelet on her left arm and a six carat emerald ring on her right hand. Joanne said simplicity was best. Green satin shoes now peaked out from under the hem. A bejeweled clutch finished the look.

"And our friend?" Joanne whispered in Sharon ear.

"Neatly and surprisingly comfortably strapped to my thigh. Don't tell Gina, I don't want to alarm her."

"Our little secret. But be judicious, there is only one extra clip in the clutch, not enough room for more."

Sharon kissed Joanne on the cheek.

"What are you two scheming about?" Gina asked as she swept into Sharon's room wearing the sapphire blue gown with its V-neck cut just low enough to show her "girls" in their best light; the lace sleeves were three-quarter length, a diamond bracelet cuffed the right sleeve. The drape of the dress made her look taller (of course the four inch heels on the dark blue satin shoes didn't hurt either), her wild black and platinum specked hair was pulled back from her face, exposing a widow's peak she'd forgotten, big soft curls lay on her shoulders. Joanne had selected large diamond earrings that hugged her ears with a ruby and diamond ring on her right hand to balance out the ensemble.

Sharon studied her friend, "I take back what I said, you are not a wench; you are a Medici princess."

Chapter 13

Somewhere in the desert, one hundred miles south of Baghdad, 2005

"Sanchez, you ready? Corporal?"

Two affirmatives rattled her earpiece. "On my mark."

O'Mara scanned the warehouses; there was nothing remarkable about them other than the five bodies in the alley where al-Jamil had left them. Two insurgents stood at each visible corner, she was sure the others had found strategic and defensive locations.

I don't like being fucked twice, either. She was beginning to understand this guy, a thug, nothing more or less. Calling him a warlord or some other crap gave him more distinction than he deserved. He was a mob boss and a butcher. Probably thinks he's al-Don Corleone or something. She'd put an end to that. As much as he was a charmer, he was also a snake.

"Now," she whispered into her headset. "Fucking now."

From high over her head, she heard the snap of the sniper's rifle. "One," Levi said. Then a steady stream of snaps, each no more than ten seconds apart. She no longer heard Levi.

Automatic fire echoed through the narrow metal canyons, flashes from explosions were absorbed into the night. She pushed her men forward.

They reached the first warehouse; Levi's man had done a lot of damage.

"Sanchez?"

"We're pinned down, one injured, a bit of shrapnel. We could use your assistance,"

"Coming. Levi?"

"You're clear for now," Levi said, then a pause. "Shit, Lieutenant, those assholes behind us are back with more men; I count at least ten. They are moving fast toward the warehouses, I'm not sure who's in the fucking middle of this fucking sandwich."

"Roger that, can you slow'em down?"

"Will try, sure as hell," Levi said, tapping the helmet of the sniper. He also pulled another thirty rounds from his bag. The kid swiveled the rifle away from the warehouses. In ten more seconds, they acquired another target, the rifle snapped.

"Sanchez, we need to push through these buildings, you ready?"

"Fucking A," Sergeant Sanchez said.

Swinging her team to the left, she pushed al-Jamil's men toward Sanchez. There was little defensive cover; their goggles lit these guys up like green ghosts. Her team took down two more as they joined with Sanchez.

"Good fucking morning to you, Sarg," O'Mara said as she covered the ass-end of her team.

"And to your horse, too," Sanchez said.

"Corporal?" O'Mara said.

"Opposite side of the first warehouse, when we opened up, some of these guys started crossing the road, heading back into the palms across the road. Maybe twenty left on our side."

"Hold there, Corporal." O'Mara said she turned to Sanchez. "I just don't get it, in and out and then this new press, I just don't get it."

"Put a light on that man," Sanchez said to the private standing next to him.

O'Mara studied the man's face in the beam from the flashlight. Clean, scrubbed, crisp beard, even though his clothes looked old, they were too clean, at least cleaner than the average Iraqi. "Shit," she muttered. "Does that man look Iraqi to you?"

Sanchez had looked at a lot of dead Iraqi faces during his tours, too many for his taste. He studied the man's features, pushed the face to one side with his boot. "Iranian, this man's an Iranian. Jamil's got the Iranian's behind him. That explains a lot, the warehouses…"

"Are not full of weapons, perhaps contraband and other

shit," O'Mara said interrupting her Sergeant. "That's why there were so few guards, my guess is that some major or colonel in the Iraqi army took control of Jamil's booty and now that asshole wants it back."

"Or Jamil caught wind of it and want's it all for himself," Sanchez said. "We're still screwed, Lieutenant, if we don't get our asses out of here."

They both turned toward another snap of Levi's sniper. "Levi?"

"Still coming, suggest that you get our men out of there, I'm taking a few rounds in the structure above me, we're okay for now, but when it's light, we're targets, dead targets. I need to be down in twenty minutes, no more."

"Got it Levi, down in twenty. Sargent, corporal, you listening?" She heard affirmatives. We can defend ourselves better at the Humvees. Work your way back to them; the Major will be here in three minutes. Then we can counter all this shit."

"Roger," she heard over her earpiece.

"Move 'em out, Sarg."

The corporal's team met them halfway, there was sporadic automatic fire from AK-47s but Jamil's men were blind. As the eastern sky seemed to brighten, the sniper rifle continued to speak its staccato one note song, for each of the enemy, it was a death song.

O'Mara heard the heavy whoomp-whoomp of the helicopters before she could see them. She knew that this was where things got dicey fast. If these were real soldiers, trained Iranians or even mercenaries, they would disappear. They died for money, not Allah or virgins. If they were insurgents or al-Qaeda, anything might happen, then again Jamil might send his men to cover the retreat of the regulars, no one knew what the hell was happening.

The roar of the Gatling guns from the Black Hawks welcomed the sun as it broke the horizon.

"Three birds, Lieutenant, never seen a better sight," Levi said from his perch.

"Get the fuck down here, it's getting too light," O'Mara ordered.

"Roger that," Levi said.

O'Mara heard the whoosh of the RPG before she saw its explosion.

"Levi, jump, you son-of-a-bitch," she yelled.

The RPG hit the tank above the two men before they could move; metal and wood shrapnel exploded from the tower, two bodies flew through the air and crumpled into the sand.

"Sanchez, find those sons-of-bitches," O'Mara ordered as she watched in abject fascination as the first Black Hawk chewed up the ground near where the rocket was fired. Secondary explosions from the area of the shooter followed as grenades and rockets were pulverized by the gunship. "Hold that, wait until they're done. Then send three men in to find out what happened."

The medic was attending to Levi and the rifleman. Both were moving. She ran to her men, "How are they?"

"Bad, a lot of shrapnel and steel splinters when those metal frames exploded, pieces cut them bad, get the choppers here fast."

"Major I have two badly wounded," she said into her headset. "Roger that," she said after his reply. "They'll be here in two, what do you want me to do, private?"

"Hold these compresses here and here on Levi, gave each got a shot of morphine, they're calming, but shit, Levi's arm and shoulder are fucked up and Jimmy's leg is bent wrong. But both are lucky, at least for now. Shit, Lieutenant, if the RPG didn't get them, then the fall should have. Two lucky SOBs, that's all I can say."

"Amen. Do what you can, get them out of here fast. The Major doesn't want his birds sitting here as targets, use whoever is available." O'Mara could read the Arabic signs on the buildings now; the horizon was an orange ball promising another day in hell. She watched two of the Black Hawks roar overhead, not more than fifty feet off the ground, the dust churned like a tornado ripping through the space between the buildings. When they cleared the two warehouses, they opened up with rockets and more Gatling fire. Whoever was trying to escape, would be dead soon.

Fuck'em, was all she could think of. *Fuck'em and that old motherfucker too.*

The Black Hawk settled about one hundred feet from her platoon, a tall grey-haired black man dismounted and passed by the men carrying Levi and Jimmy to the helicopter. He stopped and talked to each soldier as they were being placed inside. The medic jumped in after the men were set on the chopper's deck. The Major turned toward his ride and rotated his hand high over his head. The Black Hawk leaped from the ground as only an experienced pilot could do. It headed north.

"Major, welcome to my personal piece of hell," Lieutenant O'Mara said to Major Simpson.

"Thanks for the invite, those two the only one's hit?" he asked.

"Some nicks and scrapes, lucky," O'Mara answered. "This whole thing was orchestrated by al-Jamil, everything for those weapons in those warehouses. Using us to take out the Iraqi army so they could move in to clean up. Need to show you something."

They headed toward the warehouses; her teams flanked Simpson and O'Mara. They arrived beside the dead man she'd looked at earlier. "He's Iranian, I'm goddam sure about that and there are three more, there and over there. Al-Jamil was using them or they were using him, not sure which. But they wanted whatever was in these buildings."

She motioned to one of her men, the steel rolling door was secured with a large padlock; his Browning made short work of it. He slid the door open; in the early morning light it was black inside. The soldier panned his flashlight over the crates that lined the walls, past two large orange shipping containers sitting in the middle of the room. The boxes said Microsoft Xbox on the sides; others said Panasonic, Sony, and Apple. The whole warehouse was full of consumer electronics.

"All of this for junk," O'Mara said. "Now I am personally going to kill that asshole."

"Stand in line, Lieutenant, he's mine first," Major Simpson said. "This stuff is worth more than medical supplies in this country. My guess, somebody, probably government, brought it in through Kuwait; Jamil caught wind of it and decided to liberate it, with our help. He'd have sold the stuff for a hundred times what it's worth; my guess is that the Iranians were part of a buyer's group. They were here to help move the stuff to Iran. The electronics are worth even more across the border."

A soldier stood in the early sunlight waiting for O'Mara, she saw him. "Report."

"We found twelve dead north of here from the first attack, most were taken out by Levi and Jimmy; we found six more around the warehouses. There were at least five blood trails. I don't know what the Black Hawks are doing but I sure as hell would not want to be out there in the desert."

"Thank you," O'Mara said. "What do you want to do with this crap, Major?"

"Well, I'm a firm believer that television will rot your brain and turn you into a pervert. So I would suggest that a judicious application of force and power will help save young Iraqi minds for the tough job of governing this pest hole. How much C-4 do you have?"

13b

The girls glided down the stairs toward the two men; Joanne and Max stood off to one side.

"You wipe that grin off your face, Fidor Balanca," Gina said, looking sternly at the Russian.

"We have nothing like you in my country," Fidor said taking Gina's hand.

"And you remember this: No matter where Italians go, we rule."

There was an annoyed cough behind Gina, "And yes, sometimes the French can be included as well and," she added, looking at Sharon, "the Irish."

"If this keeps up, I'm sure the Scots will be in for a drubbing," Joanne said.

"You look, how do I say it, my English is so weak when it comes to this. *Vous avez l'air absolument merveilleux!*" Jean-François said with a smile. *"Absolument!"*

"He's right, it does sound better in French," Gina said taking Fidor's arm.

Sharon leaned over to Joanne and whispered the first line of I Feel Pretty into her ear.

"Every girl should, at some time in their lives. Now go have a good time, don't stay out too late and be careful," Joanne said draping a wonderful silk wrap over her shoulders; Fidor placed another over Gina's. She took a small bundle of fabric from Max's hand. "Now put these on, no one goes to a ball in Venice without a mask; these are over one hundred years old." She handed them out to everyone, then watched the four walk through the large beveled glass paneled doors and take three steps to the dock of the palazzo. Vitorio stood at the side of the launch, the line was wrapped around a Venetian barber pole painted in a red and white spiral pattern, capped with a gold finial. He couldn't contain his Venetian heritage as he let out a soft whistle.

"Thank you, Vitorio," Sharon said with a big smile, "I appreciate that very much."

The two bodyguards were the last of the party to climb aboard.

Vitorio released the line, jumped into the launch, throttled up the engine and backed away from the palazzo. "Please be seated, I don't want to get you wet or the slightest bit uncomfortable. Signorina O'Mara, please sit here, Signorina Cavelli, here. The boys can stand." With a slight objection from one of the bodyguards, Vitorio reminded him that he is the captain as he throttled up the speed a notch, causing the big man to lose his balance.

The ride lasted less than ten minutes at the slow idling pace

Vitorio set; Sharon enjoyed every building, dock and gondola they passed. The evening light was magical and with her mask she felt hidden from all the pain she'd felt recently, mostly the loss of Alain Dumont. But there was much more to hide from and the mask helped. Sometimes she wished she wasn't as good as she was, life would be so much simpler.

The launch slid between the mooring poles in front of the ornate stone quay of the Peggy Guggenheim palazzo. The structure is unlike any other on the Grand Canal, it is painted white, not an old worn out white but a fresh modern color that reflects the modern collection of art that it contains. Flat faux columns, five to each side, flank the central entrance guarded by two huge clipped shrubs. A low hedge along the edge of the rooftop terrace finishes the view from the canal. For all its appearances, it looks like a truncated Venetian castle but with its hidden sculpture garden and rooftop terrace view of the canal, it is one of the best locations in Venice for a ball. Flanking the quay, making docking intentionally difficult, were two of the AC45s, their tall wing sails dwarfing the structure. An Oracle boat was moored to the right and one of the *Luna Rossa's*, with its *Prada* signature wing sail, was tied to the left.

Vitorio idled in the roiled canal waters while others disembarked ahead of them; valets, dressed like harlequins, assisted the passengers. Sharon watched the mix of guests; they came in all sizes and styles. But there was one thing that was unmistakable, the look of money. Two young boys nimbly leaped aboard and grabbed lines at the bow and stern, they held the boat to the poles until the six passengers stood on the quay.

"Vitorio," JF said. "I will call you when we need you so have some dinner and relax."

"*Grazie*, Signore Voss, I will wait for your call." As Vitorio moved into the canal, another launch replaced it.

Standing in the quay's center, surrounded by her entourage, Bobo, Karg, and three others, Ellis Turner waved at JF and Fidor. She reminded Sharon of a huge chiffon cake, layers of foamy yellow fabric danced in the soft breeze blowing in from the Adriatic. Sharon wasn't sure about the hat or whatever someone might call it. It was a stacked confection also, type unknown. Her mask was a striking disk of modern art, two holes were punched out for the eyes; she held the mask on a stick, as was once the fashion.

"Blimey, if it's not the girls from Cali, my, my, don't you two look delicious," Turner said, her eyes masked. "You two boys are lucky. Be very good to them or I'll have to spank you."

"Spank me?" Fidor said to Turner; then he turned toward Gina.

"Later," Gina said. "Thank you, Ms. Turner, sometimes a girl just has to get dressed up."

"Isn't that just the case?" Turner said. Then she seriously upped the ante. "Do you like my dress?"

There are loaded questions in this world like... Does this make me look fat? What do you think of the European Union? Who are you going to vote for? But for one woman to ask another about her gown, especially coming from a billionaire, it requires the greatest verbal gymnastics. Bartenders are known for their eloquence and tact.

"Ms. Turner," Gina began, "Your gown is, without a doubt, one of a kind and it reflects the wonderful collection of art that we will find in this palazzo; it, like you, is unique."

Turner smiled at Gina, then kissed her on the cheek, "Thank you, my dear, you make this heart flutter in more ways than one." Then the Turner entourage climbed the steps to the museum.

Gina turned to Sharon, "Did she just make a pass at me?"

"Yes, she did," Sharon said. "Be careful, Fidor might have to use his guards to defend you as well as him."

JF and Fidor took the arms of their dates and followed the parade, led by the voluminous yellow meringue, into the palazzo. A string quartet played a violin piece by Venice's patron musical saint, Antonio Vivaldi, it was from *The Four Seasons*. The magic of the evening continued, even though it was being interrupted by a lemon meringue pie.

After a casual tour of the museum and its sculpture garden, Fidor surprised Sharon by saying that he had a Henry Moore in the garden at his dacha outside of Moscow. He acquired it from an Englishman who was in need of some quick cash, Fidor said he paid the man what he wanted and moved it the next day. He added that it portrayed a large woman with huge breasts; it reminded him of a peasant woman he once knew in the Ukraine.

"He is a man of strange tastes," Gina said to Sharon as they climbed the steps to the rooftop terrace.

"He's Russian," Sharon said. "They are all complex and misunderstood."

"Maybe, but he's quite a man. Reminds me a bit of Putin, don't you think?"

"A little but he has a great head of hair and Putin hasn't any to speak of."

"I don't care, I'm going to have a night to remember and before I forget, thanks for inviting me."

"You've already thanked me several times," Sharon answered.

"Still not enough," Gina said as they reached the terrace.

The setting sun was behind them; its last light lit the facades and towers across the Grand Canal like a golden floodlight. Windows twinkled and sparkled with reflected sunlight. The campanile in San Marcos stood like a golden sentinel over Venice. Even the most jaded billionaire on the terrace stopped and watched the sun set over the city.

"Magical, isn't it," a hard voice said from behind Sharon as she looked over the island's towers. "It would be a shame to spoil it."

Sharon turned toward Eva Karg; she stood implacably in a dark red gown, the color of spilled blood. She was alone.

"What can I do for you, Ms. Karg?" Sharon asked.

"You can make all these troubles go away. To be blunt, I know you have it and I want it. If it's money you want, no problem, tell me your price. If it's something else, we can work it out."

"I haven't a clue what you're talking about," Sharon said truthfully. "What is it you want?"

Karg studied Sharon, then said, "I don't know what your game is but I want it tonight."

Sharon took a step toward Karg as they stood eye to eye. She could tell Karg was fit and athletic; the gown removed any doubts about her sex. What her appetites were was another matter.

"I don't know what you are talking about," Sharon said. "I'm having a delightful evening with my friends, so, as the Brits say, bugger off."

"My, my, and testy too," Karg said. "As I said, I want it tonight. I know you are leaving tomorrow so I want it tonight. If you have it with you now, I'll take it, if not, I'll contact you at midnight. I have your cell number, it's your choice. Now or later, I will get it. And by the way, that man you're with is one hell of a fuck."

With that grenade, Karg turned and headed back to the small gang surrounding Bobo and some of his team. Sharon shook off the bitchy crack from Karg and looked through the crowd, she hadn't seen Mike Stroud.

"Looking for someone?" Jean-François asked, handing Sharon a flute of champagne.

"Mike Stroud," she answered still a little pissed over Karg's remark. "He said he would be here but I don't see him."

"You know what Mike says about parties, they bore him and they are waste of time," JF said.

"Yes, he told me but he also said he would be here."

"With the races beginning tomorrow, he's just running late, he'll be here."

Gina and Fidor joined both of them.

"Who was that woman you were talking with?" Gina asked.

"Eva Karg, she is an assistant to Turner, or something, not sure what exactly," Sharon said. "Wanted something, I'm not sure what. Got testy about it."

"Well, don't let it spoil your evening. Fidor, dance with me." Gina said as she took the Russian's hand and led him to the small dance floor in the corner; the band was playing another Vivaldi piece.

"You can't dance to that," Sharon said as the two walked away.

"Who cares," Gina said as they disappeared into the pack of masked revelers.

"Are you having a good time?" JF asked.

"Wonderful, but Karg's question is bugging me."

"Don't let it," and with that, he kissed her softly on the mouth. "I've invited you before."

"And I've declined, before."

"That was before, this is now."

A siren blared from the canal; everyone turned and looked over the hedge of boxwoods. A police cruiser raced its way around the southern corner of the island and headed directly toward the museum. It pulled up short and expertly slid into the vacant landing at the quay. Three uniformed *Carabinieri* leaped from the boat and headed into the palazzo, their white shoulder strap and red striped pants struck an imposing look even amongst the coated and gowned crowd. Seconds later, they appeared on the terrace. One of the managers walked toward the obvious police captain. After a brief conversation, the man pointed to Ellis Turner. The *Carabinieri* tipped his fingers to his cap in salute and walked toward Turner. Even he was stunned by the dress; it was difficult for him to get close. She hooked some of the fabric over her arm and leaned toward the officer. After a brief conversation, a stunned look appeared on her face as she frantically looked about, spotted JF and waved for him to come over to her. The officer stood to one side.

"Jean-François," Turner said, the rest of conversation was lost in the noise of the band and the crush of people.

JF waved to Sharon to come quickly to his side, "Mike Stroud's been found dead."

"Where?" Sharon asked.

"Racing team tents," JF answered.

"I only saw him a few hours ago, he seemed fine."

"This is Capitano Brescia of the *Carabinieri*. Capitano, this is Sharon O'Mara, a friend." Turner said. "They think it's foul play; he was shot."

Sharon acknowledged the Capitano, then thought for a second as she scanned the room looking for Karg, she couldn't find her in the crowd. "Is he still at the race tents?" she asked Capitano Brescia.

"Si, Signorina, we are waiting for the coroner," the officer said.

"Your English is exceptionally good, Capitano," Sharon said.

"America, you have to love their police training schools."

"I work with Ms. Turner and Mr. Voss," Sharon half-lied. "May I see the body? It is critical to the race and the events."

Not wishing to have the wrath of the politicians on his head, he agreed.

"JF, call Vitorio, have him pick us up. I need to see Mike's body, it's critical."

Gina walked up behind Sharon, "Everything okay?"

"No, Mike Stroud has been killed. There is something I need to find."

"You're not going alone," Gina said. "Fidor?"

"Vitorio will be here in three minutes, he was just across the canal," JF said. "We're all going."

"Dah," the Russian echoed, "We will all go." With that, he signaled to his men and headed toward the stairs. The tops of the dark caps of the *Carabinieri* were just disappearing down the stairs.

"Ellis, I'm sorry I told the officer I worked for you but it's important that he understands that I need the authority when I get there."

"No worries, lass. Find out who killed him," Ellis Turner said.

"I'll do my best," Sharon said, then looked over balcony. "JF,

I see Vitorio, we need to go - now."

Sharon turned quickly; she felt the steel of the Beretta rub the inner skin of her thigh. For some strange reason, it comforted her.

13c

Vitorio pushed the throttle forward hard, trying to keep up with the *Carabinieri* cruiser. They passed Santa Maria della Salute and then swung into the main channel, the Lido de Venezia. The race compound was set up near the huge cruise ship that dominated the islands during its stay. As they entered the terminal area, Sharon could see the white tents that had been erected to house the international team of Cup racers, a number of the AC45 catamarans were tied to the pier, three police boats and one that said CORONER on its gunnel were also tied to the huge concrete pier. Vitorio slid the launch into an opening between the boats. Sharon was the first one out of the boat, Gina quickly followed.

"You need to be my ears, try and remember everything you hear. We're lucky the captain speaks English. I'm not sure about the rest, so please listen and tell me what they say. Okay?"

"Never seen you this way," Gina said, putting her hand on her friend's arm. "You're like a different person, between us, a very cool person. Anything you need, just ask."

They headed directly to the captain, he cracked a smile; without a doubt, his crime scene just got a helluva lot prettier.

"Where is he?" Sharon asked. "I know this is your crime scene, Capitano Brescia but, with all due respect, I must see the body, may I have your permission?"

He had never been asked this question under these conditions, not to mention by a beautiful redhead in a spectacular green dress.

"Yes, yes, the body is this way," Brescia said as he went through the door of the second tent. The logo for Turner's contending yacht club hung over the doorway, with its scowling face, bug eyes, and tongue hanging out, all caught in a stylized

Polynesian image of war, watched as Sharon and Gina followed the officer. The rest of their group remained near the launch.

Inside was utter antiseptic organization, Sharon saw at least five techs in white jumpsuits and more police hanging about the edges; three cameras strobed incessantly and spotlights had been setup; they illuminated the yellow sheet on the floor in the middle of this investigative maelstrom. She thought that Mike would have been embarrassed by all the attention.

Capitano Brescia was talking to a man in one of the white jumpsuits and then the two walked toward Sharon. The man in the white suit puffed up a bit and pulled in his ample belly. He had never been in the presence of two women as striking as Sharon and Gina at a crime scene.

"Are all Italian men on the prowl, even at a crime scene?" Sharon asked Gina in a soft voice.

"Always, till the day they're dead," Gina said. "You should have met my grandfather."

"Ms. O'Mara, Coroner Vincenzi, I have explained the situation. You will have to dress in the whites and put on, how you say...?"

"Booties," Sharon replied.

"Si, si booties," the captain answered.

"I don't think they have an outfit that will fit over that dress," Gina said.

Even the coroner realized that; he said something to the Capitano. Gina translated.

"I have my rules," Gina said. "Sorry, I don't want anything at or near the crime scene contaminated, even for someone as scrumptious as her."

The captain looked at Gina, then said something to the coroner.

Gina smiled, "They just found out I speak Italian.

"Good, now we can move forward, Capitano?"

"Maybe he can answer your questions, Signorina O'Mara. Maybe we can start with that?"

"For a start, that may work," Sharon answered. "Where was

he shot, was it at close range?"

The captain translated, then replied, "Yes close, through the heart. He'd also had his hands crushed by a heavy boot or something similar. He also has a bruised face and, from appearances, a broken nose."

"Holy shit," Gina said looking at the yellow tarp. "You mean he was tortured, then murdered?"

"Si," the coroner answered.

Gina was turning green as she continued to stare at the tarp.

"Gina, go outside," Sharon said. "I'm sure you'll be more comfortable out there, go to Fidor." Gina did as she was told.

"Senor Vincenzi, can you check to see if he has anything around his neck? Like a necklace or a leather cord?"

The coroner walked over to the body and asked one of the techs to lower the sheet; he bent down and unbuttoned the white dress shirt, now stained crimson.

Damn it, he was going to the ball, he was wearing a formal shirt. Goddamn it, he didn't deserve this.

The coroner returned to Sharon and Brescia, *"Niente, no collana."*

"Nothing, no necklace or cord, what were you looking for?"

"This afternoon, Mr. Stroud showed me a memory stick on a lanyard that he had around his neck, it contained some important software for one of Mr. Voss's projects, now it's gone. My guess is they killed him for the stick. Now it's gone. All this for a piece of code to sail a boat; it's all wrong, something else is going on."

Ten minutes later, she joined the group on the quay, "You are looking better," she said to Gina.

"Thanks, it's not every day you get to attend a murder scene in a dress like this, can we go?"

"In a minute, JF, we need to talk," Sharon said while removing her cigarettes from the jeweled clutch. She offered one to JF.

He accepted.

They walked down the pier as a thousand lights from the cruise ship sparkled above them. Passengers leaned over their balcony rails; there was no better seat in the house.

"Mike had a copy of the software; it was the original from the boat. Whoever killed your sister thought it was on the boat when they boarded the *Cheetah*."

"The computer terminal for the stick was hidden under the seat but the stick and the program were never left plugged into the computer." JF said. "The computer was not really hidden, it was there to keep it dry. Only those who worked on the boat would have known. She didn't tell them and it got her killed."

"They would have killed her anyway, JF," Sharon said. "But something else is annoying me. An hour ago, Karg confronted me, you saw her. She wanted something; she said she knew I had it. Then I didn't have any idea what she was talking about, now I do. She thought I had the memory stick; she didn't get it from Stroud so she believes I have it. She wants it by midnight; she's involved with Mike's murder."

JF looked like he'd been struck by a boom from one of his boats. "And she may have killed my sister?"

"Very likely, my guess is she also high-jacked the boat and now she wants the software. I don't know why yet but I'm going to find out. Let's get back to the palazzo, I need a drink and I need to think this out a bit." She paused and gave JF a kiss. "JF, I do have to admit, you are a lot of fun to be around... murders, stolen high tech yachts, galas, bombs and who knows what else. The evening is still young."

The launch returned to the channel and headed toward the campanile at San Marcos. The three-quarter waxing moon cast a brilliant light over the calm lagoon. The wind caught Sharon's hair, piled high, held tight with a jeweled clasp, and tugged a few strands loose. JF wrapped his arm around her waist, his warmth felt wonderful against her body.

Fidor sat next to Gina, the bodyguards held on tight to the stainless rail that extended along the length of the open cabin.

The powerful engine pushed the boat toward the Grand Canal; its roar covered all conversation.

Suddenly, the boat carved hard to starboard, Sharon grabbed the rail and looked a Vitorio, he was grabbing his right bicep, the windscreen was shattered and blood ran between his fingers. She looked behind them, another boat, modern, low and wide, was gaining on them quickly.

"JF, I don't think she wants to wait until midnight. Everyone, get down on the deck. Fidor, get your men down."

She was a half-second too late, the larger of the two spun around, taking a round in the shoulder. His partner had already pulled his Gloch but he had to catch the man at the same time as he tumbled to the deck.

"Shit," Sharon said as she grabbed the wheel from Vitorio, she saw that the wound was a lucky nick, an inch closer and the bone in his arm would have shattered. "Vitorio, sit up. JF, help me get him down." As if to emphasize the point, a chunk of the windscreen frame exploded. She spun the wheel and turned hard up the Grand Canal. The trailing speedboat followed. More shots rang out; to her ear, it was the uncomfortable and recognizable barking of an AK-47. "Shit," was all she could add.

They raced past the Guggenheim; Sharon caught a flash of yellow confection, illuminated by a camera flash on the quay. *Still a silly dress*, flashed through her head. Another slug from the AK-47 slammed into the console, Vitorio's repair bill continued to climb. They flew past JF's rented palazzo, the Rialto Bridge, brightly lit with floodlights, crossed the canal a quarter mile dead straight ahead, its half arc *bocca* waited. Flashes, like silent gunfire from tourist's cameras along the stone docks, illuminated the way. The hostile boat inched closer; even in the confining canal, they both increased their speed. Sharon flashed on a sign stuck to a barber pole, 15km and the international symbol for NO WAKE, in bold letters, she looked at the speedometer as it bounced off thirty, the needle would stop at forty-five. Gondolas spread before them like targets at a shooting range; all she could say was, "Fuck!"

The Rialto Bridge swallowed them whole, their wakes washed over the quay and soaked tourists' Reeboks and Nikes up to their knees. One gondola, waiting to enter, came within two degrees of rolling over, thankfully the ballast of the huge German woman's butt helped keep it upright.

They roared by the empty market with its barges tied side by side, an old man standing in the bow of one was almost knocked down by the surge; he raised his arm in an Italian salute. He hit the deck when the next burst of automatic fire came from the pursuer; another boat chunk, this one inches from Sharon's right hand, disappeared. She felt the pistol under her dress, "A lot of good this will do. What I could use is an RPG and someone to steer this damn boat," she said.

"What?" JF yelled again.

"Nothing, I'm just asking for a goddamn miracle."

It arrived out of the corner of her eye. She spotted a familiar boat slowly cruising along the wharf, one hundred yards ahead of her; it was the launch from the Santa Maria della Salute, the one she saw earlier in the day. She studied the powerboat as they zoomed past it and gave a sigh of relief. As she hoped, it almost leapt from the water in pursuit of them.

"What are you smiling about," JF screamed.

"The cavalry has arrived," she answered, tilting her head over her shoulder. To the right, she also spotted the secondary canal opening they had gone through yesterday. She spun the wheel hard to starboard and aimed the bow at the dark slit between the buildings; she also prayed that there wasn't a gondola or garbage barge trying to enter the Grand Canal on the other side. As the boat dug into the water with its turn, she heard the unmistakable voice of an M4 arguing with the AK-47. From the sound of it, it was a two or three to one conversation and the Colt M4 was winning. She also saw the hostile turn to follow her.

"God damn it, give it up!" she shouted. The response was a splinter of mahogany from a bit of the rail as it exploded. She caught Gina staring at her, the look was one of fear and amazement, Sharon smiled and saluted her with two fingers from the top of her forehead. They rushed into the narrow canal; she thought she could feel both walls at the same time, they echoed like a diesel truck was racing through an alley at sixty-miles an hour. In two seconds, they flew under the Strada Nuova Bridge.

"Turn left, next canal, slow down," she heard in her left ear. Vitorio's luscious accent made it sound like a divine order from Rome. She cut left and throttled down, all she saw were boats, barges and gondolas.

"What the hell?"

"It's okay, it's my street, just you wait," he said as he waved his cell phone.

Magically, as they slid further into the canal, the other boats started to move. As the hostiles turned into the canal, all they could do was slow down, hard. First their launch slammed into a barge, bounced off its gunnel and then rammed into the wall of the canal, jamming its bow between a small skiff and the stone. Instantly, a man leaped out and started to run along the narrow quay, heading straight for Sharon. They were stuck; a barge blocked the whole canal ahead of them.

"Shit, it's the man from last night," she yelled at JF, seeing the man start toward them.

"What man?"

"The man I dumped in the canal," she answered. By this time, the Iranian was only a hundred feet away, he held a pistol in his right hand; it glinted in the overhead lamps.

"Which canal?"

"I don't know its damn name. JF, that son-of-a-bitch is going to kill us, so who the hell cares." Still fuming at JF, she reached down between her legs, pulled up the elegant gown, extracted the pistol, slid a round into the chamber and clicked off the safety. While holding up the hem of her dress, she leaped onto the quay. The man was fifty feet away; he started to raise the pistol.

Sharon dropped to one knee, swung the pistol up with two hands and fired three times. The first and second shots caught the man in each thigh, the third busted his right shoulder; his pistol flew in a high tumbling arc into the canal. He collapsed on his face.

She looked toward the end of the canal where the third boat in their parade had stopped. One of the rescue crew had just thrown a line around one of the tall striped barber poles; she watched another man jump from the boat to the quay and start toward her. He carried his M4 as only an experienced soldier would but he was still too far away. She couldn't identify him. The remaining Russian bodyguard jumped onto the quay and raised his pistol.

"No," she yelled at the man. "Nyet, he's a friend, I hope."

13d

Sharon remembered her last day in Iraq, her "Released from hell party," she called it. She'd thought that she would never leave Iraq alive, standing in the security mess in the Green Zone with more than a hundred of her comrades; she realized she could be wrong now and then.

"Sharon, we'll all miss you," Major Simpson had said, holding up a glass of Jim Beam, "and so will this man's army. In two days, you'll kiss American soil; give it a big smack for all of us."

A cheer rose from the men and women. She took a slug from the bottle of Johnny Walker Red, it t hadn't left her hand for the last two hours. She raised the bottle in the air, acknowledging their recognition.

"I can't believe that I'm leaving and all of you have to stay," she started. "But as we all know in this man's army, our lives aren't our own and, with your permission, I'll correct you Major because, as you've found out, we gals can kick al-Qaeda's ass as well as the next man." She heard a few affirmatives from the twenty female soldiers and she smiled. A lot had changed during the three years she had been in and out of Iraq. But the one grounding reality was her people; they were stronger and better. "Thanks for all this and Major, thank you for your leadership and support. Without it, a lot of us wouldn't be here. Here's to Major Simpson." She raised the bottle, another cheer rose from the ranks.

"I'm not good at goodbyes, been too many in my life. You are all a great bunch of soldiers and my friends. Someone asked me what I was going to do after the army. I haven't a fucking clue. Let me ask you, who'd hire a thirty-something broad whose skills run from rounding up drunks to policing exploded cars?"

"I would," a male voice said from the middle of the crowd.

"Thanks for that, leave your number at the door. We'll talk," laughter rolled around the room. "Seriously, I am going to miss you all, my friends are stuck here in this God forsaken land. This is the life we've chosen but it comes to an end for all of us one day. Unlike many, I'm lucky, I get to choose when. To all of us I say, HOOAH!"

* * * *

The cry sounded three times from the men and women; now, seven years later, it still echoed in her head as she stood on the stone pavement watching the man march toward her. Sharon couldn't mistake the grey hair, more silver than the last time she had seen him, but she couldn't mistake the walk and the swagger; his black skin contrasted with the white polo he wore. She heard the cheer from her team each time Major Simpson took a step closer. She looked past the Major to his boat and the hostiles. Three men in civilian clothes, all obviously military by their actions and bearing, stood over the three people in the boat. Sirens could be heard from all directions, the building canyons and canals made it almost impossible to tell where they were coming from. The man on the ground moaned.

"Lie still, you asshole, or you'll bleed to death. Not that I care. I asked you before, now I'm asking you again, who sent you? In about thirty seconds, a man will arrive who will make sure you never see Iran again." Hearing that, his eyes flared. "I was right, Iranian. Well I'm going to guess there are a few of your countrymen in Gitmo, so you won't be lonely. Now, who sent you? Was it Karg?" Again his eyes gave him away. "Shit, all this over some stupid code."

The man spit at her, blood continued to ooze from the flesh wounds she had intentionally inflicted. He was much better alive than dead. "You Americans think you own everything, you don't, not anymore. You'll see. We will show you our power and that of Allah." With his good hand, he reached inside his jacket, and pulled out a small black ball, *"Allahu Akbar,"* the man screamed.

The man tried to pull the pin to arm the grenade but it was almost impossible one handed and then he tried to pull it out with his mouth. Instinctively, Sharon kicked his hand with her right satin shoe, sending the grenade into the canal. Unfortunately, the ring had caught on the man's little finger, the armed grenade sank to about five feet before exploding; water covered everyone, soaking the boat, JF, Fidor and Gina, Vitorio, the bodyguards, Sharon and her wonderful dress. Joanne would be very pissed.

The Major stood over the Iranian and looked at Sharon. "Nice kick, Lieutenant, three points."

"No field goal, too low," Sharon answered staring at the man. "What the hell are you doing here? I thought that boat was something more than just some white guys touring Venice, so why are you here?"

"No time," the Major answered. "You get your people out of here right now or you'll be spending a lot more time in Venice and you won't be strolling the canals. The Italians aren't partial to American interference, that's what you've gotten yourself into, a hornet's nest. Get out now, Vitorio will hide the boat; it will be repaired as if nothing ever happened. You have no more than two minutes at best, Go, go now!"

She knew a direct order when she heard it and leaped into the boat. She looked at Vitorio, who had a huge smile on his still pained face. The barge ahead magically slid out of their way, he hit the throttle and moved the boat forward. She started to take in the condition of the occupants: Vitorio would be okay, really just a scratch, the injured bodyguard was being attended to by his partner, JF and Fidor were talking or at least it looked like the Russian was doing most of the talking, Gina had a big smile on her face, even though her makeup was dripping all over her ample chest and her dress. She stood and walked unsteadily toward Sharon, holding onto the busted railing.

"Wow, so this is what you do for a living," Gina said, wrapping her arm around her friend, forcibly lowering Sharon's right hand, the one that held the Beretta. "Don't think you'll need that for now, besides, the police might take a dim view of a formally dressed broad in classy jewelry absentmindedly pointing a gun at them."

The adrenalin rush was easing; Sharon sat the pistol on the console and took a deep breath. She turned to Vitorio, "We need to talk."

"Scusate la mia mancanza, io non parlo inglese."

"Vitorio, I know damn well that you speak English so cut it out. Who the hell are you?"

Vitoria continued to weave the launch in and out of moored boats and tied up gondolas. As they made a turn, a small police cruiser flew by, its lights flashing. Vitorio waved as if nothing was amiss.

"I'm waiting."

When they made another turn, suddenly finding themselves in the Grand Canal, he said, "Sergeant Vitorio Ambrosia at your service, I work for the big man."

"Special Forces?"

Gina looked at Vitorio, "No accent, none."

"My grandparents are from here; they survived the war, went to LA and raised a family. My folks made sure all the kids went back and forth to Venice almost every year. So I'm sort of your tour guide and your protector. Kind of like Special Forces Chauffer Services, but different. Mr. Voss and the others don't know, so let's keep it that way. Okay?"

"What's going on?"

"Can't say ma'am, you know the drill. But my job is to get you back to the palazzo and keep an eye on the four of you, and that's not an unpleasant duty," Vitorio said looking at the very damp Gina Cavelli. She blushed; the damp dress put her in the running for the grand prize at a wet tee shirt contest, assuming five thousand dollar dresses were required.

Max and Joanne were running down the dock as they pulled up, towels in hand as the six climbed onto the mooring. Joanne wrapped a towel over Sharon and Gina. "You gentlemen will have to fend for yourselves. Max, see what you can do help Mr. Balanca's assistants. I must get these dresses to the cleaners before they are ruined." She hurried the girls up the steps and out of sight. Sharon turned and watched Vitorio ease the boat from the dock and accelerate. He waved at her as he slid behind a large ferry.

"How did you know?" Sharon asked when they settled in her room and stripped off their wet gowns.

"I heard gunfire; I ran to the window and saw you race by driving the boat, even in the dark that dress stood out; that was not a good sign, especially with gunfire erupting from the launch following you. How did you get away?"

Sharon looked at Gina. Gina said, "Luck. Sharon turned into a canal and weaved around some boats .The chaser got stuck behind a barge or something; it was too dark for them to find us. When we found the main canal, a police boat roared by, it was so close it threw spay over all of us. It's crazy out there."

Whether or not Joanne believed her didn't matter, she dropped the questioning and while the girls took showers, she laid out comfortable clothes for the late evening. Max knocked and asked if everything was okay, Joanne said yes, they would be down in a few minutes.

"While you were in the bathroom, I took the liberty of attending to the Beretta," Joanne said. "It seems to be missing three bullets. Might I inquire as to where you lost them?"

Sharon thought for a long moment then said, "We were chased by some bad guys; let's just say they won't be chasing us anymore."

"Well done. I pegged you for a fighter, not a lover. Lovers get killed."

"So do fighters," Gina said walking into the room.

"That's true my dear but at least they put up a fight," Joanne said as she collected the gowns and jewelry. Ten minutes later, Sharon and Gina joined the men in the library. They were drinking brandy.

"Is there anything stronger, Max?"

"I have some wonderful single malts; some are thirty or forty years old," Max answered.

"I'm going to put it on ice."

"Then I have a full bottle of Johnny Walker Black Label, hot or cold makes no difference to that malt."

"Perfect, make mine a triple."

"Stoli on the rocks, I don't believe that ice will hurt that," Gina said.

"Nothing can destroy that stuff, that's why it's the king of frou-frou drinks," Max said dropping ice in a crystal tumbler.

"I heard that Max," Fidor said. "There are other vodkas that are far better but I know I can get a glass of this anywhere."

The girls sat in the huge leather chairs that flanked the oriental carpet; they both wore full slacks and crisp blouses that Joanne had scrounged. Even Sharon had to admit they looked pretty good for a couple of girls fresh from a gun fight at the Venetian corral. Max quietly slipped from the room.

"You look wonderful, no worse for wear," JF said as he slipped into the narrow space left in Sharon's chair. "Who were those men? Were they after the software?"

"Yes, I'm sure that's what they were after. Karg came up to me at the ball and demanded something; I didn't know what she was talking about. Now I do, they didn't get it from Stroud because he no longer had it. Whoever has it now is anybody's guess."

"Who were the men in the second boat? They looked like professionals. From where I was standing on the boat, you acted like you knew the black fellow," JF said.

"I do, he and I fought in Iraq. I don't know why he's here, I really don't. But I'll tell you, if I'm ever in trouble he would be the first person I'd call."

"I can understand that, he looked like the type who's always in control," JF said. "How's that cut on your arm?"

"It's fine; Joanne put a Band-Aid on it, the bleeding stopped long ago."

Jean-François took her arm, gently inspected her wound, then kissed softly. "Better?"

"Much."

"If you don't mind," Gina said looking at Sharon. "You have tuckered out this Italian lass, I'm off to bed. We have a busy day tomorrow."

"The plane for Paris leaves at 1:00 PM, Claudette will pick us up when we land. Be packed," Sharon said.

"Yes, Lieutenant," Gina said mockingly, she saluted. "I'm taking the bottle, good night all."

For the next five minutes, Fidor acted like the proverbial fifth wheel, till he finally excused himself, he grabbed the ice bucket as he walked past the bar.

"You should take something to drink if you take the ice bucket, Fidor, my friend. It's tastes so much better that way," JF said, needling the man.

Sharon was a little surprised when Fidor blushed; his white Russian cheeks flushed pink. Mumbling something, he slipped out the door as well.

"Thought they would never leave," Sharon said. "Fidor is single, isn't he?"

"Yes, I heard what you said last night; he will be kind and gentle."

"It's not Gina I'm concerned about, it's Fidor. She may be a little more than he can handle."

"That is something for him to find out, he's a big boy," JF said.

"What does he do?"

"He is an investment manager. He is connected to a dozen very successful businessmen, he handles much of their investments and he has their absolute confidence."

"Hard to find that in Russia," Sharon said.

"Very true but he also realizes that if he screws any one of them, he's dead, such is life as an investment manager in Russia."

"It's a hard world."

"Too hard but it's the life he's chosen. We all choose our lives to live. Some are handed a kick start, others fight for it. My sister and I were fortunate but all my money won't bring back Catherine. I still miss her; she would have liked you a lot. She was a lot like you, someone who takes charge and pushes through the problem. Like tonight at the canal, no discussion, no debate, no hesitation. He would have killed us if you didn't stop him."

"Maybe, but I wasn't going to let him have the chance. That's why I wounded him, I needed answers."

"Did you get them?"

"Some but not enough and now I have more questions and I don't know who has the answers. I'll find them; they've pissed me off. And I'm getting closer to the reason why your sister was killed, much closer."

"Did that black fellow have anything to do with some of the answers?"

"Yes, I think so. He was always in the thick of things. In Iraq, we spent a lot of time together; he was and still is one hell of a soldier."

"Together, as in romantically?"

Sharon looked at JF, there was a touch of jealousy in the question; she was flattered.

"No, one soldier to another, major to lieutenant, friend to friend."

JF stood, took Sharon by the hand and pulled her up to him. He placed his hands on each side of her face and slowly kissed her. As much as she wanted to fight him, she felt herself melting; his gentleness washed away the adrenaline, the blood, the smell of cordite. All that was left was a soul that needed filling. They climbed the ornate stairs hand in hand. At his door, she felt that she wanted to turn, to leave, to run. He kissed her again; her thoughts of escape fled.

"Don't be gentle, it's been a very long time,' Sharon whispered in his ear. He closed the door to his room and slowly unbuttoned her blouse.

Chapter 14

14a.

Claudette waved to the girls from the small red Peugeot.

"Bonjour Claudette, you remember Gina?"

"I couldn't forget her, especially after that long weekend in New York. *Tres, tres, rigolade,*" Claudette said kissing the girls on both cheeks. "Traffic is starting to build, even if we are going into Paris so *vite, vite.*"

Like her previous ride into Paris with Claudette so many, many months ago, Sharon took the rear seat and gave up the front to Gina who was a lot more comfortable than Kevin Bryan was after he folded his six-foot-six inch frame into the tiny car last time they were in France. Within forty minutes, they arrived at Alain Dumont's house in the 7th arrondissement. Unlike the last two times she had stayed at this apartment, while suffering from jet lag; she and Gina were awake and ready to explore.

"A simple request, a glass of Chablis at Les Deux Magots," Gina said.

"Done, it's a short walk, I'll tell you about tomorrow then," Claudette said as they strolled through one of the more delightful neighborhoods on the Left Bank. Small shops and stores lined the narrow streets, a restaurant or café sat on each corner and tourists filled the streets to overflowing. If Venice has her canals, Paris has her streets. Great trees lined Saint-Germain-des-Près and the small plaza, across from the restaurant made famous by Hemingway and the lost generation, was full of the usual students and tourists.

They were lucky; four Chinese tourists were just getting up to leave as they reached the tables and chairs that spilled chaotically across the broad sidewalk in front of the restaurant. The ubiquitous Parisian plastic cane chairs were squeezed and twisted amongst a tangled mess of bags and backpacks. For some, this was the fulfillment of a lifetime dream, just to sit at this restaurant, none gave quarter. Others were busy checking it off their bucket list. Sharon ordered a glass of burgundy, Gina, her Chablis.

Claudette sipped her coffee and said, "I have to work tonight, a client expects his software the day after tomorrow and grand-père would not approve of me getting it to the client late; even due to his own memorial service. Sharon, I miss him so much."

"So do I," Sharon said.

"Tomorrow is simple. The government has taken control of the whole ceremony. You two, Evelyn and I will be with a small group of his friends who will essentially be observing. After a brief introduction and a few short speeches, the president will say a few words…"

"The president of France," Gina interrupted.

"Yes," Claudette continued. "He never misses a chance to be photographed and this is a very uncontroversial opportunity. Unlike a state funeral or something similar, this will go quickly. It's more fuss than grand-père would have permitted but he didn't have much to say about it, other than his request to be buried near Jim Morrison at Père Lachaise Cemetery. He said Morrison was not just a wreck but an insanely creative wreck. He told me that he went to three of the Doors concerts in Los Angeles in the late 1960s, grand-père was in his fifties then and Morrison was maybe twenty-five."

"Evelyn, is she here?" Sharon asked.

"No. She has meetings with her family in Florence; she will fly in and out tomorrow. Then she heads back to the states next week, they are sorting out their spring line for next year, we are updating their software. She's added three new stores, Beijing, Rio, and Sydney. Their leather goods are in demand everywhere and she tells me they are raising the prices."

"My car's not worth as much as one of her handbags," Gina said.

"I've been in your car, you'd be lucky if it was stolen for the gas in the tank," Sharon said with a smile.

"That may be true but it's paid for and the thought of a loan for a purse is counter-intuitive. So we have the evening to ourselves?" Gina inquired.

"Yes, a car will pick you up at the apartment at 11:00, the service is at noon, then I'm buying the four of us lunch at Le Bristol. After that, you are on your own and I'm back to work. And regrettably, I have to send a car to take you to the airport, it seems work is like Paris, when it rains its pours." As if cued, the thick afternoon clouds burst into a heavy late summer Parisian deluge.

The evening was not as late as the girls hoped for. The events and chaos of Venice caught up to them and even though Gina begged to stay up to walk the streets till dawn, by midnight they were exhausted, both mentally and physically. When Sharon walked into the kitchen the next morning, she found Gina ready with a tray of Parisian pastries and cups of rich thick coffee.

"You're up early," Sharon said taking a bite.

"Slept some but told myself I'll sleep on the plane when we go home. So I walked around this morning and watched the street cleaners and the bakeries open. Those just came out of the oven. This city is so fresh and clean, I've always wondered what it would have been like a hundred years ago."

"Absolutely awful," Sharon said. "There were a million horses in this town, they washed everything into the Seine and poverty was rife. Sometimes the good old days weren't so good."

"Spoilsport. You take out all the romance; speaking of which, what did you and JF do after I left. Me, I went straight to bed."

Sharon looked at her friend and raised an eyebrow.

Gina blushed, "Well I did. And he was the perfect gentleman. Don't know about those Russians but they do have a fire burning deep in their souls. He told me he would call before he comes to California which may be late this fall; we made kind of a date. Did you sleep well?"

Now it was Sharon's turn, she coyly bit into another croissant and sipped her coffee.

"Sharon O'Mara, you didn't," Gina exclaimed. "You didn't bed that Frenchman, did you?" There was a pause; Gina did not relent. "And you call me a wench."

"If you tell a soul, I'll kill you and they will never find your body."

"Was he good? Was he like Frenchmen are supposed to be, he had big shoes you know, tell me everything."

"No. And I mean it, you will never be found."

"Please, just a taste, this is like a solar eclipse, for you having sex is so rare."

"How would you know that?"

"I'm a bartender and a psychic, it comes with the liquor license. I can instantly tell when someone has had sex. And you, my comely lass, have not imbibed for many, many years, this I know."

Sharon's smile grew into nasty grin.

"I knew it, I knew it. Sharon O'Mara has a boyfriend."

"I'll give you some of that but he is a friend and, sadly, a client. We both needed each other. It was a long day; getting shot at and then shooting back does get the blood flowing."

"It certainly did in Fidor's case," Gina said.

"It isn't always about you, Gina Cavelli," Sharon said, the grin still evident.

"Well I can and will keep a secret, rule six or seven of the bartender's code. Are you happy?"

"Now that's a question that I've asked myself a lot recently, not sure. But right now, life is better than it's been in a long time. A few more clients and a dollar or two more in the bank and we'll see. Basil always needs his bones and mom always needs her friends."

With that, she kissed Gina on the cheek, squeezed her hand and headed off for a shower.

The speeches, even for the French, were over the top. Alain would have been embarrassed. Not one politician, of the hundred or so who stood in the rain in the cemetery, had been born when Alain Dumont, in the late summer of 1945, drove the re-painted Nazi SS truck with its half ton of gold and collection of Impressionist paintings into the garage of the apartment where Sharon and Gina were staying. That grubstake, a fake French identification and passport, and a burning desire to succeed began a life that changed the kid from Pennsylvania named Robert Dupont into Alain Dumont, billionaire, financier, high tech investor and now, food for worms. As he had said, "No one gets out alive." Evelyn Lucca, Alain's goddaughter, stood close to Sharon under her umbrella; she had recommended Sharon to help Dumont return four of those paintings that arrived with Dumont in Paris soon after the war. Two Pissarro's, a Monet, and a Toulouse-Lautrec were eventually returned to the grand-children of the original Jewish owners and Sharon, while doing so, also foiled an attempt by an old Nazi to resurrect the Third Reich and retake the world.

Stick ad for Toulouse For Death Here

Lunch, as one must expect in Paris, was wonderful; Sharon was amazed, they could take a simple chicken and turn it into a miracle. The herbs, the sauce and the small stack of sliced po-tatoes just melted in her mouth. Claudette ordered a Sancerre from the private cellar that Le Bristol kept. It was a bottle from Alain Dumont's own vineyard along the Loire.

"This is the last bottle Alain made, it's only fitting for today," Claudette said. "They have asked for more but it is the last, the owners were very disappointed. I still have a number of cases of his reds but this, my dears, is the last of his Sancerre. All the vintages will have been made by others; this was the last to be bottled with his own hands." She paused a moment to gather her thoughts, "To my grandfather, Alain Dumont, the last soldier left standing. May he now rest in peace."

The girls all stood and raised their glasses, even the noisy restaurant quieted. The four women, all smartly dressed even after standing in the rain, commanded the attention of the pa-trons and the staff.

"*S'il vous plaît partagez notre toast à mon grand-père, au revoir*

Alain Dumont, bon voyage," Claudette said.

Bon voyage and *a votre santé,* echoed through the room, for a moment each patron thought of their own mortal frailty and then quickly ordered another drink. Their lives were not going to end today.

"Salute," Evelyn said as she sat.

"What happened in Venice?" Claudette asked innocently.

"You have to go back to work," Sharon answered.

"I can take some time out, what happened?"

An hour later and two bottles of Sancerre from the vineyard next to Alain's, Evelyn and Claudette sat stunned. Claudette patted Gina's hand, "Are you okay?"

"If it weren't for the almost dying from a stray bullet part, racing down the Grand Canal at forty miles an hour is was *spettacolare.* Sharon kept us safe; she's very cool under fire, you know."

"Don't we know it," Evelyn and Claudette said in unison.

"So the memory stick is gone," Sharon said. "But I don't think Karg has it, that's why she was so upset and she sent the Iranians after us. She was so sure I had it. Claudette, you were the engineering part of the code, Mike says that the genius was being able to blend the parts into a dynamic whole. Yet each part, on its own, is almost worthless. Is that true?"

Claudette thought for a moment. "When Catherine asked me to assemble my particular piece of the code, she told me it dealt with turning switches on and off. I didn't know what kind of switches but they were either on or off, I assumed it was for her boat. She said the other pieces would tell my code when and for how long. To make the boat work the way she wanted it to, you would include wind speed, anticipating changes in the wind, temperature, the tightness of the sails and everything from the height of the waves to the weight of the boat and the number of passengers. It's complicated but, then again, it's easier than flying an airplane by computer. The wrong result won't kill you."

"It killed Catherine," Sharon said.

"I thought it was an accident."

"No, someone has stolen the boat and wants the computer code to make it sail, there are at least two dead, we were almost killed and I still don't know why. It's just a boat, a Goddamn toy."

14b

Sharon had to admit she was exhausted. Someday, she told herself, she would take a vacation that was relaxing. These four and five day trips to Europe to get shot at were, almost literally, killing her. She looked at Gina in the first-class seat next to her and true to her word, she was asleep. She swirled the ice in the tumbler and thought about the last few days. A lot had changed, she knew the how and the when and the who; but what was really bugging her was the why; the most elusive part of an investigation was always the why, the motive.

"Wake up," Gina said, shaking Sharon's arm. "Five minutes and we're home."

Sharon shook her head clear, merciful sleep hit somewhere over Canada. The steward handed her a glass of ice water and a warm towel. It's always the little things that make travel better and first-class is always better.

Timing and schedules had been confirmed. Sharon had texted Kevin Bryan that they were on their way, he would confirm arrival times. He left a text to call him; he would be waiting at the cell phone lot. They grabbed their bags and after the obligatory feeling of being treated like a Pakistani immigrant going through customs, they walked through the sliding doors of the International Terminal into the cool fog rolling over the San Bruno Mountains and blowing through the San Francisco airport. A very tall good-looking guy leaned against a beige non-descript sedan.

"So you couldn't get the limousine," Sharon said to Kevin. "Are you on duty?"

"Double duty," Kevin said as he loaded their bags in the trunk. "The captain had me drop some things off at SFPD on the way, so from delivery boy to chauffer. Your ride, ladies."

Gina kissed Kevin on the cheek and climbed into the back, Sharon took shotgun.

"How's my boy?"

"Basil's just fine," Kevin said. "Somehow that dog knows when you're on your way home. For the last three days, all he did was lay about; this morning he was up and anxious, maybe what they say about dogs and being psychic is true."

"Wouldn't doubt it, someone has to take care of us humans and dogs have been doing just that for a long time," Sharon answered as she wistfully looked across the bay.

"I hadn't heard from you, so I assume the trip was uneventful."

There was a long pause, neither girl said anything.

"I also assume, from that loud silence, that I'm wrong. You know I'm a trained investigator, I can spot these things."

"Do you really want to know what happened?"

"Fire away; you're both alive so it couldn't have been too serious."

The late afternoon commute traffic was jammed at all the usual places. First, the backup over the Bay Bridge added thirty minutes, then the line at the Caldecott Tunnel added thirty more as it snaked up the hill from Oakland. Gina and Sharon needed the whole hour to tell Kevin everything, or at least almost everything. Girls have to have their secrets.

"Good God, a speedboat race through Venice, how cliché, I would have loved to have been there except for the getting all dressed up part."

"How did your trials go or are they still on?" Sharon asked.

"During one, the man plead out after the jury was selected, they scared the hell out of him, so at least he won't bother kids for a long time. The other is still ongoing. Maybe a week tops, that family is a piece of work. It was worth staying just for that. The jury is hearing the prosecution's case today, I testified yesterday so I should be done but I need to stay close."

"Gina," Kevin asked as they neared Lafayette. "Where?'

"I guess the bar; it's still early but I want to make sure it's still standing and that my staff hasn't stolen everything and run off to Mexico. I can get a ride home from Bobby."

"It was still there last night when Santinni and I stopped by for a nightcap, that new manager is cute."

"You stay away from her, Kevin Bryan; she has enough troubles without you adding to them."

"Me? What did I do? Besides, Santinni is the one who's really interested."

"Damn, that's even worse. Since his divorce, that man's become insufferable."

"Since?" Sharon added.

"He's okay, a little full of himself to be sure, but he's a good cop," Kevin said. "I'd take him as backup any day."

"You two stay away from Bobby, it took me a long time to find a manager I could trust; she's got the experience and the smarts. If either of you mess that up, I will ban you from every bar in the county and you know I have that power."

Kevin looked in the rear view mirror and smiled, "Yes, ma'am."

Standing in front of Geno's, Gina gave Sharon a hug and a kiss on both cheeks, "I'm beginning to like this European kissing thing and it's so civilized. Goodnight Kevin, and Sharon, my dear, you really know how to show a girl a good time."

Basil almost exploded into the back seat when they stopped at Kevin's house; he was all over his mistress, sniffing the seats, the back of her head, everywhere. His tail tried to rearrange the knobs on the dashboard.

"Calm down now," Sharon ordered.

It was like trying to tie down a four-year-old on a sugar high.

Basil led the way to the door of her bungalow; Sharon threw her bag inside and turned back toward her best friend.

"No mail piled on the floor, Post Office on strike?"

"I collected it. Damn, I forgot, it's at home in a bag. Want me to bring it back over?"

"No, not tonight, couldn't be anything that can't wait. Anyway, thanks for the ride."

"No problemo. You okay? You seem a little distant."

"Jet lag and I'm tired. It was a long string of days, reminded me of our three-day Paris adventure."

"Now, that was a trip! But then again, from what I heard, you and Gina may have one-upped it."

"Not my intent."

"Anything else?"

"I don't know yet, too many things in the air. I'm just exhausted. Gina wants me to stop by tomorrow evening. She had a great time, not what she expected but it was good for her."

"And for you?"

"Not sure so good night, Kevin Bryan." She kissed him on the cheek. "See you tomorrow." She ran the tips of her fingers softly across his face, turned around and went back into her cottage.

14c

The next morning, Sharon did something she rarely ever did, she slept in. She took Basil out for a quick backyard visit, then crawled back into bed and promptly fell back to sleep. After twelve hours, even she had to admit it was far too decadent to stay in bed any longer. There was nothing on her calendar; she had no appointments, nothing. She could not remember the last time she had a day with no commitments. She made coffee and found some frozen bread; it made her dream of croissants and Italian pastries. Peanut butter covered the marginally acceptable slices of toast. She was starved. Basil almost swallowed his bowl with his kibble, "Doesn't that man feed you when you're there?" she asked.

Basil stared up at her, then at the bowl, then back up to her, she dumped in another cup of food; it disappeared faster than she could pour. "It's good to be home."

A long shower, allowing her to finally wash her hair with clean California water, made a huge difference in her attitude. She brushed out her red hair, rubbed body lotion all over her skin and did some of the other usual feminine things that women do. The few days she spent in the Italian sun had warmed her tan; the Parisian rain did little to change it. Jeans and a striped top finished the upstairs, orange sneakers set the foundation.

She spent the next few hours running errands, restocking the larder, picking up dog food and bones and, on a whim, buying three huge bundles of roses. She used them to fill a large blue vase that sat on the small table in the center of the living room. The room just exploded with color. She loved art; small amateur paintings that she had bought over the years filled the walls. Many were reproductions, especially the copies of the ones she returned for Alain, she didn't mind, they were all good memories.

She spent some time making a fresh marinara sauce with Roma tomatoes and all the usual fixings, the house was perfumed with garlic and Italy. No one called to wreck her afternoon reverie. At six, she loaded Basil into the Jaguar and headed to Lafayette and Geno's. It was turning out to be one of those rare perfect days.

An empty parking space sat directly in front of Geno's; Sharon could only remember one or two times when she didn't have to walk a block or two, perfect. Basil bolted from the car and disappeared through the open door of the bar. She followed his lead.

The contrast, from the bright light of the early evening, made the interior look absolutely black. She heard Gina telling Basil to get down and laughter and jokes that started with "a dog walked into a bar." Only one man would be saying that and she wanted to know why he was here on her perfect day.

"Santinni, what the hell are you doing here?" Sharon asked one of the men sitting at the bar. "Everything was going so well today. Now you show up."

"I was here first, O'Mara, and besides, I was invited by this fellow Mick of yours," Tony Santinni said. "He invited me for a drink and thank you for that, Kevin. Gina has been regaling us with your adventures in Venice. Damn, if you did half of what she said, I would still be impressed. Sixty miles per hour down the Grand Canal."

"It was only forty," Sharon said correcting him. "I tried to go faster and I had the throttle wide open, the bullets flying by made it seem faster."

A crystal tumbler slid across the bar, stopping exactly in front of Sharon, she smiled at Gina, "Thanks."

Gina smiled back, "No, thank you, you wench."

Sharon cocked her head and started to ask a question.

"No and never," Gina said as she turned back to the bar and started to pull glasses from the dishwasher. Basil suddenly appeared on Gina's side of the bar, his huge paws directly across from Kevin like he was ready to take his order. Kevin scratched his head; the dog looked at Sharon and harrumphed, then disappeared.

"Civvies, Tony? Don't think I've ever seen you in civvies," Sharon said. "You are always in uniform."

"Got a date and Kevin is helping me to get the courage up," Santinni answered.

"A date, who the hell would date you? You're not raiding the senior center again, are you?"

"Very funny, O'Mara. No, in fact, she works in San Francisco and lives out here. Her husband disappeared a year ago with two million in funds from a small brokerage here in town. That's how I met her. Her divorce was just last month. So she's single, lives in a nice house and has no kids."

"You hit the lottery," Sharon said.

"You two cut it out, if you took the time you might actually get to like each other," Kevin said.

"Next time it snows," Sharon said, still pissed that her perfect day had been wrecked.

She pulled a stool over to Kevin.

"Sorry about Alain," Kevin said. "He was a great guy, not many of us get to leave a legacy like his."

"Thanks," Sharon said. "I'll miss him. By the way, Claudette and Evelyn say hi, we had lunch with them after the service, they are both doing great. Claudette says that you just have to come to Paris, this time, alone."

"Yes, you do a have way of cramping peoples' style. Anything more on the missing boat?"

"More than the boat is missing; seems that the software that drives the onboard computers is also missing; it was on a memory stick. They murdered the man they thought had it; I saw the stick around his neck the day he was killed. Now they think I have it. But I don't, I haven't got a clue," Sharon said. She finally had the chance to really look at Kevin; he seemed tired; he turned the glass around in his hand nervously.

"Someone is trying to kill you?" Santinni said.

"Seems to be the case, that's what the boat chase was all about," she answered, still looking at Kevin. "They wanted what they thought I had. Claudette says the whole combined software program is somewhere on a computer or a laptop. She doesn't have it. Catherine Voss was the only one who knew where it was. Even her brother doesn't know. So the memory stick is the only copy of the complete program and it's missing."

Gina continued rearranging the glasses behind the bar while she listened. She also moved the old Louisville Slugger to make room for a bunch of mint leaves for the Mojito's she was famous for. The steam still rose from the open dishwasher and the mirror behind the bar started to fog over. It was getting dark out and the street light that hung over Sharon's car cast a soft light over the window glass painted with 'Geno's' on it. A man's shadow passed by the window quickly.

A second later, the bar door burst open almost breaking away from its hinges; a man, swarthy complexion, bearded, short military haircut stood at the door, the automatic pistol in his hand suggested that he was not here for one of Gina's Mojitos. Five seconds later, another man came through the back of the bar, past the restrooms and stood still, braced with an AK-47. He was a shorter facsimile of the first man.

The first man waved his pistol at O'Mara. "Everyone stay seated, do not move. I am only here to make sure that woman does not leave. No one else move." The accent was Middle Eastern; Sharon heard a hint of Farsi in the vowels, Iranians.

Sharon looked at Kevin and Santinni.

"They friends of yours?" the first thug asked.

"No, never seen them before, just sitting here when I came in."

"Her," the misogynist tone was unmistakable.

"She owns the joint; I came in for a drink. Why are you're following me? I saw you at least three times today, driving by my house twice. I have you on at least three different cameras. God damn, you guys are just incompetent." It was all a lie but they didn't know it.

The hinge on the door squeaked like a strangling rat.

"It's the best I could do on such short notice, O'Mara. Good help is so hard to find." The unmistakable Boer-accented voice of Eva Karg filled the bar. "Yes, competence is always an issue. I see that Jean-François chose wisely when he hired you. Ever since that night at the Compton, you have been a pain in my ass. So now, please hand over the memory stick and I will be leaving. My friends may stay for a drink but I have a plane to catch."

Karg took three paces toward the bar and then pulled a Gloch, she pointed it at Sharon.

"If you don't have the memory stick, what will your Iranian partners say then?" Sharon asked.

Karg tilted her head. "That is not your concern; all I care about is the stick. We were able to find Miss Voss's laptop, the one she used to combine the lines of code. But one of our clumsy technicians tripped a security trap and the whole drive wiped itself clean. That stick is all there is now so, Miss O'Mara, the stick."

"I realize that you are either dumb-as-a-brick or deaf, I haven't made up my mind. But please listen carefully, I DO NOT HAVE IT!. Mike Stroud didn't give it to me."

"You are a liar, he had it when he talked to you earlier that day, I saw you talking to him."

"Still no prize, nada."

Karg slowly move the Gloch from Sharon to Gina, its laser sight left a red pimple on Gina's forehead. "Now, the stick, where is it?" she screamed.

Sharon watched the red dot dance on Gina's face. "At my house," Sharon said, trying to buy a minute. "You were right, he gave it to me, it's at the house. You think I'd carry it around with me?"

"That's better, you and I are leaving. These boys will help me finish our conversion. I really don't want it to be repeated so they will try to entertain the patrons."

Sharon knew what that meant, before the boys could draw their weapons, they would be cut to pieces. The only alternative was a distraction or even something worse.

"Basil, STAND!" Sharon yelled.

"What?" Karg said, looking around.

"Basil, ATTACK!"

The huge Sheppard-Rottweiler appeared as if thrown from the gates of hell. The first Iranian thug barely had time to turn before the dog had him by the arm; Karg heard the sound of breaking bone almost as soon as she heard the man scream. The second man, stunned by the dog's surge forward, swung his weapon toward the bar. Both Bryan and Santinni had drawn their service weapons as soon as Sharon said attack; they fired at the same time. The man flew against the booth behind him, two slugs in his chest; his weapon stitched a line of bullets across the ceiling.

Karg screamed something in Afrikaans and swung her pistol toward the defenseless Sharon. She heard Gina scream "DUCK," she dropped like a stone to one knee, the Louisville Slugger just missed her head by two inches as it flew like a Sidewinder missile into the face of Eva Karg, splitting her nose and leaving a permanent groove across her forehead. She dropped, like the brick she was, to the bar floor, out cold.

"Basil, OFF, HEEL." The dog released the man's arm and went to his mistress, the man's pained whimpering forced Santinni to crack, "They just don't make terrorists as tough as they used to."

Chapter 15

15a

It was after midnight when Sharon and Basil returned home, Kevin followed to make sure they made it safely. The man with the broken arm was lucky, he lived. The other wasn't, both slugs blew out what might have been called his heart if he ever had one. Karg's face had swollen to the point where she couldn't see the ceiling over the hospital bed she was handcuffed to. The police were still trying to track down the identity of the two Iranians.

"I'm glad I got twelve hours sleep last night. Not sure I would have made it this far," Sharon said as she poured herself a drink. "I've used a lot of adrenaline this last week; it's taking a toll on me. But something's eating you, Kevin Bryan, what is it?" She offered Kevin a drink, he shook his head no.

"Again I have to save your bacon, this *is* getting old. Why don't you get a job at Macy's or something? The violence level is so much lower."

"Don't change the subject. And besides, I've done that, the bored to death level is much higher. Coffee then and then you can tell me?"

"No, I have a court date at nine tomorrow, that's going to happen regardless of whatever happened tonight. That judge is strict, can't mail in my testimony. Shit, just remembered. I have your mail in the trunk, wait a second."

Sharon watched Kevin walk to his nondescript sedan; Basil nudged her hip. "You're a good boy, thanks, you're my hero." She knelt down and rubbed him behind his ears, the tough old dog's eyes glazed over.

"Here you are," Kevin said, handing Sharon a brown Safeway bag, half full. She could tell after a peak, mostly junk.

"Thanks, and I mean it, we need to talk, something's going on," she said.

"Tomorrow after all this settles. Good night, sleep well."

She waited until he pulled away before closing the door and carrying the bag to the kitchen. She was right, mostly junk and catalogs, the gaudy stamps on a manila envelope caught her eye, the stamps said Italia. Basil nudged her again, "Okay, okay, I'll get you some food." She poured some kibble into Basil's dish. He sat looking at her. "You're not hungry either; we're both tired, how about bedtime?" Basil cocked his head toward the door, stood and took a challenging stance. He had been trained to never bark when he perceived a threat.

"What is it, someone at the door?" She slid the Beretta out of her handbag, chambered a round and clicked off the safety. She stood to one side near the door, the doorbell rang. *What terrorist would ring the damn bell?*

"All right, Kevin, what did you forget?" she said, swinging the door open, the Beretta at her side just in case.

Major Simpson was standing there in a crisp camouflage uniform; another uniformed man, younger and very handsome, stood behind him. "Good evening, Lieutenant, may I come in?"

15b

Stunned, Sharon could only say, "Yes, sir. Basil, sit."

The two soldiers walked into the hallway, only then did Sharon notice the major was now a full-bird colonel.

"Can I get you a drink or something?" Sharon's nervousness was apparent.

"Just relax, Lieutenant, coffee would be great. First though, I want you to meet someone. Sharon this is Lieutenant Abdul Rashid Salim."

The young man held out his hand, Sharon looked into his eyes and immediately hugged the boy until he said, "Stop, stop, you Americans show too much emotion, stop."

"I really don't give a damn; it's so good to finally see you again. Your letters don't come that often, I didn't even know you were in the army. Major, excuse me, I mean Colonel, congratulations, but why didn't you tell me?"

"He wanted to keep it a secret. After he went to live with Habib, you remember Corporal Habib, the translator?"

"Of course," she answered.

"Abdul took well to school and with a little help, he went to a small college in New Jersey. He's not the street urchin that walked into the Green Zone anymore."

"And not so dirty either; I thought he would be too young?"

"He lied about his age when he showed up, he was sixteen. He's twenty-three now and I have him working for me. Now how about that coffee?"

The men followed Sharon back to the kitchen; Basil sniffed and harrumphed the whole way.

"Handsome dog, I understand he was vital to the success of an incident that took place in a Lafayette bar tonight."

"You don't miss anything, yes, he's my savior and my best buddy. Basil, go lie down." The dog curled up on his bed, his eyes never left her.

They sat at the table in the small kitchen, the aroma of coffee helped to perk Sharon up. It had been a long week.

"A social visit at 1:00 AM in the morning is not normal so I assume that you have been watching the house, waiting for me to come home." She looked at Abdul, "Damn, you've grown into a handsome young man. I'll bet the girls just flock to you."

She could tell she had embarrassed him. "Some do, I admit," Abdul said sheepishly. "But I have learned to be patient, to be more aware of what's happening around me. And besides, I have been too busy for women; the Colonel has kept me very, very busy." He looked at the black man who nodded.

Sharon filled their cups. The Colonel took a sip, "Damn, I could always count on you to make the best coffee and as expected, you don't disappoint. Well, to the task at hand. I expect you are wondering why I'm here and I imagine you're wondering why the hell I suddenly appeared in a canal in Venice. By the way, the Lieutenant here was driving the boat; he's become quite adaptable to the many situations and tasks I've thrown at him."

Sharon looked at Abdul, still amazed at his transition from the punk street urchin who bargained with the army to get a seat on a plane to the United States. Persistence pays off.

"First of all let me say right up front, we have been monitoring your moves for the past few months, ever since Jean-François Voss requested your services. It was on my order that no one contact you directly. I wanted to make sure that whoever was involved hadn't any idea that the US government was interested in the accidental death of Catherine Voss. But we were interested; we have been interested for almost a year. Her boat was revolutionary, besides being very cool. I sailed Hobie Cats when I kid on a lake in Indiana so her ideas intrigued me."

"More of a navy thing, isn't it?" Sharon said.

"Somewhat, but the intel came to me through some of my contacts in Iraq."

"Iraq? Intel about a sailboat, a high tech sailboat, came from Iraq?"

"True, these wings have pushed me deeper into Army Intelligence."

Sharon finally noticed the insignia on his sleeve, "Fort Lewis?"

"From sand to rain, yes, Fort Lewis," Simpson said. "We caught some chatter about the Voss boat through a mix of intercepts, it was pretty strange to see requests for America's Cup information and Voss's name kept showing up. Our first thought was a terrorist attack at a high profile venue, the races, either here or in Europe. So we passed the word along, nothing more popped up. Considering the main event is still months away, the dates for shippings and deliveries seemed strange. When Catherine Voss was found dead, my guys started looking again and that's when we intercepted an order for televisions from Korea to Kuwait."

"From sailboats to TVs?"

"Sometimes it's all about connecting the dots, even though they're thrown all over the table. The connection was the shipping container that Oakland PD had spotted; it showed up in Korea two weeks later. It was delivered to a warehouse; some of my people in Seoul took a few pictures, Abdul."

From a leather briefcase, Abdul pulled out a file and extracted some photos. "Recognize anyone?" the Colonel said.

Standing outside a large warehouse roll-up door, talking with two men, was Eva Karg, "Globetrotting bitch, isn't she?" Sharon said. "The other two look Middle Eastern, I assume Iranian."

"Good eye and yes, Iranian," Abdul said. "The one on the left is in their naval intelligence; we assumed he wasn't in Korea for the kimchee."

"I was told that Karg was a Recces, the South African Special Forces Brigade, then I assume she became a mercenary, a bitch for hire."

"That's what we found out as well, her name popped up in a couple of the seedier parts of Africa, especially the horn. She dealt in weapons, women and vehicles," Abdul continued.

"Vehicles?"

"Seems despots have a desire for fancy cars, she would get them whatever they wanted; we think this is why she knew how to move containers around the world."

"Televisions, fancy cars, sailboats, did some rich Persian want a new boat?" Sharon said.

"In a manner of speaking, the rich Iranian is the head of the Iranian defense forces. The man reports directly to Mahmoud Ahmadinejad. Karg already found a Maybach for the man, an armored one." Abdul said. "Now he wanted a sailboat, it seems."

Sharon looked at the young man and smiled, "You are a far cry from the streets of Baghdad."

"Yes ma'am, if it weren't for you and the Colonel, I would be dead. One way or another, I would have been in the wrong place at the wrong time. The Habib's were wonderful to me; the neighborhood they lived in had Iraqis and Iranians living together in peace. In Iraq, Shia and Sunni wouldn't even talk to each other but in my high school some secretly dated. It was all strange to me but Abdul is street smart and a tough guy, it got Abdul to America." He said with a grin.

"You could charm the hump off a camel, Abdul."

"I went to college, completed ROTC and when I graduated, I went directly into the Army. Skilled in Arabic and a good bit of Farsi, it helped push me along. Then I received orders to report to Fort Lewis and when I got off the bus, the Colonel was standing there waiting to meet me. Life's not been the same since."

"With the Colonel, nothing is ever the same." Sharon looked at the face of her mentor and friend; he looked a bit embarrassed.

"I'll take it from here, Lieutenant," Simpson said. "Sharon, as I said, it's about connecting the dots. Sometimes you need to look beyond the dots as well; our intel was all coming through signals from Iran, the defense minister was really nothing more than a thug who had worked his way up with Ahmadinejad; he did a lot of the dirty work for the man and we believed he was the key. He has a home on Qushm Island, near Susa. It overlooks the Straits of Hormuz, the most important thirty miles of transit space in the world. Twenty percent of the world's oil moves through this choke point, security is vital."

"Another dot?"

"One more, there's a large military base south of the city, it is one of the Iranian's lookout and listening posts. It's hard for them to fly over the Straits, which we control. So their landbased operations are key, more dots."

"The Fifth Fleet manages the tanker traffic through the Straits and provides defense, their security is critical. Since the incidents in 2008, when the fleet was harassed by Iranian speedboats, the Navy and our land-based intel has been concerned about what they might do next. The idea of the speed boats was interesting, they were fast, had low radar return, they were harriers, if you will. Not unlike the Japanese and their Kamikazes, throwing hundreds of planes at the enemy, odds are that some will hit their targets. And our ships were equipped to fight high tech weapons with high tech tactics, speedboats were low tech, adjustments had to be made and they were."

"The sanctions have started to work from what I've read," Sharon said.

"Yes, but they are also raising tensions. Tensions that our intel says is reaching a breaking point. We are concerned about the Straits. That's when a kid at Navy intelligence suggested this impossible scenario, 'What if a fleet of extremely fast sailboats attacked our fleet?' They would have almost no radar return, a one-man crew, and explosive charges in their hulls; enough of these at night could be the Iranian version of the Divine Wind of the Japanese emperor. Let's just say it was not taken seriously."

"Until you saw Catherine Voss's boat?"

"Yes, from that point forward, we watched. We were not only impressed but an admiral joked in one of our meetings that he wanted one for Christmas. We were that impressed."

"And so were the Iranians," Sharon said.

"So much that they stole it. Karg had it shipped it to Korea where it was disguised as a container full of televisions bound for Iraq through Kuwait. Then it would be smuggled across the border into Iran, where it would be replicated and moved to Suza where, at the right time, they would be deployed."

"They needed the software, the software that Mike Stroud had around his neck."

"Exactly, Karg killed him to get it. She wouldn't be paid until the whole boat was delivered; the software was the last piece and it disappeared. Her attack at the bar tonight proved it. I can only assume now that you have it and you don't know it."

Sharon looked at Simpson, then Abdul, and then put one finger up, "One second."

She walked to the kitchen counter, stuck her hand into the Safeway bag and withdrew the manila envelope. No return address but the stamps were Italian. She removed a knife from the drawer and sliced open the end of the envelope. Another smaller envelope fell out, it was lumpy.

"Mike, you son-of-a-bitch, smart man," she said as she opened the smaller envelope. It contained a note and the memory stick.

Dear Sharon,

Never was a hero, in fact a coward's path I usually took, safer. I realized that after Catherine was murdered someone was after the boat and the software, that's why I kept the stick with me all the time. Karg has been asking all sorts of questions, most of them not related to the America's Cup, never did like her, even less now. So I'm sending you the stick and getting it out of Italy, I hope that it's just some paranoia on my part. I'll see you in San Francisco when we return to watch the big boats race and we'll knock together a few beers. By the way, Turner hasn't a chance in hell to make it, Bobo is an idiot.

Cheery by,
Mike

"Smart man, unfortunate man," Colonel Simpson said.

"And a good man, he didn't deserve to die over that, he was just a sailor. Didn't give a rat's ass about politics and they killed him. What happened to the boat?"

The Colonel turned to Abdul who said, "My job was to watch the container when it arrived, boots on the ground, just another Arab kid out of work. I was in Kuwait City when the ship arrived and I followed the container after it was picked up. We let it slip through the border with only a cursory check, it's still a country run by *baksheesh*. A few dollars here and there and everything was all right. It was met on the Iraqi side by this man."

Abdul removed another photo from his case; he turned it so Sharon could see the image.

"I'll be damned, it can't be?" she exclaimed.

"Yes, I'm afraid so," Simpson said. "It's our old friend, Hakim al-Jamil, and he's talking with Eva Karg who's on a visit to Kuwait as a tourist; she came in with the container when it crossed the border. Actually, she's confirming the delivery. Al-Jamil is the middleman; he will get it into Iran."

"Damn, I knew the man was an operator but I thought we got him when they fled the warehouse," Sharon said.

"I wish," Simpson continued. "He's been a pain in the ass for the last seven years. He jumps back and forth across the border, when one side gets too hot he jumps to the other, he even pisses off the Iranians and plays them against each other."

"He doesn't look too happy," Sharon said.

"He's not, seems that Karg only gave him half of what they agreed to, she said he'd get the rest when it reached Iran safely."

"Good, screw him," Sharon added.

"The box left for Iran," Abdul continued. "It was part of a five truck convoy; I was the driver of the third truck." Abdul turned to the Coronel, "Sir, do not do that to me again please. Off the asphalt, I could hardly breathe because of the dust."

"I'll make a note of that in your file," Simpson said with a smile.

"My papers were the best you could get; in fact, they were real since our guys were doing the issuing. We drove almost non-stop for three days until we hit Bandar e Khamir near Qushm Island where the boxes were offloaded. We picked up a few containers full of frozen fish and headed back to Iraq."

"The boxes were then sent to Qushm?"

"Yes, we put a transponder on the box, kind of like the GM emergency system if you get into an accident, we could pick up the signal with the AWACS we had up over the Persian Gulf, the box was ferried to Qushm, then tracked to Suza and placed in a warehouse. Five days later, unfortunately the container and everything in it was lost when the warehouse mysteriously caught fire and exploded. Nothing remained of the trimaran; that's the report we got back."

"I assume that we were the last people to see the trimaran immediately before the unfortunate accident?" Sharon said with a bit of a smile.

"Actually Abdul was the last to see it. It is important to keep up on your insurance premiums; you never know what might happen," the Colonel said.

"It was a nice swim back to the Zodiac, the water in that area is really quite warm," Abdul said. "I have now learned that it is important to carry insurance for all contingencies."

"Al-Jamil?" Sharon asked.

"He was turned over to the government; it seems that one of the new government ministers was the owner of those TVs and electronics that al-Jamil duped us into helping him try to steal. Unfortunately for Jamil, one of the men he executed was the son of that minister. Jamil disappeared, on the way to Baghdad, after he was arrested near Basra. No one knows what happened to him."

"Justice comes in a lot different ways. What are you going to do with Karg?"

"She has been turned over to the Feds," Simpson said. "My guess is she will disappear and spend her time near the sunny Guantanamo beaches of the Caribbean. She managed somehow to slip back into this country from Europe; we were watching for her and we still missed her. We are still chasing that trick down."

"And the two men with her?"

"Iranian exchange students at Berkeley, been here for two years, no trouble, they stayed well below the radar. We will be watching others they were associated with. Both had excellent records in engineering, upper middle class, obviously true believers."

"Breakfast, I'm famished."

"Love to, but can't, we have an 0600 flight to catch from Traverse Air Base." They slid back their chairs; Basil was up sniffing their hands as they walked to the door. "Great coffee," Simpson said as he turned to Sharon. "Thanks for your help, spotting the box on the freeway and spooking Karg helped a lot," Simpson said as he kissed her. "Been wanting to do that for a long time."

"Thanks. Abdul, you listen to this man, he'll keep you out

of trouble and keep you alive, even when he throws you in the snake pit." She extended her hand; he took it, *"Asalaamu alai-kum."*

Abdul held the handshake a little longer, *"Wa alaikum assa-laam."*

She stood in the door and waited until they turned the corner and disappeared. The sky was lightening to the east, sunrise in one hour.

15c

The letter was from a law firm but she had never heard of it, not that she knew any or wanted to know of any. Sharon slipped the knife along the flap and cut. A single-page letter was enclosed. *"Dear Ms. Sharon O'Mara, as a person named in the will of Alain Dumont, you are requested to attend the reading of his will at 2:00 PM at the office of ...."* Sharon's eyes began to tear when she thought of Alain and their time together. The date was two weeks away.

"Now what do think this is all about?" she said, scratching behind Basil's ear. "Why the hell would he put me in his will?" Basil cocked his head, hunched his shoulders, then went and curled up on his bed.

Her first call was to Kevin, "Available for lunch? ...Good ... Va de Vi? ... 1:00." After she hung up, "Something is troubling him," she said as Basil watched.

Lunch at one of her favorite Walnut Creek eateries was always a treat. Great selections of wine, a decent bar and dozens of small tapas-like plates prepared with a liberal touch of pan-Pacific influence, from burgers to lumpia and Korean barbeque to sushi. All were excellent. Bryan arrived fifteen minutes late. He looked even more tired than the night before as he sat down. He ordered a Bushmills on the rocks.

"You never drink when you're working," Sharon said.

"Fuck 'em," was his terse reply, "All of them and all their damn horses too."

She had never seen Kevin this agitated, it scared her. "What happened?"

The server slid the glass in front of Kevin; he took a good swallow, "That's better."

"Now tell me what happened?"

"Well the council, in their infinite wisdom, decided they could save more money by reducing the police force. They knew they need people to enforce parking and safety and the occasional problem at the farmers market but they really didn't understand why they needed detectives. They could easily turn to the county or the state if they needed help, so why do they need personnel when other off-the-books people are available. So Sharon, my dear, this Irish mug will be out of a job in thirty days. That was why Santinni and I were at the bar early yesterday. And by the way, thanks for the evening, trouble does follow you. You have no idea what my captain said when he arrived on the scene. You missed it."

"I can imagine. This wasn't all because of me, was it?"

"No, as much as I'm sure the captain wanted to use you as an excuse, it was all due to budgets. In fact, he knows how much work will fall back on his regulars, he knows he needs us. But he'll make do, always has. Besides, Santinni also decided to retire; he's got twenty-five in and can pull a good pension. And that woman he was talking about, they are a lot more serious than he lets on, good for him." He took another sip of whiskey.

She put her hand on his, "You okay?"

"Getting there, been through too much recently. Maybe I need a vacation, a real one. A month or two, find some new wind for my sails or something. Getting a job won't be a problem, already sent out some feelers to Walnut Creek and Concord, even the county. All of them would be good gigs but this is all happening too fast. But then it always happens fast."

"You have good friends and we are all here to help you."

"I know, and thanks."

The server reappeared.

"I'll have the shrimp lumpia," Kevin Bryan said, "and another Bushmills."

Two weeks went by quickly, the final preliminary races for the America's Cup challengers were completed and Larry Ellison's *Oracle* boat, all 72 feet of monstrous catamaran, was to be unveiled the same day as the meeting with Dumont's attorneys. The contender was trying to figure out how to get their boat finished in the next six months and still find time to practice. Jean-François had called her twice and they'd had pleasant conversations, he'd still heard nothing about the hydrofoil or its whereabouts and the software never reappeared, she didn't offer him any additional information. They agreed to settle her bill for the time she spent working on the case, she cut his bill twenty percent since he paid for a first-class trip to Venice and Paris for two. She kicked herself for insisting on the reduction but then again the fringe benefits were far more than she ever expected.

The ride up the elevator to the attorneys' offices at 101 California seemed interminable. The guard had called upstairs and then placed her alone in a specific elevator, punched in a code and off she went. Twenty seconds later, the door opened into a lobby filled with overstuffed leather chairs, flowers sitting on low tables, overseen by a perky young thing in a black suit situated behind a glass desk with an earpiece and a microphone hanging off her left ear.

"Welcome, Ms. O'Mara. I will show you to the conference room." She headed down a hallway briskly. Sharon strolled behind the assistant in her dark grey knit "going to meet the lawyers," suit. Evelyn, Claudette, three others she didn't know and an old friend, Bobby Gillis were there, waiting. She hugged the two women.

"You could have called," she admonished them.

"It was simpler this way," Claudette said. "It's been difficult and the resolution of grand-pere's estate has been very complicated. He tried his best to organize it before he died but with all his investments, it has been hard and you had your own issues to deal with anyway."

Sharon turned to Bobby, her old friend during war and peace, and embraced him. He returned the gesture. Bobby helped her resolve the issues of the paintings and the Nazis, "How is your father?"

Bobby paused and took a deep breath, "He passed away about a month ago, close to the time that Alain died, in fact. Amazing it was. Alain certainly left his mark on a lot of places."

Coffee was brought into the room and then a cadre of attorneys followed, each carrying a bundle of papers and folders.

"Good afternoon, Ms. Leclair, it is good to see you again and you too, Ms. Lucca. I am Julius Diamond, the attorney representing the estate of Mr. Dumont." He walked over to Sharon and Bobby and they introduced themselves, "Excellent, excellent, coffee?" Seeing no takers, he said, "Then let us begin."

"Significant distributions and resolutions have already been made by the estate, you were not privileged to or required to attend. Most of those transactions had to do with companies and corporations that Mr. Dumont was involved in. All issues were resolved satisfactorily as Ms. Claudette Leclair, his granddaughter, can attest to. In addition, Evelyn Lucca, a close friend of the family and Mr. Dumont's goddaughter, has also been satisfactorily served as a part of these proceedings.

Sharon looked at Claudette and Evelyn; they nodded and smiled at Sharon. Good Sharon thought.

"There are only a few small issues to be completed and the probate of the will is finalized," continued Diamond. "Mr. Gillis, Mr. Alain Dumont has left you the sum of three million dollars to be used for the education of your grandfather's grandchildren and any other subsequent heirs until the fund is depleted. This money will be held in an account; you will have the sole right to distribute this money as you see fit. Our firm, if acceptable, will act as council for the trust if you desire."

Sharon looked at Bobby, he was shocked but happy, even though Alain had made a substantial gift to his family as a result of Dumont and his grandfather's partnership a half-century earlier; this was a wonderful bonus.

"Ms. O'Mara, there are two bequeaths that Mr. Dumont has left to you, the first, Ms. Leclair will give you."

Sharon watched Claudette leave the room and quickly return, a package about one foot by two feet was held in her hands. She crossed the room to her friend.

"My Grandfather wanted you to have this; he knew how much you loved it."

Sharon slowly opened the package, the small mother and child oil painting by Mary Cassatt emerged. It was the same painting that had hung in Mr. Dumont's private bunker under his home on upper Broadway.

"Oh my God," she exclaimed. "How am I supposed to accept this?"

"With a grateful smile, you wench," a voice said behind her as Gina walked in to the room.

"Thanks for coming, Gina," Claudette said.

"Thanks for the invitation," Gina said.

Sharon continued to admire the painting; it was absolutely delightful and charming. Mr. Diamond interrupted her perusal.

"Mr. Dumont also has left you a block of stock in Apple. He acquired the stock shortly after the company went public, all taxes and fees have been paid by the estate prior to this transfer. The number of shares is 5,000. They are in your name and will be transferred to an appropriate brokerage account. Just let us know which firm you prefer."

Sharon looked at the man as if he were possessed or something, she had heard the words Apple and shares and 5,000 or did he say something else? "Could you repeat that?"

"Mr. Dumont has given you 5,000 shares of Apple stock that, as of this morning, is worth six hundred and thirteen dollars a share. The value of this gift is a little more than three million dollars."

Sharon O'Mara was stunned. She looked around the table at her friends and the others, there seemed to be a soft aura around the edges of her vision, there was a pounding in her ears, she could feel her heart racing as adrenalin pumped through her body, her fingers began to shake. She reached for her handbag, a STIA handbag that Evelyn's company had made, and pulled out a pack of Marlboros.

"Do you mind if I smoke?"

Epilogue

Fireworks exploded high over Piers 27 and 29, rebuilt for the America's Cup race and its onshore activities; the festive lights, hung between the building and the lampposts, twinkled and flashed. The long buildings of the America's Cup Village, with their large glass doors, threw panels of light across the new decking; every visitor and patron looked at and pointed to the exploding fireworks.

Sharon, Jean-François, Gina and Fidor strolled among the booths and shops soaking up the gala atmosphere of the first night of the festivities of the America's Cup in San Francisco. The big boys, the huge AC72s would race for the next two weeks. Three of the AC45s were secured to trailers on the promenade; visitors ran their hands along their sleek hulls and touched the winches and lines that ran to the tops of the seventy-foot tall wing sails. Kids were everywhere, even at 9:30 PM, screaming and running around with only cotton candy for fuel. The four visitors stood at the pier's rail and watched the grand finale of thousands of explosions, flares and concussions crisscrossing the black sky below the arcs of lights strung across the full span of the Bay Bridge. The fireworks lit the faces of every man, woman and child along the railing. Oohs and ahs rose from the crowds, an occasional, "That's my favorite!" could be heard.

"It's magical," Gina said. "Magical."

"And hard to believe that it's finally here," JF said. "Catherine would have been in the middle of it all but if there was one thing she loved, it was fireworks."

The illuminations flared off the thirteen-story high wing sail tied up at the farthest end of the pier. The four wound their way through the crowds as the fireworks ended with their usual crescendo, the noise was deafening.

"Thank you for dinner last night," Sharon said, holding JF's arm as they neared the America's Cup boat.

"Thank you for the company, I'm sorry that Turner made such a scene."

"She was drunk and still upset with me for getting Karg arrested," Sharon said. "She will never believe that Karg was arrested for being a terrorist. The Compton will get over it, I'm sure the publicity caused by the fight won't hurt their business. Besides, it's not often that the police have to break up a cat fight."

"Bobo didn't help either, seems he pissed off her whole crew, at least those that were still around. He'll have a black eye, I'm sure of that; that was quite a punch you threw."

"It was an accident, his face just got in the way when I pointed at the door and told him to get out," Sharon clarified.

"I know, I know. But when Turner launched herself at you with that purple concoction she was wearing, I didn't know whether to laugh or call the fashion police. Apparently someone called the real police."

"She's upset, blames me for losing her girlfriend. All's fair in love and war."

"Wished I had said that," Gina said, interrupting.

Sharon smiled and gave Gina the bird, Gina responded by sticking her tongue out, not a lot, just a little.

"Girls, girls," Fidor said. "You Americans, I just love all your pomp and circumstance. Not like us in Russia, where everything is serious. Big parades and long speeches, then we all get drunk. You Americans act like everything is a carnival with food and music and fireworks."

"And there's a problem with that?" Gina asked.

"No, no." Fidor said. "I love it; we are such a dour people; now I know why so many have left Mother Russia and moved here, for the fireworks and cotton candy. I think even their children look better here than they do in Russia, it's so strange."

A large crowd had gathered at the end of the pier, looking at the massive Cup defender, her two sleek black hulls, seventy-two feet long and forty-six feet apart; *Oracle* was printed on the hulls and sail. The arched crossed braces supported a large intricate trampoline styled net that connected the hulls. Her wingsail reached one hundred and thirty-two feet into the black sky, floodlights made a focal point. With all sails up, she could fly over six thousand square feet of gennaker and wingsail. With the right wind, the experts thought she could reach thirty knots, after the preliminary races and training, some of the crew thought she could well exceed that estimate.

Standing in the center of the boat, microphone in hand, Larry Ellison was giving a short lecture on the boat and the competition. He talked about its one hundred and sixty-one year history. How this competition had seen the greatest financial moguls, boat designers and captains of their day compete for the right to claim the trophy, men like Ted Turner, Dennis Conner, Alan Bond, Russell Coutts, and boats like the *Stars and Stripes*, and *Australia II*. And how competing boats' lengths changed, the sail area changed, the materials changed. Sleek wooden hulls that began with the one hundred and one foot *America* in 1851, evolved to aluminum and steel, then fiberglass and later, high tech carbon fiber. Monohull designs eventually morphed into two and three hulls, then back to two. After a hundred and thirty years of American exclusivity, the Cup was finally won by an Australian boat, then it went back to America, then New Zealand, Switzerland (of all places), then America. Ellison realized that the competition could be bigger and more inclusive, that's what was behind the America's Cup World Series preliminary competitions and races, exposure, with exposure came more revenue.

Ellison waved at the four, beckoning them to the boat.

"Isn't she beautiful JF, my God, what a boat," Ellison said waving his arms about. "JF, I'm very sorry about Catherine, she was a tough competitor and a great sailor; I will miss her."

"Thanks, Larry; I want you to meet some friends of mine, Sharon O'Mara, Gina Cavelli and Fidor Balanca."

"I know Fidor, good to see you again. Gina, a pleasure, and this is the famous, or should I say infamous, Sharon O'Mara. It is a real pleasure to meet you. I've heard a little about your exploits, something about a race through the canals of Venice and some bad guys being arrested. And besides, anytime that you can get into a fist fight with Ellis Turner, well I just wish I was there. It's a shame that she had that fellow Bobo as skipper, such a putz. JF, now if your sister had been skipper it would have been different, very different."

"I'd like to think so, thanks," JF said.

"Ms. O'Mara, we're taking this boat out tomorrow, would you be interested in a ride? I'm going to watch from the helicopter."

Sharon remembered the last time she had been on one of these boats, it hadn't ended well.

"You're asking me to be the *12th Man*?"

"Yes, I am."

Sharon looked at the boat and the small seat mounted in the middle of the stern crossbeam, easily fifteen feet above the water, it looked as comfortable as a witch's dunking chair.

"Mr. Ellison, let me think about it. Can I get back to you?"

The End

A Note from the Author
The Flyer

I have tried to pare these stories into a manageable length that you can read in less than eight hours. At about 60–75,000 words, the idea is that you can read about half the book on a four-hour flight and the rest on the way home. I call them *Flyers*. But if you aren't flying, settle back, pour a good drink, and enjoy.

Gregory C. Randall was born in Traverse City, Michigan. He grew up in Chicago. Greg has never forgotten his roots. Mr. Randall makes his home in California.

Mr. Randall is the author of fiction and nonfiction works available through Amazon.com.

For more information about the other Sharon O'Mara Chronicles, and planned sequels, please visit and connect with Greg online:

www.gregorycrandall.info

See his blogs:
http://www.writing4death.blogspot.com

Other books by Mr. Randall:
Fiction
The Cherry Pickers

The Sharon O'Mara Chronicles
Land Swap For Death
Containers For Death
Toulouse For Death
12th Man For Death
Diamonds For Death
Limerick For Death

The Alex Polonia Thrillers
Venice Black
Saigon Red
St. Petersburg White

The Tony Alfano Thrillers
Chicago Swing
Chicago Jazz
Chicago Fix
Chicago Boogie Woogie

Max Adler OSS WWII
This Face of Evil
Pawns in an Ancient Game

Science Fiction and Slipstream
Sector 73
Seven Hours to Barstow

Nonfiction
America's Original GI Town, Park Forest, Illinois

Additional copies can be purchased through Amazon.com.